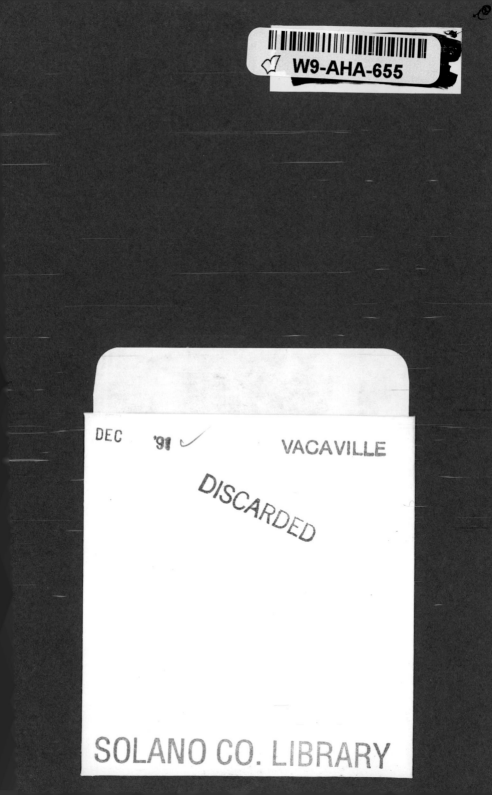

BUDDY
HOLLY

IS ALIVE AND WELL
ON GANYMEDE

Bradley Denton

WILLIAM MORROW AND COMPANY, INC.
NEW YORK

It is the policy of William Morrow and Company, Inc., and its imprints and affiliates, recognizing the importance of preserving what has been written, to print the books we publish on acid-free paper, and we exert our best efforts to that end.

Library of Congress Cataloging-in-Publication Data

Denton, Bradley.
  Buddy Holly is alive and well on Ganymede / by Bradley Denton.
    p.   cm.
  ISBN 0-688-10822-9
  1. Holly, Buddy, 1936–1959—Fiction. I. Title.
  PS3554.E588B8   1991
  813'.54—dc20   90-28537
                                                                             CIP

Printed in the United States of America

First Edition

1 2 3 4 5 6 7 8 9 10

BOOK DESIGN BY LISA STOKES

For Barbara Jean . . .

. . . these words of love

"The Midwest has a lot to answer for."

—HOWARD WALDROP, *following the August 1990 Wisconsin helicopter crash that took the life of guitarist Stevie Ray Vaughan*

PROLOGUE

In life, their names were linked for only a few cold, miserable weeks.

In death, their names became a Trinity, as if carved into the same tablet of sacred stone.

Ritchie Valens. The Big Bopper.

Buddy Holly.

Years later, we would look back with longing and say that the music had died.

We should have known better.

1 · the annunciation

1

OLIVER

I was conceived in cold circumstances in the front seat of a 1955 four-door Chevrolet in the early morning hours of Tuesday, February 3, 1959, near Des Moines, Iowa. I read about this in Volume I of Mother's diary when I was nine years old. I was terrified that she would catch me, but I needn't have worried. She was writing Volume IV at the time, and she never looked back at finished work.

The same passage in Volume I notes that the song playing on the car radio during the crucial moment was Buddy Holly's "Heartbeat." Mother wrote: *I know, now and forever, that it is "our" song. I am home in bed now, and had an argument with Mama because C. brought me back so late on a snowy night, "and a school night at that!" I cannot sleep because I hear that song over and over in my head, as if I had a radio behind my eyes. I hope to God I am not pregnant but I don't think I am because you cannot get pregnant the first time, at least that's what they say, and it all dripped out on the seat anyhow, and if you read this you can go to Hell, Mama, because you have no business snooping in my diary in the first place.*

When I first read this passage I was terribly confused, but one of the kids at school explained it to me the next day. That was the occasion of my first fight, and my first split lip.

Throughout our life together, up to and including the day she died, I was careful to never let Mother know that I think "Heartbeat" is a lousy song.

The next entry in Volume I told me that my father, referred to as "C.," committed suicide less than twelve hours after impregnating Mother . . . when he heard the news from Clear Lake. He was found in his parents' garage in the Chevrolet, a victim of carbon monoxide poisoning.

Mother was the only person in Des Moines who believed that he had intentionally killed himself. She wrote: *His mama and daddy say that C. had the engine on so that he could listen to the radio without running down the battery, but he had a radio in his room, so why would he go out to the car if the radio was the reason? He must have left me a note, but they won't let me see it. I hate them and plan to poison their Chihuahua.*

She probably did, too.

One other thing I should mention now: I have always felt that the moment of my conception must have coincided exactly with the moment that the V-tailed red Beechcraft Bonanza hit the frozen Iowa soil, smashing life from the mortal bodies of Ricardo Valenzuela, J. P. Richardson, and Charles Hardin Holley. Whenever I try to imagine what my father may have looked like, the only face I can see is that of a skinny Texan wearing glasses with black plastic frames.

I have avoided discovering my father C.'s true identity, although it would be easy to do.

That's enough to begin.

My name is Oliver Vale. I live in the one-story Kansas ranch-style house Mother willed to me. It is full of rock 'n' roll memorabilia, Japanese appliances, and Volumes I through VII of Mother's diary, dated from May 13, 1957 (her sixteenth birthday) to February 3, 1984 (her last day of life). I pasted the white date sticker on the spine of Volume VII myself. Then I called the ambulance to come and get her.

*

At 1:03 A.M. on Friday, February 3, 1989, the picture displayed by my twenty-five-inch Sony color television dissolved into bright speckles of static. I was immediately aware of the significance of the time (displayed in glowing blue numerals by the Mitsubishi VCR), and for a few moments I sat frozen in my recliner like a statue of Abraham Lincoln. Buddy Holly had died at about this moment in 1959, just as the most determined of my father C.'s umpteen zillion sperm had plunged into Mother's eagerly waiting ovum. As a multicellular process, I was exactly thirty years old, and my Sony was delivering white sparks in celebration. Mother had been dead five years.

I tried to ponder the significance of it all, and convinced myself that there *was* no significance. The Sony had been presenting static of this sort with increasing frequency over the past several weeks, and it was only coincidence that it was doing so again at this particular moment. Unfortunately, this particular moment was rottenly inconvenient, because I had remote-controlled the Sony to life hoping to see John Wayne in *The*

Searchers, the 1956 John Ford western that gave Buddy
Holly the phrase that led to his first hit single. I had
seen the movie only once before, so I'd been ecstatic when
Dish Digest told me that it was going to be broadcast
via satellite from a co-op station in Albuquerque. I had
spent a good part of the chilly evening redirecting my
creaky SkyVue satellite dish to the proper point in the
heavens, and had even popped a seven-dollar blank tape
into the Mitsubishi. Now, though, the Sony had erupted
into snow, and I was going to miss the opening credits.

Leaving the VCR running, I grabbed my ten-inch
crescent wrench from its place on the coffee table, ran
through the dining area, kitchen, and utility room, and
slammed out through the back door.

The temperature outside had dropped about fifteen
degrees since I'd finished tinkering with the SkyVue, and
the shock of the cold stopped me for an instant. In that
instant, I saw that the night was clear and beautiful.
Except for the dull orange glow of Topeka eight miles to
the north, the sky was purplish-black and full of stars.
The hills of northeastern Kansas were silhouettes that
hid all but a few of my various neighbors' mercury-va-
por yard lights, and the black outlines of the bare trees
were still. It was a different sort of night than it had
been when the Winter Dance Party had played in the
stupidly named Surf Ballroom at Clear Lake.

I shivered, and that broke the spell. If I didn't hurry,
I'd miss the Indian attack and the slaughter of most of
John Wayne's relatives, so I sprinted across the dead lawn
toward the eight-and-a-half-foot aluminum dish. It glowed
a dull white in the wash of the yard light, but that didn't
help me see the stepladder that I'd left lying on the
ground beside it. I tripped over the ladder and fell forward, banging my head on the dish's lower rim. The
SkyVue rang dully, like an old church bell.

Despite the cold, or because of it, I didn't feel much pain, so I wasted no time recovering from the blow. Instead, I set up the stepladder on the concave side of the dish, climbed it, and proceeded to use the crescent wrench to whang on the cylindrical cover of the block converter at the antenna's focus. A satellite-video specialist would cringe at this remedy, but as Mother used to say in her more lucid moments, "Whatever works." The much-cratered skin of the converter was testimony to the fact that the crescent-wrench-whanging method not only worked, but had been employed often.

The noise brought back memories. Mother had bought the dish from an obscure outfit in El Dorado in the spring of 1983, and we had developed this method of adjustment shortly thereafter (mainly because the wrench had been packed in the parts box and was handy). It had been easier when Mother had been alive, because she could yell from the house when the Sony's picture had been whanged back to normal. Since her death, I'd had to adjust the antenna by trial and error.

Currently, about twenty-five whangs seemed to do the trick. I gave it a couple more just to be sure and then jumped down from the ladder and ran back to the house. I was wearing sweatpants and a ROCK-CHALK, CHICKEN-HAWK, F*** KU! T-shirt (my movie-watching uniform), and my arms had popped out in goose pimples from wrists to pits.

I dashed into the living room and saw John Wayne on the Sony, as big as life and twice as studly. You never would have thought to look at him that he would eventually have a pig valve in his heart. I dropped the crescent wrench on the coffee table, giving the veneer another nick, and flopped into the recliner, pulling its orange afghan down to bundle myself.

It happened this quickly: A corner of the afghan,

fuzzy and fluorescent, passed before my eyes, and when it was gone, so was John Wayne. In his place, standing alone on a marbled gray plain, was Buddy Holly, wearing a powder-blue suit with a white shirt and black bow tie. A woodgrain-and-white Fender Stratocaster was slung on a strap over his left shoulder, and behind his black-framed glasses, his brown eyes looked bewildered. A pinkish proto-zit was just visible on his chin. Behind him, an enormous banded oval of red, orange, and white hung suspended in black.

I closed my eyes. This was just the sort of thing I would dream up on this night. For the forty-millionth time, I wished that I had never read any of Mother's diary, and for the forty-millionth time, I replied that it wouldn't have made any difference if I hadn't. After all, I had spent my first ten months of multicellular existence listening to "Heartbeat" over and over again (which may account for my loathing of it), and I had spent every year after that listening to the dozens of other songs that the gangly kid from Lubbock had written and/or recorded between 1955 and 1959. . . .

I opened my eyes. Buddy was still inside the Sony, looking around as though he might have dropped his guitar pick.

"Leave me alone, Dad," I said.

He looked out of the set then, straight at me. "Oh," he said. "The red light's on. Got a little distracted, Mr. Sullivan." He spoke with a down-home, West Texas twang, and his smile was shy but honest. This was clearly a boy who would offer to fix your flat tire on a long, empty stretch of road. He wasn't like your Elvis Presley or your David Lee Roth, thrusting his pelvis out there and daring the girls on the front row to touch it. This was a *good* boy.

As Mother wrote in Volume I: *Just before C. and I*

*did you-know-what, he told me that he thought Buddy
Holly, unlike all the others, spoke directly to us. Bill Haley
and Chuck Berry and Elvis Presley were great, C. said,
but they were great because they were different and wild.
(I didn't tell him that I thought Bill Haley was just plain
ugly; with all that grease on his forehead curl, it looks
like a sow's tail). Buddy, though, was special because he
wasn't so different. He was like us. And if he was sometimes a little wild, like with "Oh, Boy!" . . . well, that
meant that maybe we could be that way sometimes too.
Which I guess is how I wound up carrying C.'s little bastard, come to think of it. Not that I mind, since with C.
dead I might as well have something around to remember him by.*

Buddy began strumming his Strat and singing "Well
All Right" in a voice that was low and quiet. He had
spoken to "Mr. Sullivan," but he and the Crickets had
never performed that song on *The Ed Sullivan Show*.

I bolted from the recliner, throwing the afghan at
the Sony, and grabbed the crescent wrench from the coffee table again. Thirty-year anniversary or not, this
wasn't the show my SkyVue was supposed to be bringing me tonight. If I wanted to go crazy, I could do it
without any help from a phantom in a picture tube.

Oblivious to the cold, I charged out to the earth station, climbed the ladder, and whanged on the converter
forty, fifty, sixty times, then lost count and whanged some
more. The sound bounced back from the dish and pounded
at me as if my head were in a bucket being pelted with
rocks, and the dog at the nearest neighbor's house began
barking as if he were cursing me: "Knock off the noise!
Asshole! Have some respect! Buddy Holly died tonight!
Cat lover! Shut up! I'll mangle you! You dope!"

Finally, exhausted, numb, and afraid that the dog—
a Doberman pinscher the size of a Guernsey—was com-

ing to get me, I dropped from the ladder, scraping my shins on the rungs, and stumbled back to the house. By now, John Wayne was probably shooting the eyes out of a dead Comanche warrior (so the warrior couldn't find his way to the Spirit Land), and I was missing it.

I paused in the utility room and listened. I heard neither music nor gunshots from the living room, and I feared that in my zeal for insanity-free reception, I had whanged the block converter into electronics heaven. I was beginning to consider the benefits of spending the money for cable.

I paused again in the kitchen. From here, the Sony's static should have been as loud as hail on the roof, but I heard nothing. The whole house was quiet . . . *too* quiet. So to kill some time, and as long as I was in the kitchen anyway, I took a bag of microwave popcorn from the cabinet and tossed it into the Sanyo, which I call the Meltdown Machine because I can feel it trying to cook my eyes if I stand too close. Once, I tried to heat a Vel-veeta-on-generic-white using one of Mother's gilt-edged china plates, and the light show was something to be-hold.

I waited until the bagged kernels began to pop, and then, with that reassuring noise at my back, I proceeded into the dining area and through to the living room. The orange afghan was draped over the Sony, hiding all but one gray corner of the picture tube. The television was silent.

I approached as though the Sony were a dozing wil-debeest, and when I was close enough, I snagged the af-ghan with the crescent wrench. Then, as the noise from the kitchen became as furious as machine-gun fire, I jerked the afghan away—

—and once again stared into the face of Buddy Holly.

I walked backward, banged the side of my right knee

on a corner of the coffee table, dropped the wrench, and
collapsed into the recliner. I tried to decide whether I
should immediately call my group-therapy leader, Sharon
Sharpston, or whether I should wait until a decent hour.

My therapy group, by the way, is for Disturbed Adult
Children of Dead Rockers and Hippies. (This is my own
title. Sharon calls us "Post-Traumatic Victims of Popu-
lar Culture," or something like that.) Neither of my parents played in a band, but they both died for love of rock
'n' roll, and I figure that qualifies me. I have always been
disappointed, though, that both Mother and my father
C. passed through their crucial years before they could
have tried to qualify as hippies. I would have much preferred the name "Wheatfield in the Sun" to "Oliver."

Buddy cleared his throat and began to speak,
sounding nervous. "Well, folks, don't ask me how I got
here, 'cause it beats the heck out of me. It's only been
four or five minutes since I figured out that I ain't
dreamin' again about what a pain old man Sullivan was."
He frowned, thinking hard. "Last thing I remember, the
pilot's cussin', and the next thing I know, here I am
lookin' at a TV camera. There's a sign hangin' on it that
says 'Welcome to . . .' "

His voice trailed off, and he pushed up his glasses
with one finger against the bridge. "Sorry, it might take
me a minute to get this word. Gan—Ganil—no, that ain't
right. . . ."

"Ganymede," I said. I had seen some of the Voyager
photos in an Introductory Astronomy course before dropping out of Kansas State University, and I recognized
Jupiter in the sky behind Buddy. Whenever he tilted his
head, the Great Red Spot became visible. "Ganymede,
you dumbass Texan. And pardon me for being redun-
dant." I had decided to call Sharon just as soon as the
hallucination was over.

"Gaineemeedee," Buddy said, looking proud of himself.

The noises from the kitchen had stopped, so I went to retrieve my bag of popcorn before it scorched. I figured that the hallucination would wait for me, but when I returned, munching hot popcorn, Buddy was saying, ". . . and at the bottom of the sign, there's some smaller print that says, 'For assistance, contact Oliver Vale, 10146 Southwest 163rd Street, Topeka, Kansas, U.S.A.' So would someone out there please get in touch with that fellow for me? Thanks."

I began applauding, scattering popcorn all over the room. "Yes!" I shouted. "Oliver, you impress me! Inflated self-esteem is a major breakthrough! Sharon Sharpston will be most pleased as she ships you off to the state hospital at Osawatomie!"

Buddy took a few steps back from the camera and shifted the Strat into playing position. "That's all the sign says, but I'll repeat the address in a while in case nobody's listening right now." He looked up and around, as if watching an airplane cross the sky. "Seems like I'm in a big glass bubble, and I can't tell where the light's coming from. It's a little chilly, and I sure hope I don't have to be here long. In the meantime, here's one for your family audience, Mr. Sullivan." He struck a hard chord and began singing "Oh, Boy!" in a wild shout.

I remote-controlled the Sony into blank-screened silence. Poor Buddy. He had seemed to be surrounded by nothing worse than stars and shadows, but I remembered enough from my Introductory Astronomy course to know better. Ganymede was an immense ice ball strewn with occasional patches of meteoric rock, and its surface was constantly bombarded by vicious streams of protons and other cosmic crap whipped up by Jupiter's

hyperactive magnetic field. It was no place for a picker
from Lubbock.

The cordless Hitachi telephone on the coffee table
blooped. Wondering who could be calling at this time of
night, I leaned forward and picked up the receiver before the built-in answering machine could interrupt.
"Oliver Vale, Electronic Appliance Salesman and Messiah," I said. I thought that was terrifically witty, which
goes to show the state of mind I was in.

"Oliver, what are you trying to pull?" The voice was
female. I had parted from my long-term Relationship,
Julie "Eat shit and die, Oliver" Calloway, a month before, so this had to be Sharon Sharpston.

"Is that a Freudian question?" I asked.

"This isn't funny," she said. It was the first time I
had ever heard her sound angry, and it startled me. "At
first I thought you were only playing a trick on *me,* but
WIBW radio just said that the TV interruption is statewide, and maybe even nationwide. Didn't you stop to
think that it was against the law?"

Deep inside the damp caverns of my brain, I realized that what she was saying could only mean that what
I had seen on the Sony had not been the product of my
fruit-looped imagination after all. Primarily, though, I
was perplexed by the bizarre thought that a humanistic
individual like Sharon might be a John Wayne fan. "Were
you trying to watch *The Searchers* too?" I asked.

"What are you talking about? Bruce and I were
looking at a tape of Olympic highlights when the VCR
shut down and Buddy Holly showed up on the screen.
Who else but you would choose *that* figure as your video
persona? How did you do it, anyway? More importantly,
why did you do it? I mean, why do you *think* you did it?"

Bruce Werter was Sharon's person-of-opposite-sex-

sharing-living-quarters, a young partner in a downtown
Topeka law firm. I had first met him two years ago when
he'd come to pick up Sharon after a group therapy ses-
sion held at my house. He'd had one brown eyebrow and
one blond, and not much else to recommend him as far
as I could see. He had shown no appreciation for my collection of classic rock 'n' roll recordings, but he had
clapped me on the shoulder and told me to "hang in there
and whip those mental difficulties." I had wanted to take
up voodoo so that I could make a doll of him and stick
pins in it.

"How is Bruce these days, anyway?" I asked. "Has
he gotten that eyebrow thing cleared up yet?"

"Bruce is fine," Sharon told me. "He says that you're
probably in enormous trouble with the FCC."

"I can't be," I said. "I didn't do anything. I was just
sitting here trying to watch John Wayne shoot the eyes
out of dead Comanche warriors and save Natalie Wood
from having sex with non-Christians when Buddy came
on. I thought I was imagining the whole thing since, as
you know, I have sort of an obsession with him."

"Yes, I know." Sharon's voice was calmer now, closer
to the there-there-you're-as-normal-as-the-next-person
voice she uses during therapy. "You've taken him as your
father icon because you resemble him slightly. That's
why I know you did this TV thing even if you've convinced yourself that you didn't. You made yourself up to
look like Buddy Holly, and you converted your basement or bedroom into a set resembling a distant planet."

"Actually, a satellite of Jupiter," I said. "Ganymede."

"Whatever." In my mind's eye I saw Sharon's lips
purse, and I wanted to kiss them, Bruce or no Bruce. I
wouldn't even ask her for a blood test.

"Well, it couldn't have been Io," I said. "I didn't see
any sulfur volcanoes."

"It doesn't matter *where* you meant it to be," Sharon said. "It doesn't even matter whether you actually built a background set or programmed a computer-imaged one. All that matters is that you taped yourself and broadcasted the result. You gave out your name and address, for God's sake—clearly a cry for help—although you slipped and forgot your zip code."

"66666-6666 is hard to forget," I said. For the first time, I realized that my zip code is probably the reason why so many Jehovah's Witnesses come around. I have a full run of *The Watchtower* dating back to 1982. "It wasn't me on your TV, though. It was Buddy. My Stratocaster is solid black, and I can't play it for shit. My fingers bleed. That proves I'm innocent, doesn't it?" Something else occurred to me. "Besides, why did you assume that *I* was playing a trick on *you*? Couldn't somebody else be playing a trick on *me*?"

I felt the puff of Sharon's sigh through the cordless phone. "Oliver, no one would go to this much effort just to . . . I mean, no one would do this to you. You have no enemies other than yourself. Besides, whether you did it or not, whether you *believe* you did it or not, you're still in tremendous trouble. Bruce is listening to the radio—your tape is still jamming the TV stations, you know—and he says that the reports claim you've broken in on regular programming *worldwide,* on every channel that's been checked so far. They're describing you as—what is it, Bruce?—'An obviously brilliant but seriously disturbed computer and video genius.' And I suppose you must really *be* a genius if you did what they say."

I had no problem with the "seriously disturbed" business, but I laughed at the rest. "When it comes to video, I can connect, disconnect, or adjust it before you can blink—with the exception of my stupid off-brand satellite dish. But that's because I'm a salesman at Cowboy Carl's Computer and Component Corral in the White Lakes Mall. I sell IBM and Apple clones along with the occasional minicam, CD player, food processor, VCR, and biorhythm-charter. Does that make me a genius?"

"The news media will infer that it does, and so will the FCC," Sharon replied. "At least, that's what Bruce says."

I snorted, a noise I'd practiced since childhood and had down to near-porcine perfection. "What does Bruce know? This is the guy who thinks Eddie Cochran was a World War I flying ace."

"*Oliver,*" Sharon said irritably, and for that one wonderful moment I imagined that we were married. "Listen to me. You are *in trouble* with the *law.*"

"Deep sewage," Bruce's voice said in the background. He sounded pleased.

"Gobble it and choke, Bruce!" I yelled. If nothing else, I had learned some snappy phrases during my Relationship with Julie "Eat shit and die, Oliver" Calloway.

"I want you to come over here," Sharon said.

"*What?*" Bruce bellowed.

"We have to figure out what to do," Sharon continued, ignoring her boyfriend's shout. "If you stay home, you'll be under arrest by sunrise. But if you cut off your broadcast immediately and come over to my place, maybe Bruce and I can help with a defense to keep you out of jail. Bruce is a terrific attorney, you know."

"Oh, great," Bruce said. I heard a thump that must have been Sharon kicking him.

I liked the idea of going to Sharon Sharpston's apartment and bugging Bruce, but I was reluctant to accept the offer. In the first place, although I couldn't stop the broadcast, running to Sharon might be seen as an admission of guilt. In the second place, I hated to leave my house empty at night with no one to guard my treasures.

"I'm not your responsibility," I said.

"You became my responsibility when I allowed you into my therapy group," Sharon said. "Besides, I'm your friend."

"Christ," Bruce said. I heard another thump.

I tried to think of what Mother would suggest in a situation like this. When I had started getting beaten up in grade school, her advice had been to "run and hide." The difficulty with that had been that there weren't many hiding places on the treeless playground—and I doubted that there would be many hiding places where the Federal government couldn't find me either.

So, as attractive as running and hiding was to me (I had done it often during my Relationship), I decided to fall back on Mother's other axiom, "Whatever works." In this case, since I was probably going to be considered guilty until proven innocent regardless of what I did, that would mean taking Sharon up on her offer. "I'll be right over," I said. "Tell Bruce he can crash on the couch." I hung up before she could contradict my vision of the sleeping arrangements.

The Sony came back to life without my having touched the remote control. Buddy squinted out at me and said, "Here's that address again. I guess this Oliver Vale must be the right man for the job."

I stood up and struck my best John Wayne pose.

"That'll be the day," I drawled.

I swaggered into my bedroom wishing that someone would shoot out my eyes so that I wouldn't have to make the trip to the Spirit Land.

SHARON

Notes on client Oliver Vale, continued . . .

2/3/89; 2:45 A.M.: Oliver's transference is becoming pronounced, so offering him refuge in my home may not be good for him. However, incarceration could drive him over the brink into psychosis, and the past five years of therapy would be wasted. I have tried to explain this to my Significant Other, but I fear that he doubts my motives. Bruce, in his natural jealous anger, has even hinted that I am not truly concerned with Oliver's well-being; instead, he suggests, I subconsciously covet Oliver's collection of vintage rock and roll recordings. This is untrue. My personal feeling, in fact, is that Oliver's archives suffer from a serious paucity of Motown.

The turn that Oliver's delusions have now taken is fascinating, if frightening in its scope. Superficially, the content of his ingenious television broadcast seems to indicate a healthful realization that only he can save himself—because, as frequently noted, he often displays a strong personal identification with Buddy Holly. However, this feeling of identification is in fact a mask for Oliver's underlying delusion that Holly is his father. Thus, since the broadcast supposedly originates from another planet, I am led to the following preliminary analysis: Oliver sees himself as the savior of his father (*id est,* as the embodiment of his father's seed), which by extension implies that he also (rather uncharacteristically, at first glance) sees himself as the savior of all mankind. *Id est,* for Oliver, Buddy Holly (or perhaps what Holly symbolizes—innocence, freedom, skill, talent, love) = God the Father (who lives in Heaven, here translated as a distant planet); Oliver himself = God the Son (the Savior); and television = God the Holy Spirit (through which the Father's wishes are communicated and the Son is brought into being).

The barrenness of Buddy/Oliver's planet may be symbolic of Oliver's mother. More on this after I interview Oliver and analyze his responses.

I do not know what to make of the "Mr. Sullivan" references. I have never heard of this person, and Oliver has never mentioned him in my presence. (Oliver's real father?)

The coming legal difficulties may make further analysis haphazard, but to minimize this problem I have decided to refer my other clients to colleagues for the next week.

The Buddy Holly tape has been on television for almost two hours now. Sometimes Buddy/Oliver talks; sometimes he sings (hiccuping strangely); and sometimes he merely stands silently or sits cross-legged on the ground, which appears to be bare rock. Nothing has repeated yet. I have been taping the broadcast for the past forty-five minutes, and I expect that a detailed study will aid me in determining the future course of Oliver's therapy.

I have only now realized that I should not have told him to come here on his own; I should have gone to him and brought him back. In my surprise and shock at his unexpected appearance on my TV screen, I failed to think clearly. If he hasn't arrived in another twenty minutes, I'll drive to his home.

At this moment, Buddy/Oliver (I suppose I should really write "Oliver/Buddy") is singing a song called "It's Too Late." I fear that he is trying to tell me something.

My Significant Other is not providing as much emotional support as I would like. It will be interesting, after this crisis is past, to examine how these and forthcoming events will have affected our relationship.

Bruce persists in referring to Oliver as a "dweeb," which I find intensely irritating.

RICHTER

The buzz of the telephone woke him a few minutes after 4:00 A.M., Eastern Standard Time. He was not pleased.

"Richter?" a familiar voice asked.

"Yes." He sat up in bed, uncomfortably aware of his paunch.

"Have you been watching television?"

"No."

"You should be. Any station."

Richter touched a button on the headboard, and a fifty-inch flat screen on the far wall began to glow, gradually resolving itself into a gawky boy with a pimple on his chin.

"Are you watching yet?"

"Yes." The gawky boy began singing "I'm Looking for Someone to Love" in a happy, staccato hiccup of a voice.

The boy was Buddy Holly. Richter remembered him. He wanted to listen to the song, but it would be a bad idea to wake his bedmate while he was on the phone. He turned off the television's sound.

"It's on every channel in the world, Richter, including UHF and cable. The regular broadcasts are being wiped and replaced, apparently at the points of transmission. Even the commercial communications satellites are jammed with this thing. None of the video relays, and I mean *none,* will respond to commands. The Soviets have already protested—only two hours into it! They think we're doing it to jam Eastern bloc telecasts. But we're not, because we *can't.* And if we can't, then they can't either."

"No," Richter agreed, acknowledging the obvious.

"We don't know how to stop it. We don't even know how it's being *done.* Do you know what this means?"

"Yes," Richter said, and forced himself to add, "I believe so." He hated to waste time on any words other than monosyllables, but he also hated to be inaccurate.

"Good. You are now a sworn enforcement agent of the Federal Communications Commission. You have the same powers in this capacity as in any other. Understood?"

"Yes." Richter was perturbed. At his age, with his years of experience, he resented being told anything that he could assume.

"All right. We'll try to keep other enforcement units out of your way, but we can't guarantee that we'll be able to stop any local or state agencies that want to poke their noses into things. The suspected perpetrator, one Oliver Vale, was cocky enough to broadcast his identity, so you can begin your investigation at this address."

Richter listened to the address and scowled. Regardless of its international impact, an investigation with its focus in Topeka, Kansas, was not his idea of a cherry assignment.

"Have you finished your current business?" the voice on the phone asked.

Richter looked down at the young woman in bed beside him. She was awakening, a sleepy smile on her perfect oval face. "No," he said.

"Well, either finish it immediately or postpone it. This new matter takes precedence. If that smartass hick hacker had stuck to monkeying around with domestic transmissions, I'd leave it to the regular FCC goons, but with the Russians all set to piss in our soup, it's got to be wrapped up fast. Just be sure you find out how he did it, and how to make it stop, before you do anything else. *Before* you do anything else. Got it?"

"Yes." Richter's scowl deepened. With these restrictions, he might have to be in Kansas for an entire day.

"If you need technical assistance, I'll see that it's provided. Go."

Richter replaced the receiver in its slot in the headboard, then threw off the sheet and slid out of bed.

"Going to the bathroom?" the woman asked drowsily.

"No," Richter said. He bent down to reach under the bed, and his hand closed on his 9mm plastic pistol. It was invisible to X-rays, and he felt a strong empathy for it.

"You have a cute butt," the woman said. She had let down her guard; her accent was almost distinct.

Richter hesitated and then straightened, leaving his pistol under the bed. He had obtained all of the information from the woman that he was required to obtain, so he should put a bullet below her ear and toss her body into a dumpster on the way to the airport. But she was only a flunky, hardly a real Bad Guy at all, and if he let her live, she might be useful in the future.

He was rationalizing, and he knew it. Still, he decided to indulge himself this once. He would make up for it in Topeka.

He blacked the television screen so that the woman would not see his pistol in its glow, then dressed and armed himself in the dark.

"Are you going out?" the woman asked.

"Yes," Richter answered. He took his prepacked bag from the closet and left. The woman wouldn't want to be seen coming out of his condo by light of day, so she would leave soon too. The condo would lock itself behind her, and the computerized security system would see to it that she didn't get in again.

He really *should* kill her, he thought again as he stepped out into the cold, wet District of Columbia night.

Except . . .

He was fifty-two years old, almost bald, and gaining weight despite his workouts. He was still the best operative in the Company, but he could feel the day coming when that would no longer be true.

He should kill her. . . .

But he had a soft spot for any woman who told him that he had a cute butt.

SKYVUE

In the concrete-block snack bar/projection building of a drive-in theater near El Dorado, Kansas, two men wearing flannel shirts and bearing strong resemblances to Dwight D. Eisenhower and Nikita Khrushchev were standing at the grill. The theater was closed for the season, so they had the building to themselves.

"How long are you going to keep this up?" Khrushchev asked.

"As long as it takes," Eisenhower said, tossing a raw hamburger patty onto the grill.

"What does *that* mean?" Khrushchev asked angrily. His jowls shook.

"It means what it means."

Khrushchev brought a fist down on the grill beside Eisenhower's cooking burger. "Circumlocutionary situ-

ation-comedy bullshit!" he shouted. "We were supposed
to conduct this project together—"

"You helped with the preparatory work, Nick."

"—but now you've done this Buddy Holly thing
without so much as a word to me! And as for 'helping
with the preparatory work,' it seems that what I thought
I was doing wasn't what I was doing at all! I thought we
were opening their fleshbound little minds gently and
slowly, when all along you were planning *this*!"

"I am the leader of the project," Eisenhower said.
"As my assistant and companion, you have been invalu-
able both in your work and in helping me to survive the
isolation of being temporarily fleshbound. However, because our anti-flesh opponents have been watching, it
has been best that you not know the entire plan. Besides, you were but a child during our people's transformation, and I was a great-grandfather. Have some respect
for your elders."

"Elders, shmelders," Khrushchev said. "I'm fifteen
thousand and twenty-two and you're fifteen thousand one
hundred and seventeen. Big difference!"

Eisenhower chuckled. "Bigger than you think,
Seeker-child."

Khrushchev crossed his arms across his tremendous
gut. "All right, moot point. But—*Buddy Holly?* Just what
do you hope to accomplish?"

Eisenhower shrugged. "We'll see."

"Terrific. If you ask me, constant airing of the same
not-regularly-scheduled program is just the sort of thing
that could send the fleshbound masses over the edge.
We're talking major wastage."

"I know," Eisenhower said, flipping his burger.
"Would you like one of these?"

"You know I'm on a diet. And don't try to change
the subject. I'm still pissed."

"A consequence of your current form, no doubt."

Khrushchev rolled his eyes and breathed deeply. "Look, at least tell me this: Why did you single out that one poor jerk to take the heat?"

Eisenhower smiled. "I didn't. His mother did. She bought and used the dish, you'll remember. She almost understood."

Khrushchev shook his head. "No. She was a flake whose flakiness *looked* like almost understanding. She fooled you just like she fooled the anti-flesh infiltrators who moved in next door to her."

Eisenhower said nothing.

Khrushchev's eyes widened. "Wait a minute," he said, uncrossing his arms. "I think I know what you're doing."

Eisenhower dropped a limp slice of American cheese onto his burger. "No, you don't," he said. "But if you pay close attention, maybe you will."

Khrushchev grinned. "I'm all ears." His immense body began to sprout.

"Stop that," Eisenhower said.

"All right, then. I'm all *tongues*."

"You're making me lose my appetite."

One of the tongues hit the grill and sizzled. Khrushchev yelped.

2

OLIVER

My grandparents moved to Topeka, taking Mother with them, in June 1959. Mother had turned eighteen and had finished high school. Her graduation picture is of a sad-eyed, narrow-faced young woman with dark, cheek-length hair. Below the border of the photograph, she was almost four months pregnant and starting to show.

On the first page of Volume II, she wrote: *Mama says we're moving because Daddy can get a better job at the Goodyear plant in Topeka, but when I asked Daddy if that was true he just gave me a dirty look and went to get another Falstaff. I shouldn't have asked, because I know the real reason. They want to get out of town before people know about C.'s baby. When we get to Topeka, they will no doubt tell folks that I was married but that my husband died a tragic death, which is true in a way, so I suppose I won't deny it.*

I feel bad that they are leaving Mikey in Des Moines to live with Grandma. He is a brat, but he is also my brother and I don't like knowing that he is being left because of me, although he says he wants to stay anyway. But since when does an eleven-year-old boy know what he wants? I don't know whether he knows about the baby yet, but if he did come to Topeka he would find out soon, and I guess Mama and Daddy don't want to put him through the humiliation. I feel angry with them, but really, they are acting about as well as could be expected. At least they haven't thrown me into the street, although I can't say that I would be surprised if they did. What better place for a whore than on the street? Not that I would know.

Mother never saw Uncle Mike again. He finally started answering her letters in 1967, after he was drafted, and the two of them became closer than they had ever been when they'd lived in the same house. They probably would have seen a lot of each other when he got back from Vietnam, except that he didn't. Someone turned a Claymore mine the wrong way, and Uncle Mike, who was huddling right where he was supposed to be safe, was killed anyway.

Long afterward, I learned that some Claymore mines were stenciled on one side with the words DO NOT EAT; apparently, they looked a lot like field rations. When I related this fact to Mother, she sighed and said, "That probably wouldn't have made any difference to Mikey."

After moving to Topeka, my grandfather took a job at the Goodyear plant as planned, and the fractured family settled into a small house in the Highland Park section of town to await my arrival. Mother didn't write much in Volume II during that summer or fall, so I have only a vague idea of what those months must have been like for her. From what little she did write, I know that the tension between her and my grandparents increased in direct proportion to the size of her belly. Her sole entry for the month of August reads: *It is so hot that the insides of my thighs are covered with prickly heat and I wish I could die. Mama is a sweating, complaining bitch. Daddy drinks too much beer and smells like burning tires. I am fat and my hair is stringy. C. took the easy way out. I am going to listen to "Heartbeat" on the record player again even though Mama says it is driving her loopy. The flip side is "Well All Right" and she likes it no better, so I'll play it too.*

With Mother in this state of mind, it should have come as no surprise to her that I refused to emerge on time. I was safe and comfortable where I was, and I had no desire to splurt out into a world where prickly heat existed and "It's So Easy" hadn't even made *Billboard*'s Top 100. I was due in early November, but Thanksgiving came and went with me still barricaded in the uterus, ignoring the fact that I was getting bigger all the time and causing Mother considerable discomfort. Seventeen years later, she told me that I had been extremely selfish in my refusal to be born, and I apologized. (I was humoring her. She was wrapped up in her UFO/Atlantis "research," and I had serious doubts about her stability.)

Finally, on the eighteenth anniversary of the bombing of Pearl Harbor, Mother decided that it was time to teach me some discipline. That evening, she wrote: *This is it, you little bastard. I'm going to fake contractions and scream bloody murder until Mama and Daddy take me to the God Damned hospital. I'll figure out what to do next when we get there, but count on it, your ride is over. Ten months is about three months too many if you ask me. I want to remember C., all right, but not to the point where I fucking explode. There, I used the f word, and if you read this, Mama, f you too.*

Mother did not record the details of the following twenty-four hours, mainly because she spent much of the time anesthetized. All I'm certain of is that everybody eventually gave up on the idea that I would ever comply in a normal fashion, and the doctors performed a cesarean section.

I was dragged out of the wound into the open air on the evening of Tuesday, December 8, 1959. I wasn't happy about it. The only silver lining was that now I might get to hear something besides "Heartbeat." My birth certificate lists my official name as Oliver C. Vale. According to Volume II, Mother had already chosen my first name and initial (no full middle name), and my grandmother lied to the hospital about my last name, which has nothing to do with Jerry Vale. It's Vale as in "of Tears." Needless to say, I grew up less than crazy about my grandmother.

*

Buddy was singing "Everyday" out in the living room while I was in the bedroom pulling on a sweatshirt and swapping my sweatpants for jeans. The song didn't sound quite right without the celeste, but a celeste was probably hard to come by on Ganymede. Buddy tried to make up for it by plinking his guitar strings, and it almost worked.

I decided not to change from my worn Nikes into cycle boots because I didn't want to waste time with laces. Sharon Sharpston, convinced as she was that I was the mental equivalent of mashed graham crackers, would worry if I took too long getting over to her place. There was no way, though, that I was going anywhere on a cold night without first zipping myself into the Moonsuit. It was hanging on its peg beside the dresser, looking like the husk of an alien criminal.

The blue waffle-stitched coverall filled with goose down had been Mother's Christmas gift to me in 1983,

just a month and nine days before her death. She had
sewn "Oliver" in red thread over the left breast pocket.
The "Oli" was gone now, but the "ver" was intact.

I made sure that my wallet and keys were still in
the left breast pocket and that the garage door's remote
control was still in the right, and then I took the Moonsuit down from its peg and stepped inside. After zipping
up, I felt warm and invincible. If the G-men from the
FCC came for me, I would simply envelop each one in
an enormous hug and waffle him to death.

Walking like a bear on its hind legs, I went back
through the living room and waved to Buddy, who was
still singing "Everyday." "Bye, Dad," I said. "See you
over at Sharon's, okay?"

Buddy nodded. Given that he was there in the first
place, I wasn't surprised.

I bear-walked to the utility room and opened the
door to the garage. I switched on the light as I entered—
and there, in all of her unsurpassed and cantankerous
beauty, waited Peggy Sue.

I don't know how many adult males have either
openly or secretly given their motorcycles feminine
names, but I would bet my SkyVue that they number in
the millions. Peggy Sue is a black 1957 646 cc Ariel Cyclone, and I love her as much as it is possible for a man
to love a machine, which is an embarrassing amount.
Unlike most of my other possessions, she was not made
in Japan, but in Birmingham, England.

I acquired her in July 1982, three weeks after my
faithful flop-eared mongrel dog, Ready Teddy, was run
down and scraped up by a road grader. The bike was
sitting in some old guy's yard with a cardboard "4-Sale"
sign taped to her handlebars, and except for the fact that
the oval Ariel emblems were missing from her fuel tank,
she appeared to be in great shape. I bought her for eight

hundred dollars within two minutes of seeing her. Mother
was furious with me for wasting money on my own death,
as she put it, but I knew that I had done the right thing.
If Peggy Sue happened to be run over, she could be put
back together, unlike poor Ready Teddy, who had gone
to the Spirit Land almost instantaneously. If I happened
to be on Peggy Sue when she was run over . . . well, at
least one of us would have an afterlife.

Less than a month after buying the motorcycle, I
was looking through Mother's rock 'n' roll books and re-
discovered that Buddy Holly had owned two motorcycles
in his short lifetime. The first was a Triumph that he'd
acquired shortly after seeing Marlon Brando and Lee
Marvin beat the crap out of each other in *The Wild One*.
The second was a bike he'd purchased in Dallas in 1957
or '58 and had ridden home to Lubbock. It was a 646 cc
Ariel Cyclone.

This was yet another piece of evidence demonstrat-
ing that my life was inexorably linked with Buddy's.
Mother seemed less disapproving of Peggy Sue once I
showed her the relevant paragraphs. Even she—*especially* she—could not argue against Fate.

As I stood looking at Peggy Sue on the night of Buddy's video resurrection, the thought came to me, not for
the first time, that she was not simply a bike like the
one Buddy had owned, but that she was *the* bike Buddy
had owned. It's possible. The current title of ownership
isn't the original, but was printed by the State of Kansas in 1980. According to this title, "Boog's Hog Works
of El Dorado" purchased Peggy Sue from an unnamed
salvage source and overhauled her, retitling her soon
thereafter and selling her to the old guy from whom I
bought her. Before El Dorado, she might have come from
anywhere.

Like my father C.'s true identity, Peggy Sue's history would probably be easy enough to investigate . . . but a belief in the purposeful complexity of Fate is always more comforting than random, straightforward facts. This may be why Mother preferred to believe in Atlantis and UFOs rather than in virtually everything else.

I closed the door to the utility room, then took cowhide gloves from the Moonsuit's back pockets and wriggled my hands into them. "Ready to roll," I said with forced cheerfulness as I approached Peggy Sue. "How about you?"

Peggy Sue's answer was negative. After unbuckling the white full-face helmet from the handlebars and pulling it on, I straddled the leather seat, opened the fuel valve, yanked the choke, and jumped up and down on the kick start, but all I could coax from her were wheezes. Peggy Sue, for all her beauty and significance, can be a real bitch in cold weather. In fact, she can be a real bitch in warm weather too. Anything made in 1957 is occasionally unreliable—witness Julie "Eat shit and die, Oliver" Calloway—but Peggy Sue often seems determined to elevate unreliability to high art.

On this particular night, the night when I had to get to Sharon's before the FCC fuzz came after me, Peggy Sue was being especially petulant. The fuel tank was full and every crucial part was in place, but she didn't care. Kick. *Cough.* Kick. *Sputter.* Kick. *Urgh.* Kick. *Blatt.* After ten minutes of this, I was almost ready to go back into the living room to ask Buddy whether *he* had any ideas about what an Ariel Cyclone wanted.

I kicked Peggy Sue's starter several more times and then stopped, startled by the noise of someone pounding on my garage door. The sound was remarkably like that produced by whanging on the SkyVue's block converter.

The cold, gnarled hand of terror closed on my heart. The Authorities had come for me. I didn't know whether they were county, state, or Federal, but they were here. Sharon and her eyebrow-mutant attorney couldn't help me now.

"I didn't do it!" I cried. "I swear, I'm not a computer-video genius! I'm as surprised as you are! Honest!" Because I was wearing my helmet, my voice sounded as though I were shouting from inside a Quaker oatmeal box.

On the other side of the garage door, something began growling, and an angry female voice shouted, "What business do you have messing up our TV?"

"Yeah, what business?" a male voice cried, harmonizing with the other.

The hand around my heart squeezed harder. The people outside were not the Authorities, but my neighbors who owned the cow-sized Doberman. The growling meant that they had brought the beast with them.

"Oliver Vale has been taken to prison," I yelled, "so go away and let us do our jobs! We're dusting for fingerprints and scanning for bugging devices!"

The growl became louder, and the garage door shook as my neighbors tried to open it. I wished that I could remember their names, or even what they looked like.

"Don't give us that!" the woman's voice snarled. "We heard you trying to start your motorcycle! You're in there, all right!"

"Yeah, you're in there!" the male voice emphasized.

"May I ask who's calling?" I shouted.

"You know damn well who's calling! It's Cathy and Jeremy from next door, and we brought Ringo with us, so you'd better not do anything threatening or he'll rip open your crotch!"

"Uh . . . he'll get you," the male voice said. Jeremy was less enthusiastic about crotch-ripping than was Cathy.

I dismounted Peggy Sue and approached the garage door. "Listen, guys," I said, loud enough so that they could hear me over Ringo's growling. "I know that Buddy gave out my address, but I had nothing to do with what happened to your TV. It happened to mine too, and I don't like it any better than you do. As a fellow satellite-dish owner—down with scrambling!—I sympathize completely."

"Oh, sure!" Cathy said. "That really makes me feel a lot better about missing the World Curling Chamionships!"

"I thought we were going to watch the dirty movie channel from Portugal," Jeremy said.

"Shut up!" Cathy shrieked.

I saw my chance. "A fine pair you are!" I said. "I've a good mind to report you to Bill Willy!" Oklahoma City's infamous Reverend William Willard was, among many other things, the leader of Oklahomans and Kansans Righteously Against Pornography (OKRAP), and he and his elite "Corps of Little David" were notorious for harrassing smut consumers both at home and at their places of employment. Once, in '82, he had arranged a sit-in at a funeral home because two of its employees had been accused of removing clothing from total strangers. Mother, for reasons I never understood, sent Bill Willy a five-dollar check after this incident.

There was silence for a moment (Ringo even stopped growling) and then Cathy said, in a much calmer voice, "There's no need to call anyone, Mr. Vale. We just naturally assumed that you were responsible for the problem with the TV, since your name was announced and you're known to be handy with electronics. We're sorry to have bothered you. Come on, Jeremy. Ringo, heel. *Heel,* damn it!"

I heard their shoes and paws crunch away down the gravel driveway. My bluff had worked. Nobody wanted to risk tangling with Bill Willy.

I returned to Peggy Sue, tinkered with her throttle and choke, then mounted and tried to kick her to life again. This time, she sputtered for thirty or forty seconds before I realized that she was running, sort of. While she warmed up, I checked the chain slack and lubrication and decided that the machine would probably haul me the twelve miles to Sharon Sharpston's apartment without too much trouble.

I switched on the headlight and toe-tapped Peggy Sue into first gear, then wheeled her around and let her idle up to the garage door. She almost died when I took my right hand off the throttle grip, and I patted her fuel tank as she recovered.

Then I pushed my thumb against the Moonsuit's right breast pocket to activate the garage door's remote control, and the white aluminum wall began to rise as if it were the hull of an anti-gravity spaceship. That thought triggered another, and I wondered just how Buddy Holly could have gotten to Ganymede in the first place.

I would've thought about that further, but as the door opened, spilling yellow light into the driveway, I discovered that Cathy, Jeremy, and Ringo had returned under cover of Peggy Sue's engine noise.

Although Cathy and Jeremy were bundled in coats and stocking caps, I could see that they were an attractive WASPish couple in their forties. Cathy was taller than Jeremy, but other than that I didn't notice their specific physical characteristics. I was too busy noticing Ringo's.

The Doberman was as tall as Peggy Sue's handlebars, and he was wearing a collar of galvanized chain suitable for anchoring an aircraft carrier. His ears stood straight up, his eyes glittered, and his upper lip pulled back from teeth that looked strong and white from biting through countless femurs.

"All right, Vale!" Cathy cried. "You're going to fix our TV or our dish or whatever you screwed up, and you're going to do it *now*! You don't scare us, and neither does Bill Willy!"

"That's right!" added Jeremy.

I licked my lips. I truly would have liked to go over to Cathy and Jeremy's to do what they demanded. Under normal circumstances, I would have assumed that if crescent-wrench-whanging worked for my SkyVue, it would also work for their more widely known model. But these were not normal circumstances. There was nothing I could do for them, and I was running out of time to do something for myself. I had to get to Sharon's before someone with a badge came to take me away to less comfortable accommodations.

"Out of my way!" I shouted. "I've got to get to a psychologist in Topeka!"

I popped Peggy Sue's clutch and twisted the throttle, and—uncharacteristically—she roared and leaped forward, spinning her rear tire on the cement floor with a sound like a banshee's wail. Cathy, Jeremy, and Ringo scrambled aside, and the Ariel and I blasted into the darkness toward the Spirit Land.

As we hit the gravel, I kicked up to second gear, then kept my right hand on the throttle while I crossed my chest with my left to tap the garage door control. Glancing back, I saw that the door came down before Cathy or Jeremy could get inside, which pleased me until I noticed that Ringo wasn't with them. For the

briefest of moments I worried that the dog might have
run into the garage and been trapped there—but then,
in the pink wash of Peggy Sue's taillight, I glimpsed
the black mass that was rushing down the driveway
after me.

I faced forward and gunned Peggy Sue onto the
pavement of Southwest 163rd Street without checking
for traffic, but we weren't fast enough. As I leaned to
the left to make the turn toward Topeka, Ringo's jaws
clamped on the left exhaust pipe.

Peggy Sue and I began to go over. The front fork
twisted to the left, and I saw specks of green glass glit-
tering in the asphalt. I cried out, my voice like that of a
steer being slaughtered. My left hand came off the grip
and reached for the pavement, but my right hand
spasmed on the throttle, rapping out the engine. My eyes
locked with Ringo's, and I saw that they were nothing
like the eyes of any other dog I had ever seen. They were
black, faceted stones with blue sparks at their centers.

The Doberman's teeth were sinking into the exhaust pipe as if it were pizza dough.

My fingertips brushed the pavement.

And then everything—Ringo, the exhaust pipe, the
glass-speckled asphalt, my Moonsuited arm—began to
strobe with a scarlet glare.

Ringo jerked, lifting Peggy Sue's rear wheel into the
air and twisting me and the bike upright again. My head
snapped away from the dog and the pavement, and I saw
a car with flashing red lights top the hill a quarter mile
away. It was straddling the center line.

My left hand grabbed the clutch lever, and my right
hand reversed the torque on the throttle. Peggy Sue's
roar subsided, and I heard the sirens. The first car was
followed by a second, and a third, and a fourth. The road
to Topeka, and to Sharon's, was blocked.

Ringo, growling, lowered the rear wheel to the
pavement again. As it touched, I gunned the engine,
popped the clutch, and jerked the bike into a right-hand
U-turn. As much as the Doberman frightened me, the
four cop cars frightened me more. I didn't know whether
they contained state troopers, sheriff's deputies, highway patrolmen, or FCC enforcement officers, and I didn't
care. They were bearing down fast, and they would either
run me over or take me in.

I find it difficult to deal with Authorities.

Peggy Sue was sluggish for a moment, as if her rear
brake were on, but then she burst free and we shot away
like a missile. A half minute later, clipping along at
eighty miles per hour, I risked looking in the left mirror. The flashing lights were after me, but they were
much farther back than I had feared they would be. They
must have stopped at my driveway before figuring out
who the guy on the motorcycle was. Ringo was nowhere
in sight.

I put three hills between us and the cop cars, slowed
to forty, and cut off the bike's lights. Then we whipped
west onto the next gravel road and almost went into the
ditch because I could hardly see. The night was becoming cloudy, and if the moon was out, it was hidden.

"Make like the moon," I told myself, and turned this
way and that on gravel and dirt roads until I was sure
that the Authorities and their sirens couldn't find me.

I stopped under the bare branches of a walnut tree
beside an ice-encrusted low-water bridge, letting Peggy
Sue idle while I tried to think. My feet were freezing,
and I wished that I hadn't decided against wearing boots
for the trip to Sharon's.

That trip was out of the question now. I had stu-

pidly told Cathy and Jeremy that I was hurrying to a
psychologist, and even if the Authorities didn't question
my neighbors, they would surely decide to investigate
Sharon as soon as they found her number taped to my
phone.

I couldn't go back home either. The cops would spend
hours searching my house for evidence that I had mucked
up the entire world's television broadcasts, and even when
they found nothing, they would put the place under surveillance in the hope of nabbing me when I showed up.
I had watched enough cop operas on the tube to know
that much about police procedure.

"Whattaya think, Peggy Sue?" I asked.

Peggy Sue coughed. She didn't like to sit still, idling
in the cold. I was afraid to shut her down, though, because she might not start again. Then I'd be stuck without wheels in rural Shawnee County with no place to go
and nothing to look forward to except having my feet
amputated.

I had no family. Mother was gone, and so were her
parents and Uncle Mike. Besides, the only one I had
really known besides Mother was Grandmother, and we
hadn't liked each other. There were great-aunts and
great-uncles in the Des Moines area, but I didn't even
know their names.

Sharon wasn't the only friend to whom I could con-
ceivably go for help. There were others—coworkers at
Cowboy Carl's, mostly—but I was sure that the cops
would start watching them almost as soon as they started
watching my house and Sharon's apartment. Ditto for
Julie "Eat shit and die, Oliver" Calloway. There was no
sanctuary in the area for me.

Turning myself in to the FCC wasn't an option either.
Aside from the fact that I didn't believe I would be treated

with constitutional fairness, I wasn't entirely sure that
I wasn't guilty and that sooner or later some evidence
to that effect might turn up.

So I only had two possible destinations. On some
level, I must have known that from the first moment
that Buddy appeared on my Sony.

I could go to Clear Lake, Iowa, where he had played
his last concert. But my feet were too cold already, and
Clear Lake was four hundred miles northeast of where
I sat by the low-water bridge. Even with the Moonsuit,
I would be a fugitive popsicle before making it as far
north as Ames. Besides, what could I do at Clear Lake?
Start looking for UFOs to come down and save me, the
way Mother did? I had already made my pilgrimage there,
and there wasn't much to see. The Surf Ballroom was a
run-down brick building, and the field where the Bonanza had hit was only a field.

The other possibility was that I could try to reach
Lubbock, Texas, where Buddy had been born and raised.
The city lay a few hundred miles farther to the southwest than Clear Lake lay to the northeast, but at least
the weather would get a little warmer as I went. And
once I arrived, if I arrived . . .

Long after Buddy's death, a statue of him had been
erected across the street from Lubbock City Hall. It was
placed in the center of a large flower bed, a rarity in
that part of the country. I could go in among those flowers and stand with him awhile.

And when I had done that, there was something else
I could do.

Buddy Holly's body had been flown to Lubbock for
burial on Thursday, February 5, 1959. I knew from a
photograph in one of Mother's books that the ground-
flush headstone that came later had been inscribed with
these words:

IN LOVING MEMORY
OF OUR OWN
BUDDY HOLLEY
SEPTEMBER 7, 1936
FEBRUARY 3, 1959

To the right of those words was a carving of an abandoned electric guitar. It was leaning against a column
that looked as if it belonged in a temple of Apollo.

Until now, I had seen no point in undertaking the
long journey for so little reward. Dead was dead, and
Charles Hardin Holley would not come back to life for
me simply because I spent a day or two on the road for
him. I had seen photographs of the grave and the statue,
and I hadn't been able to think of anything the objects
themselves could do for me that the photographs couldn't.
Buddy's true legacy, after all, lay in his music, and I
could hear that anytime I liked. Compact disc technology would preserve it with crystal clarity until we wiped
ourselves out as a species, and even then those digital
codes might survive and give pleasure to whatever took
our place. Besides, who the hell wanted to go to Lubbock, Texas? Might as well head into Topeka for a hot
night at Taco Bell.

But when I tried to watch *The Searchers* and saw
Buddy instead, everything changed.

My brain knew that he couldn't really be talking
and singing from a pressurized, heated, radiation-
shielded bubble on a satellite of Jupiter; my brain knew
that someone had rigged up the fraud and had framed
me for it.

My soul, however, could feel that Buddy had come
back to life. I had seen him and heard him, and no actor
or computer-generated simulacrum could have done what

the figure on my Sony had done. He was real. He was *alive*.

So I would ride Peggy Sue to Lubbock. I would screw up my courage by going to the statue first, and then, if no one stopped me, I would go to the grave. I would discover for myself, for both brain and soul, whether his body was still there.

I turned on Peggy Sue's lights and dismounted to examine the contents of my wallet in the glare. My credit cards would be worse than useless; buying gas with Visa would be like revealing my position with a flare gun. I would have to rely on whatever cash I happened to have.

I had fifty-eight dollars and twenty-three cents. Based on Peggy Sue's usual fuel consumption, I calculated that I might make it to Lubbock if I didn't eat and if I stole a few bucks from vending machines or video games on the way. I was already a Federal fugitive, so what difference would a misdemeanor or two make?

Before remounting, I looked down at the bike's left exhaust pipe. Ringo had bitten off approximately seven inches, and a canine fang was wedged into a ragged tear in the chrome. I grasped the tooth and tugged, my gloves protecting my hands from the heat, and it came free. Examining it, I discovered that its base was not a bloody root, but a bent metal screw.

Veterinary dentistry had made strides of which I hadn't been aware. I was glad that I was miles away from Ringo and about to increase the distance.

I dropped the tooth into a Moonsuit pocket, then straddled Peggy Sue and put her into gear. It was only as I twisted the throttle that I noticed how different she sounded with the shortened, ragged exhaust pipe. The noise was as loud and raucous as that of a piston-engine airplane.

We headed south across the low-water bridge. If we

managed to make it as far as Oklahoma, I'd buy or steal
a road map. Until then, I wouldn't worry about getting
lost. I knew that my best route would pass through or
near Oklahoma City, and I had been there once before,
visiting the Cowboy Hall of Fame on an eighth-grade
field trip.

The cloud cover was thick now, and snow began to
fall. There was no wind, so the flakes fell straight and
gentle before Peggy Sue's light. We passed farms where
men in coveralls and earflapped caps were herding Hol-
steins to white buildings for the morning milking. Most
of the men waved.

"Oh, boy!" I shouted, strangely joyful.

It felt like Christmas.

SHARON

Notes on client Oliver Vale, continued . . .

2/3/89; 4:22 A.M.: Two Kansas Bureau of Investigation agents and three uniformed state troopers have just
left. They were looking for Oliver, but Oliver never arrived. I wasn't able to look for him either, because the
agents and troopers showed up just as I was heading out
the door.

I don't believe that a broadcasting violation is within
the KBI's purview, and I said so. They threatened me
with a charge of obstructing justice. Bruce commented
that if they tried that he would be forced to recommend
that I sue them until they became old and sick. That
made them still more abusive, but despite that, I was as
cooperative as my professional ethics would allow.

When I explained that I had not seen Oliver in over
a week (they didn't ask whether I had telephoned him,

so I didn't mention it), they left, muttering about a statewide manhunt.

I can only imagine what would have happened if Oliver/Buddy's initial interruption had occurred during prime time. In all likelihood, the governor would have called out the National Guard.

The KBI agents informed me that other officers were already on their way to Oliver's home. I have no way of knowing whether he left before they arrived, or whether they intercepted him en route here. I've just tried to phone him again, but after three rings his machine took the call. I recorded the answering tape, which I had not heard before:

"Hello, this is Oliver Vale. I can't come to the phone right now, but you probably have a wrong number anyway. If not, leave a message at the primal scream, and I'll send you the money I owe you. If you're one of Mother's old Flying Saucer cronies, she doesn't live here anymore. In fact, she doesn't live anywhere, because she's dead, like Jim Morrison. The only difference is that Morrison is supposedly buried in France, and Mother was definitely cremated in Topeka. As stipulated in her will, I scattered her ashes in a field near Clear Lake, Iowa. You can look for her there if you like, but I've got to tell you, it's just a field. *Beeeeep.*"

Oliver needs even more help than I had realized.

It is now 4:47 A.M. I intend to stay awake as long as I can in the hope that I will hear some news of him, and so that I can help him if he has been arrested. Bruce, however, went to bed as soon as the KBI agents left. I am angry with him for that, which is interesting, because there is no reason for anger. Oliver is my client, not Bruce's, and the truth is that I am not doing Oliver any good by sitting up by the telephone. So why should I be angry with Bruce for doing the sensible thing?

Anger = Anxiety + Fatigue.
I can hear the son of a bitch snoring.

CATHY AND JEREMY

They waited in the pale circle cast by Vale's yard
light while Ringo bounded up to them with a chunk of
chrome pipe in his mouth. He was wagging his bobbed
stump of a tail, and the blue sparks in his eyes were
bright.

"I was hoping to provoke him," Cathy said, speaking loudly to be heard over the approaching sirens. "The
fact that he simply fled presents a complication, but we
can deal with it."

Jeremy jerked a thumb toward the end of the driveway, where a blue automobile with flashing red lights
on its roof was entering. "Cheese it," he said, turning
toward their house. "The cops."

Cathy grasped his arm and gave him a look of disgust as three more shrieking, flashing automobiles
crammed into the driveway. "You still don't know the
first thing about how to handle the fleshbound, do you?"
she said. Then she put her hands to her head and began
screaming. "Oh, my God! Oliver Vale messed up our TV
and tried to attack us! After that he jumped on his horrible motorcycle and went that way!" She pointed south.

The cars stopped and the sirens' wails droned down.
The driver of the first car opened his door and began to
step out.

"That way, I tell you!" Cathy screamed.

Jeremy gave her a quizzical look. "Do we want them
after him?" he asked.

Cathy waved her arms and smacked the back of

Jeremy's head. Jeremy's right eye popped out and fell to the gravel.

The police officer who was emerging from his car stopped halfway and stared at Ringo, who still had the short length of exhaust pipe clenched in his jaws.

"Uh, I need to ask—" the officer began.

Ringo growled.

"That way!" Cathy shrieked, pointing south again.

The shriek galvanized the officer into action. "Right!" he shouted, turning to face the other three cars. "He went south! He's on a motorcycle!"

"Armed and dangerous!" Cathy cried, jumping up and down.

Jeremy got down on his hands and knees and began searching for his eye. "I really don't think we want these people to—"

Cathy collided with him, knocking him onto his side. "Well, go!" she told the police officer.

"Don't worry," the officer said, reentering his cruiser. "We have a warrant." He slammed his door shut, and one by one, the four cars backed out onto the pavement and sped away to the south, their sirens wailing again as they accelerated.

"A warrant from whom? I wonder," Jeremy said, still searching for his eye. "You'd think that the jurisdictional questions would need to be untangled first."

"Who cares?" Cathy said. "No doubt some high-powered judge didn't like having his Portuguese porn cut off. All that matters to me is that they're after him."

"Why?" Jeremy spotted his eye and crawled toward it.

Cathy reached down and plucked the eye from the gravel before Jeremy's fingers could close on it. She tossed the blue-and-white sphere from one hand to the other. "For six years we've been waiting for Vale to try to contact the pro-flesh agitators so that we could prevent him and maintain the status quo," she said, "but in all that time he's done nothing—and until now, they haven't tried to communicate with him either."

"I guess they got tired of waiting."

"They aren't the only ones." Cathy shivered. "It's going to snow, and I hate snow. Flesh gets cold, and bored. So, as long as Vale's running, I want the fleshbound police after him. If they lock him up, our problem's as good as solved, and if they don't, his fear may force him to finally act. If that happens, then either the pro-flesh experiment succeeds or we're able to foil it. But no more limbo." She slapped her legs with her free hand. "No more limbs."

Jeremy stood. "But if they don't catch him quickly, we'll have to follow him. In the Datsun, for Christ's sake."

Cathy shook her head. "Until he tries something, all we have to do is watch him." She whistled, and Ringo dropped the tail pipe, wagging his stump and giving her a wide Doberman grin.

"Aw, look," Jeremy said. "He lost a tooth. I'll see if we have a spare."

Cathy squatted and pressed her thumb against the side of Ringo's right eye until it popped out. "There's no time to bother with that," she said, pushing Jeremy's eye into Ringo's empty socket. Now the dog had one black eye with a blue spark, and one blue eye with a black pupil.

Jeremy clapped a hand over his own empty socket. "Yag! I'll get dizzy and throw up!"

"So take out your left one too," Cathy said. She picked up the length of exhaust pipe and held it against Ringo's nose. "Ringo! Go follow!"

The Doberman sniffed, then loped away, turning south as he reached the road.

Cathy stood. "That's all we need to do right now. I doubt that Vale will find a way to call on our misguided brothers without returning here first, and in that case we can stop him."

Jeremy lurched off the driveway and began staggering across the dead yard. "Oh, dog, not so fast," he moaned.

Cathy caught up with him and inserted Ringo's eye into his socket. "This should improve your reception and balance. Keep me apprised of what he sees. Six years of fleshbound life are riding on this."

"Some life," Jeremy said. "I don't even have working genitals."

Cathy took his arm and steered him toward their house. "That's a psychological problem."

"So my psychology doesn't work either."

She patted his hand. "Maybe we won't have to put up with any of it much longer. How's Ringo doing?"

"He's stopped to urinate on a tree. Oh, disgusting— I can *feel* it!"

Cathy sighed. "Bitch, bitch, bitch."

3

OLIVER

I remember little of my infancy. I do have a vague recollection of being breast-fed, but according to Volume II of Mother's diary, I was strictly a bottle-baby. Even back then, it would seem, I had an active imagination.

On the whole, I am thankful for my lack of memories from this period, because Volume II depicts my early years as having been horrific. Grandfather plunged deeper and deeper into the Falstaff well from which he would never emerge, and Grandmother became a bitter, wounding harpy—while Mother, as a teenage single parent in 1960, had no choice but to live with them until I was old enough for full-time school. To make things worse, I contracted every ailment known to babyhood— colic, diaper rash, croup, measles, mumps, impetigo, ear infections, you name it—and all before my first birthday.

It is a lousy way to start, Mother wrote while I was crusty with impetigo. *How is he catching all of this stuff, anyway? We never go anywhere except to the doctor's office.*

Meanwhile, Grandmother took every opportunity to preach to Mother about how this was what always happened to babies born out of sin: The sin stayed with them, staining them with illness, for their entire lives. Mother would have liked to take a job in order to escape this refrain for at least eight hours a day, but that would have meant leaving me with Grandmother (no day care in Topeka in 1960), which she was not willing to do. *There's no telling what Mama might do in one of her moods,* she wrote.

This may not have been paranoia. My first clear memory, from when I was perhaps two years old, is of Mother preventing Grandmother from smacking me in the face because I had ralphed up my Cream of Wheat. The first complete phrase I learned was "drowned at birth."

Mother kept the radio in our bedroom tuned to the local rock 'n' roll station. *It is the one thing in my world that offers any joy,* she wrote. *Despite what happened to Buddy Holly, despite even what happened to C., this music makes me feel as though I and my son might live forever.*

Which we wouldn't.

I remember when I realized this. It was lunchtime on a Saturday, four days after my fifth birthday. I liked Saturdays because there was no kindergarten. (I was the youngest kid in Mrs. Johnson's morning class, and the other kids called me "the baby.") Mother and I were in our room listening to the radio and finishing off the last of my chocolate birthday cake. As a song ended, the disc jockey said, "Now let's spin a few in tribute to the late Sam Cooke, who died last night in Los Angeles at the age of twenty-nine."

The radio started playing "You Send Me."

Mother was sitting on the floor with a piece of cake

in her hand, staring at the radio on her dresser. She was so still and quiet that I was scared.

"Mother?" I said.

She didn't acknowledge me. She just kept staring at the radio.

I crawled onto her lap and hugged her. She didn't hug me back.

"Everything dies," she said.

I pressed my face into her sweater. She smelled of baby powder, and the sweater made my eyes itch. I began to cry.

She held me then and stroked my hair and face. Her hands were cold. My grandparents didn't believe in wasting money on heating the house.

"Not you, Oliver," Mother murmured as she rocked me. "Not you, baby, not you."

I could hear the lie.

I knew what death was. I had seen a squirrel run over in the street. It had lain there for weeks until it had become a virtual part of the blacktop. That had happened to Sam Cooke. That was going to happen to me.

Years later, I learned that Sam Cooke's demise had been even less glorious than that of the squirrel. In the reported version of reality, he was shot three times by the owner of a motel where he had been trying to make it with a woman who didn't want to be made.

But even if I had heard that and had been able to understand it at the age of five, the knowledge wouldn't have made any difference in how I felt. After all, I wasn't mourning for Sam Cooke. His voice was still alive, and I would hear it again and again. I wasn't even mourning for Buddy Holly, because Mother had told me that he still lived inside me, and that his music was immortal.

I was mourning for Mother. I was mourning for me.

We were not immortal.

This was not an easy revelation for my five-year-old
self. I had nightmares for months afterward. They usually involved my being run over, like the squirrel, while
"You Send Me" echoed in the street as I was mashed.

That day in the bedroom, my chocolate cake sticky
in my throat, I learned that only the music lasts. From
that moment on, I paid closer attention to the songs on
the radio, listening for the secret of eternal life.

Volume II reveals that Sam Cooke's death was a
turning point for Mother as well. It was the impetus that
started her down the path to true weirdness. She wrote,
*All things beautiful are doomed. The purer the voice, the
truer the vision, the more vibrant the song, the sooner
death comes for the perpetrator.*

*The only way to escape this truth is to deny the real-
ity from which it has been created, to exist in some other
universe altogether.*

*So it is time to believe in flying saucers. Dianetics is
worth serious consideration. Lee Harvey Oswald acted
alone. Mississippi welcomes visiting Jews. Vietnam will
become the fifty-first state. My son Oliver is the reincarnation not only of Buddy Holly, but of the Buddha. Mama
is the reincarnation of Lot's wife. I can fly to the moon if
I tape a photograph of John Glenn to my forehead.*

Rereading that passage makes me realize something: The mention of Lee Harvey Oswald is the only
reference to the assassination of John F. Kennedy in any
of Mother's diary entries, and I have no recollection of
November 22, 1963, even though I was almost four years
old at the time.

Maybe if Kennedy had cut a record.

*

Seven hours after Buddy appeared on my Sony, Peggy Sue and I found ourselves 115 miles southwest of there, riding through a treeless prairie on U.S. 54, aiming for the city of El Dorado. (Pronounced El Doraydo, not El Dorahdo. This was still Kansas.) We had traveled farther than 115 miles, though, because whenever possible we had taken county roads and state highways to avoid the troopers cruising the U.S. highways and the Kansas Turnpike. The snow had stopped at dawn and hadn't accumulated, so the roads hadn't been bad, but the cold had been harder on me than I'd expected. My body was chilled almost to the point of numbness, and my feet were already there. The dull gray sky wasn't helping me think warm thoughts.

In addition, Peggy Sue was thoroughly grumpy. She'd started sputtering and stumbling a few miles south of Emporia, and switching the fuel valve to the reserve tank hadn't helped. I begged her to hold out just long enough for us to find a hiding place for the day. I didn't want to keep traveling while the sun was up because we might be spotted by a Kansas Highway Patrol airplane, and if we had to stop on the prairie, we were as good as caught.

The Ariel's engine died a half mile short of the El Dorado city limits sign, but we were able to coast into a self-service gas station. The hands of a cracked Pepsi-Cola clock attached to the FUEL-U-PUMP sign said that the time was twenty minutes past eight o'clock. Cowboy Carl's would open in forty minutes, and the boys would wonder why I was late for work again. I had not slept in twenty-six hours.

The red column of mercury in a Dr Pepper thermometer on the stucco building topped out at forty-one degrees. That was almost twenty degrees warmer than it had been at home when I'd left, but even inside the

Moonsuit I felt as though I had spent the night packed in dry ice. Dismounting was an adventure in pain because my knees didn't want to bend back straight and because putting weight on my feet was like stabbing them with pickle forks. I was beginning to suspect that there was no way in hell that Peggy Sue and I could make it to Lubbock.

I filled the bike's tank from the lone Regular pump, then staggered into the building and gave five dollars to the shriveled man behind the counter. That left me with a little over fifty-three bucks. A radio beside the cash register was playing mournful country music, heavy on the steel guitars and slow on the beat.

I had removed my gloves to accept the few cents of change due me, but my cold fingers fumbled the coins and dropped them. The counterman peered at me through inch-thick eyeglasses and said, "You okay to keep riding that Harley?"

My faceplate was fogging, so I flipped it up as I squatted, knees popping, to retrieve the coins. "It's not a Harley," I said.

He glanced out the smudged window. "Triumph?"

I lost my balance and fell onto my rump, realizing that I shouldn't have corrected the old man. I should have let him think Peggy Sue was anything but what she was. "Yeah," I lied. "A 1962 Triumph Thunderbird."

He frowned as I scraped up the coins and lurched to my feet. "I see you've got a Shawnee County sticker on your plate," he said. If his eyes were sharp enough to see that, they were sharp enough to see that there were no Triumph emblems on Peggy Sue's fuel tank. At least there were no Ariel emblems there either.

My right hand knotted around the coins, and their edges bit into my fingers. "Yeah," I said, heading toward the door.

"Bet you could use a cup of coffee," the old man said.

I shook my head and pushed open the door.

"Only fifty cents," he called after me. Just then the country music stopped and a news bulletin began: "For those of you who haven't turned on your TV sets yet today . . ."

I hurried outside, shoving my change into a Moonsuit pocket and pulling on my gloves. As I straddled my bike and snapped up the kickstand, I thought, *Everyone is an enemy.*

Peggy Sue didn't want to fire, and I jumped furiously on the starter. I was sweating now, and my eyes stung. My body's numbness had disappeared and been replaced by an itching heat. I glanced at the stucco building and saw the old man staring out at me.

I dismounted, grasped the Ariel's handgrips, and pushed. If I could find a hill, I might get up enough speed for a clutch-popping start—but at that moment I didn't care if I had to push forever as long as we got away from that gas station. I felt the old man's gaze drilling into my back as I shoved Peggy Sue's five hundred pounds out of the drive and began trudging down the shoulder of the highway. I was breathing hard, and for the first time I noticed that the air was tinged with a stink of burning crude oil.

I stopped beside the city limits sign and tried to kick-start the bike again, but all she did was sputter. Inside the Moonsuit, my clothes were sticking to my skin, and inside my helmet, my hair was wet. Even my feet were hot. I resumed pushing.

A few hundred yards inside the city limits, we passed a windbreak of evergreens that lay perpendicular to the highway on the north side. West of that windbreak was a two-story white building with seven gray doors visible on each floor. A flaking sign out front displayed the words

FIFTY-FOUR MOTOR INN REASONABLE RATES outlined in dead
neon tubes. The "Vacancy" appendage hummed and
flickered, but it was a redundancy. The only vehicle in
the parking lot was a battered Pinto in front of the door
labeled "Office" at the west end. As I paused, an obese
woman carrying a plastic trash bag emerged from around
the building's southeast corner. An access road branched
off from the parking lot there, running between the motel and the trees. That might mean that there was a
second lot and more rooms on the north side, hidden from
the highway.

I began pushing Peggy Sue again, but I kept watching the woman. The bike and I were barely thirty yards
away from her, but she didn't even glance at us. She
was gazing down at the concrete walkway, mumbling
words that I couldn't make out. When she reached the
office, she took a keyring from her coat pocket, unlocked
the door, and went inside. The curtains over the window
beside the door stayed closed.

I looked behind me and saw that the highway had
curved so that the FUEL-U-PUMP station had vanished behind the row of evergreens. Even if he was still watching, the old man wouldn't see me now, so I guided my
motorcycle onto the sparse gravel of the motel parking
lot. To my helmet-encased ears, the noise made by her
tires sounded like thunder.

I parked the bike beside the Pinto and approached
the office cautiously to observe and evaluate my enemy.
If the obese motel manager caught me, I would never
make it to Lubbock. I would never discover whether
Buddy had truly arisen, and I would never know why
his image had singled me out for persecution or glory.

Understand: I didn't *want* to break into a room and
sleep there without paying. Despite what the FCC
thought of me, I had never willingly broken any law ex-

cept the occasional speed limit or controlled substances statute. I had never stolen from anyone. At least, not much. But fatigue and fear go a long way toward breaking down the superego.

There was just enough space between the curtains to let me see into the office. The woman was lying on a couch below the window, watching the snow-speckled screen of a color TV atop the registration desk. Buddy was on the screen, and the sound was turned up loud enough that I could hear him doing his version of "Bo Diddley." The Great Red Spot floated above his tousled hair like a halo.

The woman lay as still as a lump of dough; the volume of the television had kept her from hearing my bike's tires on the gravel. I returned to Peggy Sue, pushed her down the length of the building to the access road, and sure enough found an empty northern parking lot and fourteen more rooms.

At the lot's far edge, a chain-link fence threaded with dead vines marked the boundary of a salvage yard. The scabrous skulls of three GMC pickup trucks grinned at me through the links. Their windshields were intact. They had made it to the Spirit Land.

A blue dumpster with stenciled letters indicating that it was emptied on Tuesdays sat in the lot's northeastern corner. I hid Peggy Sue behind it.

"Talk to her if she gets lonely," I told the nearest truck skull.

Then I crossed to the motel and climbed metal stairs to the second-floor walkway. I was feeling an echo of the primitive urge for height, of our ancestors' need to see danger approaching at a distance . . . which made little sense in my situation, because once inside a room, I would keep the curtains drawn. Also, if my enemies blocked the stairs, my only escape would be to jump over the walkway railing. Ignoring these facts, I chose the corner room, number 15.

As I had hoped, the FIFTY-FOUR MOTOR INN REASON-ABLE RATES had lousy door locks, the kind that will open to a credit card slid between the jamb and the spring bolt. Unfortunately, I was so tired that my coordination was screwed, so after a few tries I gave up on that method and rammed the door with my shoulder. The wooden jamb was rotten, and the bolt ripped through it as if it were moist cardboard. The break-in made only a small noise, so I didn't think the woman at the other end of the building could have heard it.

Once inside number 15, I fumbled in the gray light filtering through the curtains and chained the door. Then I started laughing. The base plate of the chain was nailed into a jamb with the strength of frozen pudding, and *I had chained the door.*

I laughed so hard that I was barely able to unbuckle and pull off my helmet, and I collapsed face-first onto the bed to muffle myself. The pebbled bedspread smelled like day-old dinner rolls. The bedsprings sagged and squeaked. I laughed until the only sound I could make was a strangled wheeze. My abdomen ached. Tears tickled my nose. I couldn't move. I slept.

I was awakened by pain in my crotch. I hadn't stopped to piss during the ride down from Topeka, and Peggy Sue and the road had pounded my bladder and kidneys the whole way. I'd been so cold and tired that I hadn't even been aware of the problem until now.

I sludged out of bed, supported myself with a hand on the wall, and shuffled around a corner into the closet-size bathroom. When I flipped the light switch, a buzzing white fluorescence almost slammed me to the floor. The glare wouldn't be seen outside number 15, but from where I stood, it hurt almost as much as the urine pressure.

I threw my gloves into the main room, squirmed out of the Moonsuit and kicked it after the gloves, then shoved my jeans and shorts to my knees in a panic. I was grateful that the toilet didn't have a lid. The relief was momentary, however. My guts twisted, and I had to finish in a hurry in order to turn around. Diarrhea. An ache began pulsing behind my left eye.

After flushing the toilet, which made ominous gurgling noises, I tried to throw up. All I could do was heave. The last thing I'd eaten had been a few handfuls of microwave popcorn just before leaving home.

When the heaving stopped, I struggled up from my knees, pulled up my underwear and jeans, and saw my face in the speckled mirror over the sink. My hair was rumpled, and I looked a lot like Buddy might look without glasses, except that the whites of my eyes were tracked with crimson veins. I glanced at my wristwatch; the time was a little after 3:00 P.M. I had been wearing my gas-permeable contact lenses for thirty-two hours. With that realization, I experienced a sensation like having Comet shoved under my eyelids.

I removed the lenses and rinsed them in the ochre water that jitterbugged from the faucet. I had neither a storage case nor wetting solution. Sharon Sharpston wore the same type of gas-permeable lenses, so I had planned to borrow those things while I stayed at her apartment.

What might Sharon be doing at that moment? I wondered. I pictured her sitting on a straight-backed chair in a police station in Topeka, her chopped auburn hair standing at attention, her violet eyes looking down her impossibly straight nose at the Authority who was trying to question her.

"My professional ethics prevent me from discussing

my client's psychological profile," she would be saying.
"However, I can tell you that he is an intriguing person
whom I find tremendously exciting sexually. Now, if you
badger me any further, my boyfriend Bruce will give you
a sound thrashing with the Constitution."

The pain behind my left eye increased. In the almost three years that I had known Sharon, I had never
been able to visualize her naked. Bruce always came into
the picture before I was able to unfasten anything.

I went back into the main room and placed my contact lenses on the palm of one of my gloves, which had
landed beside the TV on the desk. The set was an ancient black-and-white Zenith, and when I snapped it on,
it filled the room with pale flashes. Only one channel
displayed a viewable picture, but one channel was all
that I or anyone else would need today.

"—Southwest 163rd Street, Topeka, Kansas," Buddy
was saying. His fuzzy image scrolled up a few times, then
came to an unsteady rest. "You know, folks," he continued, shaking his head, "it's no fun being stranded. I'd
appreciate some help soon, please, either from this Oliver
Vale or from whoever can think of anything."

He took a deep breath, then shook his head again
and began playing "What to Do."

I sat on the foot of the bed, staring at the screen
and feeling guilty. We hadn't even managed to hustle
our lazy butts to Mars yet, so how could we ever hope to
get to Ganymede to save a kid who couldn't do much for
us anyhow except write songs and play the guitar?

At that thought, I became afraid that I knew what
the pain behind my left eye was. It was apeshit insanity
trying to bore up into my forehead and spread through
my brain like a metastasizing carcinoma.

It couldn't be sane to think of the video-Ganymede
as reality. It made much more sense to believe that the

image on the Zenith, and the one at home on my Sony, were random outpourings of electrons following the same logic as the infinite number of monkeys with the infinite number of typewriters cranking out *Julius Caesar* and *I, the Jury*. In a universe chockful of chaotic energies, didn't the Uncertainty Principle and the Laws of Thermodynamics predict that a televised rock 'n' roll ghost was bound to pop up sooner or later?

I wished that I had toughed it out in my one attempt to take physics at K-State.

Not that an answer would have made any difference. Even after six hours of sleep, my soul's belief in Buddy was as strong as it had been beside the low-water bridge. I would have to learn to live with the pain behind my eye.

The guilt was another matter. Madness I can handle, but guilt sucks.

I had decided to go to Lubbock to discover the truth of what had happened, but if Buddy had truly arisen, I would have to do more. I would have to find a way to rescue him. If his ascension to Ganymede meant that he had become immortal in life as well as in music, I would have plenty of time.

The pain behind my eye increased, and I leaned forward to shut off the TV. The Zenith crackled and glared with a bright dot, but unlike my Sony, it didn't turn itself on again. I thanked it for that.

A few hours remained before it would be dark enough for me and Peggy Sue to leave the FIFTY-FOUR MOTOR INN REASONABLE RATES. I wasn't sleepy anymore, though, so to kill time I turned on the pink plastic radio that sat beside the lamp on the nightstand. I was careful to keep the volume low in case the woman in the office had turned off her television.

"—last seen driving south on a county road near To-

peka. Registration records describe the vehicle as a black
1957 Ariel Cyclone motorcycle, a model that resembles
Triumph motorcycles of the same era. Vale apparently
fled spontaneously, so his destination, if any, is unknown. Police, county sheriff's deputies, state troopers,
and highway patrol officers are scouring the eastern half
of the state—"

"It's a dirty job, but somebody has to do it," I
muttered.

"—and their counterparts in Oklahoma, Nebraska,
and Missouri have been alerted. Once again, any citizen
who sees anyone fitting the description of Oliver Vale is
urged to contact the nearest law-enforcement office at
once. According to reports, the 'Buddy Holly' television
intrusion is nationwide, and late reports are that normal broadcasts in foreign countries, including the Soviet
Union, have also been displaced. State Department
sources warn that we may find ourselves embroiled in a
serious international incident if this situation is not resolved quickly. The White House has no comment."

The newscast ended, and the reporter was replaced
by a disc jockey. "Well, friends and neighbors," the dee-
jay said, "it looks to me like we're livin' in peculiar times,
yes indeedy. One thing you can count on, though: KOWW
ain't ever played that rock and roll noise, and we ain't
ever going to. So this is the place to get away from what's
on your TV."

A song turgid with steel guitars began playing. I
twisted the tuning knob, and it fell off.

I listened to the steel guitars. Curiously, the whiny
music soothed me, and I relaxed more with every drunken
note. Maybe it was because the songs and rhythms with
which I had grown up had been mostly frantic and loud.
Whatever the reason, though, I lay back and slept again.
I even had a pleasant sexual dream about Julie "Eat

shit and die, Oliver" Calloway in which she more than
repented for earning her nickname.

When I awoke, the news announcer was back, saying the same things he'd said before. I turned off the
radio and sat up, stretching. My watch said that it was
six o'clock. Almost time to go. I stripped off my clothes
and, with only a rotten doorjamb protecting me from the
world, went naked into the bathroom. The water emerged
from the shower head at a fast dribble, alternating between chilled and scalding. I washed with a sliver of
brown soap that smelled like turpentine and dried with
a towel that was covered with old cigarette burns.

I had left the bathroom and was still toweling when
a metallic booming noise echoed outside. It was the sound
of something bumping an empty dumpster.

Someone had found Peggy Sue.

A smart person would have paused to think. A smart
person would have inserted his contact lenses and peeked
out between the curtains to see what was going on. A
smart person would have put on his pants.

"Oliver," Mother once told me, "you are sensitive,
sweet, and loving, with good taste in music, but you will
save yourself a lot of trouble if you remember that what
you are _not_ is smart. No reflection on you. It's genetic."

I was out in the forty-degree air and down the stairs
before the dumpster had stopped vibrating. It was only
as I stepped on an especially sharp bit of gravel halfway
to the dumpster that I stopped and noticed my situation.

It was cold. I was nude. The sole of my right foot
was stinging. An enormous out-of-focus man with wild
red hair and a beard to match stood beside the dumpster. His features were blurry, but it was obvious that
he was looking at me fiercely. He was wearing a Harley-
Davidson cap and oil-stained overalls. As I squinted at

him, he reached into a bib pocket and pulled out a crescent wrench much like the one I keep on my coffee table.

All I had with me was the cigarette-burned towel.
"Get away from my bike," I said, twirling the towel into
a rat tail, "or I'll snap you into a coma." I was hoping to
make him think I was crazy. Even accomplished fighters
hate to mix it up with lunatics.

The big man glanced behind the dumpster. "I wondered who belonged to this," he said in a voice corre-
sponding to his size and hair. He looked back toward
me. "Go put on some clothes, boy. I ain't gonna hurt
your machine. I was screwin' around in the salvage yard,
and I had to hop the fence when I saw the bike. A six-
fifty Ariel is rarer than a disease-free fuck with a
porno queen."

I was nonplussed.

"Well, go on," he said, gesturing toward the motel
with his wrench. "Don't just stand there with your dick
shrinking."

I took a few steps backward, then turned and began
to wrap the towel around my waist as I walked.

The obese motel manager came around the corner
of the building before I had covered my crotch. She was
too far away for me to see her expression, but her scream
told me all I needed to know. I began sprinting for the
stairs, and she spun and ran, thinking I was after her.
Indecent exposure and attempted sexual assault were
about to be added to the list of my crimes.

As I charged up the stairs to number 15, I heard the
red-haired man's laugh. It was the sort of laugh elicited
by The Three Stooges and Wile E. Coyote. It was the
sort of laugh that said, *Oh, sweet Jesus, am I glad that
isn't me!* I couldn't hold it against him.

I jabbed my contact lenses into my eyes and yanked
my clothes on, not even pausing when I saw that my

briefs were inside-out and backward. I was imagining
the progress of the motel manager's phone call to the El
Dorado police and estimating their response time. As I
zipped up the Moonsuit, I decided that I had a slim chance
of making it out of town if Peggy Sue started right away.

Peggy Sue never started right away.

I clattered down the stairs, pulling on my helmet as
I went, and ran to the dumpster. The red-haired man's
crescent wrench was back in his pocket, and he stuck
out an open hand as I approached.

"Boog Burdon," he said.

"A pleasure," I said, touching his hand as I dashed
around him to my bike. The Ariel was nosed into the
narrow space behind the dumpster, so I would have to
roll her out before trying to start her.

"Couldn't help but notice the Shawnee County tag,"
Boog said. "You the dude Buddy Holly mentioned on the
Today show this morning?"

"That wasn't the *Today* show," I said, wrestling
Peggy Sue out backward and turning her to face the access road.

"Well, he was in that fuckin' time slot," Boog said.

I mounted Peggy Sue, opened the fuel valve, and
began jumping on the kick starter. "I'm not responsible," I said as I jumped. "I didn't bring him back to life
or send him to Ganymede, I swear it."

Boog took out his crescent wrench again. I screamed
a string of nonsense syllables.

"Shut up," Boog said. "I'm just gonna take off your
goddamn license plate."

I stopped kicking. "Huh?"

Boog moved to the rear of the bike, squatted, and
fitted his wrench to one of the bolts that held the plate
to the rear fender. "Radio says various fuzz are after your
ass, and if this bike don't draw their attention, the tag

sure as shit will." He squinted up at me. "You're kind of stupid."

"It's genetic," I said, and jumped on the starter again.

"Sit the fuck still," Boog said. "Soon as I get this off, I'll start the bitch. I remember her." He scowled. "Christ, what'd you do to the left exhaust? Let an alligator suck on it?"

I remembered now that Peggy Sue had been owned by "Boog's Hog Works of El Dorado" before being purchased by the old guy from whom I'd gotten her. "It was bitten off by a dog," I said.

"A fuckin' lesson for us all," Boog muttered, grunting as the license plate came free. He twirled the bolts back into the empty bracket and stood, flinging the plate over the truck skulls into the heart of the salvage yard. "Soon as you can, swipe an out-of-state tag," he said.

Then he nodded in the direction that he had thrown the plate. "Coupla old dead Indian cycles in there. Can you fuckin' believe it? Nobody knew they was there until they hauled out some DeSoto bodies yesterday and found 'em underneath." He shook his head. "Poor old bastards ain't much but rust now."

A siren shrieked in the distance.

"You said you could start my bike?" I asked.

Boog turned back and gestured for me to get off. Reluctant but desperate, I dismounted. He got on and kicked the starter a few times, harder than I could, but Peggy Sue still refused to start.

The siren was getting louder.

Boog whanged on the fuel valve and carburetor with his crescent wrench. I began to like him.

"A bike gets old, crap flakes off in the tank," he said as he whanged. He didn't seem to have noticed the siren. "You gotta start using better gas, make sure you don't get none of that alcohol junk, and change the filter screen a couple of times a year. It's like when people get old, they're supposed to eat more broccoli and bran flakes, but their asses get clogged up anyhow so they gotta take Ex-Lax." He stopped pounding, then gave the starter three King Kong-class kicks, twisting the throttle hard.

Peggy Sue roared. Boog dismounted, letting the engine idle down, but stood in my way as I tried to take his place.

"They ain't here yet," he said, "so give me a fuckin' minute. You're heading south, right?"

I nodded. "I've got to get to —"

Boog thunked me upside the helmet with his wrench. "Don't tell me where you're going. If the fuzz ask me, I want to say I don't know. Now listen up: Head west on fifty-four and blast through the first five stoplights. At the sixth light, hang left. That'll get you out of town quick. It turns into a country road that'll take you clear the fuck to Winfield, and from there it's less than twenty miles to the state line."

He moved aside, and I got onto the bike. "You hand out silver bullets too?" I asked. I would have sped away then, but he still had a hand on the handlebars.

"That ain't the way it is," Boog said. "I got no altruistic impulses." He looked off toward the heart of the salvage yard. "But I was seventeen when that goddamn plane went down. Maybe a guy young as you don't know what that means. But the first time I ever felt really good, I was listening to 'Oh, Boy.' I stripped down and rebuilt my first bike listening to 'Tell Me How.' I got to home plate with my first chick listening to 'Maybe Baby.' "

"I understand," I said, and maybe I did. He was the same age as Mother would have been.

"You owe me now," Boog said, fixing his eyes on mine. "You owe me, and you're gonna fuckin'-A pay me back."

Should have known, I thought. "How much?"

He scowled. "Fuck that."

The siren was no more than a half mile away now. "What, then? What?"

Boog took his hand off Peggy Sue. "Help him," he said, and stepped back.

I sat still for an instant, thinking that I should say something. Then Peggy Sue went into gear and we ripped past the motel, spraying gravel all the way out to U.S. 54.

As we accelerated westward, a wailing patrol car passed us heading in the opposite direction. In my mirrors, I saw it swerve into the driveway of the FIFTY-FOUR MOTOR INN REASONABLE RATES. I cranked the Ariel's throttle and ran two red lights. The next four were green. We turned south.

The town gave way to bare hills and dead trees, and a mile from the turn we passed an oil refinery. White tanks like humongous aspirin tablets hulked along the east side of the road, and in their midst stood a complicated tower, all pipes and girders and incomprehensible shapes. A smoking yellow flame burned at its apex, making the thing look like an inverted starship. This was the source of El Dorado's distinctive smell.

Less than a quarter mile past the refinery, the ramshackle screen of a drive-in movie theater stood with its ribbed back turned to the road, displaying a white marquee with red letters that spelled SKYVUE. On the dead grass between there and the ditch, satellite dishes sprouted like cockeyed mushrooms. A sign leaning against one of the dishes read "SkyVue Drive-In Theater and Earth Station Emporium/Theater Closed for the

Season/Buy a 200-Plus Channel Dish to Cure the Winter Blahs/All Antennas Built on the Premises/Inquire at Snack Bar."

I let up on Peggy Sue's throttle. I was driving past the place from which Mother had ordered the dish that had relayed Buddy Holly's image to my Sony. My chest felt hollow. My head hummed as if with sympathetic vibrations.

I didn't know how or why, but the SkyVue Drive-In Theater and Earth Station Emporium was important to my quest. I downshifted and hit the brakes.

I had just begun the left turn into the theater's driveway when I glimpsed a car with flashing red and blue lights approaching fast from the city. It wasn't using a siren, and it was still far behind, but I was sure that the Authorities inside had seen me.

I leaned back out of the turn, and Peggy Sue accelerated hard, nearly jerking me from the seat. Boog and his crescent wrench had done a good job. If the Authorities behind us were locals, they would have to give up soon because we would be out of their jurisdiction. I hoped.

My attitude had changed from that of a law-abiding citizen to that of a law-breaking fugitive in less than a day. "It's so easy," I told Peggy Sue, amazed.

SHARON

Notes on client Oliver Vale, continued . . .

2/3/89; 6:22 P.M.: I gave myself the day off and have slept almost seven hours, so I'm thinking more clearly than I was in the early morning. I believe I know what to do.

I have an advantage over the authorities who are searching for Oliver. I know his psychology, which means that I should be able to predict his actions.

Oliver was last seen heading south. But all of his friends are here in Topeka, and his few remaining relatives live in Des Moines. According to the most recent radio news report, the Kansas Highway Patrol believes that Oliver traveled south only a short distance, then doubled back and slipped into Topeka, where he is now supposedly hiding out. In my opinion, the highway patrol is trying to save face because they haven't caught him yet. If Oliver were in Topeka, he would have come here. Because I asked him to.

He has not come here, which means that he is still heading south. The reason the KHP hasn't captured him is because he's in Oklahoma by now.

Oliver is heading for Lubbock, Texas, the birthplace—and gravesite—of his hero and father figure.

The one thing I can't predict is the route he will take. The only way I can help him, then, is to get to Lubbock first and meet him when he arrives.

It isn't as simple as that, of course, because I also have to get there secretly. I'm sure that I'm being watched, and my telephone might even be tapped. If I were to buy plane, train, or bus tickets, I would be pointing a bright red arrow right at Oliver.

So I'll have to drive, and I'll have to take a route as tortuous as the one Oliver is probably taking. If I can persuade Bruce to come along—without telling him where we're going, or why—then we can use one of his firm's two Chevrolets, and the authorities might not even realize I've gone until I've reached my destination.

Bruce has just come into the apartment. He's had a tough Friday with a difficult lawsuit, but he says that he is in a good mood because he's taking the weekend off to be with me. He ignores the fact that Buddy Holly is still on our (and everyone else's) TV. He thus also ignores the fact that my client and friend is still in trouble.

I can deal with this, however. I'm no longer fatigued, so I'm not susceptible to useless anger. Bruce is simply being Bruce. And that's fine.

"Let's go away for the weekend," I'll tell him.

"Sounds great," he'll say. "Where to? Chicago? Minneapolis? Denver?"

We'll snuggle on the divan. "Let me surprise you," I'll murmur.

I know *his* psychology too.

RICHTER

A woman wearing a black sweatsuit met him at the Kansas City International Airport, handed him a keyring with two keys, and walked away without speaking. Richter appreciated that. A slip of paper taped to the keyring was printed with the words "Lot F, Row 17, sixth space from the fence. Perpetrator has fled area, but investigate residence." Richter tore off the paper and ate it for practice.

The automobile was a black two-door Jaguar equipped with a compact disc player, a police-band scanner, a telephone, and a computerized map display. In the glove compartment Richter found directions to Oliver Vale's home, a driver's license photograph of and fact sheet on Vale, and a leather card case with a card identifying "S. I. Richter" as an agent of the Federal Communications Commission. Richter skimmed the fact sheet and then started the Jaguar to begin the eighty-mile trip.

The disc player filled the compartment with Chuck Berry songs. Richter smiled. If one had to work in the Midwest, this was the way to do it.

He arrived at Oliver Vale's home in the late afternoon, feeling refreshed. His mood soured, however, when two policemen emerged from their cruiser, which was parked in the driveway, and told him that he would have to leave. They looked at the Jaguar suspiciously.

"FCC," Richter told them, and produced identification from an inner pocket of his suit coat.

The shorter officer opened the card case and scowled. "This ID says FBI," he said.

"Yes," Richter said, careful to mask his anger with a calm, measured tone. He was furious with himself for having blundered. He had always been the kind of man who neither made mistakes nor tolerated the mistakes of others. The FCC card case lay heavy in his pocket.

"Oh, you're with both, huh?" the officer said, looking him over. "Guess you're about big enough to be two people."

"Not enough hair for one, though," the taller officer said out of the side of his mouth.

Richter took back the FBI card and handed over the correct one. He wished that he could simply kill the two policeman, but to do that would be to allow his mistake to have consequences.

The shorter officer sneered as he looked at the new card. "I suppose you're CIA too, ain't you?"

Richter allowed himself a frown, but he said nothing. He put his hands into the pockets of his gray overcoat to keep them from the policeman's throat.

The taller officer reentered the cruiser. "I'm gonna have to call this in for confirmation, Mr. FBI-FCC-CIA."

"Very well," Richter said, imagining the two policemen's headless bodies spurting blood onto the ground.

He stood silent while the taller officer drawled into a microphone and listened to the squawks that answered.

"Awright, ten-four on that," the taller officer said at last. He stepped out of the cruiser and squinted at Richter. "Go on in. Dispatcher said he just got word you were comin'." The shorter officer gave Richter a glare, then walked around the cruiser to the passenger door.

Richter held out a hand. "Key," he said.

The taller officer handed him a key to the house. "Dispatcher says you can pick up a hard copy of our investigation progress report at the sheriff's office, but we don't have much yet. There's nothing here, unless the KBI boys found something." He joined his companion in the cruiser and shut the door.

Richter turned his back on them and walked up the driveway to the house, his shoes crunching gravel. As he walked, he took latex gloves from his pockets and pulled them on. The locals had probably ruined all but the most obvious pieces of physical evidence, but it didn't hurt to be careful. He was determined that his mistake with the ID card would be his last.

The lights were on in the living room, as was the television set. Buddy Holly was hiccuping and strumming his guitar on the screen. Richter gave the image a cursory glance. It didn't vary in any significant aspect from what he had already seen on his bedroom wall.

A greasy plastic bowl lay on the floor beside a brown recliner, and popped popcorn kernels were scattered on the carpet. Richter picked up a kernel and sniffed it. It seemed ordinary, but he would order a chemical analysis anyway. For now, the only thing the bowl and the scattered kernels told him was that Vale had left the house in a hurry. The rest of the room was tidy.

The items on the coffee table in front of the recliner drew his attention: The latest issue of *Rolling Stone*. A water pistol shaped like an electric guitar. A ten-inch crescent wrench. A paperback novel entitled *Power Chord,* by an author he had never heard of. A cordless combination telephone/answering machine. A liquor-bottle statue of Elvis Presley. A lucite photo cube containing trimmed magazine pictures of Buddy Holly, Sam Cooke, Otis Redding, Janis Joplin, and John Lennon. The sixth space on the cube contained a snapshot of a dark-haired, sad-eyed woman standing in front of a satellite dish. Richter knew from the fact sheet that this was Vale's deceased mother.

Next he examined the telephone. A piece of white tape on the receiver cradle read "Sharon S.: Speed Dial 01, or 234-0793." The fact sheet had said that Vale was a client of a psychologist named Sharon Sharpston, but the piece of tape put a new light on the relationship. Vale was either totally dependent upon Sharpston's counseling, or he was in love with her . . . which perhaps amounted to the same thing. He would keep her in mind.

Upon playing the answering-machine message, Richter decided that Clear Lake, Iowa, was a possible destination for the fugitive. If Vale had scattered his mother's ashes near there, it was obviously an important place to him, notwithstanding his assertion that it was "just a field."

Richter went through the rest of the house quickly but methodically. In the living room, dining room, and largest bedroom he found state-of-the-art stereo systems and libraries of record albums, tapes, and compact discs. In one of the two smaller bedrooms he found a microcomputer, a laser printer, and shelves containing hundreds of books, many of them devoted to rock 'n' roll history and criticism. In the third bedroom (the windowless one, with a mussed bed) he found posters, concert paraphernalia, a black Fender Stratocaster and amplifier, and a worn hardbound biography of Buddy Holly. Richter let the book fall open three times, and each time it opened to a page containing a photograph of Holly's gravestone. Then, flipping through the book, he came across a photo of the snowy Clear Lake crash site in which hunch-shouldered men stood around the wreckage of the Beechcraft. In the margin someone had written, *Why seek ye the living among the dead?*

Also in this room, Richter found seven notebooks with stickers listing volume numbers and dates on their spines. The first page of the first volume was signed "Michelle Renee Cranston," but each of the others was signed "Michelle Vale." Richter skimmed the volumes for thirty minutes.

In the kitchen he found only appliances, utensils, dishes, and food. In the utility room he found only a washer and dryer. In the attic he found only pink insulation. In the garage he found only a lawnmower and a box of tools that looked new. In the basement he found more rock 'n' roll albums and memorabilia, including a computer-generated rendering of Buddy Holly and the Crickets and a black-velvet painting of a fat Elvis wearing a fringed jumpsuit and rings the size of hand grenades.

Richter stared at the painting. It struck him as sad that a man who had once had so much talent had tried to keep on going past his prime. Maybe Holly had been lucky. He hadn't had the chance to become a bloated caricature of himself.

Outside, Richter found a brown lawn, leafless trees, and a satellite dish that looked like the scores of others he had seen during the drive from Kansas City. Upon close inspection he discovered that the aluminum shell that housed the dish's electronics was covered with dents.

He went back into the house and tapped and pounded the walls, searching for secret panels. There were none.

He was finished. In his opinion, this house did not contain sufficient equipment to override either terrestrial or satellite video transmissions. He would recommend that the earth station and microcomputer be dismantled and examined by a technical team, and he would also recommend that the compact discs be scanned for codes, but he didn't think that such measures would yield results. He had smashed the guitar and amplifier himself and had found nothing out of the ordinary.

Also in Richter's opinion, Oliver Vale was not a genius and therefore was not the person responsible for the worldwide TV disruption. However, it was clear that Vale was obsessed with Buddy Holly, so it was possible that he was acquainted with whoever *was* responsible. That was all Richter needed to know for now, because he was eighty percent certain that he knew where Vale was going.

He left the house, locking it, and walked past the police cruiser without returning the house key to the officers. They glowered at him, and he ignored them.

Once inside the Jaguar, he picked up the phone receiver and punched a long sequence of numbers. His call was answered by the voice that had given him his orders that morning.

"Richter?" The voice sounded agitated.

"Yes," Richter said. "No macroscopic clues as to the how of it, although a tech team should examine household electronics. But I have an idea of where he's gone." Richter's throat began to hurt. For him, this was a long speech.

"Then go get him, and hurry. Circumstances dictate that you act alone if possible."

Richter wanted to shatter the phone. He had been hoping that he would be ordered back to D.C. "Sir, I think it best that another operative retrieve him. He's fleeing several hundred miles, en route to—"

"Classify it!" his superior cried. "This satellite channel may be monitored, and we do *not* want the Bad Guys getting to Vale first. We had believed that he was nothing more than a hacker, but we were wrong."

"Yes?" Richter prompted.

He heard a rasp of breath. "Richter," his superior said, "preliminary radio telescope data indicate that the primary source of the Buddy Holly broadcast is indeed located on Ganymede. They're picking up pulses that translate into a dork playing an electric guitar. Do you have any idea of the implications of this?"

"Yes," Richter said, starting the Jaguar. He was tired of talking, and of listening.

"It means that an extraterrestrial intelligence has infiltrated our solar system."

"Yes," Richter said. He held the phone wedged between his cheek and shoulder as he put the Jaguar into reverse and backed onto the street.

"And since these aliens—God, *aliens!*—have fingered Vale as their contact, then he's either an alien himself or he's been chosen to— Well, hell, you saw all those Spielberg movies. So get to him fast, and request backup only if you're in danger of failing. In that event, use a pay phone with a command sequence to keep the information on earthbound lines." The voice paused, then said, "Any reason to think you can't handle this by yourself, old pal?"

"No," Richter said stonily, pivoting the Jaguar so that it faced south.

"Good. Don't fly, whatever you do; too conspicuous.

But drive like a demon was chomping at your butt. Assume that this conversation has been overheard. And by the way, there's to be no elimination of Vale. Understood?"

"Yes," Richter said. He put the Jaguar into first and stepped on the accelerator. The automobile sped forward smoothly.

"Unless he's about to be taken by the Bad Guys, of course."

Richter said nothing.

"My God, Richter, just think of it! *Little green men.* A tech squad's on its way to examine every molecule in Vale's house, and who knows what we'll find? I don't know about you, but I'm excited!" The phone clicked dead.

Richter hung up the receiver, shifted to second, and switched on the police-band scanner. He wasn't excited. A hacker who could take over satellite transmissions might also be able to generate spurious radio-telescope data.

Richter didn't believe in little green men.

As for keeping Vale alive . . .

Upon finding his quarry, he would learn what he could, make an evaluation, and act accordingly. Then he would tell his superiors whatever they wanted to hear, just as he always had.

Old pal, his ass. Damn straight he could handle it by himself.

His throat felt as if it had been rubbed with steel wool. He resolved to revert to his practice of speaking only in monosyllables until he either found Vale or reached Vale's intended destination: Lubbock, Texas. The final resting place of Buddy Holly.

CATHY AND JEREMY

Cathy lowered the binoculars and took off the earphones. "The guy in the Jag is a U.S. government spook," she said. "His boss thinks that extraterrestrial aliens are behind the broadcast."

Jeremy was crawling around on the Congoleum floor, occasionally bumping his head against the refrigerator or a table leg. "In other words," he said, "you goaded Vale into running, and now the feds who have come to look for him are one house away from finding us out."

Cathy sighed in exasperation. "Oh, they are not. They don't know thing one about us. Seekers aren't aliens."

"Technicality," Jeremy said, snuffling at toast crumbs at the base of the counter. "We've been gone so long that Earth is hardly our home, now, is it? They could figure that out."

"If they do, it isn't *my* fault. I didn't generate the broadcast, did I? And I didn't goad Vale into running away. I simply decided not to stop him."

"That's not what you said this morning. You said you wanted him pressured to act so that we could get this thing over with. You said—"

Cathy stepped past him, kicking his ribs and knocking him over as she did so, and sat down at the table. "Don't worry about it. The G-man may even kill the poor schlub. How do you think our cousins in El Dorado will react to that?"

Jeremy lay on his side, staring under the microwave-oven cart. "They'll try again."

"Maybe, but by that time someone besides you and me will be stuck with this mess."

Jeremy closed his black dog-eye and looked up at her with his blue human-eye. "You don't really want Vale killed, do you?"

Cathy pursed her lips and looked away. "If I did, I'd be no better then the fleshbound. But if he *is* killed, I won't have had anything to do with it."

"It would be nice to think so," Jeremy said, getting to his hands and knees. "But one who knows how to prevent a death is guilty of murder when that death occurs, regardless of the active agent. Wouldn't you say?"

Cathy did not respond.

"Well, then, would you like a status report?"

Cathy nodded.

Jeremy closed his blue eye and opened the black one. "Vale has left the motel. He isn't in sight, but the scent of the motorcycle indicates that it's only a few miles ahead of Ringo's current position."

"Is that all?"

Jeremy cocked his head. "No. Ringo's lonely."

"*Lonely?* He's a construct!"

"He's also part Doberman pinscher. Just as you and I are part flesh."

Cathy stood. "If you're going to get nasty, I'm going to watch TV." She left the room.

Moments later, she was back. "I forgot," she said. "Buddy Holly's on every channel."

Jeremy smiled warmly. "Imagine the ratings he must be getting. Probably beating hell out of the last episode of *M*A*S*H*." He resumed snuffling the Congoleum.

RINGO

He had reached the motel at midmorning and had dozed among the evergreens until awakened by the siren. Now he sniffed around the base of the dumpster, sorting through the odors of rotten vegetables and burning crude oil.

There: The motorcycle had headed back toward the highway. The wailing automobile that had been here briefly was now following it.

Ringo began trotting away from the dumpster, tracking the Ariel.

"Hey, ol' dawg!" a voice called behind him. "Where'd you come from?"

Ringo paused and looked back. Across the fence, among ruined and rusted machines, stood a man with wild red hair. Ringo knew that the hair was red because his new eye gave him images in color. Sometimes it also gave him a glimpse of the bricklike Congoleum in Cathy and Jeremy's kitchen, but mostly it showed him what he was looking at.

"You hungry, boy?" the man asked, reaching into a pocket on his chest. "I got some beef jerky." The man came close to the fence and held a strip of dried meat between the links. "My name's Boog. What's yours?"

Ringo's implanted chips understood the man's words, and although his modified body did not require food, the dog part of his brain longed to accept a morsel from a human hand. He approached the fence and sniffed the meat. His processors analyzed the odor and concluded that it smelled good.

He took the strip and gulped it down, then pressed his nose against the fence so that Boog could scratch his muzzle.

"You're a *big* motherfucker, ain't you?" Boog said. "How come I never seen you around here before?"

Ringo grunted. The scratching felt wonderful.

"Man, what's with your eyes?" Boog asked.

Ringo closed his eyes for an instant and saw Cathy looking at him sternly.

He gave the big man's fingers a lick, then pivoted and ran for the highway, his chain collar jingling.

"You come back anytime, now," Boog called after him.

Ringo wished that he could stay longer. He liked Boog.

He ran to the other side of the building, then slowed as he saw a fat woman coming toward him on a concrete walk. She was carrying a bucket, and she smelled of bacon. Maybe she was bringing him a treat, as Boog had. He trotted toward her to find out.

She screamed and pulled a bottle filled with blue liquid from the bucket. Ringo stopped, realizing his mistake, but he was too late. The fat woman squeezed a lever on the bottle and sprayed him in the face.

Ringo bolted for the highway, sneezing as he went. His artificial eyes had not been hurt, but his Doberman nose was burning. His processors analyzed his olfactory responses and told him that the blue liquid was called Windex, but he didn't care what it was called. All he cared about was sneezing it away. He needed his nose clear to follow the scent of the motorcycle.

The fat woman had taught him a lesson. He must concentrate on his mission. He could not afford to indulge his desires for affection and snacks. He would try to forget the man named Boog.

Ringo ran down the shoulder of the highway, ignoring everything in the world except the trail of the Ariel. The twilight became night.

SKYVUE

Khrushchev sat on a Naugahyde-covered bench in the projection room, his eyes closed and his face puckered in concentration. Eisenhower lounged beside him, munching popcorn while watching Buddy Holly perform on a five-inch color TV that hung from the film projector.

Khrushchev's eyes opened abruptly, and he clambered to stand on the bench and look through the projection window. Gazing across acres of speaker poles, he said, "There goes your boy, right past us. Did you plan that?"

Eisenhower swallowed. "No. It's Fate."

"And here come the cops after him. Is that Fate too?"

"Don't be sarcastic."

Khrushchev turned away from the window and sat down with a thud. "I'm not being sarcastic. I'm merely curious as to how much of this you're orchestrating and how much you're just letting happen. I mean, since I'm not directly *involved* anymore, curiosity is all I have."

Eisenhower gave him a look of sympathy and sincerity. It was an extremely presidential sort of look. "I'm orchestrating nothing. Everyone is free to react to the broadcast as he or she wishes."

"In that case, we might as well give up on these people and convert back to noncorporeality right now."

Eisenhower's expression became stern. "You sound as though you're on the anti-flesh side."

"Not at all," Khrushchev said, folding his arms. "I believe in the right of the fleshbound to attain Seeker status. However, I admit that I do understand the anti-flesh position."

Eisenhower nodded sagely. "As do I. That's why I prefer not to intervene in whatever events the broadcast may foment. Nevertheless, because I selected the catalyst, I must accept responsibility if the outcome is tragic."

Khrushchev's eyebrows rose. "How so?"

Eisenhower looked back at the TV and stuffed a handful of popcorn into his mouth. "I shall pay the price along with them," he said, his voice muffled.

"You mean *death*?" Khrushchev exclaimed. "Are you *nuts*? I should open your head and—" He stopped in midsentence and climbed up to look through the window again. "There goes the opposition's canine computer."

"He isn't theirs," Eisenhower said. "He does their bidding, but he belongs to himself."

"If you say so. But maybe we ought to divert him before he catches your boy and chows down."

Eisenhower shook his head. "He won't do that. At least, I don't believe so. In any case, he too is part of Fate's random plan, and therefore we shouldn't interfere."

" 'Fate's random plan'?" Khrushchev said. "Sounds like more bullshit to me. I mean, how can a plan be random? How can randomness be planned?"

Eisenhower leaned forward and turned up the TV's sound. "Let's stay tuned and find out, shall we?"

Khrushchev sat down again. "You've been here too long, Ike. Your brain's turning to video kibble."

"Hush. I want to hear whatever Buddy's going to play next."

"You don't already know?"

"Of course not." Eisenhower picked a popcorn hull from his teeth with a fingernail. "*He* belongs to himself too."

2 · the **pilgrimage** of the **physically** fit

4

OLIVER

My grandfather died in April 1965 as the result of an accident at the Goodyear plant. No one would tell me what happened, and Mother didn't explicate it in her diary, so I have always imagined that he went to work drunk (as he often did), fell into a vat of bubbling black goo, and ended up rolling down the highway under somebody's Ford. The closed casket at the funeral made a hollow sound when I knocked on it, so I wasn't convinced that he was in there.

Five-year-olds do things like that. At least, I did. Four months had passed since Sam Cooke's demise, and a portion of my fear of death had metamorphosed into an intense curiosity about just what it was that separated death from life. So I knocked on the casket to see whether anyone was home.

Fortunately, Grandmother was talking with the pastor in the vestibule when I did that. If she had witnessed it, she would have whipped the snot out of me.

As it was, the only witness was Mother, and she knocked immediately after I did.

"Knock, knock," she whispered.

"Who's there?" I asked. I had become a skilled straight man at knock-knock jokes.

"Coffin," she said.

"Coffin who?"

"Coffin your handkerchief or don't coffat all!"

I giggled. I was only five.

On Mother's birthday, Thursday, May 13, Grandmother left for Des Moines for a two-week visit with Uncle Mike, who was supposed to have come to Topeka for the funeral but who had missed it because the Greyhound bus bringing him had broken down. Mother and I were specifically not invited along on Grandmother's trip, because she felt that our sinful and illegitimate presences would have a deleterious effect on her seventeen-year-old son.

Mother cried the night before Grandmother left. She had not seen her brother in six years, and now he was almost grown up and she didn't even know him.

Being denied a trip to Des Moines turned out to be only a prelude. As we said good-bye to Grandmother at the bus station, she informed Mother that by the time she returned, we had better be out of the house.

I remember that much. For further details, I must refer to Volume III of Mother's diary:

So there I was this afternoon, just turned twenty-four without so much as a Happy Birthday, waiting with Mama and Oliver at the bus station. Oliver was sitting on the floor playing with his Matchbox fire truck, and Mama said, "Get that child off the floor, Michelle, what's the matter with you? He'll catch a disease." So I picked him

up and held him on my lap, although he's getting big.
It's always best to let Mama feel like she's running things.
Which she is. Except for not getting to go see Mikey so
that Oliver could meet his uncle, I was looking forward
to the next two weeks without her.

Then the man with the microphone announced the
bus, and we all stood. I was still holding Oliver, so I
hugged Mama with one arm. She didn't hug back, which
has been typical for a long time now. She is still Mama,
though, just like Daddy was Daddy and I miss him even
though he was pretty awful the last five years.

Mama picked up her little blue suitcase and said,
just as if she were commenting on the weather, "When I
come back, you have to be gone."

I said, "Huh?"

"You are an adult," Mama said, but in a tone of voice
that meant Like Hell You Are. "You have a child. It is
time you took responsibility. Out of respect for your father's feelings, I tolerated you under our roof. But your
father was a more generous Christian than you had a
right to expect, and he's gone now, God bless him. You
can go to work and take care of yourself. You and your
things and your boy had better not be in the house when
I get back."

As she walked for the bus, I hurried after her, still
carrying Oliver, who was fidgeting. "Just let us stay until
he starts first grade in the fall," I said. "How could I get
a job before then? What would we live on?"

I shouldn't have done that. I shouldn't have crawled
to her. She is my mama and somewhere in my chest full
of hate I must still love her a little, but I should never
have crawled to her.

She looked back at me and said, "I don't know, but
if you think you'll use some of your father's insurance

*money, you can forget it. It all comes to me, and I might
give a few thousand to Mikey if he needs it, but never to
you. Not after what you did."*

*Mama got on the bus and went away. She should be
in Des Moines by now. She's probably giving Mikey and
the relatives all of the smiles and hugs she's been hoard-
ing since we came to Topeka.*

*Oliver is asleep as I write. He doesn't look like a bas-
tard. Just before I put him to bed, he hugged me around
the legs and said, "Happy burfday, Muvver." He can talk
better than that, but not when he's sleepy.*

Absolutely, I thought. Happy goddamn birthday.

How am I going to be able to alter this *reality? If I
deny Mama's existence, will she be unable to come back
and throw us out?*

*I had thought that it would be nice for me and Oliver
to have the house to ourselves for a while, but I was wrong.
I can smell Daddy's cigarettes and beer even though he
is dead and buried. I expect to see Mama frown at me
when I get a glass of milk even though she has gone to
Des Moines. Even when they aren't here, they're here.*

*Time for us to go, Oliver. Where to, though, beats the
hell out of me.*

*I wish we could go to England. That's where all the
rock 'n' roll is these days. All you need is a rubber soul,
baby, and I surely do have that.*

I was a ball and chain bolted to Mother's ankle. If
it hadn't been for me, she would have gone to London.
She would have found a way.

As it was, she had to pick me up from kindergarten
every day and then take me along as she searched for a
job. That alone ensured that she was rejected by several
employers who might not have rejected her otherwise.
Amazingly, though, she found something a few days be-

fore Grandmother was to return. A small pop radio station happened to need someone to handle paperwork at
just the time that Mother happened to be looking, and
thus she became the lone secretary at KKAP, "The
Hop of the Heartland." The management and disc jockeys were stuck in 1959, but that was okay because
Mother was too. (Not quite fair. At this point in her
life, Mother was as progressive as it was possible to be
in Topeka. It was at her suggestion, in fact, that KKAP
finally decided to take a bold step forward and start
playing the Beatles.)

That solved one problem. Mother had a job, and she
was scheduled to start with a training day on Friday,
May 28, the day after Grandmother was to return. That
left only two other problems: where to live, and what to
do with yours truly.

Neither was solved by the time Grandmother showed
up. She came home from the bus station in a cab on the
evening of May 27, and Mother began to tell her about
the job.

"And I suppose you want me to baby-sit your brat
while you're off making your fortune," Grandmother said.

"Well, no," Mother said, looking at me anxiously.
She still didn't completely trust Grandmother alone with
me, and I felt the same way. "But tomorrow's his last
morning of kindergarten, so maybe you could just have
him tomorrow afternoon. That would give me the weekend to find a regular sitter."

I wanted to scream, *No! Not even one afternoon!* but
I knew that wouldn't help matters. Either that, or I was
just too scared of Grandmother.

"You're forgetting one important thing, Michelle,"
Grandmother said grimly. "You and Oliver don't live here
anymore. You not only don't have a free baby-sitter, but
you've lost your free housekeeper as well."

Then she went back into our bedroom, pulled the drawers from the dresser and bureau, and began flinging our clothes into the hallway.

Some crying and screaming followed, but the next thing I remember clearly is that Mother and I ended up standing on the front walk while she struggled to hold four grocery sacks full of clothes.

I was bawling. When I could, I sobbed, "Grandmother doesn't mean it, does she?"

"No, she doesn't," Mother said. Her voice sounded firmer than I had ever heard it before. "She thinks she'll let us stand out here for a few hours or maybe overnight, where the neighbors will see us. She thinks I've never been properly repentant, so she wants us to feel humiliated and learn our lesson. Then she'll let us back in and expect us to be grateful and humble."

Mother paused. I looked up and saw her glaring at Grandmother's house. Her eyes flashed with wet heat.

"Well, *fuck that*," she said.

She strode off down the sidewalk, and I toddled along with her, wondering what she had meant. She dropped one of the grocery sacks, so I picked it up and carried it with both arms, hugging it as if it were a stuffed animal.

We took a city bus, and the driver and passengers stared at us. Mother stared back, and they stopped.

We went to the radio station, a small brick building north of the Kaw River. By the time we arrived, only three people were still there. The two-to-six disc jockey was just coming off the air, and the six-to-ten man was just going on. The engineer was dozing in the control room, letting the deejays fend for themselves.

The two-to-six man was a skinny, stooped guy with pale skin. His name, Mother told me, was Jeff. We met him as he came out of the booth.

"Hey, that front door's supposed to be locked after five," Jeff said.

"It wasn't," Mother replied. "I'm the new secretary. I start tomorrow. This is my son Oliver."

Jeff looked at us. "So you're bringing in sacks of clothes?"

"We need a place to stay," Mother said.

"Well, you sure can't stay here," Jeff said. "Better call in some favors from friends."

"I've been too busy raising my son to make friends," Mother said.

"That's me!" I said brightly. I had surmised that this occasion called for cuteness.

"Isn't he something?" Mother asked, tousling my hair. She dropped one of her sacks in midtousle, and it spilled onto the floor. It was her underwear.

We spent the next sixteen nights on the couch in Jeff's apartment. He even saw to it that I made it to my last day of kindergarten (which I could have done without) and took me to the radio station that afternoon, where I spent four boring hours in a corner of the lobby.

Beginning the next Monday, Mother went to work every morning at eight, and Jeff stayed with me until ten. Then he went to work too, and his sister, whose name I've forgotten, came in and baby-sat until Mother returned at about five-thirty. Jeff's sister was a high-school junior on summer break, and she charged fifty cents an hour to watch soap operas on her brother's black-and-white Motorola.

That Motorola changed my life.

My grandparents had never owned a television, so the space program had never been more than words to me. But on Thursday, June 3, 1965, I saw Gemini 4 lift off amid black-and-white smoke and flame. Then, a few days later, I saw Edward White floating above the Earth, holding his propulsion unit before him like a crucifix against the void.

Okay. At age five and a half I couldn't have come up with anything as pompous and meaningless as "a crucifix against the void." What I did come up with, though, was the feeling that I would give anything to trade places with Edward White, to float in nothingness far from Topeka, Kansas. Far from anything.

If anything besides rock 'n' roll could confer immortality, leaving the Earth would be it.

Meanwhile, according to Volume II, Grandmother was calling Mother at KKAP twice a day and asking her to come back home. Mother refused.

Mother found an apartment for us through a friend of a friend of the KKAP station manager, and we moved out of Jeff's place as soon as she received her first two-week paycheck. Rent, food, a used TV set, and a down payment on the money we owed Jeff and his sister, and that was it until the next check. Jeff's sister agreed to continue baby-sitting on an I.O.U. basis—for longer hours now that Jeff wasn't with me mornings—provided that she got a raise to sixty-five cents an hour. Mother, having no choice, agreed.

During this period, Mother underwent something of a spiritual revival as a result of her job. Her obsession with Buddy Holly had flagged due to her depression at the death of Sam Cooke and her subsequent recovery as she discovered the Beatles, but one day while she was cataloging tapes, she came across an interview with Buddy Holly and the Crickets that had been recorded during a multiband tour stop in Topeka in 1957. A copy of that tape, dubbed onto a cassette, is now part of my collection.

The interviewer's questions are pedestrian, so Holly's answers reveal little about himself or his band . . . but his voice itself is another matter. He makes no effort to hide his West Texas drawl. Nor does he try to hide the fact that he is less comfortable talking than he is singing. While his singing is sure and brash, his speaking voice is uncertain and even shy. Here is the final exchange:

ANNOUNCER: "That's all the time we have for this interview with the Crickets, and we want to thank them for taking time out of tonight's busy schedule for talking with us for just a few moments."

BUDDY: "Well, uh, we'd like to thank everyone that, uh, listens and, uh, everyone that, that requests and likes our records, and, uh, we'd like to thank you boys for playin' 'em."

No genius is evident. For Mother, that was the beauty:

He sounds like a scared kid, she wrote. *He sounds like I feel. But then there are his songs, and just like C. said, they sound like I feel too even though they're so different. So despite that difference, they aren't hard to connect to the Buddy in that interview. Unlike other singers, other stars, he is one of us, and he is grateful that we like his music and that we like him. He is neither above us nor below us, but on a level with us—listen to how he thanks "you boys for playin' 'em."*

And now he is gone, and the records that everyone requests have been cut by a band from across the sea, a million miles from Lubbock or Topeka. Yet look at their name: "The Beatles." Not so far from "The Crickets." And listen to their songs: Is "I Saw Her Standing There" a million miles away from "I'm Looking for Someone to Love"?

If I could hear the Beatles speak the way I have just

heard Buddy speak, I know I would hear their Liverpool accents just as I have heard Buddy's Lubbock drawl. They have not taken his place; they have not usurped his kingdom. They have inherited it. They are his disciples.

And listen, listen, listen to this new record that just came to the station this week! A new band, also from England, calling themselves The Rolling Stones. And what song are they singing? "Not Fade Away"! It is both a tribute and a transformation.

It is almost a resurrection.

Thus, consciously or unconsciously, Mother gave me religion. In the pantheon of her beliefs, Buddy Holly was God, Chuck Berry was the Holy Spirit, John Lennon was the new Pope (replacing the martyred Pope Sam), and Paul, George, and Ringo were cardinals. Otis Redding, Bob Dylan, and the up-and-coming Stones were priests with terrific parishes. (In 1965, Mother may have been the only white person in the entire state of Kansas who knew who Otis Redding was. She was also one of the few people anywhere who openly predicted that Dylan was about to go electric.) The Messiah—Buddy reborn in flesh—was still to come.

The tiny walk-up apartment in central Topeka, the first home that Mother and I called our own, was where we worshiped for the next six years. I grew up in the Church, and I learned its liturgy: Oh yeah, baby, baby, oh yeah. Can't *get* no satis*fac*tion. Amen, *unh.*

Christians, Jews, or Muslims might conclude that this Religion of Rock and Roll is either facetious or deliberately offensive. It is neither.

Mother and I relied upon our Church and our God just as any other religionists rely upon their Churches and their Gods. Of course, everyone believes in the superior power of his or her own particular God . . . but for those who doubt that the God whom Mother and I worshiped had any power at all, I offer my memory of Wednesday, June 8, 1966:

I was six and a half years old. The U.S. manned space program had been proceeding rapidly and magnificently (except for a minor malfunction that had cut short the mission of Gemini 8), leading me to the conclusion that human beings were in control of Nature, that the Universe was under our dominion and command. All we had to do was go out there and take it.

On that Wednesday evening, the sky darkened early. A few minutes after 7:00 P.M., the temperature dropped sharply. Civil defense sirens went off. Mother turned on the TV, and an announcer told us that a tornado was heading for the city.

We had no basement. Mother put me into the bathtub, then brought the mattress from my bed and covered me with it.

"Stay there," she said. "Don't move for anything."

She started to leave, and I poked my head out from under the mattress, asking her where she was going.

She stopped in the bathroom doorway. "It's stupid," she said. "It's awfully stupid. But I have to go to the roof."

She left, and I waited. The wind picked up and the lights went out. I yelled for Mother, but she didn't come, so I got out of the tub, stumbled through the weird green light, and clambered onto the fire escape through the living-room window. The walnut tree beside the fire escape was trembling.

I climbed up to the flat tar-and-gravel roof, and there stood Mother, her hair blown back, her dress snapping behind her knees. She was facing southwest.

I tried to shout to her, but either I made no sound or it was lost in the growing rumble. The wind rammed

down my throat; the noise of a bass drum the size of a
mountain shook me; and I saw what was coming.

Tornadoes occur in any number of sizes and in a
surprising variety of shapes. There are funnel tornadoes
and diffuse tornadoes, needle-shaped tornadoes and wa-
terspouts. Most people who have never seen one assume
that they all look like the one in *The Wizard of Oz*. Long
and snaky—a twisting, dancing devil.

The tornado in *The Wizard of Oz* is a mewling in-
fant.

What I saw coming toward us that evening was the
king of kings, Odin, Yahweh, Allah, and Shiva; it was
the rage of every madman of every race of all history,
compressed and raised to the billionth power; it was a
churning mass that laughed at the puniness of volcanoes and earthquakes. It was an impossibly immense, un-
swerving cone of utter black insanity that covered a third
of the southern sky.

The cruelty of the universe had come down to Earth
again. Seven years before, it had killed Buddy Holly.
Now it would kill Mother and me. It wouldn't even notice.

Mother raised her right middle finger to it.

I ran to her, pulled her arm down, grasped that finger, and strained to drag her toward the fire escape. Instead, she picked me up and carried me, and then we
were in the bathtub, the mattress heavy and smelling of
my nighttime accidents. The tornado's rumble lived in
the porcelain that pressed cold against my cheek.

Mother began singing "Love Me Do."

I joined in, my voice a panicked squeak. I knew all
of the words.

By the time we finished the song, the building was
shaking.

Mother began singing "Everyday," yelling so that I

could hear her over the rumble that had become a dragon's roar.

"A-hey, a-hey, hey!" we shouted in unison.

We alternated between Buddy Holly and the Beatles, taking turns singing at the top of our lungs into each other's ears, yelling the choruses into the mattress. We stayed there and sang for a long, long time, until a distant siren sounded an all-clear, and it was over.

When we came out from under the mattress, both of us so hoarse that every breath hurt, we saw that the window over the tub had exploded. Neither of us had heard it happen. Nor had we heard the mirrored door of the medicine cabinet fly open and shatter. Shards of silvered glass were stuck in the top of the mattress.

Every window in our building had broken, and the walnut tree outside our living room was stripped of its leaves and most of its bark. The buildings on either side of ours, and across the street, were gone. Dead birds and splintered boards lay all over the street. Four people on our block had been killed.

The tornado had not left us untouched, however. Mother wrote, *It is an omen. Nothing that enormous and malevolent can be meaningless, and it came right for me. It is only because of my son and the songs that I still live. But because the thing could not have me this time, it will try again, perhaps by trying to take something I love.*

I will not let it take Oliver.

Mother's belief that the tornado was an omen of more bad things to come was soon to be strengthened. For one thing, Bob Dylan suffered a motorcycle accident in August that was to silence his increasingly vital voice for more than a year. And then, soon after Christmas, we learned that Uncle Mike was being drafted. By the time Mother could arrange for time off work to visit him in Des Moines, he had already been shipped to boot camp.

But on June 8, I knew neither that Mother saw the
tornado as an omen nor that her brother was destined
to be sent to Vietnam. All I knew was that on that day,
I had been saved by the power of prayer.

So you pray your prayers to your God, and I'll pray
my prayers to mine. May the best chorus win.

*

The cop car from El Dorado stayed on my tail for so
many miles that I almost stopped to give myself up.
Raising a finger to Authority is all well and good, but
you can't hold it up there forever.

But Peggy Sue slowly began to gain a little ground,
and then a little more. Finally, when it had been several
curves and hills since I'd last seen the red and blue lights
in the mirrors, I pulled off onto a dirt sidetrack and
scooted Peggy Sue under a railroad trestle, where I turned
off her lights and waited.

I waited a long time, but the cop car never came
past me, although a few other cars did. As I had hoped,
the El Dorado Authorities must have stopped soon after
the bike and I left their official jurisdiction. I turned on
Peggy Sue's lights and pulled back onto the paved road.
I knew that we still weren't safe, though, because the El
Dorado boys had probably alerted the Authorities of
whatever jurisdiction we did happen to be in.

Less than two miles later, I passed a black Jaguar
that was parked on the shoulder of the road with its
lights off. I recognized it as one of the cars that had passed
while I'd been hiding under the trestle. Probably just a
couple of rich kids making out, I told myself.

The car's headlights came on, flashing from the
Ariel's mirrors into my eyes, and began following us. I
cranked Peggy Sue up to eighty and held her there, but
the Jaguar kept pace, staying within a half mile. Al-

most an hour later, after our road had bypassed Winfield and Arkansas City and had taken us into Oklahoma,
the headlights were still shining in the mirrors.

I'd had enough of them. Peggy Sue and I took a sharp
left onto a strip of blacktop with a sign that said TO KAW
RESERVOIR. A forest crowded both sides of the road, and
the Ariel's headlight beam threw crooked shadows among
the trees.

The road curved back and forth as the leafless forest
became thicker, and I had to reduce our speed to keep
us from jumping off the blacktop and ramming a tree
trunk. During a rare stretch of straight road, I glanced
at a mirror and saw the Jaguar's headlights emerging
around the previous curve.

The road was angling down toward the reservoir. I
sped up a little despite the danger, hoping to put at least
two curves between us and the Jaguar, but the headlights never dropped back quite far enough for me to
pull over and hide in the trees.

The forest ended abruptly, and the road was swallowed by a wide, sloping apron of asphalt. As Peggy Sue
and I passed through on open gate onto the apron, the
bike's headlight beam wavered among the aluminum
masts of sailboats docked at a marina. The sky was still
covered with a thick shell of clouds, so neither moon-
light nor starshine broke through to gleam on the water.
The lake was an unbroken sheet of black stretching
toward the horizon.

I turned the Ariel around and accelerated back onto
the road. Then I braked hard, kicking down the stand
at the same time, and dismounted, running back to the
open metal-bar gate. I pulled the gate across the road
and jumped back onto Peggy Sue just as the Jaguar came
around the last curve. Its headlights almost blinded me,
and I had to guess whether the Ariel and I had enough

room to shoot past without running off the road.

The bike's left mirror scraped against the driver's side window, and then we were past and running hard. I heard the Jaguar's tires squeal, but I didn't look back to see whether it had hit the gate. Either way, the driver would have to get out and open the gate so that he could drive onto the apron; the road was too narrow for the Jaguar to turn around.

I remembered where most of the curves were, so the bike and I were able to go faster than we had coming down to the lake. When we had almost reached the main road, with no sign of the Jaguar behind us, I stopped, killed the Ariel's lights, and rolled her into a clump of trees and dead brush on the inside of a tight left-hand curve.

The Jaguar came by about thirty seconds later. Its tires shrieked on the curve and its lights shone into the trees across the road from us, and then it was past. A moment later I heard it burn out onto the main road and roar an angry twelve-cylinder roar—heading south, I thought. The driver was pushing it hard.

We waited until I couldn't hear the Jaguar anymore, and then we waited a few minutes longer. The sound didn't return.

I whooped and slapped Peggy Sue on the tank, then pushed her out of the trees and remounted. If I could continue to be devious for a few more days, we might make it to Lubbock after all, especially since I was starting to get used to riding in the cold.

We went out to the main road again and headed south, but I started looking for more obscure side roads so that we could start zigzagging. I didn't want to risk running into the Jaguar again.

Miles of back-road zigzagging later, after having passed ghost towns and windowless farmhouses, dark-

ened bait shops and abandoned filling stations, I saw a
pair of headlights in the rearview mirrors. They were
several miles behind us, but even at that distance they
looked familiar.

I twisted Peggy Sue's throttle, and as we sped faster
and faster, the headlights behind us dropped back farther and farther. I relaxed a little and slowed to a safer
speed. The occupants of the vehicle behind us didn't care
who we were or what we did. Those headlights didn't
belong to the Jaguar, but to some rural vehicle carrying
its occupants home from a late night in town.

A few miles later we reached an intersection with a
north–south state highway, and I decided to risk it. The
back roads were rough, and my butt was sore. I knew
that Peggy Sue appreciated the smoother pavement too,
because she began running better than she had since
leaving home.

That gave me the confidence to pull in at a convenience store/gas station in one of the myriad small towns
that dot eastern Oklahoma. Since Peggy Sue was in such
a good mood, she would probably start again if I shut
her off for a few minutes. I checked my watch as we
stopped beside the Regular pump and saw that it was
12:30 A.M. The Ariel had been running for over six hours
since leaving the motel in El Dorado. Almost twenty-
four hours had passed since Buddy Holly had first appeared on my Sony.

As I filled the tank and tried to get the kinks out of
my knees, I realized that while I wasn't especially cold,
I was starving. Not only had it been almost twenty-four
hours since Buddy had appeared, but it had also been
almost twenty-four hours since I had eaten anything—
and that had been a couple of handfuls of microwave
popcorn. I needed carbohydrates, and I needed them now.
Junk food was the only answer.

I finished refueling Peggy Sue and then went into the shop, removing my gloves but leaving the helmet on, and saw that I was in the right place. Nowhere in the world can you find a wider variety of empty calories than at any American convenience store. While the clerk was busy waiting on a man who was paying for a tankful of unleaded and a pouch of Red Man, I strolled up an aisle and stuffed the pockets of the Moonsuit with as many brightly colored bags and rectangles as they could hold.

By the time the clerk looked up, I had the pockets zipped and four dollar bills in my hand. Casually, as if it had taken me this long to make up my mind, I selected a bag of CornNuts and took it to the register.

"That and the gas be it?" the clerk asked. He was nineteen or twenty and bored out of his skull. He wouldn't have cared if I had shoplifted the ice-cream freezer and the cash register.

"Yeah, unless you've got some contact lens soaking solution," I said. My eyes were stinging again, although the sharper pain behind my left eye had not come back. Eluding the Jaguar had made me feel good. Even my feet were confortably warm.

"Sorry," the kid said as he took my money. "You ought to wear glasses. Less expensive, less trouble." He tapped his own wire frames.

I grunted, thinking of my black plastic-framed glasses lying entombed in a dresser drawer at home. I had put them away in 1978.

"Twenty-three cents your change," the kid said, shoving the coins across the counter.

As I looked down at the counter, I saw the stack of Tulsa newspapers beside the register. The one on top had a headline reading SUSPECTED MARXIST AGITATOR TAKES OVER TV AIRWAVES. Below the headline was a reproduction of a photo from the last Cowboy Carl's employee party. A red circle surrounded my head.

"Want a paper?" the kid asked.

I pocketed the twenty-three cents and looked up. "Nah," I said, trying to sound indifferent. I was glad I had left my helmet on. Even so, I felt exposed, and I had to stop myself from putting a hand in front of my faceplate. "Nothing but bad news anyway."

"Got that right," the kid said, a faint light of interest brightening his eyes. "Say, do you know whether that TV stuff is true? I'm working a double shift, so I ain't seen any tube since yesterday evening."

"Me either," I said, turning to go.

"You come back now," the kid said, not caring whether I did or not.

As I turned, I found myself faceplate-to-chin with a fierce-eyed young woman with curled, dark blond hair. She was more than three inches taller than me, making her at least six-one. She was wearing worn Reeboks, red nylon warm-up pants, and a blue tank top that left her arms and shoulders bare. Her skin was goose-pimpled, and her muscles and veins stood out in tight cords. She looked as if she could bench press a tractor. She had a backpack slung over one shoulder, and I had the impression that it was filled with cannonballs.

"You," she said, jabbing me in the chest with a forefinger.

Even through the Moonsuit, the jab left a dime-size spot of pain below my collarbone. Worse than that, though, was the look of contempt on the woman's face. She knew me. She knew who I was. I was dead.

I tried to run down an aisle, but she sidestepped to block me.

"You own that putrid motorcycle?" she asked. Her voice was a normal woman's voice except for the edge it had, the edge that said, *Answer politely or I'll break your wrists.*

My next thought was that this woman was the driver of the Jaguar that had been following me. I had unwittingly committed some offense against either her or her car, and she had been following me ever since to exact payment. Either that, or she really did know my identity and was just making sure before bashing me unconscious and hauling me off to the Authorities.

"Uh, I'm sorry," I said. "Which motorcycle is that?"

I had never before seen a sneer of such loathing. "There's only one here, roadapple," she said. "The one that's blocking the Regular pump so that I can't get my truck to it."

Relief made me chuckle. The woman didn't know who I was. She was nothing more than a powerfully muscled grouch who would hurt me if I didn't move Peggy Sue. Now.

Her eyes narrowed to predatory green slivers. "Something funny?"

I shook my head, the helmet strap scraping across my chin. "No, ma'am," I said. "I'm sorry I took so long. I'll get my bike out of your way right now."

She jerked a thumb at the door. "So hurry up. You cycle jerks are the most inconsiderate cruds in the world."

"I'm sorry," I said again, starting toward the door. I held my bag of CornNuts out to her "Want some?"

She snatched the bag from me, opened it, and poured the contents into her mouth. "Fangksh," she said, handing back the empty husk.

I went out and dropped the bag, watching it slide away with the breeze. I was already a fugitive and a thief, so I didn't think I could do much more damage to my soul by becoming a litterbug.

The woman came out and ran after the bag. "Rancid

pukebucket!" she yelled back at me, spewing CornNuts
onto the concrete. Her vocabulary was starting to remind me of Julie "Eat shit and die, Oliver" Calloway.

I walked into the pinkish-yellow glow of the lights
that hummed over the gasoline pumps and pulled on my
gloves. Peggy Sue was waiting in front of a dinged-up
white GMC pickup that looked as bad as the ones I'd
seen at the salvage yard behind the FIFTY-FOUR MOTOR
INN REASONABLE RATES. The bike's exhaust pipes were
making soft ticking sounds.

I was still ten feet from the Ariel when the headlights came on across the highway and a V-12 engine
bellowed. I put my head down and ran.

The black Jaguar squealed across the highway and
into the convenience store lot, stopping broadside in front
of Peggy Sue just as I reached her. The driver's door
opened, and a bald man wearing a long gray coat
emerged. He was big. The Jaguar growled.

I had never seen the bald man before, and I had no
idea who he was. I didn't want to either, so I jumped
onto Peggy Sue and kicked the starter. The Ariel sputtered and chugged to life, but the stranger grasped the
Moonsuit and yanked me from the bike before I could
put her into gear. While Peggy Sue coughed helplessly,
the bald man dragged me toward the Jaguar.

Scrambling, I got my feet under me and threw an
off-balance punch at my captor's face. I knew that he
might be an Authority, but he hadn't identified himself
as one. So as far as I was concerned, I was being as-
saulted, and I was within my rights to defend myself.

Bullshit. I was terrified. I would have swung at him
regardless.

My gloved fist hit the man's cheek, and I elbowed
him in the ribs with my other arm. He paused and glared
at me, so I swung my fist again. This time, he let go of

the Moonsuit and blocked the punch with a forearm. Simultaneously, his free hand shot under my helmet and gave me a stiff-fingered jab in the throat.

It was as if a grenade packed with nails had gone off in my larynx. I stumbled back against the Regular pump and clawed at my helmet's chin strap, then slid down and sat on the concrete island.

The bald man kicked me in the helmet, and I fell onto my right side. Then he leaned down, grasped me under the armpits, and began dragging me toward the Jaguar again. I struggled, but I couldn't get my feet under me. The inside of my head sounded like a chain saw, and the spikes in my throat were cutting off my breath.

In the midst of the noise and pain, I heard a woman's voice ask, "What do you think you're doing, bozo?"

I'm being killed, that's what, I tried to say, but all I could do was wheeze.

The voice came again. "Could you stop screwing around and move your car? I've been waiting a long time. I mean, try to overcome your slime-licking alpha-male instincts and show some consideration. . . ."

The chain-saw buzzing began to subside as the woman talked, and I was even able to swallow past the nails. I could tell that the bald stranger was ignoring the woman.

"What is it, anyway? Just because you guys have balls you think that the poison they put into your systems entitles you to act like walking porta potties?"

I had an inspiration. I sagged forward as if I had become unconscious, and then I snapped my head back and up. My helmet rammed into the stranger's crotch with the desired effect: He dropped me.

I rolled away, lurched to my feet, and ran for the idling Peggy Sue. The muscular woman with the backpack was standing beside her pickup truck with her arms crossed.

"I've just about had it," she said.

I was hit from behind and fell facedown, my helmet bouncing off the pavement. The stranger landed on top of me, grabbing my right wrist and pulling my arm behind my back. Only the thickness of the Moonsuit kept him from twisting it out of its socket.

A pair of Reeboks walked past my face. "I'll move them both myself, you adolescent armpit kernels," the woman said.

The stranger yanked me to my feet, which hurt a lot, and spun me so that I faced the Jaguar. The muscular woman was entering the car.

"No!" the bald man shouted, shoving me aside so that I collided with the Regular pump again.

I grabbed the pump to keep from falling, and then I turned to try to get to Peggy Sue. As I did, I saw that the man had produced a pistol and was aiming it at the woman, who was now behind the wheel of the Jaguar.

She didn't wait to find out what he would do next, and neither did I. She ducked, and the Jaguar bellowed and sped backward. I jumped onto Peggy Sue, kicked her into first gear, and opened the throttle.

The stranger fired his pistol as Peggy Sue and I rammed him. A small hole appeared in the Regular pump, and the bald man hit the concrete. Peggy Sue ran over his arm, and the pistol skittered away.

The Jaguar laid rubber in reverse in a semicircle around the gasoline pumps, and I glanced at my right mirror just in time to see the car crunch trunk-first into the GMC pickup's right front fender.

At that point, Peggy Sue and I missed the driveway and dropped into the ditch, adding a bitten tongue to my aching head and throat. I hung on tight as the bike churned up to the highway, spraying dirt and dead grass. By the time I regained control, we were a few hundred feet down the road. The mirrors showed me that the Jaguar, with the muscular woman at the wheel, was whipping out of the convenience store lot in the correct fashion, via the driveway.

Well, if she wanted to steal an Authority's car—if the bald man *was* an Authority—that was her business, and her problem. Peggy Sue and I accelerated and got the hell away from there.

And the Jaguar kept pace with us. No matter how fast we went or what side roads we ducked down, those headlights wouldn't fade away. I tried to pray for them to disappear, but my throat and tongue were too sore to sing.

SHARON

Notes on client Oliver Vale, continued . . .

12:46 A.M. Bruce and I are in bed in a Ramada Inn in Wichita. He is angry with me for a number of reasons. One of these reasons is that I have just told him where we are going and why, and he does not like it. Neither does he like the fact that we are using one of his firm's Chevrolet Celebrities. He tells me that to use it for this purpose is unethical.

I disagree. After all, Oliver will almost certainly become Bruce's client once we find him, so we are at least partially on legitimate business.

What Bruce is most angry about, though, is the fact that I have cajoled him into this trip but do not want to make love. After all our time together, he still has not managed to grow beyond the notion of sex-as-reward. His attitude seems to be that as long as he is doing something for me that he does not want to do in the first place, the least I could do in return is give him head.

I'm not in the mood. I too am angry. I'm angry because he insisted that we stop here after traveling such a short distance. At this rate, Oliver will reach Lubbock, do something foolish, and be arrested long before we can get there.

I have to do *something* to help Oliver, though, so I am watching Oliver/Buddy perform on the room TV. I keep hoping that he will do or say something that will give me an insight into how best to direct his therapy.

Not much luck so far. But, my God, can he play the guitar and sing!

Can that really be Oliver?

I am beginning to wonder.

RICHTER

He rose from the pavement and watched the Jaguar's taillights disappear down the highway. Vale and his motorcycle were somewhere ahead of them.

Richter looked down at his right arm and probed it with his left hand, then flexed his right fist. The forearm was going to bruise where the motorcycle had run over it, but nothing was broken or sprained. He would still be able to squeeze a trigger.

That was one thing he would do sooner next time, he promised himself as he stooped to pick up his plastic pistol from where it had fallen.

This was the second mistake he had made in twenty-four hours, and it had been far more serious than the

first. He had lost an opportunity to apprehend Vale, who
now knew him by sight and would be watching for him.
Worse still, he had allowed a bystander to interfere with
his duties. She had even stolen his Jaguar, which was
government property . . . although it couldn't be traced
as such.

Richter had gone to a great deal of trouble only to
let it be wasted. He had been driving south on the Kansas Turnpike when his police scanner had told him that
Vale was being pursued by a sheriff's deputy on a county
road near El Dorado, so he had left the turnpike and
had used the Jaguar's computerized map display to guide
him there. He had then driven at dangerous speeds until he had overtaken the patrol car and forced it into the
ditch. Having eliminated the competition, Richter had
continued driving at a high rate of speed, confident that
he would overtake the motorcycle in twenty or thirty
seconds.

He had not, which meant that Vale had left the road
to hide from the pursuing deputy. Richter had pulled off
at a picnic area to wait, and sure enough, Vale had come
by several minutes later. Richter had begun following
him then and had come close to apprehending him at
the Kaw Reservoir, but Vale had hidden again, almost
evading Richter entirely. Richter had been more cau-
tious after that, hiding the Jaguar behind an abandoned
farmhouse until Vale had passed him a second time.
Richter had resumed following the motorcycle then, but
had kept well back, waiting for Vale to stop and dis-
mount before attempting a capture.

It had almost worked. Richter had caught up with
Vale at the convenience store and had parked across the
highway while the other was inside, planning to nail
him when he came out. Then the woman had butted in.

The bitch. Not only young, but strong too. And here he was, his arm throbbing, his eight-hundred-dollar coat covered with sand and glass, his breath coming in hard puffs. Without his car.

He replaced his pistol in its shoulder holster and looked toward the glass door of the convenience store. The counter was visible, but there was no one at the register. That meant that the clerk was hiding somewhere and telephoning the local uniforms because of the violence outside.

Richter grimaced. As if he didn't have enough problems.

Brushing himself off, he walked to the woman's pickup truck and climbed inside. The keys were in the ignition, so he started the engine, pulled up to the pump that his bullet had hit, and got out to fill the tank. The pump hummed to life when he flipped its lever, so at least he wouldn't have to go inside and possibly kill the clerk just to turn it on from the counter.

The tank took eighteen gallons. When it was full, Richter let the nozzle fall to the pavement. He climbed inside the truck and started it again, then drove onto the highway and headed south.

The truck rattled and shimmied, and as Richter pushed it up to highway speed, it rocked as if an anvil had been dropped into the bed. Its headlights were dim, and the speedometer and fuel gauge were broken. The muffler, if there was one, was so full of holes that the cab reverberated with a perpetual metallic cough. The engine was firing on only five or six of its eight cylinders.

The GMC was worn out, and Richter was furious that he had to use it. He didn't know how he would find Vale now that he didn't have the Jaguar and its equipment, but he swore that he would. His body might be older and softer than it had once been, but he still had his instincts.

Things had become personal now. He owed Vale. Even more, he owed that interfering female citizen.

He hoped that she would stay close to Vale for a while. She had humiliated him, and that could not be allowed. He had never enjoyed discretionary killing, but sometimes it was necessary.

His considered opinion—*damn* them for making him feel so old—was that this was one of those times.

RINGO

Ringo was bored. Occasionally, after making sure that the Ariel's scent was so strong that he couldn't lose it, he had cut cross-country for variety . . . but that had made things worse. It was awful to come across a rabbit hole without being able to stay and bark awhile.

So he was glad when the motorcycle stopped at a convenience store. Maybe it would stay long enough for him to have a little fun. He would have to remember, though, not to interact with humans any more than necessary. He would have to remember the lesson that the fat woman with the Windex had taught him.

He circled the convenience store's parking lot outside of its circles of yellow light so that the motorcycle's rider (Cathy and Jeremy called him Vale) would not notice him, and then he loped behind the building to see whether he could find anything interesting in the trash.

Ringo rose up on his hind legs and put his front paws on the rim of the store's dumpster. He looked inside, sniffing, but found only boxes and papers. What he really

wanted, he decided, was food. His insides had been modified so that he didn't have to eat, but he liked to do it
anyway. Boog's beef jerky had reminded him.

The Doberman dropped back to the ground, and as
he did so, he heard an automobile drive into the parking
lot and slam on its brakes. He cocked his head to listen
and also heard the motorcycle's engine start, then human voices and other noises. But the motorcycle wasn't
going anywhere yet, so he could putter here a bit longer.

He trotted past the dumpster and found the store's
back door. When he sniffed at its edges, he smelled
hundreds of wonderful things: potato chips, peanuts,
chocolate, cheese, salami, fish sticks, corn dogs, pretzels,
donuts, frozen pizzas, gumballs, sesame crackers, and—
yes!—beef jerky.

Drooling, Ringo nosed the steel door. It didn't move,
so he nosed it harder and whined, hoping that someone
would let him in. No one did, so he nosed harder still.
The door buckled in the middle and fell inside.

Ringo blinked. He hadn't meant to do that, but as
long as it had happened, he might as well go on in.

He padded through a storage room as a youthful human male looked in from the doorway that led to the
shop. The youth's mouth opened and his eyebrows jumped,
and he turned and ran. Ringo hurried after him, making
sounds in his throat that he hoped would be reassuring.
"Don't be afraid!" he wanted to say. "I just want some
beef jerky! Please don't spray me with Windex!"

The young man ran past a counter to a glass door,
but then he stopped and made a squeaking noise. He
turned to face Ringo, made a squeaking noise again, and
then sprinted to a big metal case that sat against the
wall. The young man slid open a transparent lid on
top of the case, climbed inside, and pulled the lid shut
over him.

Ringo looked out through the glass door and saw
two humans, one of them Vale, locked in a weird dance.
Another human, a female, was standing beside a white
pickup truck and yelling. The situation didn't look like
anything that was any of the dog's business, so he am-
bled over to the big metal case to see what the deal was
there.

The young man lay on his back among colorful
cardboard cartons and cylinders, peering up at Ringo
through the lid. A circle of fog had formed on the glass
over his mouth.

Ringo sniffed, and his processors told him that the
cartons and cylinders inside the case were filled with ice
cream. No wonder the young man had jumped in there.
The stuff smelled terrific. But Ringo didn't want to be
greedy. He would let the human have the ice cream.
There were plenty of other things to eat.

He trotted down an aisle and gulped a jumbo bag of
sour-cream-and-onion potato chips, then found a refrigerator chest containing packages of bologna and cheese.
He wolfed down several of each, wrappers and all. Next
he nosed open an upright case and pulled out a cluster
of red-and-white cans labeled "Budweiser." He popped
the first can between his teeth, and the foam tickled his
nose. He swallowed the other five for safekeeping, then
munched a frozen pepperoni pizza.

When the pizza was gone, Ringo went to the counter
for dessert. The beef jerky was inside a plastic jar beside
the cash register. He tore open the jar and ate every
salty, delicious strip.

Now that his hunger was sated, he thought to look
outside again. Vale and his motorcycle were gone. Caught
up in his revelry, the Doberman hadn't even heard the
Ariel leave. The man with whom Vale had been dancing

was at one of the gasoline pumps, holding a hose to the side of the pickup truck.

Ringo started toward the door, but paused beside the ice-cream case. He had told himself to have as little to do with people as possible, but the young man had allowed him to eat, and Ringo couldn't leave without acknowledging that favor. He nosed back the case's lid and licked the whimpering human on the face. The nose was cold; a good sign.

That done, Ringo went to the front door, shouldered it open, and trotted out, belching because of the Budweiser. He sniffed the air and discovered that the motorcycle was still heading south.

The pickup truck was leaving now, and it too was going south. Ringo hesitated, cocking his head and considering, then bounded after the truck. It would have been no physical strain for him to continue after Vale on foot, but he had always found it pleasant to lie down and snooze after a meal.

He leaped into the truck bed as the noisy vehicle accelerated, and its body bounced and swayed as he landed. Hunkering down so that the driver wouldn't see him, the Doberman curled up below the cab's rear window.

His olfactory processors would alert him if the Ariel got too far ahead or if the truck deviated from the motorcycle's path. For now, though, he could nap.

He coughed up one of the Budweisers and popped it with his teeth, first savoring the foam and then chewing on the can. He was content.

5

OLIVER

1967 began as though the world were coming to an end. A fire during an Apollo test killed Gus Grissom, Edward White, and Roger Chaffee on January 27, and I lost one of my most treasured dreams. Edward White had been the man I had first seen floating above the Earth, an atmosphere away from all of the trouble below. With his death, I realized that even space was not a refuge. To get there, you had to find a way to leave the planet, but the planet did not want to let you leave. If it could, it would kill you first.

Mother saw the tragedy as another omen, like the tornado of seven months before. She was certain that still worse things were yet to come.

They took their time, but they came.

That summer was the Summer of Love. At least, it was in San Francisco. In Topeka, it was the Summer of Sweat. The city was sticky and miserable, and so was I.

My baby-sitter from the summer before had now

found better things to do than spend eight hours a day with a kid, but Mother could neither quit her job nor leave me home alone. Thus it was that I spent June with first one baby-sitter and then another, and finally with something that made even first and second grades seem pleasant in retrospect:

Vacation Bible School.

Every Protestant church in the Midwest runs one of these. Some last only a few weeks, and some last the whole damn summer, but all have several things in common: A lack of air-conditioning. "Bible Heroes" coloring books. "This Little Light of Mine," an inspirational song written for three-year-olds but forced on persons up to the age of ten. The Children of Israel's Escape from Egypt. Blue-haired teachers with fat arms and cheek rouge the color of red M&Ms. The walls of Jericho. King David. Construction paper. The baby Jesus. Elmer's glue. The adolescent Jesus. Crayola crayons. The adult Jesus. Rounded-tip scissors. The crucified Jesus. Severe discipline for the unruly. The dead Jesus. Warm Kool-Aid and stale cookies. The resurrected Jesus. Bible-quiz contests ("What is Jael best known for?"). The ascended Jesus. Why the Devil (aka Satan) is bad and how to avoid him. Jesus, Jesus, Jesus.

I was furious with Mother for sending me to a place like that, but she had little choice in the matter and did the best she could in picking the church. She enrolled me in the Vacation Bible School that was operated by the Central Shawnee County United Methodist Church of God in Christ of the United States of America, which she probably figured was the Vacation Bible School that was the least like an ideological concentration camp in all of Topeka. We were given two bathroom breaks and one snack period per six-hour day, and twice a week we were allowed to go outside to play sinners and saints in the church parking lot. (Sinners and saints was a religious version of the playground staple called dodgeball or bombardment. My class of Vacation Bible Schoolers would count off, one, two, one, two, and the teacher would designate the ones as saints and the twos as sinners. The sinners would line up against the brick wall of the church and try to dodge the melon-size red inflate-o-balls that the saints threw at us. I always tried to be a sinner, because if a sinner managed to catch a ball that was thrown at him, the saint who had thrown it was either out of the game or had to become a sinner—and I was good at catching.)

It really wasn't too bad, as long as I turned off my ears during the lectures and focused on artistic perfection during the crafts periods. I wasn't allowed to draw, paint, or cut-out-and-glue just anything that I wanted to, of course, but had to follow Mrs. Stummert's assignments. Thus I had to find what joy I could in the work itself. Once I drew a picture of David and Goliath that I thought was almost good enough to be in *Mad* magazine, and another time I did a finger painting of Jesus Walking on the Water that might have been done by Salvador Dali when he was my age (seven). Mrs. Stummert generally frowned whenever she took a look at my finished work, but she could hardly complain because I had done what she had asked to the best of my abilities. She couldn't punish me just because my interpretations happened to be a little bizarre.

My masterpiece was going to be a huge construction-paper collage of the Destruction of Sodom. Mrs. Stummert had told us to reconstruct a biblical scene that illustrated the Power of God in Action, and for me the choice was easy. In my opinion, turning Lot's wife into a slab of rock salt while simultaneously wasting a city was the best trick God had ever pulled.

The beginning of the end of my Vacation Bible School career came as I was putting the finishing touches on the collage one Friday in late July. I had worked on the project during crafts period for five days in a row, lavishing care on details and striving for perfection as I had never done before. I had cut the buildings of Sodom out of purple and red paper, the smoke from gray and tan, the flames from orange and yellow, the tiny screaming Sodomites from brown, and Lot's wife from white. I was finishing by carefully pasting each piece on a big sheet of black, and I thought it looked terrific. I actually felt happy.

I should not have let myself feel that way. Not in Vacation Bible School. When I felt happy, I hummed or sang without being aware of it, and the songs I hummed and sang (although they were my prayers) were extremely secular in nature.

Several weeks earlier, Mother had brought home a new Beatles album: *Sergeant Pepper's Lonely Hearts Club Band*. Ever since she had first played it, the lyrics had been jostling about in my head like soccer players. One of them scored a goal that day while I was working on the Destruction of Sodom, and I sang.

To me, it was nothing more than a happy song about being in good ol' Sergeant Pepper's band. But to Mrs. Stummert, it was something else. It was a sign that the long-haired freakish enemies of all that was good and decent had invaded Topeka.

"What are you singing?" she asked. She was standing behind me, her voice quavering over my head with outrage and doom.

I had learned enough in grade school to know when a teacher had already made up her mind that you were in trouble. The only defense in that situation was to act humble while displaying as much ignorance about your supposed crime as possible.

In this case, I really *was* ignorant of my crime. I knew that I was in trouble, but I didn't know why.

"Just a song," I said in a tiny voice.

"What *kind* of song?" Mrs. Stummert demanded.

"A Beatles song," I squeaked.

Mrs. Stummert clamped my right arm in one fat red hand, pulled me out of my chair, and marched me around the table where my entire Vacation Bible School class was working. The kids were all staring, although they kept their heads down and tried to pretend that they weren't.

"Please continue working, children," Mrs. Stummert said. "This is none of your business." She propelled me into the hall, and the church echoed with the sound of the heavy wooden door banging shut behind her.

Still holding my arm, Mrs. Stummert put her free hand under my chin and tilted my head so that I had to look directly at her rouged face.

"Where did you hear that song?" she asked fiercely. "Were some older kids playing their radio where you could hear it?"

"No," I said, my voice distorted because Mrs. Stummert's fingers were clamped on my jaw.

"Where, then?" she said, shaking me. "Where did you hear filth like that?"

I twisted my head out of her grasp and tried to pull away altogether, but she held my arm tight. "It's not filth," I said, my voice shaking with the tears that were climbing up my throat to my eyes. "It's just a song about being in a band. Sergeant Pepper's band."

Mrs. Stummert's eyes bulged, and her flaccid lips trembled. "Oliver! Do you know who Sergeant Pepper is?" She said "Sergeant Pepper" as though she were spitting out something rancid.

"Just a sergeant, I guess," I said, hating her. "One who runs a band."

Mrs. Stummert shook her head, and her cat's-eye glasses went crooked. "No, Oliver! It's another name for someone who sells bad drugs, and that song and all of those other Beatles songs are about people who aren't married but who all live in the same house together and, and—" She gulped for air.

Meanwhile, I was pissed. "Says who?" I yelled. When Mrs. Stummert insulted the Beatles, she might as well have been insulting me and my mother. After all, the Beatles were Buddy Holly's disciples, and so were we.

At that point, Mrs. Stummert took off down the hall like a speeding blimp, dragging me to the pastor's office. Naturally, he was in.

He was a broad, big-bellied man with a pockmarked nose and hair as black and gleaming as shoe polish laced with Vaseline. He wore a dark blue suit with a tightly knotted necktie that was partially covered by the pouch of skin under his chin. "Well, well, what have we here?" he said as Mrs. Stummert yanked me forward to stand in front of his desk. I swear, that's what he said.

"We have a young man who has been singing hippie drug songs in Bible School," Mrs. Stummert said.

The pastor's eyebrows pulled together, his eyes narrowed, and his face darkened to a deep red. He stood and came around the desk to stand towering over me. "Is this true, young man?" he thundered. I swear: He *thundered*.

When you're a kid, this is what they do to you. One adult accuses you of a crime, and another demands, "Is this true?" If you say no, then you've just called adult number one a liar, and you're in for it. If you say yes, then you've confessed your guilt to adult number two, and you're in for it.

Come to think of it, that process stays pretty much the same after you've grown up. Damned if you do and damned if you don't, between a rock and a hard place, good cop/bad cop, Scylla and Charybdis.

I said nothing.

"I asked you a question, son," the pastor said.

"I'm not your son, fat butt," I blurted.

"Fat butt" was an insult I had learned in second grade. I was horrified at myself for having used it on the pastor, who for all I knew would kill me; but regardless of that, it was appropriate.

Mrs. Stummert shrieked and shook me, telling me that I would wind up in either Hell or reform school and nearly dislocating my arm. The pastor raised his hand as if he were going to swat my head from my shoulders, but then he walked around the desk and sat down again. From there he glared at me with the most intense expression of hatred that I have ever seen. I became scared.

"Mrs. Stummert," he said.

Mrs. Stummert stopped shaking me. "Yes, Pastor?" she asked. Even she sounded a little frightened now.

"Please bring me your record book," he said. "I need the boy's home number to call his mother."

"Yes, Pastor," Mrs. Stummert said, pulling me toward the door.

"Leave him here," the pastor said.

Mrs. Stummert released my arm and left the office, closing the door. I stood before the pastor's desk and rubbed the red spots her fingers had left.

"Stand still," the pastor said.

I stopped rubbing and stood still.

The pastor stood again and came around the desk. He put one meaty hand on my head.

"You little piece of dogshit," he said. His voice was a low growl. "You're going to grow up like those others, aren't you? The un-Christian, un-American ones in California and New York with their dirty hair and filthy clothes and their diseased whores who commit perversions with their mouths."

My stomach tightened with a sick terror. Even what I had felt at the sight of the tornado the year before was better than what I felt now. I wanted to run, to get out of there and never go back, but I couldn't move.

"If your teacher would just wait a few minutes before coming back," the pastor continued, "I'd show you what it'll be like for you. That'd teach you."

He pulled my head toward him, and my terror snapped back to anger. I kicked his shin and then flailed away from him, backing up against the wall.

"Stay away from me or I'll kill you!" I screamed.

The pastor went back to his chair. He didn't seem to have felt my kick. "Boys who say things like that get sent to reform school, just like Mrs. Stummert says," he said in a voice that was now weirdly calm. "So do boys who tell tales. Be sure not to tell any tales, son. No one would believe you, and you'd end up sorry you'd done it."

I stayed against the wall, breathing hard, tears on my face, my fists knotted, even after Mrs. Stummert returned with her record book.

She hardly gave me a glance. "His mother has a job outside the home, apparently," she said, holding out the book to the pastor. "She gave two phone numbers and wrote 'work' beside one with a circle around it."

The pastor took the book. "Where do your father and mother work, son?" he asked.

"I don't have a father," I said, "and I don't need one either."

The pastor and Mrs. Stummert gave each other looks

that made me want to pound their faces into pulp.

"What about your mother, then?" the pastor asked.

"KKAP radio," I said.

This time the pastor and Mrs. Stummert looked at me. Their expressions were mixtures of disgust and smugness.

"Might have known," the pastor said. He picked up his phone.

Mother came quickly. I don't know how she was able to drop everything at the station and take off, but she did. I loved her for it.

Still, I wanted to make my position plain from the outset. The moment that she stepped into the pastor's office, I said, "I'm not coming back here. Not ever."

She squatted before me so that our eyes were on a level. "Why? What happened?"

Mrs. Stummert and the pastor took turns lecturing Mother then, talking as if I were a hundred miles away. Mrs. Stummert told Mother what I had done, and Mother asked what was so bad about that. The pastor replied that so-called music like that Beatles poison was destroying the Christian fiber of the nation. He also said that any radio station that played things like that was under the influence of Communists and drug addicts.

Mother told him that *she* worked for a radio station that played things like that, that no one she knew was either a Red or a junkie, and what the hell made him think he knew his head from his ass, anyway?

The pastor almost exploded. "We don't need you LSD hippies in our community!" he cried, his face shaking. "We won't let you raise your bastard children to destroy us! We can tell the Authorities about you! We have Jesus on our side!"

"I'll bet He's just thrilled to pieces about *that*," Mother replied, taking my hand. "Let's get out of here, Oliver.

You won't have to come back. I'll either find baby-sitters, or you can come to work with me. We'll hide you in a filing cabinet."

As we left, I looked over my shoulder and yelled, "Fat butt!" at the quaking pastor. Ordinarily, Mother would have disapproved of that out of a sense of maternal duty, but this time she looked over her shoulder and yelled the same thing.

Once we were inside our creaky old Ford Falcon, Mother gazed at me with a seriousness that startled me.

"Oliver," she said, "this is important: Did they hurt you? Did they hurt you at all, in any way? Did they even just scare you?"

I opened my mouth to tell her about my arm, which was probably going to bruise where Mrs. Stummert had grasped it, and about the pastor grabbing my head.

"Because if they did," Mother said before I could speak, "we'll *get* them."

There was an edge to her voice that made me stop. Considering, I asked, "How do you mean?"

She stared out the windshield. "That depends on what they did to you. At the very least, we'll slice their tires. We'll put sugar in their gas tanks. We'll break into their houses and flush explosive chemicals down their toilets. We'll put dead skunks in their ovens and set the temperature at five hundred degrees. We'll capture pigeons, feed them blueberries for a week, and set them loose in their living rooms. We'll telephone them and blow police whistles. We'll send them cow poop by fourth-class mail. We'll hound them until they go berserk and do something crazy and *die*."

I thought about the pastor saying, *We can tell the Authorities about you.* I wasn't sure who the Authorities were, but if they were meaner and more powerful than the pastor, I didn't want to find out.

"They didn't hurt me," I said. I didn't want Mother
to go to jail, or worse. "We don't have to do any of that
stuff. I just don't want to go back there, that's all."

Mother looked disappointed. "Okay," she said. "Let
me know if you change your mind."

Her summertime entries in Volume III indicate that
she was indeed disappointed, and not just about the fact
that I had vetoed the fourth-class-mail cow poop.

*That bloated walrus called me a hippie, she wrote.
Would that it were so. If I could, I would go out to San
Francisco and find out what this Movement is all about,
and whether there might be a place in it for me. I would
even try LSD. Wouldn't that be something to shock Mama;
I would do it just for that. I could probably try it right
here in Topeka, Kansas, if I wanted, because Ted at the
station has hinted that he knows people over in Lawrence
who can get him pretty much anything.*

*But I'll never do it. I have Oliver. He has me. If I
dropped acid and went tripping tra-la-la across the roof-
tops and danced at the peak of the Statehouse dome, what
would happen to him? Mama would probably get custody
of him, and Great Chuck Almighty, I don't want that.*

*Besides, I'm twenty-six. I'm too old to be a hippie.
Another four years, and no one in Haight-Ashbury will
trust me. I'm not sure that they would now.*

Mother's frustration at being a single parent trapped
in Topeka in 1967 is in evidence throughout the rest of
Volume III, which she completed late that fall. She began to buy more and more books and magazines devoted
to UFO investigations and speculations concerning the
lost continent of Atlantis, apparently figuring that if she
couldn't indulge in hippie-type weirdness, she'd settle for
any kind of weirdness she could find.

And there was plenty to be found, as illustrated by

the diary entry Mother wrote on October 21:

Today is the day that the Pentagon will rise one hundred feet into the air and that its evil spirits will be exorcised. I cannot be there to see it, but I will be here adding my energy to the effort, humming and chanting whatever feels right for a levitation spell. They sent Mikey to Vietnam last month, but maybe if we can do this thing, they will bring him back and he won't be killed. In the name of ancient Atlantis, in the name of Zeus and Poseidon, in the name of the star creatures who visit in their ships of light, we command you, arise.

The Pentagon either didn't budge an inch or only rose a mere ten feet, depending on who you ask.

The Apollo tragedy, the Vacation Bible School incident, Mother's growing weirdness, and the general state of Everything in 1967 served to make me one miserably confused little seven-year-old boy. I began to throw tantrums, break things, and stick pencils down my throat to make myself throw up. It was a good thing that Mother and I almost never saw Grandmother during this time, or I might have really gone crazy. Sharon Sharpston has suggested that the lack of a positive male role model during this period might be the primary reason for my behavior, but I think that this theory is largely manure.

After all, I did have positive male role models. Always, I had Buddy. I also had the Beatles, and along about this time, The Who. Townshend and Daltrey were added to our pantheon, and Mother and I sang "I Can See for Miles" every night one week while she was cooking supper.

I had one other male role model, although I had never met him and had never heard his voice: Uncle Mike. Mother had been receiving letters from him since February, some of them with snapshots included, and she

read them to me. At least, she read all except the parts
that she thought I shouldn't hear.

Here is one of those letters, which I found stuck into
Volume III. I remember Mother reading it aloud one
evening in November. I do not remember the fifth para-
graph.

> *Dear Sis,*
>
> *Well I sure feel bad I couldn't see you before I
> got sent over but that's the way it goes sometimes I
> guess. I'll make up for it when I get back. I especially
> wish I could see that boy of yours, I bet he's some-
> thing.*
>
> *I have been here at Da Nang for two weeks now
> and know most of the guys pretty good. The food is
> mostly bad but it was in Des Moines too ha ha ha.
> Say you haven't learned how to cook yet have you?
> because if you have some cookies or something would
> sure make me popular around here hint hint.*
>
> *The weather here is about like at home only hot-
> ter and wetter. Another week here and then my unit
> goes out to do stuff like making sure the enemy stays
> clear of strategic roads. That should be easy because
> I hear they mostly hide out in the jungle anyway.*
>
> *So how are things at the radio station? We got
> one guy in the unit, Pete is his name, who is a real
> Rolling Stones fan. He says you must have the best
> job in the world. He says to tell you "better than our
> jobs, anyway." He is just joking since we haven't had
> to work too awful hard yet.*
>
> *The only tough thing so far was I saw two dead
> guys yesterday. It was two guys who got caught in
> some kind of booby trap that blew up on them. They
> got put into plastic bags, not even boxes but bags,
> and the guys doing it couldn't figure out which feet*

*went with which guy so they had to guess. Don't worry
I won't end up that way you can bet because they
taught us at camp new methods how to tell booby
traps when you see them.*

    *Say hi to that Oliver kid of yours for me and tell
him I'll give him all my medals when I get home.
Pete says the only medal he wants is the Meritorious
Eating Prize. He is the one who made me ask you to
send cookies.*

                                     *Your brother,
Mike*

I didn't understand Vietnam, or the levitation of the
Pentagon, or any of it. The whole business was one of
those things that I figured I would understand once I got
older.

I was wrong. Since I had been born in 1959, I had
lucked into the eye of the hurricane. I would never have
to worry about being drafted or about seeing my friends
drafted. War was not something I would ever have to
deal with in a direct, personal way.

Why do I feel guilty about that?

Back then, Uncle Mike's letters were nothing more
than the words of a stranger in a faraway land. They
had no more effect on me than the incomprehensible
events Walter Cronkite described on the evening news.
Death is meaningless unless it happens to someone you
know.

It happened to someone I knew on December 10, two
days after my eighth birthday. Otis Redding and four of
the Bar-Kays were killed when the twin-engine Beechcraft in which they were flying crashed into a lake near
Madison, Wisconsin.

Mother and I sat silently in our tiny living room

when we heard the news. I was on the floor beside the
furnace vent, and the hot air coming out dried my eyes
so that I couldn't cry. I don't know whether I could have
anyway; I was almost more scared for myself than I was
sad for Otis.

He had died within a few days of my birthday, just
as Sam Cooke had three years before. In addition, Otis
had died a death eerily similar to Buddy Holly's. (Buddy's plane hadn't gone into a lake, but it had crashed
near a town named for one, which struck me as being
almost the same thing.) And Mother had told me any
number of times that Buddy and I were spiritually linked.

I began to fear that the link was Death, which made
me wish that I would never grow up. The more birth-
days I had, the more gods we would lose.

Mother, however, had another explanation for Otis's
death.

I was right about last year's tornado, she wrote in
her final entry in Volume III. *It was a harbinger of more
horrible things to come. The fire that killed the astronauts (itself an omen). Mikey in Vietnam. The war getting worse, the police and military cracking down on
public assemblies. People like that pastor at the church
gaining more and more power. Otis Redding dying. The
station getting threatening mail for playing "hippie-nig-
ger" music.*

*Come for us, O wise flyers of the bright ships of an-
cient Atlantis. Come and take me and my son away with
you to live among the giant blue stars. You won't be sorry.
We aren't like the rest of these dumbfucks.*

But the bright ships of ancient Atlantis did not come.
Neither did anything else. Mother and I remained in Topeka, waiting to see what could possibly happen in 1968
that had not happened already.

*

Dawn on Saturday, February 4, 1989, was a signal for cold drizzle to enshroud the state of Oklahoma. That was all I needed to make me want to curl up in the nearest ditch.

Peggy Sue and I had spent the night zigzagging among back roads, trees, and barns in an effort to shake the Jaguar off our tail. The woman who was now driving the beast had proven to be even more tenacious than the bald man had been, and the bike and I had both been pushed to our limits. I had tried doubling back, hiding under bridges, and outright speed, but still the woman had stayed within a mile of us.

Finally, I had killed our lights and cut cross-country, running the bike over a downed barbed-wire fence and bouncing across a pasture. It had been a dangerous move, because we could have run into a gully, a badger hole, a cow, or a coyote, but it had worked. The mirrors had shown the Jaguar's headlights standing still at the place where Peggy Sue and I had left the road.

As soon as we'd put a hill between us and the car, I had switched the bike's lights back on, found a cowpath, and followed it for a couple of winding miles until it intersected with an oil-pumper road. That in turn had taken us to a township road of graded red dirt, and I had steered Peggy Sue in the direction that I was pretty sure was south.

By that time, the bumps of the pasture had almost neutered me, Peggy Sue sounded as if she were choking, and we had made no progress toward Lubbock. Then the sky brightened from black to gray, and the drizzle started. The Moonsuit and the bike were both splattered with red mud before we found pavement again.

It was time to find a place to hide for the day, but first I had to figure out where the hell we were. A shotgun-peppered road sign read "Kingfisher, 6 miles," and although I didn't know where that was, it was definitely somewhere.

Kingfisher was at the junction of a state highway and a U.S. highway, and the map I swiped from a box outside a closed gas station showed me that I was only about thirty miles northwest of Oklahoma City. That was as close as I wanted to get. Aside from the danger of the usual Authorities, Oklahoma City was the home base of the Reverend William Willard and his Corps of Little David, who had probably not appreciated having their ministry preempted. The Bill Willyites would be marching in the streets today.

I studied the map for a few minutes—luckily, Kingfisher was as still as death this early in the day—and then Peggy Sue and I headed west on the state highway. Despite my fatigue and soreness, I had resolved that our hiding place would not be within city limits this time.

The drizzle worsened, and I had to wipe my faceplate every fifteen seconds. Maybe leaving Kingfisher hadn't been such a good idea after all. The combination of my weariness, Peggy Sue's occasional stumbling, and the cruddy weather were going to add up to Oliver Vale smeared on the pavement if I didn't stop soon.

Ten miles out of Kingfisher, we reached a blacktopped crossroad with a sign indicating that the "Chisholm Trail Rest Stop Waterbed Motel" was only a short distance south. I swerved the bike onto the crossroad, and a few miles later we reached the promised motel.

The FIFTY-FOUR MOTOR INN REASONABLE RATES had been a luxury resort compared to this place. The wooden building leaned, its paint was a peeling yellow-gray, and

the parking lot was mud. Surprisingly, though, the lot
was packed with cars and pickup trucks. I wouldn't be
able to pull the same get-a-room-free trick that I had
pulled in El Dorado. I rode Peggy Sue to the south end
of the motel, shut her down, and then pushed her behind
the building (where there were no rooms). She would
have to sit parked in mud, but at least she wouldn't be
seen from the road.

Now I would have to pay for a room and hope that
I wasn't recognized. The wet, muddy ride had probably
helped me in that regard; the Moonsuit hardly looked
blue anymore, and my face couldn't have been more than
a blur behind the helmet faceplate. I slogged around to
the front of the building and tracked red mud down the
crumbling sidewalk to the office. As I passed occupied
rooms, I heard noises and comments from within: "Not
again, honeybunch, I gotta sleep sometimes, don't I? Ow!"
"Wazzat a motorsickle outside? Goddamn it, my wife's
brother rides a motorsickle." "Gonna ask for half our
money back. Ain't no poochy on the TV." "Where's the
beer? What happened to the fuckin' beer? Did you drink
all my fuckin' beer, bitch?" "Sorry, baby, if you're out of
rubbers, you're out, period. This girl don't take no
chances." By the time I got to the office, I had a good
idea of why the Chisholm Trail Rest Stop Waterbed Motel was well off the main road.

There was a doormat outside the office, but wiping
my feet on it only made my shoes muddier. I shouldered
open the swollen door and found myself inside a closet
filled with cigarette smoke. Through the haze, I saw an
ancient man in need of a shave sitting on the other side
of a low counter. His eyes were fixed on a black-and-
white TV watching Buddy perform, but he might have
been seeing anything.

"Need a room," I said, taking my wallet from a
Moonsuit pocket. My tongue was still sore from having
been bitten.

"Six dollars for four hours, ten for eight," the old
man said without looking at me. His voice was phlegmy.

I put a ten-dollar bill on the counter.

"Tape machine ain't working today," he said.

"That's okay."

He took the ten and unhooked a key from one of
twelve cardboard clock faces on the wall, then adjusted
the clock's hands to read three-thirty. "Room eleven," he
said, dropping the key on the counter. "Second from the
end. Have a good time." He still hadn't looked at me.
My head and body ached, but I felt lucky.

Room 11's door banged into the waterbed as I entered, and when I found the light switch, I saw that the
room was the same size as the office and that it had not
been cleaned since its previous occupants had left. Beer
cans, whiskey bottles, cigarette butts, condom wrappers,
and a few used condoms were scattered on a grimy,
colorless surface that had once been a carpet. The bed
was unmade, and one glance at the sheets told me that
I didn't want to lie on them. The smell of the place was
reminiscent of stale smoke, beer puke, and soured bodily
fluids. At least the heat was working.

All things considered, I couldn't have asked for a
better hideout, I thought as I removed my helmet and
gloves and shrugged out of the junk-food-laden Moonsuit. Only a pervert would think to look for me here.

After taking two stolen plastic tubes of breath mints
from the Moonsuit, I scrunched around the waterbed,
bumped against a shelf that held a small TV set, and
squeezed into a bathroom that was the same size as the
wall indentations that once held ironing boards. There
was no shower or mirror, and the sink was set into the

wall above the toilet tank. It was impossible to sit without thunking my head.

After flushing the toilet and washing my hands (no soap), I poured all of the breath mints into my mouth. While I was sucking on the pellets, I popped out my contact lenses and dropped each into one of the empty plastic tubes. Then I filled each tube with water, hoping that I would remember that peppermint was right and wintergreen was left. Again, I wished for my glasses.

I set the tubes on the toilet tank and returned to the waterbed cubicle, where I kicked the mess on the floor into one corner, suppressing screams when things stuck to my shoes. Once that chore was done, I put on my gloves again and stripped the sheets and pillowcases from the bed, throwing the resulting wad into the same corner as the rest of the trash. I saved one pillowcase to wipe the mud from the Moonsuit.

Finally, I pulled off my shoes and lay on the waterbed (which was so underfilled that my rump touched the floor), wrapping myself in the bedspread and a blanket. These had been tangled at the foot of the bed and seemed cleaner than the sheets, but I kept my clothes on anyway. Once I was bundled, I curled up on my side with one bare pillow under my head and the other under my hip. Despite my stinging eyes, a headache, a bitten tongue, a sore throat, various bruises, and a *thumpata-thumpata* noise coming from room 10, I fell asleep quickly. My last conscious thought was that although I lay in squalor, my mouth was minty fresh.

I had several interlocking dreams. First I was riding Peggy Sue down a highway that melted to become a broad gray plain; then Jupiter rose, and the Great Red Spot winked and fluttered its eyelashes; a satellite-dish-headed creature appeared and began chasing me, firing

popcorn and breath mints from its block converter; I tried
to accelerate and flee, but discovered that I was twisting
Sharon Sharpston's right ear instead of Peggy Sue's
throttle. Sharon reached up and flipped me onto my back
in the dust, then sat on my chest and began choking me.

"Buckethead," she said.

I awoke thrashing, and found that it was not Sharon
Sharpston who sat on my chest, but the curly-haired,
muscular woman whom I had thought I had eluded.

"Snakefart," she growled, squeezing hard and shaking me. "Dirty thieving criminal welfare cheat."

I tried to beg her to stop, but the only sound I could
manage was a squeak. My head felt as though it were
about to pop open like, well, like a head being popped
open.

"Lousy ratfink *motorcyclist*," the woman said.

My hands slapped her arms, beating out a coded plea
for mercy. The thought of slugging her in the face crossed
my mind, but I didn't have the strength. If I had, and I
had actually tried it, she probably would have killed me.

"You want to say something, lizard piss?" she asked,
loosening her grip on my throat enough for me to breathe.

"Please get off," I wheezed.

"Why? You got me mixed up with a guy with a gun,
didn't you? You ride a motorcycle, don't you?"

"Well, yes," I said, answering the second question.

"All right, then," the woman said. "I *hate* motorcycles. I hate men who *ride* motorcycles. My ex-boy-
friend rode a motorcycle. At least, the ancient Mongolian
entity he channeled for did."

"I'm sorry to hear that," I said. I was sorry to hear
anything that made her want to kill me.

"Whenever I come across a motorcycle under five
hundred cc," she said, "I throw it against a wall. Whenever I come across a motorcycle bigger than that, I kick

it over. I should have kicked yours over last night
when it was in my way, but now I've made up for it. I've
kicked it over in the mud."

That fired up my adrenals. I sat up, and the muscular woman tumbled onto the floor between the bed and
the wall, landing beside her backpack. "You kicked over
Peggy Sue?" I yelled. "What'd she ever do to you? If you've
got a problem, it's with me! Leave my bike out of it!"

The woman rubbed the back of her head. "Take it
easy, groutbreath," she said, sounding less angry. "It
landed soft."

I struggled out of my cocoon of blankets and rolled
away to stand on the opposite side of the bed. "You're
going to clean it up!" I shouted. "That motorcycle's like
a dog to me!"

She stared. "You guys are all bughouse nuts," she
said. "It's a machine, for God's sake. It's not like I kicked
over your mother or something."

"A lot you know!"

She stood. "You act like I'm the one who's the criminal here. *You're* the one who wouldn't move your motorcycle from the pump. *You're* the one the guy with the
gun is after. *You're* the one who fixed things so I'd have
to steal his car."

The unfairness of these accusations pissed me off. I
was having a tough enough time without being held responsible for this woman's problems. "I didn't make you
do anything," I said. "If you weren't such a hothead, you
wouldn't have tried to move his car and he wouldn't have
pulled his gun."

Her face took on a thoughtful expression. "Maybe,"
she said. "Who is the Bald Avenger, anyway? A cop?"

"I don't know," I said, rubbing my throat to let her
know that it hurt. "He could be, I guess. But cops are
supposed to identify themselves, and he didn't."

"I noticed. That's why I have to give you to him."

I tensed. "How do you figure?"

"Simple. If he's not a cop, he's something worse. And if he's something worse, he's the kind of guy who won't go crying to the real cops that his car's been stolen. He'll just find me and shoot me. But if I return you and his Jag, maybe he'll leave me alone."

"And maybe he won't," I said, estimating my chances of getting to my contact lenses, the Moonsuit, my shoes, and my helmet and then dashing out before the woman caught me and beat me senseless. I estimated that I had no chance at all. "Maybe he'll just shoot you because he feels like it."

The woman took a few steps and leaned against the door. "Yeah. It's a problem." She smiled humorlessly. "Thought you'd lose me with that cross-country trick, didn't you? But here I am, and you've got to tell me what the deal is with you and the Avenger. You've also got to convince me that you're not lying. Once I know what's up, I can decide what to do."

I realized then that she didn't have any idea of who I was.

"Have you watched any TV recently?" I asked. "Since, say, Thursday night?"

She scowled. "I've been on the road since Thursday morning. I was trying to get my worthless GMC to take me from Minneapolis to Houston. Just my luck that the tags are expired. If they weren't, I could've stuck to I-35 and I wouldn't have been anywhere near you."

"Truck have a radio?"

"Broken. You're not trying to be evasive, are you, crudball?" She looked as if she might be thinking of clamping her hands around my throat again.

In most Life Situations, the truth is irrelevant. Once in a great while, however, it's the only thing you've got.

I sat on the floor and told the woman my name and everything that had happened to me, and because of me, since 1:00 A.M. Friday morning. I also threw in some stuff about Mother, UFOs, Ready Teddy, and my job at Cowboy Carl's Computer and Component Corral to provide color and verisimilitude.

The woman stood against the door with her arms crossed. Her face was as impassive as an anvil.

I stopped the story at the point where I met her in the convenience store. She was looking at the floor now, and her tongue began moving around inside her cheeks. I guessed that she was trapped in a limbo between belief and disbelief, so I got onto the waterbed and crawled down its length, *thud-slosh thud-slosh,* so that I could turn on the television set.

Buddy fuzzed into existence. He wasn't singing, but was strolling around and strumming his guitar idly. Occasionally, he stopped short as if he had bumped into a transparent wall, then changed direction and continued walking. He was exploring the parameters of his bubble, which was proving to be about the size of the inflated Moonwalks you can still see at small-town carnivals. The camera was at the center of the circle, and it tracked Buddy all the way around. Jupiter came in and out of view like an enormous striped UFO.

The woman had stepped away from the door to come closer to the TV. I flipped around the channels to show her that the same scene was on all of them.

"This is just a tape the motel is playing," the woman said. "It's a sci-fi smut flick, and any second now a naked space bimbo is going to show up."

As she spoke, Buddy approached the camera and read my name and address again. Then he started singing "Dearest."

I crawled off the bed, fetched my wallet from the

Moonsuit, and showed the woman my driver's license.

She looked at it for a few seconds. "Glad to meet you, Ollie," she said in a faraway voice. "I'm Gretchen Laird."

"Glad to meet you too, Gretch."

Her back stiffened, and she glared at me. "I hate being called 'Gretch,'" she said.

"I hate being called 'Ollie,'" I said.

She looked back at the TV and turned down the sound. "The way I figure it," she said after a minute or so, "the Bald Avenger must be a foreign agent—say Russia or Poland. If he were American, he'd be driving a Ford or GM product, right? Besides, I took a look in the Jag's trunk and there are about thirty different license plates." She paused. "Guess I might as well keep it. Nobody's going to care that I swiped a car from a Communist."

"What would Russia or Poland want with me?" I asked.

"Well, you're obviously a valuable guy if this stuff is coming from another planet," Gretchen said, gesturing at the TV. "If I were a president or a dictator or whatever, I'd sure want to be the first to get hold of you and dissect you. It'd be a real feather in my cap."

For the first time, it occurred to me that I might have more than domestic Authorities to worry about. I grabbed the Moonsuit and began pulling it on.

Gretchen frowned. "What are you doing?"

"If you found me, he can too," I said as I struggled with the Moonsuit's flapping arms. "He probably took your truck when you took his car."

She grinned. "If he did, he didn't get more than twenty miles. The radiator leaks like a rhinoceros pisses. I've had to stop and refill it every forty miles ever since Kansas City. I was gonna take care of it right after getting gas, but the Jag showed up. Right about now, the Bald Avenger is stranded with no idea of where we are."

I stopped struggling with the Moonsuit. "So what was all that crap about turning me over to him?"

"That's still an option," she said. "And that's why I'm not letting you out of my sight for a while. See, I'm a capitalist, and capitalists are realists. I'll do whatever's necessary for my own best interests."

I sat down on the bed, my rump hitting the floor hard. "Why's a capitalist driving a truck with expired plates and a busted radiator?"

She gave me a dark look. "That isn't my fault," she said, and proceeded to tell me the story of her life.

I lay down and wrapped myself in the blankets again. As long as she didn't try to strangle me anymore, I didn't much care what she did. Besides, it was kind of nice to have some company.

Gretchen told me that she had been born in 1967 to San Francisco flower children who became embarrassingly wealthy marketing lava lamps. Unfortunately, by the time Gretchen had turned fourteen, the bottom had fallen out of the lava-lamp market, and her parents had cut off her allowance. As a result, she had rebelled against their liberal politics and had become a hard-core conservative. She had left home after graduating from high school at the age of seventeen (her parents had "gone back to the land," which had disgusted her) and had been wandering from city to city ever since, a materialist without material, a money-lover without money. She had garnered enough grants and loans to attend college, but had dropped out of the University of Illinois during her sophomore year.

"This fruit of an English professor wanted us to write a twelve-page paper on the Beat poets," she told me. "You know, Ginsberg, Kerouac, Burroughs, that bunch?"

"I've heard of them."

"They were a bunch of faggots and junkies," Gretchen said vehemently. "So I asked the prof, why should I want to write about drugged-out, left-wing, unpatriotic mental popsicles? Besides, what did any of that literary Bob Dylan crap have to do with my double major in Business Administration and Physical Education, I'd like to know?"

"It's a puzzle," I acknowledged.

After dropping out of college, Gretchen had worked for the Illinois Republican Party for a year and had found it emotionally, if not financially, rewarding. Then she had become romantically involved with a law student and had quit her job to move to Minneapolis with him. She had supported him with her savings account while he worked on his J.D., confident that when he graduated and passed the bar, she would at last have the secure, conservative life she deserved.

Unfortunately, the young man's studies had slipped when he had become a trance-channeler for a member of Genghis Khan's horde who had a penchant for expensive motorcycles. At first, Gretchen had embraced the New Age channeling phenomenon, for although she had long been certain of her politics, she had never been able to decide upon an appropriate spiritual life. Her trust and belief had been crushed, however, when her Mongolian-possessed boyfriend had cleaned out their bank account, stolen her Penney's credit card, and left her for a middle-aged vegetarian Democrat.

"So here I am," Gretchen told me. "My politics are beyond reproach, and I'm in perfect physical shape. Yet I'm almost broke and spiritually void. Even if I were to get hold of lots of money, I have this sick feeling that I'd still be unhappy. I've been trying to get to Houston because a college friend just opened a health spa there and might give me a job, but even that doesn't thrill me.

Nothing seems to matter much these days." She gave
me a piercing look. "At least, nothing seemed to matter
until I ran into you last night. You gave me something
to care about, to get mad about."

"You're welcome," I said.

"But now that we've talked, I don't feel mad anymore," she continued. "Instead I feel, I don't know, *an-
ticipation*. I feel like maybe it was Fate that I met you."

That made sense. Fate and I go way back.

Gretchen nodded at the TV. "I mean, there's something spiritual about Buddy Holly coming back to life,
isn't there? Didn't he die a long time ago, back in 1963,
like Kennedy? It has to mean something, doesn't it? And
him reading your name—that has to mean something
too, right?"

"He died in 1959," I said. "And, yeah, I think his
resurrection must 'mean something' . . . if he really has
been resurrected." I hesitated. "That's why I'm going to
Lubbock. To find out whether he's arisen."

Gretchen slapped one of her rock-hard thighs. "That
settles it. The Jag and I are going to Lubbock with you."

I shook my head. "I appreciate the offer, but I don't
think—"

"That's right," Gretchen said, leaning over me and
flexing her right arm. A vein popped up on the biceps.
"From here on, *I* think. You need help. And if you bug
out on me between here and Lubbock, you'll need more
help than you can get on this planet, skunknuts."

I resigned myself. "Whatever you say."

"Got that right. Now get off the bed. It's my turn. If
you try to leave while I'm asleep, I'll hurt you."

"I've only got the room until three-thirty."

"Okay, I'll chip in my share and keep it until seven
or so," she said. "We shouldn't travel until after dark."
She went to the door. "Be off the bed when I get back."

When she was gone, I went to the window and pulled back the dirt-stiff curtains to watch her walk to the office. Her tight, round rump was sharply defined by her red warm-up pants.

"Forget it," I told myself.

I was on the floor with a blanket and a pillow when she returned. Buddy was singing "It's So Easy."

"Hey," Gretchen said, "isn't that an old Linda Ronstadt song?"

I turned away from her. She stepped on my leg on her way to the bathroom. I closed my eyes when she came out.

The TV snapped off, and the waterbed sloshed as Gretchen lay down. "One more thing, mushface," she said. "I'm your worst castration anxiety come to life. Don't try anything cute with me just because I'm horizontal."

"Well," I said, "all right."

I considered telling her not to try anything cute with me either, but thought better of it. She might have started strangling me again.

RICHTER

The rattletrap GMC pickup overheated only fourteen miles from the convenience store. Richter brought it to a halt straddling the center line, but he left the lights on. He wanted someone to stop, not crash. He climbed out of the truck and walked across the road to stand on the west shoulder.

The first three vehicles to come by swerved around the pickup and drove on, but the fourth, a candy-apple-red Ford crew-cab truck, came barreling down from the north and squealed to a stop. The Ford's right front fender came within six inches of hitting Richter.

Richter walked around to the driver's side. The window slid down as he approached.

"Hey, skinhead!" the driver yelled. "Got a problem?"

Richter came close to the window and saw three men in the green glow of the dashboard lights. They were laughing. Each held a quart bottle of beer.

"Yes," Richter said, resigning himself to the fact that he would have to speak an entire sentence to get what he wanted. If he simply drew his pistol at this point, the Ford's driver might be quick enough to escape. "A whore has passed out drunk on the seat of my pickup."

Richter stepped back as the crew cab's doors flew open and its occupants scrambled out, spilling beer.

"Shit!" one of them said. "That sounds bad!"

"Yeah, she could drown in her own puke!" another cried.

As the three men headed for the GMC, Richter climbed into the Ford, closed and locked both doors, and rolled up the windows. The vehicle was an automatic, so he put it into Drive and stepped on the accelerator. As he did so, he glanced in the rearview mirror to see whether any of the three furious men had produced firearms.

What he saw was a two-weapon gunrack in the crew cab's rear window, and beyond that, an enormous Doberman pinscher with a galvanized chain collar jumping into the truck bed. The vehicle rocked as the dog landed and lay down.

Richter wondered whether the dog belonged to one of the three men, or whether it had been in the GMC without his knowing it, or whether it had just happened along at that moment and decided to hitch a ride. Whatever the case, he decided, the animal's presence was an irrelevancy. If it bothered him, he would shoot it.

When he was well down the road, he reduced speed
and took an inventory of the truck's accessories. He had
gotten lucky. A CB radio and a police scanner were bolted
to the underside of the dash. If he kept his cool, his superiors need never know that two jerk-off civilians had
made a veteran operative look like a fool.

After switching on the CB and the scanner, Richter
glanced back to see what else he had gained. The gunrack held a Remington 20-gauge shotgun and a Win-
chester .30-06 rifle, either of which might come in handy.
His 9mm plastic pistol was only effective at close range.

Richter turned off the cab light and pushed the Ford
up to seventy, then took an amphetamine from the silver case he kept in his coat. He listened to the crackly
voices on the radios, alert for any mention of a black
Jaguar or a blue-coveralled man on a motorcycle.

The Doberman in the truck bed shifted his weight.

Take it easy, Fido, Richter thought. *Be a good dog,
and I'll give you their bones.*

CATHY AND JEREMY

Jeremy lay under the kitchen table while Cathy sat
with her feet on him, reading the Saturday *Capital-
Journal* and listening to a transistor radio.

"I suppose it was only a matter of time," Cathy said.
"Look at this." She tossed the front section of the newspaper under the table.

"I'm not talking to you," Jeremy said. "You're forcing me to live like a dog."

"One of us has to be the link, and Ringo likes you
better."

"He doesn't like either one of us. Neither do I."

"Look at the top story on page two, will you?"

Jeremy read, " 'New Mexico Radio Astronomer Says Ganymede Broadcast May Be Genuine.' So what?"

"Don't you see?" Cathy said. "Now that the flesh-bound population is about to find out that the broadcast isn't Earth-based, we can count on them to show their true maniacal colors. Listen to the radio: Scientific, sociological, and religious 'experts' are fighting with each other about what it might mean if the signal turns out to be from space. Sounds pretty good."

"Yeah, great," Jeremy said, scratching his neck with a heel. "World leaders are behaving like lobotomized dingos, the public is reacting with shock, anger, and fear, and a number of religious cults, including the Reverend Bill Willy's, are girding their loins for Armageddon."

"Isn't it wonderful?" Cathy said. "With all of that going on, our pro-flesh cousins will realize that they've misjudged the fleshbound. We'll be out of here by Valentine's Day."

Jeremy crawled out from under the table. "Don't start packing yet. Didn't that scientist on the box say that if the Holly broadcast *is* from Ganymede, that it's 'a wonderful opportunity to expand human knowledge'? That's a point for the opposition, wouldn't you say?"

Cathy made a noise with her lips and tongue that she had learned from watching reruns of *All in the Family*. "How many members of the fleshbound masses do you think will listen to him? He's making sense, and they don't respond to that. I'm telling you, they're going to prove themselves to be complete wankers." She paused. "I just hope they don't hurt themselves. Not that it's our fault if they do."

Jeremy cocked his head. "In other words, the fact

that we've come back to our place of origin doesn't imply
that we have accepted any responsibility for our fellow
humans' fate?"

"They aren't our fellow humans. They've remained
fleshbound. Now shut up, will you? I want to hear what
the police are saying."

On the radio, a Kansas State Trooper was explain-
ing that the search for Oliver Vale was no longer a
priority. "I'm sure that any officer would take Vale into
custody if the suspect happened to show up," he said,
"but frankly, we now have to view the situation as a
strictly Federal matter. The rest of us are going to have
our hands full keeping folks from panicking and looters
from taking advantage."

"Taking advantage of what?" a reporter asked.

"Well, with no TV programs to speak of," the trooper
said, "we're projecting that people will be going out of
their homes more, leaving their possessions vulnerable
to burglars, vandals, and malcontents."

Cathy laughed and clapped her hands. "This is great!
Modern humanity at its finest—that is to say, *terrible!*"

Jeremy lay belly-down on the floor with his head on
his hands. "I'm worried about Vale," he said, "and I think
it's our ethical duty to go after him and protect him. It
isn't his fault that the El Dorado faction broadcast
his name."

Cathy snapped off the radio. "He'll be fine," she said
irritably. "Didn't you hear? The police aren't after him
anymore."

"What about everyone else?" Jeremy asked. "What
if the public goes nuts for fear of an alien invasion and
takes it out on him? And what about that Federal agent?"

"I thought you said that Vale got away from him
last night."

"Temporarily. The agent must still be close, because

if he weren't, Ringo wouldn't be riding in the back of the truck he stole."

Cathy sighed and began reading the comics page. "My ancient love, this thing is almost over, and you yourself just said that Ringo is on the job. If the G-man finds Vale again and does something dangerous, you can use the eye-link to order Ringo to block it—"

"I'm not sure he'll respond."

"—but otherwise, as long as we know where everyone is, more or less, I see no reason to run all over the countryside. Being in the flesh is bad enough without exposing it to the elements."

Jeremy rose to his hands and knees and crawled under the table again, where he curled into a tight ball and shivered.

"Tell me about it," he muttered.

6

OLIVER

Volume IV of Mother's diary begins gloomily. The year was 1968. Frankie Lymon (a minor deity, yet still a member of the pantheon) died in February . . . but his death was not like that of Buddy or of Otis, who had both died at the hands of Fate. It wasn't even like that of Sam Cooke, who had died at the hands of a mortal. Instead, Frankie Lymon's death was his own doing. His and heroin's.

Not that he was the first pop star to die from self-destructive behavior. Johnny Ace had blown out his own brains in a game of Russian roulette in 1954, and Bobby Fuller had died of either carbon monoxide poisoning or drugs (reports varied) in 1966. Even "country" Hank Williams had booze-and-pilled himself to death as far back as 1953.

But Frankie Lymon was the first one to check out after the Summer of Love, and although he had been something of a has-been for a decade, the nature of his death seemed to Mother to be yet another omen.

No one will pay much attention to his passing, she
wrote. *He was "Why Do Fools Fall in Love?" not "Strawberry Fields Forever" or "Rainy Day Women #12 & 35."
He wasn't part of the Movement, part of the new g-g-gen-
eration. And even if he had been, well, he didn't die of
the hip drugs, of acid or grass. He died of heroin. In the
newspaper it says that heroin has been a problem for big-
city Negroes for decades. Big-city anybody is my guess.*

*Things are only going to get worse. I keep hoping for
the UFOs to come for me, but sometimes I think that they
never will. 1968 will be a bad year.*

I was eight, and I remember most of it: The USS
Pueblo was seized by North Korea. The Tet offensive
made Vietnam even bloodier. Martin Luther King, Jr.,
and Robert Kennedy were assassinated. Police in Chicago went berserk.

And then, in early September, Mother received a
telephone call from Grandmother. It was the first time
they had spoken in almost a year. Grandmother had just
been told that Uncle Mike was dead.

His death was "accidental," the result of a mistake
with a Claymore. But *how* Uncle Mike died meant nothing. Dead is dead. Even at eight, I knew that. I had not
forgotten what I had learned from the death of Sam
Cooke, from the reality of a squirrel smashed in the
street.

For Mother, though, it had become easier to forget
what was real and to hope for what was not.

*Buddy, Sam, Otis, and even Frankie are not dead at
all,* she wrote. *They are still alive because I can still hear
them sing.*

*But I can't hear Mikey. Except for a few times on the
phone, I haven't heard him in nine years. Does that mean
that he's gone forever? Or can the letters he wrote serve
the same purpose as 45 rpm records? If I read those let-*

*ters over and over, will he still be alive? If you can think
of someone, picture him as solid as flesh, can't you say
he's really here?*

*Even if you can't, what does that matter? I can't pic-
ture the other soldiers in Mikey's unit, but that doesn't
mean that they don't exist. Nor can I picture the ancient
Atlanteans or their machines of flying light, but others
have, so I don't have to. They exist as surely as I and
Oliver do, as Buddy Holly does, as President Johnson
does, as poor sweet C. does in my heart.*

*Say hello to C. for me, Mikey. Take a ride together
in a machine of flying light and tell me what you find.*

Even though I had never known Uncle Mike, I was
sad that he was gone. Many times in the months after
his death, I would awaken at night with the idea that
there was a young man in an Army uniform sitting beside my bed, looking at me.

Things seemed better in October when the nation's
long hiatus from space ended with the successful flight
of Apollo 7. Then, in December, Apollo 8 went all the
way around the moon and back, and I was ecstatic. (I
wished that they hadn't done the Bible reading, though.
It reminded me of Vacation Bible School.)

During the Apollo 8 launch, Mother said something
like "If the government would put money into UFO research, they wouldn't have to spend so much on those
rockets."

"You're crazy!" I shouted, watching the Saturn
booster rise on a pillar of smoke and flame.

When I finally glanced at Mother, her eyes were wet.
I looked back at the TV.

1968 was a bad year.

1969 was worse.

School was dismissed early one Wednesday in April

because of a sewer backup that flooded the halls, and I found myself at home alone at 2:30 in the afternoon. My after-school baby-sitter would not arrive until a quarter to four, and Mother would not come home until six.

I did what any nine-year-old would do. I took the opportunity to get into things I wasn't supposed to get into.

I had long been curious about Mother's black note-books. She had told me that they were her diary, but she had also told me that their contents were none of my business. You don't tell a kid that. At least, you didn't tell me that. I knew that she kept her current volume in the top drawer of her dresser, but I was afraid she might notice if it were disturbed; so instead, I searched for the volumes already completed.

I found them in a box under her bed and began to read Volume I, stopping every few seconds to look at the alarm clock on the nightstand. I was terrified that my baby-sitter would catch me and report my perfidy.

Volume I began at Mother's sixteenth birthday, and its early entries were boring: who liked whom, who was mad at whom, who was taking whom to the sock hop, etc. I began flipping pages to see whether I could find anything that Mother might have written about her husband, my father, about whom I knew almost nothing except that he had died before I was born. Mother always deflected my questions with answers like "No, he wasn't a soldier." "Yes, he was a nice man." "No, I don't have a picture I can show you." "Yes, you look a little like him."

What I found was the description of my conception. I didn't understand all of it, especially the sentence in which Mother wrote *it all dripped out on the seat*. But I knew that I had discovered something that I would wish I hadn't.

I read further, feeling sicker and sicker, all the way
to my birth. Then I went back and read it all again.

It seemed to say that Mother and my father had not
been married. But that wasn't possible. People who
weren't married couldn't have babies.

The apartment's front door opened while I was still
sitting on the floor of Mother's bedroom. Panicking, I
crammed the notebooks back into the box and shoved it
under the bed, then rushed into the living room. My baby-
sitter had just come in. I blurted that I had just been to
the bathroom, and she gave me a look that said she didn't
really care about my bodily functions.

That evening, Mother felt my forehead. I was flushed,
and she was worried that I might have a fever. I told
her that I felt fine, honest. I was fine, school was fine,
everything was fine. She said that I didn't have to get
so agitated about it. She believed me.

The next day at school, I sat atop the monkey
bars with my best friend, Steve, during morning recess.
Steve had other best friends besides me, but he was my
only one.

Pretending that I had read it in a book I'd found on
a sidewalk, I described the things from Volume I that I
had not understood. Steve was smart, and I figured that
if anyone could explain those things to me, he could.

He laughed. "You found a dirty book! Didn't you
know that? Was there a naked lady on the cover?"

"No."

"Well, there should have been," Steve said. "Did you
read the whole thing?"

"Most of it," I mumbled, climbing down to the ground.
I didn't want to talk anymore.

Steve followed me. "Did the girl in the book get
pregnant? My brother says that a chick who'll do it in a
car is a slut, and that sluts always get pregnant."

I started walking toward the building. My face burned as if it had been stung by wasps.

"Come on," Steve said, hurrying to walk beside me. "Tell me about the book. Did the slut have a bastard baby?"

I turned and hit him in the mouth.

He stared for a few seconds, and then his face contorted and he swung a fist, hitting me in the left eye. I fell on my rump in the dirt, and Steve dropped on top of me, pounding furiously. I pounded back, and we rolled over and tore at each other's clothes. Two teachers pulled us apart and dragged us to the principal's office.

What happened there was the same thing that has happened in principals' offices ever since there were such places. When it was over, Steve was no longer my friend, and my nickname at school, said in whispers when no teacher could hear, became "Ollie the Bastard Baby."

The principal telephoned Mother that day, of course, and she had to leave the radio station early to come to the school. She didn't seem upset, though. She simply listened to what everyone had to say, and then she said that she would punish me.

When we got home, she cleaned my scrapes and said, "No skydiving for a month." She didn't ask me what the fight had been about. Her mind was on other things.

A few days later, on Saturday evening, my baby-sitter showed up while I was watching TV, and Mother appeared from her bedroom wearing a dress and makeup. She was going on a date, and she had told me nothing about it.

I glared at her as she sat on the divan to wait. She asked me to stop it, but I wouldn't. My baby-sitter sat cross-legged against the wall and pretended to read a magazine.

The doorbell rang, and Mother went to answer it. The man she let into our apartment was tall and had bristly blond hair, a reddish mustache, and freckled skin.

"Oliver, this is Keith," Mother said. "He's the new midday on-air personality at the station."

"I'm at school at midday," I said, trying to make it plain that this Keith person had no place in my world and never would. I kept hearing Steve say the word *slut*.

Keith squatted and held out his hand. "How ya doin', pardner?" he asked.

"Watching television," I said, turning to face the screen. I kept my eyes fixed there until they were gone.

"He seems real nice," my baby-sitter said. "He sounds different than he does on the radio, though."

"Big deal," I said, and didn't speak again that evening.

Mother dated Keith from April to July, and I did my best to be a brat about it. I even turned our radio dial away from KKAP so that I wouldn't have to hear Keith's voice on commercials. Mother turned it back a few times, then let me have my way.

Fortunately, I didn't see what Mother wrote in Volume IV during those months. Most of the entries are so erotic that the ink virtually smokes. Even now, I can't read those passages without experiencing a weird nausea that I can only describe as voyeuristic-Oedipal shock:

I had forgotten what it was like to feel reality. Fingers touching, stretching the skin of his back, breasts pressed to chest, strands of my hair sticking to our faces, my calves locked over his— Those are real. UFOs, Vietnam, Atlantis, Mikey's death, Mama's hate, my son's pain, Nixon's jowls— Those are unreal. At least, they seem that way when I'm with Keith. Nothing exists at those times except the touch, the kiss.

I am never so alive as when lying with Keith. Noth-

ing else makes the universe so sharp and clear. Nothing else makes me feel so sane.

Reading that now, I know that Mother was trying to heal herself of Buddy's death, of my father C.'s suicide, of Grandmother, of everything. She might have done it too, if she had been blessed with a different son. Or a different mother.

Mother's Relationship with Keith came to an end in July.

They were both scheduled to work on the Fourth, so they were given Thursday, July 3, off and had planned a long date for that afternoon and evening. My existence created a problem because my usual baby-sitter was out of town and there were no others to be found. I insisted that I was old enough to stay home alone, but Mother disagreed. At first, she suggested that I accompany her and Keith on their picnic, but I replied that I wouldn't go anywhere with the two of them even if it meant that I would die if I didn't.

Her next suggestion was that I spend the holiday weekend with Grandmother.

She wasn't deliberately sending me into the lion's den, because things had changed between Mother and Grandmother—at least, they seemed to have changed. Ever since Uncle Mike's death, they had spoken to each other on the telephone at least once a week, and recently, Grandmother had been expressing a wish to know her grandson better.

So that Thursday afternoon, Mother drove me to Grandmother's house. I was to stay until Sunday evening. I refused to kiss Mother good-bye when she left.

"Well, young Oliver," Grandmother said when she had me seated at the kitchen table, "what would you like to do today?" Her voice was so stern that I had the impression that I wasn't supposed to like to do anything.

I shrugged. I saw no reason to treat Grandmother any better than I was currently treating Mother. In fact, I could think of several reasons for treating her worse.

Across the table from me, Grandmother frowned the way that God must have frowned when He heard about Adam and the apple. "A polite young man answers when he's asked a direct question," she said.

"I guess I'm not a polite young man."

She reached across the table and smacked my ear, almost knocking me out of my chair.

I cried. I hated myself for that, but I couldn't help it. Too much had happened—my discovery of Volumes I through III, the fight with Steve, "Ollie the Bastard," Mother and Keith, and now this.

"A polite young man does not talk back," Grandmother said. "Neither does he bawl like a baby when punished." She stood. "You will sit here and think about that until I say you may get up." She left the kitchen.

I put my head on the cool tabletop. When I couldn't cry anymore, I kept my head down and imagined that I was a poisonous turtle. I would dart from my shell and bite off the hand of anyone who came close.

After a long time, Grandmother returned.

"Have you learned anything?" she asked.

"I hate you," I said.

She raised her hand to smack me again, but I was ready for it and didn't cringe. She lowered her arm without hitting me.

"You'll go without supper until you apologize," she said. "You'll remain at the table."

She went away again. The sky outside the kitchen window became dark. I had to pee, but I swore that I would explode before I would ask for permission to go to the bathroom.

Finally, Grandmother came into the kitchen with

her purse on her arm and her car keys in her hand. "Get up," she said. "I'll not put up with a sinful child. You're going home."

That was fine with me. If Mother wasn't back from her date yet, I would watch TV late into the night.

Grandmother made me sit in the back seat of her car while we crossed the city. The pain in my abdomen was so awful that I was afraid I might pee my pants, but I clenched my jaws and held it. I wouldn't give Grandmother anything else to say about me.

When the car stopped, I flung open the door and ran for our building. As I reached the main door, I could hear Grandmother telling me to wait, but I ignored her and went inside, charging up the stairs to the apartment.

Mother kept a spare key hidden in a crack beside the doorjamb; so I grabbed it, put it into the lock, and opened the door. I wanted to get to the bathroom fast.

I stopped after two steps. A lamp was on in the living room, and Mother and Keith were clutching each other on the floor. They were naked.

Keith saw me first. "Oh, shit," he said.

Then Mother saw me too, but she didn't say anything.

I stumbled out backward, slammed the door, turned, and collided with Grandmother. She was staring at the apartment door, her lips pursed. She had seen. I was sure that she had seen.

She went down the stairs and out to her car. I stood alone on the landing, dizzy and sick, and would have vomited if there had been anything in my stomach.

After a while, Mother came out, wearing clothes, and took me inside. Keith left as soon as I was in. Mother closed the door behind me, and at that sound I looked down and saw that I had wet my pants.

Mother did not go out with Keith again. Instead,

she bought more books on UFOs, Edgar Cayce, and spiritualism.

She had been healing herself, and I had destroyed it.

Yet even while Mother was slipping back into weirdness and I was roiling with anger and guilt, there was something in which we both rejoiced: On Sunday, July 20, Neil Armstrong stepped onto the surface of the moon.

I bounced around the apartment trying to duplicate a moon walk, and I jumped off a kitchen chair to simulate the "giant leap" off the LEM. Meanwhile, Mother sat in the living room, watching the television and smiling wistfully.

"Maybe they'll let us join them now," she said.

I was bounding through the living room. "Who?"

She didn't answer, and I bounced into the kitchen again.

She wasn't able to go to Woodstock.

*

Gretchen Laird took command of the pilgrimage. She told me what to do, and I did it. It was comforting, because it relieved me of responsibility. Yes, officer, I fled to Oklahoma, but after the Chisholm Trail Rest Stop Waterbed Motel, I was only following orders.

We prepared to leave the motel at eight o'clock Saturday evening. Gretchen would drive the Jaguar and choose our route, and I would follow on Peggy Sue. According to Gretchen, the Jaguar had a computerized map display in the dashboard, so it only made sense that she should be in charge of navigation. In addition, she said, if I attempted to take off on my own, she would hunt me down and break my fingers and toes.

The bathroom in our odious room had no shower, so I tried to make do with dunking my head in the sink.

As I did so, I became aware of the itch caused by the stubble on my throat and cheeks.

"Hey," I called, "do you shave your legs?"

Gretchen, who had been watching Buddy on TV, appeared in the bathroom doorway with murder in her eyes. "What's it to you?"

I tried to look ingenuous. "I thought I could maybe borrow a razor."

She glared a bit longer and then left, returning in a moment with a disposable razor. "Think fast," she said, tossing it. It landed atop the toilet tank beside the plastic tubes containing my contact lenses.

"Anything clsc?" Grctchcn asked sardonically.

"You wear contacts?" I asked. "I need some wetting solution."

"I have perfect twenty-twenty vision," she said. "I have perfect everything. Now hurry it up. The night won't last forever." She left the doorway again.

The bathroom had no mirror, so I shaved blind with soap and water, scraping my throat in the process. As I finished, a small plastic bottle flew past my head and landed in the grungy water in the sink.

"Eye drops," Gretchen said behind me. "The kind that gets the red out. I figured it'd be better than nothing."

I thanked her and took my lenses from the tubes, rubbing them with the eye drops before inserting them. They still hurt.

Then, with Gretchen telling me to get the lead out of my ass, I left the bathroom and pulled on the Moon-suit. For breakfast, I took a squashed package of chocolate cupcakes from a pocket, wolfed one, and offered the other to Gretchen.

She sneered. "No wonder you're in such rotten shape. I've got trail mix in my backpack, and I'll eat in the car so you don't try to swipe any. Can we please get going now, junkgut?" She dropped the room key onto the bed for the manager to find.

I pulled on my helmet and gloves, and we got going, leaving the TV on. Buddy watched us longingly as we left. He was singing "Send Me Some Lovin'."

Outside, I saw that the Jaguar was the only vehicle in the parking lot. Apparently, eight o'clock was still too early for the Chisholm Trail Rest Stop Waterbed Motel's Saturday night trade to begin. Gretchen got into the car and started it while I went around back for my bike.

Peggy Sue was leaning over in the mud, looking battered and bruised. "Bitten by a Doberman and kicked over by an Amazon," I said as I pulled her upright. "And I bitch when you don't feel like starting. Some life, huh?"

I rolled her down the sloppy path to the parking lot. Inside the Jaguar, her face lit by the bluish glow of the dash displays, Gretchen looked impatient.

I had hoped that by speaking words of sympathy, I would persuade Peggy Sue to start with a minimum of difficulty, but it was not to be. I kicked the starter thirty or forty times before Gretchen emerged from the Jaguar and ordered me to let her try. As she straddled the bike and started kicking, it occurred to me that I could enter the idling Jaguar and be gone. But that would have meant abandoning Peggy Sue.

The bike's engine started on Gretchen's sixth or seventh kick. "Oh, sure," I said as Gretchen walked past me to the car. "It was easy after I got her primed." She did not reply, but reentered the Jaguar and took off. I climbed onto Peggy Sue and switched on the headlight, and we followed. The Ariel sounded ragged. I worried.

Gretchen's route soon became incomprehensible to me, and I had to take it as an article of faith that we were making progress toward Lubbock. My sense of direction was destroyed by the turns, twists, and back-tracks of the Jaguar, and the cloud cover made it impossible to regain my bearings by looking at the stars.

A few hours away from the motel, we stopped for gas at a self-service store in the middle of nowhere, and I filled Peggy Sue's tank without shutting off the engine. The way she was sounding, I was more afraid of trying to restart her than I was of blowing up. I even asked Gretchen to reduce speed for the rest of the night because the Ariel was having trouble cruising any faster than fifty. Something was going wrong, and I didn't think that crescent-wrench-whanging would make it right this time. Even if I'd had that tool with me.

I was glad to finish refueling and get back to the highway. Out there, the only things that existed besides me and Peggy Sue were the road, the cold wind, and the red lights that we followed. Occasionally, other lights would pass us from either direction, but they were only temporary phenomena. They were hardly even here before they were gone, like UFOs. I saw them, but I had no proof that they were anything but illusions. Neither did I have any proof, other than phantom memories, that Buddy Holly had ever appeared on my television, or even that there was such a thing as television.

On a motorcycle at night (even a sputtering motorcycle that might die at any moment) the rest of the world fades toward noncorporeality; toward the Void. The rider becomes an astronaut in a Moonsuit, shooting through that Void on a rickety space sled.

It's wonderful.

Just as I was beginning to feel truly separate from the planet, as if Peggy Sue and I were fusing to become a meteor, the Jaguar's taillights left the highway again and entered a roadside park in a cluster of trees. I didn't want to stop, but if I went on, Gretchen would hold to her promise to find me and break my fingers and toes. You cannot control a motorcycle if you have broken fingers and toes. I slowed Peggy Sue and leaned into the paved split that the Jaguar had taken, and we were surrounded by the dark cones of evergreens.

The Jaguar had stopped on a sandy patch beside a picnic table with a concrete canopy, and I steered Peggy Sue in beside it. The car's lights went off.

"What's wrong?" I yelled as Gretchen emerged from the Jaguar. Peggy Sue's engine was still running, and I had to shout to be heard over the coughing.

"Nothing, dork," Gretchen answered, stepping over to stand in the bike's headlight beam. She was wearing a blue warm-up jacket and carrying her backpack. "Turn that freaking thing off before it gives me a headache."

"If I do, she might not start again," I said. "She's not running right. I think we should keep going while it's still dark."

Gretchen reached out to Peggy Sue's right handlebar and hit the kill switch. The engine wheezed and died. I switched off the headlight, snapped down the kickstand, and dismounted. "She's not going to like this," I said.

" 'She'?" Gretchen spat. The park had no lights, but I didn't need to see Gretchen's expression to know what it was. "You call a machine 'she'? I thought I heard you do that before, but I didn't want to believe it. It's insulting, degrading, and perverted. Men like you make me blow chow. You think with your dicks, and what your dicks think is that you can fuck an internal combustion engine."

"Sorry," I said, backing away.

"Why the hell a supernatural being would come on

TV and name *you* as someone special is beyond me," Gretchen said.

"Me too." I paused, in case she had anything further to add on the subject of my unworthiness, and then asked, "Why did we stop? I'm not protesting, understand. Just curious."

Gretchen made a dangerous noise in her throat. "I feel weak and cramped," she said. "I haven't had a workout since I left Minneapolis, and if I'm going to face God or whatever when we get to Lubbock, I want to be in shape." Her dark form went to the picnic table and set the backpack on it. "Not that you would know anything about that, big butt."

"I do *not* have a big butt."

"Tell it to God when we get there," Gretchen said, unzipping the backpack. "We'll see what Her opinion is."

"Buddy Holly is male," I pointed out.

"Most errand boys are."

"Buddy isn't an errand boy. He's a rock and roll pioneer."

"Yeah, yeah, yeah. Look, I'm snapping on earphones to blast some old Whitesnake, and if you come close enough for me to hear you, you'll get smacked with a hand weight. I suggest you get into the Jag and take a nap. The seats recline. I'll take a short rest on my side when I'm finished out here, and then we'll get going again."

The noise of latter-day heavy metal (shrunk to munchkinlike decibel levels) began pulsing from Gretchen's head, and I blundered away to a shadow that proved to be an open-pit rest room. When I had finished there (tricky business in the dark), I returned to the Jaguar and entered on the passenger side. When the door was closed, I stretched my left leg across the center con-

sole to touch the brake pedal, and adjusted the mirror
so that I could see out the back window.

Gretchen was exercising on the narrow strip of
pavement behind the car, and I watched her dance in
the red glow for a few seconds. Her back was to me, and
I don't think she knew that I could see her. Her hair
bounced to a rhythm that I couldn't hear, and as her
arms swung, her jacket stretched across her shoulders
and back. Below that—

"Forget it," I told myself again.

I pulled off my helmet and then fumbled with the
console until I found the switch that made the seat recline. The compartment was warm, and I would have
fallen asleep immediately had I not started worrying
about Peggy Sue's increasingly poor performance and our
overall lack of progress. The Ariel and I had only fled a
total of four hundred miles in forty-eight hours, and
thanks to the zigzagging nature of our route, some of
that distance was wastage. At best, we were now halfway to Lubbock—and here I was counting on Gretchen
Laird, a potentially homicidal stranger who was currently bouncing around in the cold night like a spastic
kangaroo, to get me the rest of the way there.

It made as much sense as anything else.

The next thing I was aware of was a blaring noise
and a bright light, and I woke up yelling, "No, Julie!
Don't run over me!" I had apparently been dreaming of
Julie "Eat shit and die, Oliver" Calloway.

Julie was long gone now, but the blaring noise and
the light were real. They belonged to a Peterbilt semi-
tractor-trailer that had pulled into the rest stop and that
was now being stared down by Gretchen Laird. Using
the mirror, I saw that Gretchen was standing in the center of the access road exactly where I had last seen her.

Her arms were crossed, her hair was darkened with
sweat, and her eyes gleamed. The semi's headlights gave
her a whole-body halo.

I looked at the rig and saw the trucker emerge and
amble toward the open-pit toilet I had visited earlier.
He seemed to be ignoring Gretchen, Peggy Sue, and the
Jaguar, so I lay back again and closed my eyes, expect-
ing that he would leave soon. I hoped that Gretchen would
see the wisdom of getting out of the way and letting the
Peterbilt drive on through.

She must have, because when I heard her voice
threatening the trucker's life, it was coming from the
picnic-table shelter. I opened my eyes, knowing that I
would hate whatever I saw.

The trucker had returned from the toilet, but he had
not reentered his truck. I had been wrong in assuming
that he had ignored Gretchen.

"Get away from me or I'll rip off your balls and stuff
them up your nose," she told him.

He grinned down at her. Gretchen is a large person,
but the trucker was larger. He was Bigfoot in blue jeans
and a down vest. I scrunched down in my seat and prayed
to Chuck Berry (a former hairdresser) that the trucker
would decide Gretchen was ugly. If he didn't, the idiotic
masculine imperatives that had been conditioned into
me by both DNA-triggered testosterone and society would
demand that I get out of the Jaguar and be killed.

"Now, sugarplum," the trucker said in a voice like
a bull's. He reached out to stroke her face.

Gretchen grabbed his thumb and twisted. The
trucker went down to his knees like a man who had sud-
denly gotten religion, and Gretchen, still holding his
thumb, began walking toward the idling semi. The
trucker was forced to shuffle on his knees across the picnic
table's concrete pad, and then across the dead grass to

the road. When they were on the pavement, Gretchen
released him and started back toward the table.

The trucker got to his feet and said something, but
he was far enough away now that I heard it only as an
angry mumble. Gretchen kept walking and said nothing.

He went after her, and I began fumbling for the door
handle without having any idea of what I would do when
I got outside. I may have had a vague hope that the
Moonsuit would make me look bigger than I actually
was and that the trucker would flee upon seeing me.

But before I could get the door open, the trucker
had grabbed Gretchen's arm, and she had popped her
elbow into his face. He released her and staggered away,
but this time *she* went after *him*. When she caught him,
she knocked him down with a shove, grabbed his ankles,
and bounced his head on the pavement twenty or thirty
times. Then she dropped him and returned to the picnic
table, where she put on her headphones, picked up her
hand weights, and resumed her exercises. Slowly, the
trucker got to his knees, and then to his feet. For a moment I thought that he was considering another try at
Gretchen, but then he turned and went to his semi. He
did not walk there in a straight line.

The semi hissed, then roared away. When it was
gone, the only sounds left were those of my own breathing and of Gretchen's aerobics. I tried to sleep again, but
Gretchen was huffing closer to the Jaguar now, and I
found my respiration rate accelerating to match hers.

Hoping for distracting music, I leaned forward and
twisted various knobs on the dash until I found the radio. When it came on, it told me that civil unrest had
begun in major cities across the nation and around the
globe as the result of the Buddy Holly broadcast. The
video takeover was in its fiftieth hour, and people were

beginning to realize that it was more than a prank. Already it had deprived them of *Dallas, Saturday Night Live,* several basketball games, and countless other necessities, and they were getting pissed. TV stations the world over were being picketed despite the fact that the nonvideo media had made it clear that the broadcasters were not responsible.

Along with their anger over the lack of regular programming, various citizens were also concerned about the details of the Buddy Holly broadcast itself. One of the loudest of these, as I had expected, was the Reverend William Willard of OKRAP fame. His voice blared from the Jaguar's dash with the following words:

"When I saw that my ministry, the Resurrection Television Network, was being crippled by this disruption, I prayed. And when I prayed, the Lord answered, saying, 'William, this Satanic rock and roll broadcast is a sign of the Last Days. The figure on your television screen is a Cuban atheist who has disguised himself as a dead man by means of a rubber mask. He is the herald of the Antichrist, and with his own words he has identified the Antichrist himself—Oliver C. Vale of Topeka, Kansas.' Thus, our course is clear. We must do battle with the Beast and destroy him."

So now I was not only a Federal fugitive, but the Antichrist to boot.

I had been minding my own business, trying to live my life in as nonlethal a manner as possible, and trouble had come gunning for me all the way from the neighborhood of Jupiter. It wasn't fair. Despite my weird upbringing, I was no different from any other ordinary guy. I was looking for peace, security, beer, and a decent stereo. I was looking for my predestined share of sexual encounters. I was looking for—

Gretchen opened the driver's door and got inside. "What are you trying to do, jughead? Run down the battery?"

"No," I said. "I'm looking for someone to love."

In the glow of the dial, I saw Gretchen's sweat-slick face take on an expression that was mostly pity.

"Forget it," she said, and snapped off the radio.

SHARON

Notes on client Oliver Vale, continued . . .

After midnight, early Sunday morning, and I'm writing in the car. Bruce is driving us south into Oklahoma City, or trying to. It's impossible to go faster than ten miles an hour because of the crowd of both automobiles and human beings that is packing I-35. I *told* him that I didn't want to take the interstate.

On either side of the freeway is an open field, and in each of those fields, circus-type tents and canopies have been set up. They glow orange and yellow as if they were about to catch fire. Thousands of people are packed around the tents like cattle at a stockyard, which must mean that the tents themselves are already full. I have the impression that the tents are mobile slaughterhouses where the waiting people will eventually be turned into hot dogs and braunschweiger.

I have finally found an Oklahoma City radio station that tells me what is going on here. This is a massive tent revival organized by the Reverend William Willard and his Corps of Little David. Its purpose, the radio says, is to concentrate as much "prayer power" as possible at one focus. Willard's faithful have begun holding what

they claim will be a continuous vigil until the Antichrist is defeated.

This strikes me as overly optimistic.

But now the radio reports that Willard believes
Oliver is the Antichrist who must be vanquished.

Armageddon is around the corner, the people in the
fields are shouting. The Rapture will occur at any second. (Good. Then maybe they'll all disappear and we can
get through this traffic jam.)

I've changed the radio station, and the news on the
new one is no better. Vigilante squads of angry TV
viewers are being organized to search for Oliver. Some
of these are Willard-inspired, but most are led by secular couch potatoes who simply resent having their freedom of choice taken away.

The Federal Communications Commission has become the smallest of Oliver's worries.

"If the vigilantes find him first," Bruce says, "there
won't be enough left of him to prosecute." Bruce sounds
matter-of-fact, and it makes me angry at him again.

I must remind myself that he is an attorney. He isn't
supposed to get emotionally involved.

As a professional, I'm not supposed to get emotionally involved, either. But when you spend your life listening to other people's pains and fears, how can you
stay unaffected? Transference works both ways.

I am terrified for Oliver. I am afraid that he will die
before I can find him. I am afraid that I will never find
him at all.

I am afraid that I will never be able to ask him
whether he really has spoken with beings from other
worlds. I am afraid that I will never be able to ask him
what they have told him.

Bruce drives on. The jam clears a bit, and we pick

up speed. But it isn't enough. We will never reach Lubbock in time.

Bruce points to a brilliantly lit white structure on a
distant hill and tells me that it is the Cowboy Hall of
Fame. I tell him big fucking deal.

RICHTER

After hours of monitoring the Ford's CB radio on
Channel 19, he finally heard a trucker complain about
"a rich bitch in a Jaguar."

Richter picked up the microphone and thumbed the
key. "Y'all mind sharing that rich bitch's ten-twenty?"
he asked, affecting a drawl. "She owes me money."

"When I run into her," the speaker answered, "she
was at a roadside crapper on Oklahoma 17, about three
miles east of Sterling. Maybe fifteen minutes ago."

"She have anybody with her?" Richter asked.

"There was a motorcycle," the trucker said, "but I
didn't see nobody with it. Could've been inside the car."

"Ten-four," Richter said.

He stopped at an all-night convenience store, where
he used the rest room and bought a sandwich, a Coke,
and an Oklahoma map. As he came outside again, the
Doberman jumped out of the Ford's bed and ran past
him. He saw a blue spark in one of the animal's eyes.

Richter watched the dog run out to the highway,
turn south, and disappear into the darkness. He was short
of sleep, but even so, he did not think that he had imagined the spark.

He reentered the crew cab and studied the map while
gulping his sandwich and Coke. He was only twenty-five
miles from the rest stop that the trucker had indicated,

so it was time to prepare for battle. He took down the shotgun and rifle and loaded them with the shells he had found in the glove box, flicked off the safeties, and replaced the guns on their rack. Then he started the Ford's engine.

He had driven only a mile when his headlights illuminated the Doberman running down the shoulder of the road. The dog glanced back, then put its head down and ran hard. It pulled away from the glare and became part of the night again.

Richter looked at the truck's speedometer. He was driving seventy miles an hour.

His instincts told him that the dog was connected to Vale somehow, which meant that he and the creature would meet again. He was glad that he had loaded the rifle.

CATHY AND JEREMY

Jeremy was lying under the kitchen table, chewing on a boot. Cathy was pacing from the table to the refrigerator and back again.

"Okay," she said. "Okay, okay, okay."

Jeremy grunted.

"You were right," Cathy said. "There. Does that make you happy? You were right."

She stopped at the refrigerator and turned on the radio that she had placed atop it. The news was the same as it had been for hours: Protests. Vigilante squads. Lunacy.

She snapped off the radio and resumed pacing. "Well, at least that'll convince the pro-flesh faction that these fleshbound maniacs aren't worthy of higher learning."

"Ought to," Jeremy said around a mouthful of leather.

Cathy paused by the table. "How close is that G-man to Vale now?"

"Close," Jeremy said.

"Maybe he'll just take him into custody. Then the citizenry won't be able to get to him."

Jeremy dropped the boot and crawled out from under the table. "No. I didn't see the whole thing because Ringo was busy ransacking a store, but I think that when the agent almost caught Vale last night, Vale made him look like a fool. The guy lost his car and had to steal two pickup trucks. I don't think custody is what he has in mind anymore."

"Nonsense. He's a Federal agent. He has to follow orders."

Jeremy cocked his head. "What planet have *you* been living on?"

Cathy stopped pacing and slumped into a chair. "It won't do any good for us to go down there. If the agent is close, he'll have Vale before we're out of Kansas. And if he doesn't, the Bill Willyites or other nasties will. Oklahoma is crawling with them."

"Stop trying to talk yourself out of it," Jeremy said.

Cathy rubbed her eyes and stood. "Grab anything you think these stupid bodies might need. I'll go warm up the damn Datsun. We'll use your eye-link to guide us, so stay sharp."

Jeremy whined. "Couldn't we just go to the basement and become noncorporeal? We could zip to Oklahoma in no time then."

"And what would we do when we got there?" Cathy asked. "Whisk around and make pretty lights while they lynch the poor bastard? Only flesh can touch flesh."

Jeremy scratched his ear. "I forgot. There are actually a few things flesh can do that nonflesh can't."

"Nothing worthwhile," Cathy said, and went out to the garage.

RINGO

Ringo caught up with the motorcycle after a twenty-minute run. The Ariel was parked with a black automobile, but no people were in sight.

He trotted to the car's left front window and peered in. Sure enough, Vale was asleep in the far seat . . . but in the driver's seat was a woman who was awake.

The window slid down with an electric hum, and Ringo backed away. He remembered the Windex incident.

"I thought I heard someone out here," the woman said softly. "It was the nose print on the window that gave you away, though."

Ringo cocked his head as he listened. The woman's voice sounded neither afraid nor threatening. Instead, it was almost like a higher-pitched version of the voice of the man called Boog.

"Are you hungry?" the woman asked.

He wasn't, really, because he was still saving treats from his raid of the night before. He took a step forward anyway.

The woman rummaged in a pocket of Vale's thick outer garment. Vale shifted in his sleep and mumbled. There was a rustle of cellophane, and the woman pulled out a package of Twinkies.

"Yucch," she said as she turned back toward Ringo. "You wouldn't want this junk, would you?"

Ringo whined. It seemed like the polite thing to do.

The woman unwrapped the Twinkies and tossed one to the dog. He caught it in midair and swallowed it whole.

"I'll have the other one myself," the woman whispered. "Just don't tell bugbrain here. It'd ruin my image." She bit into the cake.

Ringo watched her for a little while, wagging his stump, and then trotted away. The woman seemed nice. He was glad that he had broken his rule about getting close to human beings.

He crossed the asphalt strip that cut through the park and then lay down in a clump of evergreens, where he dozed until the sound of an engine woke him. He recognized it as that of the second truck in which he had ridden.

Ringo raised his head and pricked his ears as the truck's headlight beams speared through the trees. It stopped twenty yards from the car and the motorcycle, and as it stood there idling, the smooth-headed driver emerged and stood between the lamps. He was carrying a rifle.

The woman who had given Ringo a Twinkie stepped from the car, and Vale appeared on the other side of the vehicle. The woman looked angry, and Vale looked frightened.

The rifleman cocked his weapon and aimed it. Ringo leaped to his feet, but the man was already squeezing the trigger.

The sharp crack echoed among the trees as the man cocked the rifle again. The black automobile's right rear tire had gone flat, but Vale and the woman were still standing. The rifle cracked again, and the car's left rear tire exploded.

"Run, stupid!" the woman shouted at Vale, and then she sprinted for the black air beyond the reach of the headlight beams.

The rifleman cocked his weapon a third time and swung the barrel toward the running woman.

Ringo bolted from the trees as the man began to squeeze the trigger, and his jaws closed on the man's left forearm. The dog's momentum drove the man backward, pinning the gun to the hood of the truck, and the bullet flew far from its target.

"Son of a *bitch!*" the man yelled.

Ringo jerked his head, flinging the man to the ground. The rifle skittered away, and the dog released the man's arm to go after it. His plan was to chew it to pieces, but as he reached the rifle, he heard the man scrambling back to the truck. He remembered then that he had seen a second weapon in the rack while riding in the bed. Leaving the rifle where it lay, Ringo whirled and ran past the man, beating him to the truck. Once there, he faced the man and growled, amplifying the sound electronically.

The man turned and dashed for the rifle. Ringo followed at a lope, still growling.

As the man bent to scoop up his weapon, Ringo heard the motorcycle grind, choke, and begin running raggedly. At a glance, he saw that Vale, now wearing his helmet, was lugging the machine onto the road.

Ringo turned his attention back to the bald man, who now had the rifle and was aiming it at Vale. The dog leaped and knocked him down, then clamped his jaws on the left arm again. He was careful not to bite all the way through.

The motorcycle, with Vale aboard, sputtered past Ringo and the bald man to the highway. Seconds later, the crew-cab truck pulled up beside them.

The passenger door opened, and Ringo saw the woman leaning toward him from the driver's side. "C'mon, doggie," she said. "Just leave him there."

Ringo considered. If he jumped into the truck, the man might shoot at them as they left, and the bullet might hit the woman. Ringo supposed that he could destroy the rifle first—but now he smelled another weapon inside the man's coat, and he was afraid that the man might be able to use it before he had finished splintering the rifle.

The only way that he could go with the woman and still ensure her safety would be to kill the man. He tried to make himself do that, but it was impossible. The necessary circuitry wasn't there. He could knock down, shake, and even wound, but he couldn't kill.

With the arm still clamped in his mouth, he lay down on the man's chest and sighed. The man groaned.

"Damn it, dog, come on," the woman said. "I've got to go before Ollie gets too far ahead!"

Ringo sighed again, making a *whuff* sound that he hoped would communicate his regret. Then he closed his eyes to indicate that his decision would not change.

The truck left. Ringo lay still for several minutes, and then he opened his eyes, released the man's arm, and stood. He took a few steps away from the man and stood watching him.

The man rolled onto his stomach and rose on his hands and knees. Then, breathing hard, he grasped the rifle and stood up. He was stooped over, as if his back pained him.

There were no lights in the park now, so Ringo brightened the blue spark in his black dog-eye to ensure that the man would see him. He had changed his mind about his dealings with people. Regardless of whether they were kind or cruel, he would not back away from them anymore. He would not run.

The man straightened his back and cocked the rifle. He pointed it at the Doberman and fired.

Ringo's processors flashed, and without even knowing that he would do it, he caught the .30-06 bullet between his incisors.

The man stared for a moment, then cocked the rifle again. Ringo sucked the bullet into his mouth, took a deep breath, and spat.

The slug entered the man's right thigh, and he staggered backward, dropping the rifle. Ringo stayed until the man got down on his hands and knees and began crawling toward the black automobile. Then, sure that the man would survive, he loped out to the highway.

The motorcycle's scent was strong and easy to follow. The crew-cab truck's scent was strong too, and Ringo was glad to find that the woman was following Vale as she had said she would. He was looking forward to seeing her again.

As he ran, he belched up a Budweiser and popped it with his teeth. He wished he'd done it earlier; that would have *really* freaked the man with the gun.

SKYVUE

Khrushchev stood beside the county road, his cloudy breath whooshing from his nostrils as if from a cartoon bull. His flesh quivered. He was enraged.

The theater's marquee was lit, and there, in gargantuan red plastic letters, were words announcing that the Reverend William Willard of Oklahoma City would hold a rally here, in person, on Monday evening, February 6. Khrushchev had not known about it until this moment. He had been watching Buddy Holly on the five-inch TV in the snack bar when he'd heard the racket, and he had come out here just as the people who had put up the letters were driving away.

Eisenhower emerged from the darkness below the marquee and walked toward Khrushchev.

"Did you let them do this?" Khrushchev bellowed.

"They paid a reasonable fee," Eisenhower said as he came close.

Khrushchev kicked off his right shoe, snatched it from the frozen ground, and began beating Eisenhower on the forehead with the heel.

"Is there a problem in there?" Khrushchev shouted. "Hello? Can you hear me? Jesus Christ!"

Eisenhower crossed his arms. "You're going to give me a bruise."

Khrushchev flung his shoe across the road. "There's mob violence in the cities, world leaders are accusing each other of provocative acts, and now you've rented out SkyVue to the Bill Willyites! They're calling your boy the Antichrist, did you know that? They'd like to lynch him, did you know that? They're using your Buddy Holly stunt to grab power, did you know that? They're *mean,* did you know that? They're going to ruin the chances of all their fellow fleshbound, did you know that?"

Eisenhower turned away and began walking down the drive toward the theater lot. "They have a constitutional right to assembly," he said. "If we're going to make our case for the fleshbound people's worthiness, we have to demonstrate that they deserve the rights they already have."

"But *these* people are fanatics!" Khrushchev cried. "The ordained psychopaths of the Corps of Little David could hurt somebody!"

Eisenhower paused and glanced back, rubbing his forehead. "You should talk," he said, and then continued down the drive.

Khrushchev stood looking after him and felt ashamed.

He had struck a friend in anger.

It was appalling what flesh could do to a person. He would be glad to go home again, to return to the blessed state of noncorporeality that had given the Seekers their freedom.

He stood in the cold for a few more minutes and then began limping toward the snack bar. He had decided not to look for his lost shoe.

3 · the **oklahoma** kamikaze

7

OLIVER

Reading Volume IV of Mother's diary, I see myself and the culture in which I was raised through the eyes of a woman being driven crazy by both of them. Volume IV chronicles the end of my first decade of life, and the end of the sixties. Both of us were stinkers.

My most vivid memory of 1970 is of April, when an oxygen tank in the command module of Apollo 13 ruptured. At school, we had a Moment of Silence every day to pray for Lovell, Haise, and Swigert as they went all the way around the moon with a crippled ship, using the oxygen and power reserves of the lunar module to substitute for what the command module no longer had. For the only time in my life, I willingly said the same prayers that everyone else did.

And then they were back, haggard and drained, but heroes, and I felt again as though human beings could accomplish anything, that all in the universe was ours.

I was ten years old.

Mother, of course, saw Apollo 13 and its message in a different light.

The ancient Atlanteans, they who fly the ships of light, have done this, she wrote. *They crippled the ship to teach us our weakness, and they brought it safely home to teach us that our lives are dependent on chance, on Fate.*

The astronauts were closer to death than we have been told. The coupling with the lunar module should not have worked, but the celestial Seekers saw to it that it did. They are warning us of our frailties while exhorting us to become pure of heart so that we may overcome those frailties.

It is yet another omen. They are trying to tell us that we are close to disintegration, to self-destruction.

The command capsule of Apollo 13 returned to Earth on April 17, 1970, and Mother wrote the preceding words the next day. Two and a half weeks later, four people were shot to death on the campus of Kent State University in Ohio.

They carried no weapons. They were killed by bullets shot from the rifles of National Guardsmen—by definition, their protectors.

Disintegration. Self-destruction.

Some animals, when caught in a trap, will chew off parts of their bodies in order to escape. As the decade came to a close, my nation was caught in such a trap, and it began to devour itself. A few kids at a time.

I was ten years old.

There was no prayer vigils in school for those who were killed, and none for those killed a few days later at Jackson State.

Mother wrote, *I am changing my opinions of those who fly the ships of light. Some of them must be malevolent. It must have been one of these who whispered into a Guardsman's ear, "Shoot, or they will kill you!" It is*

*the only explanation. Why else would a youth with a rifle
kill another youth who does not have one? Human beings
would melt into pools of blood before we would do such
things of our own wills.*

*We could not massacre children as it is said was done
at Mylai. After all, we are not only humans, but Americans. We are the Good Guys. We would not beat people to
death or hang them from trees. We would not kill unless
we were made to do so by a force against which we could
not stand.*

*Some blame Nixon. I do not. He is not strong enough
to do this to us. He may not even exist.*

*Somewhere in the Void, a battle is raging. The aliens
who love us are fighting those who despise us, and while
the battle rages, spies of the malevolent ones whisper in
our ears. They know that we can be made to destroy ourselves.*

*Yet some of us, especially those who make music of
power, are not so weak as the rest. They have joined in
the battle against the malevolent ones, and in them I place
my ultimate hope.*

Which was more hope than they could handle. In
the fall, Jimi Hendrix and Janis Joplin died of drug ov-
erdoses within weeks of each other. Willingly or not, they
and their music had become symbols of the countercul-
ture and of the struggle for justice, and they had blown
it. Big time.

Shortly after Mother had taken her job at KKAP,
she had begun the album collection that now forms the
core of my own. She began with the Crickets and proceeded through the late fifties and early sixties until she
had caught up with the year, and then she had bought
whatever music she could afford. By 1970, she owned
virtually all of the most important rock 'n' roll albums
ever pressed.

Then Hendrix and Joplin offed themselves.

They lied, Mother wrote. *They promised life, and they gave us death. They listened to the malevolent ones. Jimi played guitar like he came from a planet where a guitar is part of your body, and then he drowned in his own puke. Janis had a voice that could make you feel love and pain and life and sex all at the same instant, and then she filled her body with shit and fell on her face.*

Fuck them and the bus they rode in on.

She went through her record collection and pulled out everything that had been pressed after 1965, boxed them up, and sealed the boxes with duct tape. She wanted to retreat to the late fifties, when Buddy Holly was still alive and all seemed right with the world.

"We'll take these to the dump," she told me, and I was horrified. *Sergeant Pepper* was in there.

The boxes sat in the living room while Mother immersed herself in the music of the fifties and in paperbacks about UFOs and ancient civilizations. I listened to acid rock under the covers in my bedroom.

Then, on her thirtieth birthday, Mother wanted to hear "Eleanor Rigby," from the Beatles' *Revolver* album, which was pressed in 1966. The box containing that record came open, and the others soon followed. She played them all, even the ones by the Jimi Hendrix Experience and Full Tilt Boogie. Mother could get righteously angry with the best of them, but even she had a hard time holding a grudge against the dead.

Still, things always get worse before they get better. The year of Mother's thirtieth birthday was a signal for all of the evil on the planet to squirm out into the light. 1971 began with the conviction of Charles Manson and three members of his "family" for the slaughter of seven people. The murders were two years in the past, but it was only with the trial that the sickening details were revealed. Then, as if that weren't horror enough, a court-martial told the world that Lieutenant William L. Calley, Jr., was guilty of the murder of *twenty-two* South Vietnamese civilians. Our *allies*.

One night soon after the conclusion of the trial, flipping from one radio station to another, I chanced upon a country music station playing a song that praised Calley as a hero. I was confused by this and asked Mother to clarify the situation for me. She refused. If she had her way, she said, I wouldn't hear anything about what was going on out in the world in the first place.

Laos was invaded by South Vietnamese and U.S. forces in February, and thousands were killed. Jim Morrison died of a "heart attack" in France on July 3. North Vietnam was bombed in December.

And, paradoxically, while the world was filled with pain, there were triumphs. Apollo 14 and Apollo 15 went to the moon in January and July, and I felt pride so massive I thought my chest would explode. Space had tried to stop us, but we had come back. We had conquered another planet.

I was eleven years old.

There would be two more lunar landings in 1972, but then we would abandon our new planet, won at such high cost, without so much as a good-bye.

The Vietnam war and the Apollo program had more in common than was clear at the time.

By the end of the year, Mother had begun to talk openly of her beliefs concerning the ancient Atlanteans, their ships of light, the Cosmic Battle, and the malevolent ones. I laughed and told her that she was dreaming.

I thought that I knew better than she did, that my

A in science meant that I knew far more of what the Universe was about than she with her fantasies ever could.

Obviously, I knew less than nothing.

That, at least, hasn't changed. Everything else has.

*

Miraculously, Peggy Sue started when the Bald Avenger attacked at the roadside park, and we escaped. I would like to think that I would have gone back to help Gretchen, but I didn't have to face that decision. As I was slowing down to consider it, the Ford crew cab that the Bald Avenger had been driving barreled past. Its interior light was on, and I saw Gretchen at the wheel. I followed.

Now that Peggy Sue, Gretchen, and I had survived and would continue to survive for a while (the Jaguar's rear tires had been shot flat, so the Avenger couldn't come after us), I began to wonder how my neighbors' Doberman had happened to show up in the middle of Oklahoma. Ringo's size and his galvanized chain collar had identified him beyond any doubt.

He had appeared some four hundred miles from where I had last seen him.

As I rode, I listened to the ragged noise emanating from Peggy Sue's semi-amputated left tail pipe. Ringo had bitten through it, and I still had the threaded tooth he had lost doing so. I had seen his eyes, and they had burned with blue sparks.

The conclusion I came to was weird enough that Mother would have been proud of me: Ringo was a doggy robot, or a canine android, or something like that. Therefore, he had stamina beyond that of mortal Dobermans and could follow me indefinitely. Unless the Bald

Avenger had killed or deactivated him, I would be seeing the beast again.

That made me unhappy. Ringo scared the piss out of me.

As did the Bald Avenger. I hoped that they had managed to waste each other, because I figured that was the only way I'd have a shot at making it to Lubbock unscathed. So far, the regular cops hadn't been a big problem, so as long as I could get the Avenger and the Doberman pinscher cyborg off my tail—

I would still be in trouble. Ringo belonged to Cathy and Jeremy What's-Their-Name, which had to mean that *they* were something weird too. (The astute reader will recognize that I should have figured all this out two days earlier when Ringo bit through hot metal. I plead extenuating circumstances. Buddy Holly had just come back from the grave and had read my name on TV. I was preoccupied.) I was being pursued by things beyond human ken. I began to wonder whether Mother might have been on to something all along.

Such were my thoughts when Gretchen's truck pulled onto the shoulder. I stopped alongside, and she rolled down the window.

"Goddamn cheap-ass ratmeat," she said.

I flipped up my faceplate. "What'd I do now?"

"This junk Ford is out of gas. I abandoned my backpack to get to it—my *backpack,* with my weights and tape player and everything—and now it's stranded me in Oklahoma at two-thirty in the morning with a dorkus on a *motorcycle.*"

I patted the portion of Peggy Sue's seat that extended behind me. "Room for a passenger," I said.

Gretchen's face contorted. "I'm wearing warm-ups over a tank top and shorts. I'd freeze."

I shrugged and revved the Ariel's engine. It didn't sound good, which diminished the effect I'd been hoping for. "Up to you," I said, "but I'm going on to Lubbock." I put the bike into gear.

Gretchen poked a shotgun barrel out of the window. "You take off without me, and I'll shoot 'Peggy Sue' right in the motor," she said.

I stopped. "How'd you know her name?"

She opened the truck door and stepped out. "You talk in your sleep," she said, climbing onto the bike behind me. She put her left arm around my waist and cradled the shotgun in her right.

"You sure you want to keep that?" I asked. The shotgun was aimed at the back of my knee.

"Positive. Just like I'm positive that I was crazy for deciding to go to Lubbock with you. What do I care if Buddy Holly has risen from the grave? What's he gonna do for me if he has? Just take me to the nearest town with a phone, yorkface, and I'll get my friend in Houston to wire money for a bus ticket."

"What about your lack of spiritual fulfillment?"

"Screw it. I'm alive, and I won't be if I stick with you. Our association is ended. Let's go."

I flipped down my faceplate, and we went. I hadn't seen any distance-to-next-town signs since leaving the roadside park, but it couldn't be more than ten miles. Gretchen would survive the ride, and then we would part. It made me a little sad, even though I had a sense that we would each be better off without the other. Gretchen would be warmer, and I wouldn't have a shotgun threatening to shorten my leg.

I should have remembered: Things get worse before they get better. A mist began to fall, and then, six miles from where the Ford had stopped, Peggy Sue lurched and died. I clutched and let her roll.

"What's going on?" Gretchen shrieked. "What the
bloody damn stupid pissant hell are you doing?"

"I don't know," I yelled. We coasted to a stop on the
shoulder.

Gretchen dismounted and began stomping back and
forth, shouting curses that were unintelligible because
she was shivering. This went on for twenty seconds or
so, and then she cocked the shotgun and pointed it at
Peggy Sue's fuel tank. "Get off!" she bellowed.

I was rigid. "No."

She turned away and aimed the gun across the ditch
at an empty field. A spike of blue fire roared out, and
then another and another. A plastic shell bounced off
my helmet. "Goddamn goddamn goddamn goddamn goddamn!" Gretchen cried, cocking and firing, cocking and
firing, until the chamber was empty. She threw the gun
into the field.

I switched off Peggy Sue's lights and put down the
kickstand. "Feel better?" I asked as I dismounted.

Gretchen punched me in the stomach, but because
of the Moonsuit and a layer of cupcakes, it didn't hurt
much. I stood with my hands on my knees, and the mist
turned to rain.

Gretchen flipped up my faceplate. Despite the darkness, I could see the water soaking her hair and running
down her face. "My parents put you up to this, didn't
they?" she said.

When I was able to stand upright, we started walking. I pushed the bike. Gretchen set a fast pace, and occasionally I ran in an attempt to catch up. Peggy Sue
was heavy, though, and before long Gretchen was far
enough ahead that I couldn't see her. When I did spot
her again, it was because she was illuminated by the
headlights of a vehicle coming from the north.

My first thought was that the Bald Avenger was after

us again, but as I looked back I saw that the headlights
sat too high to be the Jaguar's. I stopped walking and
straddled the Ariel to pretend that nothing was wrong,
hoping that the unknown vehicle would pass by without
slowing. I was more afraid of being hauled in than I was
of being stranded in the rain.

Gretchen, however, was running down the shoulder
toward me, waving her arms.

"Stop it!" I yelled. "We don't know who that is!"

"I don't *care* who it is," she said.

I grabbed Gretchen's wrists as she came close, but
by then it was too late. A Winnebago slowed to a stop
beside us. Lights came on inside, and the door opened.

An elderly couple smiled out. The husband, who was
driving, asked, "You folks having trouble?"

"No," I said, while Gretchen said, "Yes."

"Need a lift?"

"Please," Gretchen said, pulling away from me and
starting toward the open door.

The wife's eyes widened. "Dale, the radio, it talked
about a motorbike, a blue suit . . ."

The husband's face switched to an expression of
shocked recognition. He put the Winnebago into gear and
hit the gas.

Gretchen ran after it, keeping pace with the open
door for fifteen or twenty yards. "I'm not with him!" she
cried. "I've never seen him before! Wait, goddamn it!"

They didn't. I got off Peggy Sue and began pushing
again. When I reached Gretchen, she said, "I hate you."

"You can't," I told her. "You're my accomplice."

I had judged that she was in too much discomfort to
hit me this time, and I was right. She began walking
beside me and the Ariel, calling us names now and then.

*   *   *

Another vehicle, a flatbed farm truck, came upon us from the same direction several minutes later, and it too slowed and stopped. Gretchen stared at it sullenly.

"What's up?" the driver asked. His cab light wasn't on, and I couldn't see his face. I could, however, see the faces of a teenage boy and girl sitting beside him.

"Just some mechanical difficulty," I said. "I can handle it, thanks."

"You sure?" the man asked. "Nearest town's Pumpkin Center, and there's nothing there. There's Lawton, of course, but that's another twenty miles."

I considered. Twenty miles might as well have been fifty or a hundred. The Moonsuit was wet and heavy, and my Nikes were drenched.

"Well, I'd hate to leave my bike out here," I said.

"Got a ramp," the man said. "Don't think she'll fall over if you ride back there with her. There isn't enough room up here for more than one more anyway."

"That's me," Gretchen said.

The passenger door of the truck opened, and the boy jumped out. "Hop in," he told Gretchen, and she did. Then he nodded toward the back of the truck and said, "I'll give you a hand with your motorcycle, sir."

I rolled Peggy Sue backward as the driver emerged. He was broad-shouldered and walked as if he were strong. He and the boy dragged a sheet of plywood from the flatbed and propped it on the tail.

The man vaulted up onto the bed. "Push her up, and I'll grab the handlebars when she's high enough," he said.

Peggy Sue and I were at the bottom of the ramp now, but I hesitated. It had occurred to me that I had no idea of what I was getting myself into.

"You sure you want to take us all the way into Lawton?" I asked.

"If you want," the man said. "To tell you the truth, though, it's awful late, and we live just a couple of miles from here. I've got a shop, so I could probably fix you up for less money than they'd stiff you in town."

I became suspicious. "Why would you want to do that?"

"I'm getting wet," the boy said.

"Be polite, son," the man said as he waved for me to bring the bike up. "We've got a spare room. You and your wife look honest, and you could probably use some sleep. I promise we aren't thieves or backwoods cannibals."

I pushed Peggy Sue up the ramp, and the man reached down to help. When we were almost up, I slipped and fell to one knee on the wet plywood, but the man caught the bike and kept her from falling.

"I'm Pete Holden," he said as I scrambled to my feet.

"Thanks, Pete," I said. "I'm—Charles Hardin. I owe you one."

"At least," the boy muttered.

I rolled the bike to the front of the flatbed and propped her on the kickstand while Pete and his son shoved the ramp in after me. I would have to crouch beside the bike to hold her steady.

"I'll take it slow," Pete said.

As they walked past on either side, my suspicion increased. They hadn't asked what Gretchen and I were doing out here. They hadn't asked why she was wearing such inadequate clothing. They were being far too helpful to possess entirely altruistic motives.

"Seen any TV lately?" I blurted.

Pete got into the cab without answering, but the boy paused and looked up at me.

"Television is the new opiate of the masses," he said. "It tells them lies of peace and prosperity while they're slowly crushed by the iron heel of an oppressive and greedy aristocratic minority." He got into the cab.

The truck started moving, and now I couldn't escape without abandoning Peggy Sue. All I could do was huddle in the cold rain as a stranger drove me toward whatever would happen next.

Soon, the truck left the highway for a muddy road and proceeded through countryside that alternated between flat, open fields and stands of soggy trees. The silhouettes of oil pumps nodded like rocking horses. The truck turned twice onto muddier, bumpier roads, and I was afraid that Peggy Sue and I would be jostled into the ditch. My arms, shoulders, and back ached from holding the Ariel, and my fingers were numb.

Finally, the truck turned into a rock driveway that entered a grove, and I saw a mailbox with an attached sign that read "Holden Welding and Motor Works." Far back in the trees stood a one-story frame house with a porch light that illuminated a separate garage and a satellite dish. The truck stopped beside the garage, and I let go of the bike. When Gretchen, Pete, and the two kids came back to the bed, I was lying on my side.

"Rough ride?" Pete asked.

Gretchen didn't give me a chance to answer. "Hey, pinbrain, did you tell this guy that I was your wife?"

I felt so lousy that being killed by Gretchen wasn't such a horrible prospect. "No," I croaked. "I told him you're my concubine."

Pete stepped between Gretchen and the bed before she could grab me. "If we get your bike into the garage," he said, "it'll be dry by the time we're ready to work on it."

I forced myself up and helped Pete and his son with the ramp and with Peggy Sue. The girl pulled open the garage door, and I pushed the Ariel inside onto a con-

crete floor. There was a fast-looking white car occupying
one quarter of the garage, and most of the rest of the
place was cluttered with toolboxes, welding equipment,
and electronic and mechanical doohickeys that I couldn't
identify. Pete called for me to come into the house and
get warm.

I patted Peggy Sue on her fuel tank and went out.
The girl closed the door, and then Gretchen and I followed the Holdens to the back door of their home.
Gretchen thumped my helmet with the side of her fist
to demonstrate her displeasure with my "concubine"
remark.

We entered the house through a mud room, and I
hung my helmet and the Moonsuit on pegs that Pete
indicated. It was at this point that I had my first clear
look at the Holdens. Pete was tall and ruddy, with blue
eyes and sandy hair cut down to bristles; the girl had
the same coloring, but wore her hair in an anachronistic
ponytail; and the boy, who was shorter and more slender
than the girl, was darker than either his father or sister. The way he looked at me made me feel as if he were
judging my life at a glance.

The girl, who introduced herself as Laura, gave
Gretchen a robe so that she could get out of her wet
clothes, and the boy, whom Pete called Mike, brought us
each a towel. I took off my Nikes and socks, hanging
them with the Moonsuit and helmet, and dried my feet.

"I hate to ask since you're already doing so much,"
I said, "but do any of you wear hard contact lenses? I,
uh, lost my case and soaking solution."

"We all wear 'em," Pete said. "We can probably
scrounge up what you need."

"I want the new kind," Laura said. "The kind that
you can wear for weeks or months without taking them

out. But Dad says they cost too much."

Mike looked at his sister disdainfully. "How can you ask for luxuries when the majority of the human race lives in conditions of poverty and oppression?"

Gretchen leaned close to me and muttered, "Jesus, this kid sounds like my father."

"Here's the bathroom," Pete said, leading us into a hallway and stopping beside a door. "There are new toothbrushes in the drawer under the sink, and I'll see if I can find a case for your lenses, Mr. Hardin. Come down the hall when you're finished, and I'll set one of you up in the spare bedroom and the other one on the living-room couch." He and the kids went on.

"I have dibs on the john," Gretchen said, shoving past me. "And guess which one of us is taking the couch." She entered the bathroom and shut the door.

I leaned against the opposite wall and thought again that there was something wrong here. Normal people simply weren't such Good Samaritans. Not without a reason.

Pete reappeared and handed me a plastic contact lens case. "There's soaking solution in the medicine cabinet," he said, peering at me. "You okay? You look dizzy."

"I'm fine, I'm fine," I said, too loud. "I'm just tired. Cold. Wet. You know."

Pete turned away. "Hope the soaking solution's your brand," he said, and left.

I dropped the plastic case, and my fingers could hardly pick it up again. I had come to the conclusion that a reward had been offered for my capture, and that Pete Holden was planning to collect it.

Gretchen came out of the bathroom wearing the robe that Laura had loaned her. "Your turn, bozo. I hung my clothes on the towel rack, and I've memorized their exact positions, so if you touch them, I'll know."

"They're going to turn us in," I said. "It's the only explanation."

She shook her head. "I talked with them in the truck, and they don't seem the type to do that." Her eyes hardened. "Besides, what's this 'they're going to turn *us* in' crap? There is no *us*, bud. I've severed our association, remember? It's only coincidence that we're stuck together for now. And as soon as I get some sleep, I'll take care of that." She started down the hall.

"Good night," I said.

"Up yours," she answered.

When I had finished in the bathroom, I walked down the hall barefoot and blurry-visioned with my sweatshirt draped over a shoulder. The hall took me to the kitchen, and I went through to a small dining area. From there I could see Pete sitting on a couch in the living room. I could also see a big Sony TV set like mine. Its screen was dark.

"Feel better?" Pete asked as I approached.

"Some," I said, eyeing the Sony. Surely it had been turned on at least once in the past two days, and surely the satellite dish beside the garage had fed it the same thing from every channel in the world. . . .

Pete squinted at my T-shirt. " 'Rock-chalk, chickenhawk,' " he read. "Eff blank blank blank KU. What's that mean?"

"I've never been sure."

He pointed past me. "That's my bedroom on the other side of the dining room. If you need anything, just give a knock."

"Sure," I said. "Great." The Sony was staring at me.

"And you don't need to worry that the kids'll bother you before morning," Pete said, jerking a thumb at a door beside the couch. "Their rooms are in the basement."

"Oh. Good." I began to inch backward.

Pete stood. "I'll get you a blanket."

"Terrific," I said, still inching away. I was too great a coward to run.

Pete sighed. "All right, then." He looked at my eyes. "I know that your name is Oliver Vale, but you can hide here without being afraid that I'll turn you in."

I stopped inching. "How do I know that?"

He reached into a back pocket and pulled out a wallet. "Here," he said, removing a photograph. "I would've told you about this when I found you, but I was afraid you'd think I was making up a story to lure you. Not everyone believes in Fate."

I took the photo and held it close to my face so that I could see it clearly. It was a black-and-white snapshot of two young men in Army fatigues. Their faces were dirty and sweat-streaked, but they had their arms around each other's shoulders and were grinning.

"Your mother's name is Michelle," Pete said. "I used to read all of her letters."

I handed the photo back. "Thank you," I said, and lay down on the couch. Pete brought two blankets and a pillow, then turned off the light and went to his room.

I covered myself with the blankets and noticed for the first time that the Holdens' house smelled as if a pot roast had been cooked there within the past twenty-four hours. Pot roast had been Mother's specialty. It was the only thing she could prepare that didn't taste like everything else she had ever cooked.

I hadn't felt so safe in years.

When I awoke, the room was lit by filtered sunlight, and Laura and Mike were standing over me. They were both wearing jeans and sweatshirts, and Mike was holding a thick Sunday newspaper.

"You snore," Mike said.

"Try sleeping on your side," Laura suggested.

I mumbled an apology, and they moved away and sat cross-legged on the floor to read the paper.

"You'll be happy to hear that you're still the top story, Mr. Vale," Mike said dryly. "You've managed to make everyone with a television set forget everything in the world except you and Buddy Holly. You've made them forget the thousands of innocent people being murdered by neo-Nazis and oligarchical theocrats in Chile, South Africa, Israel, El Salvador, Afghanistan, Iran, Ulster, and Sri Lanka. All of the major protest marches and riots this past weekend were the result of worldwide anger over the current homogenous state of video entertainment."

"You know who I am too?" I asked, sitting up.

"Mind like a trap," Laura muttered.

"Of course we know who you are," Mike said. "We found you last night because we were looking for you. What did you think we were doing, riding around in the middle of the night because we enjoyed it?"

"How—" I began.

Laura dropped her section of the paper. "It wasn't tough. In fact, I'm surprised we got to you before anyone else did. Once we decided that you must be heading to Lubbock, Texas—an obvious choice, and I don't know why the authorities have only now started to consider it—"

"They have?" I asked. Mike tapped a front-page headline and held it up close enough for me to read: TEXAS OFFICIALS THINK VID-PIRATE COULD HEAD FOR ROCK STAR'S HOMETOWN. It wasn't the lead story, but it was there.

Laura was still talking. "—calculated that the odds were seven to three that you would pass within fifty miles of here sometime between Saturday noon and Sunday morning, so I monitored various CB, police, and two-way bandwidths, and when I caught a CB signal that suggested you were near the transmitter, I metered it and calculated your approximate distance on the basis of signal strength."

"Which was silly," Mike said, "because the guy came right out and said where you were."

Laura glared at him. "And you said that he wasn't even talking about Mr. Vale. You said that the motorcycle in a roadside park beside a 'rich bitch's' Jaguar was a coincidence. I, on the other hand, calculated that the odds were three to two that a motorcycle in that location at that time would be Mr. Vale's. And I was right."

My stomach tightened. "You didn't go to that park, did you?"

"Sure," Mike said. "We got there via the road that Dad figured would be your first-choice route after leaving the place, and when we didn't see you there or at the park, we came back on the highway, which was where we found you."

"Did you see anyone at the park?" I asked. "A bald man with a gun, a huge robot dog with electric eyes?"

Laura and Mike exchanged glances. "We saw the Jaguar," Laura said, "but its back tires were flat and no one was inside. We honked our horn and yelled, and when no one responded, we left. We didn't see a dog."

I slumped and closed my eyes.

"I was surprised at your choice of companions when we finally found you," Mike said. "This Gretchen person strikes me as being a self-centered, materialistic tool of the gluttonous consumerist profiteering machine."

My eyes opened. "How old are you?"

"Thirteen," he said. "How old did you think?"

Laura grinned. "You're boring enough to be sixty."

"And you're politically naive enough to be a Baby Boomer."

Pete's bedroom door opened, and Pete shuffled out.
He was wearing baggy coveralls. "Damn it, I was up late
last night," he said, his voice thick with sleep.

"Sorry, Dad," Laura and Mike said in unison.

I stood. "Why'd you do it?" I asked Pete.

He looked at me groggily. "Do what?"

"Search for me. Bring me here. Granted, you knew
my uncle, but . . ."

He shuffled toward the kitchen. "Coffee. Food. Maybe
a shower. Then we'll talk." He wrinkled his nose. "And
do your laundry."

I followed him. The mention of food had made me
smell the pot roast again, which in turn had made me
hungry. The mention of laundry had made me realize
that I'd been wearing the same pair of briefs since
Thursday, which in turn had made me itch.

"Should we wake Miss Laird at any particular time?"
Laura asked.

I shrugged. Gretchen had made it plain that she no
longer wanted anything to do with me, so I saw no reason to have anything to do with her.

"Let the fascist sleep," Mike said.

After putting in my contacts and having breakfast
(pancakes and sausage), I put on a pair of coveralls that
Pete loaned me and threw my other clothes into his
Kenmore. Then he and I went out to the garage, and I
gave the Ariel a few test kicks while he listened to her
wheeze. Then he took a toolbox from a shelf and got to
work. "Sounds like fouled plugs," he said, fitting a spark-
plug socket to a ratchet and squatting beside the bike.

I grunted and looked away. It's embarrassing when
someone else has to do your work for you, no matter
what the circumstances. My eyes lit on the white car.

"Nice vehicle," I said.

Pete began loosening a plug. "Yeah, that's the Oklahoma Kamikaze. A 1968 Barracuda with a 426 Hemi. My special project."

"It isn't finished?"

"Oh, yeah, he's finished," Pete said. "But a Hemi always needs adjustments. He's temperamental, like a stud thoroughbred."

"He?"

"Named after your uncle." The plug came free. "See, look at that spark gap—carbonized all to hell."

I looked. It was. "I'd sort of figured that your son was named after my uncle," I said.

"He is. But he's also heavily into politics, which the old Mikey definitely was not."

"Young Mike's into politics? Never would have guessed."

Pete chuckled. "He says he's a founder of a club called the New Radicals, and he claims that the 1990s are going to be the sixties all over again. He's his own man."

He pointed at the Barracuda. "Now, *that,* on the other hand, is my old friend. We called him Kamikaze Mikey— Jesus, twenty-one years ago. He was going to move down here after we got out, and we were going to go into the welding business together. He said he was going to be- come the *Oklahoma* Kamikaze."

"Why 'Kamikaze' in the first place?"

"Because he was, man. Full-bore, all eight cylin- ders hammering, wild-assed, look-out-motherfuckers-I'm- heading-down-your-goddamn-throats, bug-eyed, shit-fire crazy."

"I don't remember his letters being anything like that."

"Well, I guess not," Pete said, loosening the second plug. "I read them all before he sent them, and some- times I made him do them over again so they'd sound

normal. Now, don't get me wrong; he could be as sane
as anyone. But he knew when a situation called for *in-*
sanity, and it wasn't something he could just turn off
like that." Pete snapped the fingers of his free hand.

Something like recognition welled up in me. "I remember you! I mean, I remember him writing about you.
You were the guy who thought about food all the time."

Pete nodded. "Uh-huh. We all had our things. Some
guys had women or pot or whatever. Mikey had crazi-
ness. I had food. Would've gotten fat if I hadn't had the
shits so often." He grinned. "Except near the end of my
tour, we got some stuff in dinky cans that, God, had to
have been Korean War surplus. Cheese stuff with bacon. We called it choke-ass. First few guys who ate it
got so constipated that no one but me wanted any."

He held up the second plug, and it was worse than
the first. "Think they'll be okay if we clean them?" I
asked.

Pete shook his head. "Better get new ones if you
want to make it to Lubbock without breaking down
again."

I was disgusted. "Does everybody in the world know
where I'm going?"

"Maybe," Pete said, standing and tossing the cruddy
spark plugs into a bucket of junk. "Laura knew right
away. She'd no sooner seen the broadcast on Friday when
she asked me all sorts of questions about Buddy Holly.
When I said that I thought he was buried in Lubbock,
she said, 'Then that's where Oliver Vale is going.' "

"Smart girl."

He walked to a rack of drawers and began opening
and closing them, looking inside each. "Yeah, she's only
sixteen, but she'll graduate from high school this spring,
a year early. Then she figures on heading off to MIT.
She already knows more about computers than most en-

gineers, and on top of that, she's just a solo flight short of her pilot's license. She wants to be an astronaut, if NASA ever gets its act together again, and she figures that flying'll be a good complement to brain power." He looked at me. "Sorry. I tend to go on about my kids."

"Sounds like they're something to go on about. Besides, you're fixing my bike, so I'll listen to anything."

He turned back to the drawers. "Well, I *hope* I can fix it. I'm more comfortable with things that run on a decent number of wheels. Tell you what, though—if we can't get the bike up and chugging again, I'll run you to Lubbock in the Kamikaze." He looked into the last drawer. "I don't have the right plugs, so I'll have to go to town. You won't be able to leave until tonight at the earliest. Assuming nothing else is wrong."

"Wouldn't count on it," I said. "Peggy Sue's old, and I'm not much good at preventive maintenance."

"Peggy Sue, huh?" Pete scratched his neck as he gazed at the bike. "What happened to the left pipe?"

"Doberman pinscher cyborg. A big one."

"It'd have to be."

We walked back to the house, and Pete told Laura and Mike that he was going into Lawton for parts. While he was gone, they were to treat me and Gretchen as honored guests.

I followed Pete to the mud room, and as he was putting on his coat, I again asked, "Why?"

"Why what?"

"Come on, Pete. The same 'why what' as an hour ago. Why treat me like an 'honored guest'? Why search for me in the first place?" I hesitated. "Look, if you knew my uncle, you also know that he and I never met, so it doesn't make sense for you to do this for his sake. We were related by blood, but nothing else."

Pete stared at the floor. "You were related by things

stronger than blood," he said, "but I'm not sure I can put
a name to any of them. Not and have them make sense."
He opened the door, and the rush of cold air made my
eyes water. "There's a metal box on the desk in my room.
It has all of the letters your mother wrote to Mikey. He
told me to keep them if something happened to him, because he knew I liked reading them as much as he did."

"You've kept them twenty-one years?"

"Couldn't throw them away. Emily, my wife, was
going to once, because she thought they were from an
old girlfriend. But I explained it to her, and she let me
keep them. Still, she always knew that she was right,
in a way."

"You fell in love with my mother?" I was starting
to shiver, and I hugged myself.

Pete was silent for a moment. "Not love," he said
then. "Fascination. I fell into fascination with her, with
all of that wild stuff about Atlantis and space beings
who flew around in bubbles of light. Stuff about how you
were the spiritual reincarnation of Buddy Holly. I got to
feeling like I was as much your uncle as Mikey was."
He shook his head. "Never had the guts to get in touch
with either of you after I made it home, though. I was
afraid that the reality wouldn't live up to the fascination. Boy, was I wrong." He started to close the door.
"Go read the letters. Me, I've got to buy some off-size
spark plugs."

The door closed, but I opened it again. Pete was
walking toward the flatbed truck.

"Mother died five years ago," I blurted.

He stopped, saying nothing.

"I didn't know whether you knew," I said.

Pete looked back. "I knew," he said. Then he went
to the truck and drove away.

*   *   *

    I wandered back through the kitchen and dining area. My eyes avoided the door to Pete's room.

    "Is everything all right, Mr. Vale?" Laura asked as I came into the living room and sat on the couch. She was lying on the floor reading a book filled with diagrams and equations.

    "Fine," I said. "Except for the worldwide chaos that's being blamed on me, I mean."

    "Glad to hear it."

    Mike came into the room from the basement. "It's ten o'clock," he said. "Does Ms. Laird always perform auto-erotic acts at about this time?"

    "I wouldn't know," I said. "How do you?"

    "I was wondering how she could sleep so long, so I went downstairs and used a stethoscope to listen to the spare room's floor. A lot of thumping and bumping."

    "She's probably exercising. She seems to place great value on having a strong body."

    "I'm not surprised," Mike said. "Right-wingers have little else of value in their lives."

    Laura looked up from her book with a sour expression. "Give it a rest. You don't know anything about her."

    "I know enough."

    "Dad said we were to be polite."

    "And I will be, when she shows her face. If you weren't so concerned with numbers and gadgets, you might have some small awareness that people like her are responsible for most of the world's pain and suffering, not to mention the decline of art and culture."

    As Laura retorted, I stood and crossed into the dining area. Then, before Mike retorted to Laura's retort, I opened the door to Pete's room and stepped inside.

    The light was on. The room contained only a bed, a bureau, and a desk with a wooden chair. On the desk was a PC and a metal document box.

I closed the door and stood still, unwilling to go to the desk. When I had first read the passage in Volume I that described my conception, my life had changed, and not for the better. Then, after Mother's death, I had read the entire diary, and that had changed things further. Again, the change had not been for the better . . . assuming that "better" means increased happiness and peace of mind. Reading Mother's words had never given me either of those.

Now here I was again, with more of her words before me, knowing that the things she might have said to a brother she missed terribly, a brother trapped in a world of shit, might reveal things about her, and about me, that even her diary had failed to reveal. If I read these words, I would again be changing all the changes of my life.

I stepped forward and opened the box. I always had.

SHARON

Notes on client Oliver Vale, continued . . .
Sunday, February 5, 1989. 10:20 A.M.
I should never have tried to do this thing with Bruce. He isn't the only lawyer in the world.

Once we made it through Oklahoma City (after hours of struggling through crowds and traffic jams), I told Bruce, who was driving, to take a state highway that I hoped would not be well patrolled. I was afraid that the authorities might be looking for us by now and that someone in the city might have spotted us.

Bruce refused. The mess in Oklahoma City had been the last straw, he said. If I wanted to go to Lubbock,

Texas, fine, but we wouldn't skulk about like fugitives.
"That," he said, "is a method I'll leave to your friend
Oliver the Geek."

Despite my protests, he turned the car around and
drove north to I-40, where he turned west. We would do
the sensible thing, he said, and drive directly to Amarillo, then south on I-27 to Lubbock.

I tried to explain. The KBI agents had told me to
stay in Topeka. If we were caught—

Bruce scoffed. The KBI had neither placed me under arrest nor delivered a court order requiring me to
stay put, so they didn't have a legal leg to stand on.

We reached the Texas border about 7:00 A.M., and a
mile after we crossed it, we encountered a Texas Highway Patrol roadblock. The patrolman who looked in at
us said, in a West Texas drawl, that he was sorry for
the inconvenience, but that it was the opinion of the
Texas Highway Patrol that the Federal fugitive known
as Oliver Vale might be headed for Lubbock, and as of
this morning the patrol was stopping traffic on all major
highways coming into the state. Could he please see our
identification, and had either of us seen anyone riding
an old motorcycle or fitting Vale's description?

We had no choice. Bruce and I both had to show him
our Kansas driver's licenses. He took them and asked us
to wait a moment.

While traffic began to pile up behind us, the patrolman went to one of the four cruisers sitting on the highway and spoke into a microphone, reading from the
licenses. I rolled down my window to hear the reply, but
all I could make out were static-filled squawks.

When the patrolman returned, three of his colleagues came with him. "Would y'all step out of the vehicle, please?" the patrolman said.

Bruce scowled his best don't-harass-me-you-fool-I'm-an-attorney scowl. "What is this?" he demanded. "Are we under arrest?"

"No, sir."

"Then we're not stepping out," Bruce told him. "I'm a lawyer, and I know my—"

"Sir," the patrolman said, interrupting, "you aren't under arrest *now*. However, if you refuse to cooperate with the Texas Department of Public Safety in our efforts to apprehend a possible felon, we'll have just cause to suspect you of aiding that felon. *Then* we'll arrest you."

"This is coercion!" Bruce thundered.

The patrolman smiled. "No, sir," he said. "This is Texas."

They put us in a cruiser and took us to a Texas DPS building in the town of Shamrock (assuring us that Bruce's car would follow via tow truck), and that's where we've been for almost three hours now.

Every fifteen minutes, two suit-and-tie Texas Rangers come into the room and ask the same questions.

Do you know Oliver Vale?

Is Oliver Vale responsible for the takeover of television communications?

Did you help him do it?

What are Vale's intentions?

Why Buddy Holly?

Are you going to Lubbock? Is that where Vale is heading? Why?

Each time, I answer their questions as honestly as I can. Yes, I know Oliver. I don't know whether he's responsible. I didn't help him. I don't know his intentions. He identifies with Buddy Holly, but that doesn't mean that he did it. Yes, we're heading to Lubbock. Maybe. I don't know.

The Rangers can only hear me part of the time. The

rest of the time, Bruce is bellowing about deprivation of civil liberties and massive legal retaliation.

The way I feel now, I myself may retaliate by depriving myself of Bruce.

RICHTER

After the slug was removed and the stitches and bandage were in place, Richter got down from the table and pulled on his pants despite the doctor's advice.

"You should rest for a few hours," the doctor said. "You had quite an ordeal, waiting all that time out there. Lucky for you that you had a car phone."

"Yes," Richter said, sitting on the table again to put on his shoes.

The doctor coughed. "Um, you should also stay because, um, I have to report a bullet wound to the police. They'll want to ask you how it happened."

"No," Richter said, and limped out of the cubicle past the wide-eyed nurse. He had too much to do to waste more time here, and he didn't think that the doctor would have much of a chance to call the police.

He had to push his way through the packed Emergency waiting room toward the exit. Lawton was not a large city, but it was currently experiencing an epidemic of physical injuries ranging from scrapes and broken bones to almost-severed limbs. The Bill Willyite/Couch Potato Riots were in full swing here. One of the ambulance attendants had told him that a large number of soldiers from Fort Sill had been given weekend passes and that they had become enthusiastic contributors to the violence of the demonstrations.

"Hey, is your name Richter?" a voice boomed over the noise in the waiting room.

Richter saw a beefy policeman pointing at him from a doorway. He kept moving toward the exit, but his leg slowed him down too much, and he didn't make it. The policeman's hand clamped on his shoulder.

In this crowd, it would be difficult to break free and stay free without killing his opponent. It was unfortunate, but . . .

"You've got a phone call," the policeman said, pulling Richter toward the doorway from which he had come.

Richter shook himself from the officer's grip, then followed him down a hall to a bank of pay telephones where another officer was holding a receiver. Richter took it, and both officers walked away.

He leaned against the wall to take the weight off his right leg, and he spoke into the receiver, "Yes?"

"Richter." It was his superior. "I thought I would call and save you the bother. You *were* going to call when you were out of surgery, weren't you?"

"Yes," Richter lied.

"Mmmm. I wondered, because the credit card you gave the towing company and the hospital receptionist is one that you obtained using an alias that we did not assign to you. If I didn't know better, I would suspect that you didn't want us to know you were in a hospital in Lawton, Oklahoma. Nor that you had been shot. Nor, by extension, that you were having difficulty with your assignment. That wasn't the case, was it?"

"No," Richter said. He was weary. The amphetamines had long since worn off, and he ached in more places than his leg.

After the Doberman had run off, Richter had crawled to the Jaguar and had been about to get inside when a flatbed truck had pulled into the rest area. Richter had belly-slid under the car and had drawn his pistol, waiting there while the truck's occupants had honked their horn and shouted, "Is anyone here?," a hundred times. Richter had nearly passed out, but even so he had been certain that he had heard someone yell, "Is Oliver Vale here?" He hadn't had a chance to investigate that, though, because the truck had left.

He had crawled out from under the car, gotten inside, and called for an ambulance and a tow truck. Both had taken over an hour to arrive, with the tow truck showing up ten minutes before the ambulance, but he was fortunate in that his wound had bled only a little. He had known that he wouldn't die. It was a small comfort.

"I'm glad to hear that you haven't forgotten me, Richter," his superior said, "for I certainly haven't forgotten you. You are my best operative and have been for a number of years—"

"Yes," Richter said.

"—which is why I regret to inform you that you are removed from your assignment. Other arrangements will be made about the matter. As soon as your vehicle is repaired, you will proceed to the Will Rogers World Airport in Oklahoma City and fly home."

Richter smoldered.

"You can't be surprised, Richter. Did you think that I would speak with you via an unsecured telephone line if I were going to say anything else?"

"No," Richter said. He tried to keep the anger out of the word and did not succeed.

The tone of his superior's voice became consoling. "Sometimes the simplest-looking jobs turn out to be the most complicated, my friend. This one wasn't your type, anyway. Come home, and I promise something good for you. You aren't so old that we're putting you out to pasture. There's an individual representing a certain foreign company who has been taking advantage of the current social disorder to engage in unfair business practices. You may be able to persuade him to desist. Yes?"

Richter almost said "Yes," but stopped himself.

You aren't so old that we're putting you out to pasture.

It was a lie, but it contained the truth.

They weren't going to give him a sanction when he had failed at an apprehension. An operative only failed once, and then he was no longer an operative. Usually that was because he was dead, but there were a few who survived and were merely considered incompetent.

"Problem," Richter said. His throat began hurting.

"What is it?"

"Leg's hemorrhaging. Request two days recuperation."

There was a long silence. At last his superior said, "Very well. We'll assign another man to the business problem. I assume you'll be coming home for your R and R."

"No. Possible concussion. Dizziness. Don't want to fly until it's gone."

Another silence. "Your order to return home will be in force in forty-eight hours." The line clicked.

Richter hung up the phone. Whatever happened now, his career was over. His life was over.

They had done it to him. Vale. The woman. The dog.

The dog that could catch bullets in its teeth and spit them out again.

Richter didn't care. Nobody did to him what they had done. Nobody made him look like a fool.

He limped down the hall to Emergency and struggled through the packed bodies again. He had paid the men in the tow truck quadruple their usual rate in exchange for a promise that they would replace the Jaguar's blown tires and bring the car to the Emergency parking lot. He found that they had fulfilled that promise.

Richter slid behind the wheel and sat for a few minutes until the throbbing in his leg subsided to a tolerable level. Then he reached under the seat and took his weapon and shoulder holster from the compartment where he had hidden them. He removed the pistol from the holster, ejected its ammunition clip, and checked the action. Then he replaced the clip and started the Jaguar.

Amphetamines would not relieve his fatigue now, so he would take some time to recuperate, just as he had said he would.

But not much.

CATHY AND JEREMY

Jeremy sat on his haunches in the passenger seat of the Datsun and scratched himself behind an ear. "We should've had this car fumigated when we bought it," he said.

"Which way at the next light?" Cathy said, holding her nose with one hand and steering with the other. The stench of crude oil was heavy even thought it was Sunday morning.

"Left," Jeremy answered. "Past the refinery."

"Wonderful," Cathy muttered, taking the corner and accelerating.

"Sorry. This is the way Ringo went."

Cathy's eyebrows rose. "I just had a thought. Can you see where he is now?"

Jeremy closed his human-eye and opened the other.

"He's caught up with Vale again. He's lying among some trees and watching the house where Vale's hiding."

"Great. Let's buy a road map and just *go* there. There's got to be a more direct route."

Jeremy shook his head. "I can see what Ringo sees, so in one sense I know where he is—but I don't know *where* he is. I couldn't even figure out his current location by trying to trace his route on a map, because he doesn't care about north or south, east or west. He just follows the motorcycle and occasionally looks at the scenery. So the scenery's all I've got to go by."

They came upon the oil refinery tower, its flame burning bright orange in the gray dawn. Cathy shuddered. "How can they stand it? All these odors flooding their senses for their entire lives. . . ."

"Human beings can get used to anything." Jeremy stiffened as he spoke and looked to the east.

"What?" Cathy asked. "What's wrong?"

"Pull onto the shoulder and stop."

Cathy did so, then looked out to see what Jeremy saw.

"Can you feel them?" he asked.

She nodded. "I knew they were here somewhere, but the stink kept my senses occupied."

"So this is SkyVue," Jeremy said.

"Not an impressive place."

"Impressive enough. Read the marquee."

Cathy did, and grimaced. "Bill Willy? Here? Are the pro-fleshies *trying* to defeat themselves?"

"Sort of looks that way. Should we drop in and say hello?"

Cathy steered the Datsun onto the road again. "Why? To gloat? With all that's happened in the past two days, our point's been proven. The fleshbound peoples of Earth aren't ready for the responsibility of noncorporeality. All that you and I have to do now is see to it that Vale remains unharmed, and our consciences are clear."

"What about the rest of the world?" Jeremy asked. "A lot of people besides Vale stand to get hurt. Some already have been."

Cathy jerked her left thumb at the receding drive-in theater. "That's the responsibility of our two cousins back there. The only part of it that you and I have had anything to do with is Vale. And he's going to be fine. Right?"

"I hope so. When the Fed tried to shoot him, I was afraid that we'd waited too long, but—"

"But Ringo responded to your commands, as I predicted."

Jeremy frowned. "Maybe. . . ."

"Whattaya mean 'maybe'? He stopped the attack, didn't he? He gave Vale the chance to escape and hide, didn't he?"

Jeremy began scratching his ear again. "Yes. But it felt as if he might be acting on his own."

"He's not smart enough to do that," Cathy said. "The hardware didn't include any free-will circuits, and the rest of him is plain old dog."

"Maybe 'plain old dog' has more to it than we thought. I didn't tell him to put a bullet into the Fed's leg."

"That was just a reflex, and no real harm done. Vale escaped, and the G-man survived. All's well that ends well."

"It hasn't ended yet. The agent won't quit."

"But he won't get to Vale again before we do."

"Assuming our car holds up."

Cathy pounded on the dashboard. "Damn it, why'd you have to say that? The heater's stopped again! What an existence—putrid stenches, bodies that ache and collapse, machines that don't work. How do the fleshbound stand it?"

Jeremy shrugged. "By taking one day at a time, I suppose, so the agony doesn't accumulate. That's no more than a guess, mind you."

Cathy gritted her teeth. "Just a little longer," she said. "Just a little longer, and then we can go back to taking life the civilized way—one *millennium* at a time."

Jeremy squirmed and began biting his shoulder. "Right now," he said around a mouthful of his shirt, "I'd settle for taking life with no fleas."

8

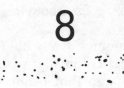

OLIVER

In 1974, when I was fourteen and Mother was working on Volume V, we moved to the house south of the
city where I still live. The move came as a surprise to
me, for I had always assumed that Mother's salary barely
covered necessities and record albums. Somehow, though,
she had saved enough in nine years at the radio station
to cover a down payment. (Of course, a down payment
in 1974 was somewhat less than the fortune required
now.) We moved in the spring, right after the end of the
school year. I had finished junior high, and it was a good
time for change.

The Apollo program was over, and while the Skylab
missions had been fascinating, they hadn't been as exciting as the lunar adventures, and my interest in space
exploration had waned. That waning, however, wasn't
entirely due to the change in NASA's priorities, because
my own priorities had shifted. By the end of my ninth-
grade school year, if a genie had given me the choice of
becoming either the first man on Mars or the first man

to fornicate with Valerie Frackner from my English class, I would have agonized for about six seconds and then tackled Valerie.

It was a good summer. I was old enough that Mother trusted me to take care of myself while she was at work, and I was young enough that I didn't have to find a job of my own yet. I spent my mornings either reading in my new room or shooting a basketball at the hoop over the garage door, and on every sunny afternoon I changed into swim trunks and rode my bicycle nine miles to the community pool on the city's south side. There I could lounge with three or four other males my own age, drinking soda pop and swimming, but mainly ogling the seventeen-year-old female lifeguards.

I had been wearing black-framed glasses for over a year, but those afternoons at the pool made me yearn for contact lenses. For one thing, I was the only boy my age who knew, or cared, who Buddy Holly had been, and the fact that my glasses made me look like him was an irrelevancy in my social circle. For another thing, the guys told me that the glasses were dorky, and that the girls thought so too.

Mother told me that what with house payments and everything, contact lenses were just too expensive, especially since our optometrist said that my eyes were still changing. She was afraid of spending a few hundred dollars just to have to do it all over again. "Besides," she said, "your glasses make you look like Buddy." Mother and Buddy had been on a first-name basis ever since he had died.

I was beginning to resent the dominating influence of Charles Hardin Holley in my life in much the same way that other adolescent males resented the dominating influence of their fathers in theirs, and sometimes at night I would lie awake and curse him. I wanted to live in 1974, not 1958; I wanted to be Oliver Vale, not an avatar of a man who had been dead for fifteen years.

And yet, just as the adolescent male who resents his father will fight when his father is slandered, so I fought when Buddy was slandered. One afternoon at the pool, someone had a transistor radio tuned to KKAP's Oldies Hour, and one of the oldies was the original version of "Rave On." A guy I didn't know asked what sort of crap that was supposed to be, and the radio owner answered that it didn't matter because the singer was dead.

"Good riddance," answered the other guy.

I shoved him into the water. Neither of the life-guards saw me do it, but they *did* see him come up out of there and punch me in the face, busting my glasses at the bridge. He was thrown out and forbidden to re-turn for the rest of the summer, and a bikinied lifeguard named Shelley came to me while I was holding my nose, put her hand on my arm, and asked if I was hurt.

I was struggling to keep the pain from bringing tears to my eyes. "Nah, he didn't hit me hard," I said, leaning close so that Shelly's left breast touched my shoulder. What I wanted to do then was drop my hand from my nose and gaze into her eyes, but what I had to do instead was turn away and head for the shower room. The tears had come anyway. Pain had defeated sex.

By the time I had recovered enough to emerge from the shower room, the guy with the radio had ratted on me, and I was thrown out too—but just for the after-noon, since no one in charge had any hard evidence against me. Riding my bike home while trying to hold my busted glasses on my injured face was tough, but I felt triumphant. I had kicked butt, had mostly gotten away with it, and had brushed against a seventeen-year-old girl's boob.

It was a good summer.

*   *   *

Nixon resigned on August 9, and I didn't care. I was fourteen and had better things on my mind.

Mother's attitude wasn't much different. She wrote, *Nixon has resigned. Big deal. He was only a figment of my imagination anyway.* Not surprisingly, she had shown more interest in the death of Mama Cass Elliot eleven days before. She had written, *Despite the sadness that I feel, I must admit that after all of the overdose deaths of the past five years, it is refreshing to see a pop star phase herself into another plane of existence via a ham sandwich.*

Then the summer was gone, and I started high school with a new pair of black frames and my first truly hideous pimples. With the move to the house, my school district had changed, and instead of going to Topeka High, I wound up at a rural unified-district school. My classmates were strong, rawboned farmers' kids, and I didn't fit in too well. Not that I would have fit in any better elsewhere. The summer of 1974 was the only oasis in the desert of my early adolescence, and it would have been so no matter where I had gone to school.

My grades were okay—no A's, but not many C's either—and my social relationships were about the same. I made a few friends, but none were close. I made the junior varsity basketball team and played for a total of fifteen minutes in five games. None of the girls I wanted were disgusted by me, but none were attracted either.

If I was the reincarnation of a rock 'n' roll star, I thought, I was not living up to it. It was only later, after Mother bought the first biographies of Buddy to hit the stands, that I discovered he hadn't been a superstar in high school either.

Like every other male I knew, I spent my days in agony. My hard-on would start on the school bus in the

morning and take only five-minute breaks between then
and my arrival home in the late afternoon. My blue jeans
were a torture chamber. Basketball practice helped, but
only when we didn't have to share the gym with the
girls' team.

These were not the sort of things that I discussed
with Mother. Yet for my fifteenth birthday, she gave me
two presents: a mongrel puppy and a box of condoms.

I was delighted at the first and horrified at the second. Rubbers, for the love of Christ. Peacocks, made down
the road in Kansas City. From my mother. For my
birthday. As if I had a use for them. Didn't I wish.

I named the scruffy black-haired pup Ready Teddy,
after the Little Richard song that Buddy had covered à
la rockabilly, and I took both him and the condoms into
the backyard. While Ready Teddy growled puppy growls
and chewed on my shoelaces, I removed the twelve prophylactics from their packets and stuffed them inside each
other until I had a rubber ball. Then I taught Ready
Teddy to chase it, and chew on it, and play keep-away
with it in the cool December air.

When Mother came outside to tell me that it was
time for supper, she saw what I had done, and for the
one and only time in her life she became furious
with me.

"Do you think it's a joke?" she shouted. "Is that it,
Oliver? Do you think it's a goddamn *joke?*"

In those days we had no neighbors closer than a
quarter mile away, for which I was grateful. "I don't
know," I said sullenly. Ready Teddy was at my feet
chewing on the condom-ball.

"You don't know," Mother said. "You *don't know.*
Fucking-A *right* you don't know!"

I yelled back at her. "Don't talk like that! Other
people's mothers don't talk like that!"

Her hands became fists. "I'm not other people's mother, shithead! And I didn't give you those to be funny. I gave them to you because you're fifteen. I gave them to you because in the next few years things are going to *happen*. I gave them to you because I want you to take *responsibility* for those things. Do you understand?"

I glared. "No." It was a lie, but I was pissed.

Some of the fury went out of Mother's eyes, and when she spoke again she didn't shout. But the words cut deeper than the yelling had. "That's the only box I'll ever buy for you, Oliver," she said. "You have to buy the next one yourself. Whether you think it's worth it, or whether you take the trouble, is up to you. But know this: If you get a girl pregnant, you no longer have a home. Got it?"

I squatted to pet my puppy, not wanting to look at Mother anymore.

"I asked you a question," she said.

"Don't worry," I said. Ready Teddy nipped at my fingers. "I'm never going to be stupid enough for that." This last was a slap at her, because she *had* been stupid. Even as I said it, though, I was thinking, *I'm never going to be* lucky *enough for that.*

A long silence followed as I petted Ready Teddy and pretended that I couldn't feel Mother's eyes on me.

Then she said, "Promise."

I couldn't help looking up. "Promise what?"

Now she was the one who looked away. "Promise that you won't get anyone pregnant. If you don't promise, I'll have to leave. On a UFO. A ship of light. The world is hard enough as it is. I couldn't stay knowing that my son had made it worse."

I picked up my dog and stood. "I promise," I said. It seemed the quickest way to get the whole scene over with.

Mother looked at me again and smiled, her eyes

glistening. "You're a good boy," she said, turning to go inside. "Come in and eat. Pot roast and baked potatoes."

Of all the meals we ate together, that is the one I can still taste.

*

Reading Mother's letters to Uncle Mike was a lot like reading Volumes III and IV, except that her isolation comes through even more strongly. She missed her brother, and in seven of the twenty-two letters she even tells him that "sometimes I miss Mama almost as much"—a statement that has no equivalent in the diary. Yet it rings true, especially since Mother and Grandmother did begin to spend time together after Uncle Mike's death (a trend that was destroyed, of course, when Grandmother brought me home to find Mother and Keith making love on the carpet).

I sat at Pete's desk going through the letters for two hours and was beginning to think that perhaps I would emerge from the experience unchanged. Parts of the letters were tough going, but I hadn't come across anything startling.

Then I came to the last letter in the stack, dated August 29, 1968. It could not have arrived in Vietnam until after Uncle Mike's death.

It begins with the usual letter-from-home news, but concludes with this:

I am going to tell you something now, Mikey, that I have not told anyone else. I have not even put it into my diary because I don't want to read it again after writing it down, but I have to let it out this once because it has been preying on my mind. When you come home, pretend I never told you.

I had a dream during the Democratic National Convention that did not seem to be a dream at all. I dreamed

*that I was walking along a sidewalk in Chicago when I
became trapped between a mob of anti-war protesters and
another mob of riot police. Both sides converged on me,
and a policeman, thinking that I was one of the protesters, clubbed me. I fell, and they all began trampling me.
I tried to crawl away, and then there were bodies falling
on me, smothering me. There was blood on my mouth
and nose. My eyes were closed. I was being killed. The
whole world was watching.*

*Then, just as I could feel the last of my life about to
be crushed, all of the weight disappeared, and I floated
up, up, up. I opened my eyes and saw that I was suspended in the center of a sphere of light high above the
street. I could see through the sphere, and I looked at the
riot below me. The shouts and screams had become one
loud rumble.*

*I thought that I was dead, that I had left my body.
But then I felt a vibration in the sphere that surrounded
me, and a voice burrowed into my head, saying, "You
must remain until twenty-five years have passed."*

*The sphere carried me higher and flew me home, de-
positing me in my bed here in Topeka. When I awoke the
next morning, there was blood on my pillow from a cut
on my lower lip, and I had a bruise on my forehead. I
covered the bruise with makeup and went to work.*

*I have thought about it a lot, and I am sure that I
know what the sphere of light meant: I am to die on the
twenty-fifth anniversary of the death of Buddy Holly.*

*It is not an easy thing to know when you will die,
even if it will not happen until 1984. That is why I had
to tell you, Mikey—you, who must think of death every
day and find a way to live with it. I am sorry to give
you more.*

*And now that I have written it, I will find a way to
live with it myself. Pretending that I don't know will, I*

think, be the wisest course. Whatever works.

I read those paragraphs over and over again.

"Why didn't you tell me too?" I murmured.

But I knew that Mother never would have told me anything that she wasn't even able to tell her diary. Besides, I had been eight years old. I couldn't have understood. Now I was twenty-nine, and I still couldn't.

When I heard Pete's truck drive up outside, I gathered the letters and replaced them in the metal box, glad that I had finished before he had returned. Then I stood and opened the blinds over the window to the left of the desk. Pete had stepped out of the truck and was petting an enormous Doberman pinscher with a galvanized chain collar.

I yelled and burst out of the room, colliding with Gretchen, who shoved me into a wall. "Watch where you're going, lardbrain," she said.

Mike and Laura appeared in the kitchen doorway. "Is something wrong, Mr. Vale?" Laura asked.

"Do you own a rifle?" I gasped.

"Dad has a shotgun," Mike said, "but I hid the shells so he wouldn't hurt himself."

"Find them! My neighbors' dog is here!"

The sound of the back door slamming shut echoed through the house. "Hey, kids, look what I've got," Pete called. "I gave him a piece of jerky, and he seems to have decided that I'm God." A moment later he came into the dining room with Ringo trotting by his side.

I tried to become part of the wall. "Are you crazy?" I shrieked. "That's the monster that bit off my tail pipe!"

Pete looked at me and back to the dog. "No kidding?"

Gretchen got down on her knees and began petting the Doberman. "I don't care," she said. "He saved my butt from the Bald Avenger, and yours too."

"Only so he could have us for himself," I said. "It was one killer battling another."

"Yeah, some killer," Gretchen said, reaching up to scratch behind Ringo's ears. His eyes were closed, and his bobbed tail was wagging.

"He's beautiful," Laura said, joining Gretchen in petting him.

Mike crossed his arms. "Looks like a four-legged Gestapo officer."

"Oh, shut up," Laura said. "He can't help that."

"Who's the Bald Avenger?" Pete asked.

"Somebody who's after me," I said. "Just like Ringo's been after me."

Mike gave me a look. " 'Ringo'?"

"I told you, he belongs to my neighbors. That's what they call him."

Mike looked back at the Doberman. "I don't see the resemblance. Still, a dog named Ringo isn't likely to be a fascist." He joined Gretchen and Laura in stroking the animal, which quivered with pleasure.

"Don't trust him," I said. I was beginning to feel foolish for standing against the wall while everyone else was falling all over the creature. "I'm telling you, this dog ate a chunk of my motorcycle and has been following me ever since."

Pete went into the living room and sat on the couch. "Oliver, are you claiming that Ringo left Topeka at the same time as you and followed you all the way here?"

"That's right."

"I see. Do his owners mistreat him?"

"I have no idea," I said, "but I don't see how they could. *Look* at him!"

Pete did. "He's big, but that doesn't mean much. I

know dogs, and I wouldn't have let this one into my home if he hadn't given me good vibes."

"*Good vibes?* From a Doberman that bites through—"

"Yeah, yeah, yeah," Gretchen said. She was still petting Ringo. "You know, Vale, you're a real eighties kind of guy—a complete pussy."

"Can we keep him, Dad?" Mike asked. "The dog, I mean."

"I knew who you meant," Pete said.

"Well, can we?" Laura asked. "You've been saying ever since Puck died that we ought to have another dog."

Pete leaned back and looked up at the ceiling. "If Ringo has run this far from home since Thursday night, he either really hates his owners or really loves Oliver. And since he and Oliver don't seem to be pals, I guess it's the former. If he wants to stick around here, he's welcome."

Mike and Laura made various noises of thanks while Gretchen went to sit beside Pete. "Good decision," she said, patting his knee.

"Look at his eyes!" I cried.

Laura took Ringo's massive head in her hands. "Come on, boy," she said. "Let's reassure Mr. Vale. Open your eyes. Mike, stop petting him or he'll keep them closed."

Mike stopped petting, and Ringo opened his eyes. He looked at me, and I saw that his left eye was as I remembered—black, with a blue spark in its center. The right eye, though, had changed. It was blue, and almost human-looking.

"Dad, did you notice these before?" Laura asked. She turned Ringo's head so that he was facing Pete.

Pete frowned. "Didn't look straight at them until now."

"Me either," Gretchen said. She sounded less brash
than usual.

Laura held Ringo's eyelids open with her thumbs.
"There, boy, it's all right, I just want to look closer. That's
a good— Oh!"

Ringo's right eye had popped out and was rolling
across the carpet.

Mike picked it up. "Hey, it isn't slimy."

"And Ringo doesn't seem to mind that it's gone,"
Laura said. The Doberman was licking her hands and
wagging his stump so hard that he swayed back and forth.
"In fact, he seems glad about it."

Gretchen shuddered. "God, how gross!"

"Spoken like an eighties woman," Mike said dryly.

I relaxed a little. "Laura, you're the scientist," I said.
"Is the mutt a robot?"

She was probing gingerly around Ringo's remaining
eye. "Well, that might explain how he was able to bite
through metal, if in fact he did. . . ."

I remembered that I still had Ringo's missing tooth
in a Moonsuit pocket, so I ran back to the utility room
to retrieve it. When I returned, Mike was shining a penlight into Ringo's eye socket, and Laura was peering inside.

"It's pink," she said. "But there's a crosshatch of fine
silver wires set into the flesh."

"And the rear half of the eyeball has a silvery coat-
ing," Mike said.

Ringo was standing stock-still. "That's one patient
dog," Pete said. "Hard to believe he attacked you, Oliver."

"I have evidence," I said, holding up the tooth.

Laura took it from me, examined it, and then pushed
her fingers in between Ringo's lips.

I started toward her, intending to pull her away from
those Doberman jaws, but Mike pointed the penlight at

my face, stopping me. "She knows what she's doing, Mr. Vale," he said. "She knows animals, like Dad. Besides which, she's a genius."

"That's the first compliment you've ever given me," Laura said as she pried Ringo's mouth open.

"It wasn't a compliment," Mike said. "Both of the traits I mentioned are inherited, so you aren't responsible for them. In all things for which you *are* responsible, such as social duty and political awareness, you're a miserable failure."

"Uh-huh," Laura said. "Look, there's the same silver crosshatch on the roof of his mouth. And the upper right canine is missing." She began screwing the tooth back into place. "Some of the socket threads are stripped, but it's going in. It'll be a little crooked, but I don't think it'll jab his lip."

"If he's a robot, what would it matter?" Mike asked.

Laura stood and patted Ringo, who nuzzled her hand.

"He's not a robot," Laura said. "He acts like a dog, smells like a dog, and slobbers like a dog." She wiped her hand on Mike's shirtsleeve, and he pretended to ignore it. "Dad, I'd like to take him to my room and try a few experiments. Nothing physical, just radio-frequency stuff. I want to see if that crosshatch is an antenna. Also, I should try to reinsert his eye."

"Be sure you don't hurt him," Pete said. "He's got a sweet disposition, but that doesn't mean he won't get mad."

Laura nodded. "C'mon, Ringo, let's see what makes you tick." She started for the basement door, and Ringo followed.

"I'd better go along to keep her humane," Mike said. "She might cut his skull open just out of curiosity. Besides, I have the eye." He went into the stairwell after Laura and Ringo, shutting the door behind him.

Pete stood and started for the kitchen. "He's probably hungry and thirsty. I'll see what I can find." As he
passed me, he said, "Oh, yeah—I got your spark plugs."

Gretchen followed him. "Need a hand, Mr. Holden?"
she asked.

"Sure, if you like," he answered. "When we're done
with this, I'll call the Lawton depot for tomorrow's bus
schedule. I thought about driving you in when I made
my trip this afternoon, but I didn't want to wake you."

"There's no hurry," Gretchen said, sounding bi-
zarrely sweet.

I went to the couch and sat down, picking up the
remote control for Pete's TV from an end table. As long
as I had to wait a bit longer for Peggy Sue to be repaired, I wanted to see what Buddy was up to. He might
even take my mind off the fact that I was in the same
house with Ringo. Vibes or no vibes, I still didn't trust
the beast.

The Sony wouldn't come to life when I punched the
button on the remote, and when I went to the set to investigate, I discovered that it was unplugged. I remembered then that my own remote-controlled Sony had
refused to stay off for more than several seconds, while
both of the nonremote-controlled motel televisions I had
seen since leaving home had turned on and off with no
trouble. Whoever or whatever had taken over video
broadcasts had also managed to take over remote con-
trols, perhaps by periodically zapping the planet with
split-second bursts of infrared radiation. Except that infrared radiation couldn't go through walls. . . .

I stopped trying to figure it out. What was, was. *How*
was irrelevant. That would be a bad attitude for someone like Laura, but for me, it was the only one possible.

I plugged in the set and returned to the couch while

the picture tube resolved into an image of Buddy lying on his back in the dust. His hands were clasped behind his head and his knees were raised; his guitar lay beside him. As I watched, he crossed his right ankle over his left knee and began humming. His right foot bobbed.

I had never before heard the tune that he hummed. When he stopped and started over again, changing some notes, I realized that Buddy Holly was writing a new song before my eyes. I leaned forward, fascinated, and hardly noticed when Pete and Gretchen walked by and went downstairs.

Softly, Buddy began to sing. "I got a girl from Jupiter, she comes from outer space." He paused, scratched the bridge of his nose under the glasses frame, and sat up cross-legged. Then he picked up the Strat and began strumming. "And if she had a mind to, she could change the human race."

He stopped playing, frowned, then began again, faster. "And I'll sing, whoa-oh! fly a little bit higher, gonna ride a rocket with a flame so bright. Whoa-oh! gonna let her take me with her, gonna ride a ragin' rocket to the stars tonight."

Buddy stopped strumming, then looked out and grinned at me. "Could be worse," he said.

I grinned back, feeling as though I were up there with him.

Then somebody pounded on the front door, and I snapped back to Earth. I hit the remote, and Buddy disappeared.

"Hey, Pete!" a deep voice boomed. "Pete Holden! You home or what?"

I stood to head for another room, and as I did, I caught a glimpse of the man outside through the translucent curtain over the picture window. He was wearing a uniform and a gun.

The TV popped on again. Buddy was strumming.

The stairwell door opened, and Pete and Ringo came into the living room. Ringo's ears were stiff, and his left eye was open wide. His right eye was still missing.

"Maybe you ought to go downstairs," Pete said to me, gesturing toward the stairwell with his thumb.

I stepped onto the landing, shutting the door behind me. I didn't go downstairs, though, because I wanted to hear what happened.

The front door opened. Ringo growled.

"Hello, Pete," the deep voice said. "Sorry to bother you on a Sunday, but the boss says deputy sheriffs ain't got a Sabbath."

"That's okay, Curt. You want to come in?"

"Better not take the time. Your dog doesn't seem to want me to anyway. How long've you had him?"

"Just today. He's a stray, but I think we're going to keep him. He and the kids hit it off."

"Well, good. How are your kids these days, anyway?"

I was going nuts. Why couldn't the guy just get to what he wanted, the way city Authorities did?

"The usual," Pete said. "Laura's brilliant, and Mike's gonna change the world."

The deputy chuckled. "If he were brilliant too, he'd know better."

Buddy began singing his song about the girl from Jupiter again, at a faster tempo. I heard Pete walk across the room, and Buddy stopped abruptly. Ringo was growling steadily now.

"Uh, guess I'd better not waste too much more of your time," the deputy said as Pete returned. "I just need to ask if you've seen anyone on a motorcycle."

"Lots of times. The Harrisons down the road own four."

"Yeah, right, but see, we got a report this morning

from some snowbirds on their way to Texas. They said
they saw Oliver Vale—you know, the one who did *that*"—
I imagined him nodding at the TV—"about eight miles
from here, out on sixty-five. Wondered if you'd seen anything like that."

Pete clicked his tongue. "Curt, folks are getting so
upset over doing without their boob tubes that they'll
think anybody on a bike is Vale. Those snowbirds probably saw one of the Harrisons."

The deputy coughed. "Well, uh, Pete, I talked to the
Harrisons and looked at their motorcycles. Didn't fit the
description. Besides which, they don't ride at three in
the morning, do they?"

"No, I guess not."

"Me neither. And, well, Pete, Mrs. Harrison said you
drove your truck past at about that time. She had in-
somnia and was in the kitchen, and when the truck went
past, she looked out and thought she saw something in
the back that might've been a motorcycle."

There was a brief silence. "Let me get this straight,
Curt," Pete said then. "You think I'm actually Oliver
Vale and that I took over every TV in the world because
I'm a Buddy Holly fan."

The deputy chuckled again, but nervously. " 'Course
not, but I've gotta check things out."

"Okay, you've checked."

Another silence. "You know, Pete, I remember that
back in high school you used to get out of trouble by
taking the teacher's question and giving it a sort of judo
throw. You never lied, but you never answered quite
straight. You're doing the same thing now."

Ringo snarled, and his collar rattled.

"Hey, down, boy!" Pete cried. "Sit! Good dog!"

"He doesn't like me much, does he?" the deputy said.

"Guess not."

The deputy sighed. "So I guess I'll go check out another report. To tell you the truth, I don't want to catch
the sumbitch even if he is around here somewhere. People in town are so foul-tempered about this business that
we're thinking about asking for Guard troops to keep
'em from busting things up. If we apprehended Vale and
tried to keep him in temporary custody in our jail, we'd
be buried in the rubble before the Federal boys could
catch a plane."

"Sounds like it's lucky for you that you haven't found
him," Pete said.

There was a final silence, and then the deputy said,
"Yeah, real lucky. See you, Pete. And congratulations
on the new dog. He ought to keep the place good
and safe."

"You know it." The door closed.

I waited, listening to be sure that the deputy was
gone. I was poked in the ribs from behind and almost
fell down the stairs.

"He's gone, turkeybutt," Gretchen said.

I went into the living room. Pete was standing beside the closed front door, scratching Ringo behind
the ears.

"Think Curt is satisfied?" I asked.

Pete shook his head. "He won't be back today, but
he'll keep thinking about it until he's sure you're here,
and then he'll show up with a buddy or two. Tomorrow
afternoon, maybe. We'll have you out of here by then."

Unexpectedly, Ringo, who had looked relaxed, jerked
his head away from Pete and pricked up his ears. Then,
with a sharp bark, he bounded past me and Gretchen
and barreled down the basement stairs.

"What's with him?" Gretchen asked, as if Pete or I
should know.

Pete followed Ringo. "Mike! Laura!" he shouted as he entered the stairwell. "Everything all right down there?"

Laura answered. "Sure, Dad. I've been broadcasting a beep signal on different frequencies to see if Ringo would respond, and he just did."

Pete came out of the stairwell, and then Laura, Mike, and Ringo appeared as well.

"He won't let us put the blue eye back," Mike said.

"Because it isn't his," I said. "Both of his eyes used to be like the one he still has. I don't know how he came to have the one that popped out."

"If he doesn't want it back by tomorrow, I'm taking it apart," Laura said. "In the meantime, I'll see if I can rig a radio dog whistle. A garage-door remote would be perfect, but Dad's always been too cheap to buy an electric opener."

"Now you know why," Pete said. "You'd have torn it apart and put it back together as something else, and I'd still have to open the garage by hand."

I went to the Moonsuit and retrieved my garage-door remote control. I figured that I might as well let Laura have it, since I doubted that I had a house or garage left anyway. An enraged populace had surely torn the place apart by now. I mourned for my record collection.

Laura accepted the remote control with what seemed to be uncharacteristic shyness, and then she, Mike, and Ringo disappeared downstairs again.

Pete stretched. "Well, Peggy Sue won't fix herself." He looked at Gretchen. "Miss Laird, I hope you don't mind staying another night. I'd take you to Lawton now, but getting Oliver on the road again is more urgent."

Gretchen smiled brightly. It looked weird on her. "I don't mind at all, Pete," she said, "but I wish you'd stop calling me 'Miss Laird.' As long as I'm freeloading, you might as well call me by my first name."

Pete glanced at me. "Uh, sure," he said.

He and I went out to the garage. "Looks like you've got a girlfriend if you want one," I said.

Pete grunted and turned on the lights. "She's a little young for me. Like about twenty years."

"She doesn't seem to mind."

He gave me a narrow-eyed look. "You're a lot closer to her generation than I am. Why don't *you* make a move?"

"Because one, she hates my guts, and two, she scares the piss out of me."

Pete laughed. "Well, she doesn't scare me, but she sure makes me feel old. She was probably nursing at her momma's breast in a condo while your uncle and I were sucking on reefer in a pit latrine." He shook his head. "Too much distance there."

"I'm not so sure," I said, nodding toward the Oklahoma Kamikaze. "I think she could relate to a '68 Barracuda. She respects physical power. And mentally, she's closer to your age than she is to mine. It's clear she prefers you."

"You sound jealous," he said, taking the new spark plugs from a paper bag. "No reason you should be, though. After all, she's only a mortal. Why should you want that when you have an Ariel?"

"Don't let Gretchen hear that comparison. She's already accused me of preferring motorcycles to women. I think her basic assumption is that men, or at least men who ride bikes, are all misogynist perverts."

Pete squatted beside Peggy Sue. "I wasn't comparing women and motorcycles. I was comparing natural with supernatural, using Gretchen as an example of the natural and your Ariel as an example of the supernat-

ural. Even if Gretchen were to attach herself to you, her
aid would only be physical. But with the Ariel, why,
you're Prospero—you can command your airy spirit to
conjure up a tempest."

I stared at him. "Pretty mystical for a welder who
drives a Barracuda."

"Not really. I don't smoke dope anymore, but when
I did, I smoked a *lot*."

"And that gave you insight into the supernatural?"

He shrugged. "I don't know. But I get feelings for
things. For example, when Laura figured out that you
were in the area last night, I was already getting ready
to leave, because I *knew* you were close. I was even pretty
sure which stretch of road we'd find you on."

"Did you know Gretchen would be with me?"

"Nope. She was a surprise."

Pete finished inserting and connecting the plugs
while I thought about what he had said about Ariel and
Prospero. I had taken a Shakespeare class at KSU before dropping out, and *The Tempest* had been one of the
plays I'd read. It began to come back to me.

"Peggy Sue isn't like Prospero's Ariel," I said. "This
Ariel is only a machine."

"Is that why you gave her a name and call her 'she'
instead of 'it'?"

"It's not like I really believe it, Pete. *I* never smoked
a lot of dope."

"Maybe you should have." Pete stood, wiped his
hands on a rag, and gestured at the bike. "Give her
a try."

I got on and gave Peggy Sue a few kicks. She didn't
even come close to starting. "Think the choke needs help?"
I asked. Pete nodded and found a screwdriver, and I got
off the bike so he could tinker with it.

I watched, chewing my lip, and finally said what I

was thinking. "Prospero had to set Ariel free at the end
of the play."

"That's true," Pete said. "But only after Ariel had
done everything he'd asked of it."

" 'It'?"

"What would you call an airy spirit?" He stood and
gestured for me to try the bike again.

I straddled the motorcycle and put my foot on the
starter. "I'm not sure," I said.

"Liar."

He was right. I would call an airy spirit "she."

Peggy Sue started on the first kick. She sounded
better than she had at any moment since we'd left home.

I killed the engine. "Guess I should be going," I said,
and found that I didn't want to. My fervor to reach Buddy's gravesite had been subdued by comfort and security.

"Not just yet," Pete said. "You should wait until deep
night. Besides, it's almost time for supper."

We returned to the house, where Mike and Gretchen
were preparing salad and baked chicken. They weren't
getting along. As Pete and I came into the kitchen,
Gretchen said that the country would never find another
president to match Reagan, and Mike responded by saying, "Yeah, cue-card readers are hard to find."

I think Gretchen was about to stab Mike with a car-
rot peeler when Pete upbraided his son for being rude.
He concluded by saying, "Political arguments have no
place in the kitchen. Kitchens are for food." This was
directed as much toward Gretchen as it was toward Mike,
and I was glad to see her look abashed. She could do it
better than I would have guessed.

While waiting to eat, Pete and I sat at the table and
listened to the kitchen radio. The latest news was not
good. The riots in the cities were getting worse—an un-

determined number of people in New York City had been killed—because mobs hungry for Sunday evening movies had stormed theaters and fought over tickets. And now the U.S. Naval Observatory had confirmed reports that the primary Buddy Holly broadcast signal did indeed originate on Ganymede. The worldwide frustration of having no TV (other than Buddy) was rapidly becoming compounded by the fear of an extraterrestrial invasion.

"Personally," Pete said, "I would've been surprised if they'd discovered that the unknown Buddy Holly fan *wasn't* an alien intelligence."

"All I know is that *I* didn't have anything to do with it," I said. "In fact, with this news, even the FCC must realize that I'm innocent."

"Either that, or they think that you're an extraterrestrial," Mike said. "And they won't be the only ones. If I were you, I'd watch out for the Corps of Little David and for Bavarian villagers carrying torches."

"And for the Bald Avenger," Gretchen said.

"In any case," Mike said, "if the news media have only now confirmed the source of the signals, you can bet that our government and others have known it for a day or more. Your pursuers don't want to incarcerate you; rather, they want to hand you over to the latter-day equivalents of mad scientists and have you dissected."

Laura came into the kitchen. "Who's dissecting what?"

"Here's one now," Mike said. "Run for your life."

Laura gave him a puzzled look, then came to the table and sat in the chair beside me. She put my garage-door remote control in front of me.

"You can call Ringo from up to half a mile away," she said, pressing the bar.

Ringo romped into the room, put his front paws on the tabletop, and nosed the remote control into my lap.

"Impressive," Pete said.

"Uh, yeah," I mumbled, drawing back from Ringo's fetid breath and picking up the remote. "You should keep this, Laura. Ringo's staying with you, right?"

Laura frowned. "Aren't you too, Mr. Vale?"

Pete cleared his throat. "Oliver's got to get on to Lubbock, honey."

"I know," she said. "But he's coming back, isn't he? Since he's your friend's nephew, I thought . . ." Her voice trailed off.

Pete gave me a meaningful look. "He's welcome here any time, as one of the family. But he has his own home too."

I wasn't sure that was true anymore, but I didn't say so. Instead, I held out the remote control to Laura.

She shook her head. "I want you to have it. You can use it whenever you visit. It'll help you and Ringo become friends." She stood and patted the dog, who lowered his front paws to the floor, and then she crossed the room and looked into the oven.

I left the table and went to the utility room to replace the remote in its Moonsuit pocket. Pete followed.

"She has a crush on you," he said.

"I don't know why."

"Me either. Hell, what father ever knows his daughter's mind? But my guess is that she sees you as some romantic, questing Don Quixote figure."

"Don Quixote was a deluded fool."

"Uh-huh."

"Don't worry about it," I said. "I won't do anything to encourage her. Even if she weren't your daughter, she's way too young."

"Got that right," Pete said. He looked at the floor

and stroked his lower lip. "Y'know, it just occurred to me that there's a smaller age difference between you and Laura than there is between me and Gretchen."

"Laura's sixteen. Gretchen's twenty-three. The comparison isn't valid."

"Maybe not, but it's still a sobering thought."

"Not as sobering as the thought that the human race is trapped under the thumb of extraterrestrial video dictators."

"Says you. Bug-eyed monsters are easy compared to women."

I disagreed. It seemed to me that they were about the same.

From the kitchen, Mike called, "Supper!"

During the meal, I had no thought of the rioting in the cities or of those who might be behind it. I sat with the Holdens, and with Gretchen, and even with Ringo, and savored the chicken. Whatever would happen to me was coming fast, and time was draining like water, but I relaxed in that house in Oklahoma and took my time. Time, after all, is an illusion. At least, that's what they say.

CATHY AND JEREMY

Jeremy clapped a hand over his dog-eye and gasped.

Cathy glanced at him as she drove. "What is it?"

Jeremy swallowed. "He's gone. The eye-link has been removed."

Cathy clutched the steering wheel. "You can't feel him? You can't see what he sees?"

Jeremy shook his head.

Cathy drove on for another mile, then said, "But you

know how he got to where he is now, right?"

Jeremy popped out the dog-eye. It glistened in his palm like a black jewel. "I think I saw the whole route in his memory. I think I can remember it."

"All right, then. Are we still on track?"

Jeremy looked out at the countryside. "We're in Oklahoma," he murmured.

"I *know* that. Are we still on Ringo's route?"

"I think so."

Cathy glared. "I wish you'd stop saying that. Saying 'I think' is like saying 'I'm guessing.'"

Jeremy replaced the dog-eye in his socket. "Still nothing. Damn it, Cath, I might as well be guessing. Even if I can get us to where Ringo and Vale were when the link was cut, Vale won't be there anymore."

"If he's not, we'll catch up at Lubbock."

Jeremy gave her a grim look. "He'll never reach Lubbock. If he leaves his current hiding place, he'll be lynched before reaching Texas."

"You don't know that."

"If I don't, then what am I doing here? And if you don't, what are *you* doing here?"

Cathy's jaw muscles bulged. "I'm driving," she said. "And you're whining."

Jeremy popped out the dog-eye again and placed it in his shirt pocket. "Not anymore," he said.

RINGO

The girl named Laura gave him the supper leftovers, and although he wasn't hungry, he ate enthusiastically. While he was eating, the boy, Mike, attempted to replace the human-eye, but Ringo turned his head so the thing wouldn't go in. With its removal, the last of his wariness of these people had vanished, and he had realized that the eye was what had made him suspicious of people in the first place. He had only used the Windex incident as a rationalization. His reaction to the man named Boog had been the true one.

He had made up his mind: He would stay with the Holdens. He wouldn't miss Cathy and Jeremy.

The only uneasiness that he felt now was a sense of guilt for having damaged Vale's motorcycle. Pete, Laura, and Mike Holden all liked Ringo, as did the woman named Gretchen, but Vale was still wary.

So when the people went to lounge in the living room, Ringo trotted in and lay at Vale's feet. Vale stiffened. To reassure him, Ringo sat up and licked his hand. Vale made a noise in his throat, and Ringo realized that the man thought he was being tasted.

Gretchen laughed and called Vale a name.

Ringo knew now that it would take more than friendly gestures to make Vale his friend. It would take a gift.

He belched his last can of Budweiser onto Vale's lap. All of the people were immediately interested.

"Looks like a peace offering," Pete said.

Ringo barked to indicate that Pete was right.

"Uh, well, uh, thanks," Vale said. He was still nervous, but at least he was smiling.

"Well, aren't you going to open it?" Pete asked.

Vale picked up the can and popped the tab, and beer sprayed everywhere. The people yelped like puppies.

When the can stopped spraying, everyone was spattered with white flecks. Mike and Laura went to the kitchen for paper towels. Ringo sniffed the can in Vale's hand and found that it was empty.

He lay down and put his head on his paws. His gift

had been worthless. Vale would dislike him more than ever now.

Instead, Vale leaned down, laughing, and patted Ringo's back. "Listen," he said, "it's the thought that counts."

Ringo raised his head and let his tongue hang out. He had been forgiven. Everything in his world was good.

9

OLIVER

I graduated from high school in 1977 at the age of
seventeen. It had been a good spring, the highlight being
when a friend and I drove to Lawrence to hear Lynyrd
Skynyrd on the KU campus. Seeing Ronnie Van Zant
and the band perform their fourteen-minute-plus concert version of "Free Bird" was a transcendental experience. I was probably the only member of the audience,
though, who felt guilty because he hadn't brought his
mother along. She would have appreciated the show more
than most of the people there.

Following commencement (my four-year GPA was
2.8; I was forty-third in a class of a hundred and twelve),
I went to work hauling hay. Tossing bales at four cents
apiece was dirty, sweaty, itchy work . . . work to sweat
the poison out, as my custom-cutter boss said. I and the
other four guys on the crew alternated between complaining that the baler was packing the bales too heavy,
and bragging about how well we were going to do with
the women come fall. All of us would be going away to

college, and none of us were able to think of that event
in any context other than sex. Or if we were, we didn't
talk about it.

I was heading for Kansas State University in Manhattan. The campus was only fifty-five miles west of Topeka, but Mother seemed to think it was on the dark
side of Neptune. She couldn't believe that I was grown-
up enough to leave home. (This was the same woman
who had given me a box of prophylactics for my fifteenth
birthday.)

Mother's UFO/Atlantis/occult obsessions had been
getting worse, leaning toward spiritualism and entrail
reading, and as my departure date drew near, she began
holding seances in the basement. I made it a point not
to learn the names of any of the middle-aged women who
joined her for these things, and I counted the minutes
until I could jump into my '69 Dart and head west.

It's easy now to look back at my seventeen-year-old
self and feel ashamed, particularly after reading some
of Mother's thoughts as recorded in Volume VI:

I am thirty-six years old. I have no husband or lover.
Since 1959—except for one brief interlude with a man
named Keith—only three things have mattered in my life:
my son; rock and roll; and a belief that beings with pow-
ers beyond those of Earth will someday come in their ships
of light to transform the world. Now my son is leaving
home (hard to comprehend that he is the same age that I
was when I became pregnant with him), and I am too old
and solitary to make a life of rock 'n' roll, for it is the
music of youthful tribes. In fact, because he was con-
ceived in that energy, the last of the music may leave me
when my son leaves. All that will be left is what Oliver
calls my "weirdnesses." All that will be left is the hope
that human beings will not be allowed to mangle them-
selves.

I'll still have my records. But what is music if you listen to it alone?

Even if I were younger, I couldn't rejoin the tribes, for the tribes have dissolved. The stuff the kids listen to these days ("disco") would drive me to self-evisceration in a matter of hours. Even KKAP plays it; I wear ear-plugs at my desk. I have begun haunting used record stores after work so that I can buy the artifacts that may soon be extinct. Thank Chuck, my son was raised right. He is leaving, but he is leaving with the Beatles, not the Bee Gees, in his heart. C. would be proud.

I will miss him.

Meanwhile, I was having the best summer of my life. I was making money, and the work became easier as the summer progressed. My stamina increased each day and made the bales seem ever lighter. Hard work does that for you when you're seventeen. Shirtless, I swung my hay hook as if it were a part of me and tossed seventy-pound bales onto a flatbed as if they were made of cotton candy. My arms and back became brown, and my sweat smelled of salt and prairie hay.

What was mainly responsible for my joy, however, was a girl named Cheryl. She was the cousin of one of the guys on the hauling crew, and on Friday, July 1, she came out to the field where we were working and, as a favor to his mother, gave him the lunch that he had forgotten that morning.

Sun-blonded. Tanned skin. Cutoff jean shorts. Long legs. White blouse not buttoned all the way.

"Owwww," one of the guys groaned as we watched her crossing the greenish-brown expanse of the field.

All of us, with the possible exception of her cousin, wanted her—and I, with my ridiculous black-framed glasses, was the one who got her. I asked her out before

I knew what I was doing, and she said yes.

Cheryl and I went out every Saturday night for the next seven weeks, and starting with Week Two we clambered into the Dart's back seat and screwed like maniacs. The first time really was my first time. She was patient up to a point and then aggressive. I was grateful.

I had always thought that I would have to rely on pity to have a First Time, but the actual event was more like a delirium-induced coincidence: Cheryl and I happened to meet while we were each experiencing intense late-adolescent summer horniness, and so neither of us had a choice, nor wanted any. It would never happen that way again.

I used a condom the first time, and most of the others. My fifteenth birthday present notwithstanding, I'd had too many nightmares about accidental babies to do otherwise. On August 13 (Week Seven), however, Cheryl and I had the luxury of her bed because her parents and siblings were at the movies, and we were stripped and tangled before I realized that the Peacocks were still out in the Dart. Cheryl, undaunted, untangled and dashed from the room, returning with a can of foam from her parents' dresser. I was horrified, but she only laughed and gave me my next lesson.

There was one week of hay hauling left, and I would leave for Manhattan the next Sunday, so after making a mess with the foam, Cheryl and I made plans for a last summer romp together. We would meet on Saturday, August 20, drive to Perry Reservoir, and spend the night there. It would be our last time together until I came back to Topeka for a weekend visit. Then we would pick up where we left off.

So we told each other; but Week Seven, in Cheryl's bed, was the last. If I had known, I would have stayed

longer and made love to her again despite my fear that
her parents would return.

But I didn't know, for I had no way of divining that
in Memphis, Tennessee, the forty-two-year-old King of
Rock and Roll had less than three days left to live.

On Tuesday, August 16, the hay crew hauled late
into the evening because we were all leaving the next
Sunday and still had several fields to clear. The portable
radio's batteries died before sundown, so I didn't hear
the news until I got home. Ready Teddy greeted me, as
always, by performing a mad dance punctuated by yips.
He had grown into a cocker-spaniel-size, dustmop-col-
ored mutt, and I loved him. I would miss him while I
was at K-State. He and I went into the house, and I
headed for the bathroom.

But Mother was in there, and she had the door
locked, so I went into the kitchen to have a can of soda
and to wait. I waited thirty-five minutes, and at a quarter
to ten I returned to the bathroom and knocked on
the door.

"Are you all right?" I called.

Silence.

Heart attack, I thought. *Stroke. A slip in the tub.
Concussion. Coma. Death.*

"Mother! Answer me or I'll break down the door!"

The latch clicked, the knob turned, and the door
opened. Mother stood in the doorway, still wearing her
radio-station-secretary clothes.

I rolled my eyes and leaned against the wall. "Jesus, Mother, I thought you were dead or something."

She looked at me steadily, and I saw that the rims
of her eyelids were red.

"Why do you always call me 'Mother'?" she asked.
"Why haven't I ever been 'Mom'? Not even once, not even

when you were little, have you ever called me 'Mom.' "

"I, uh, I don't know," I said.

She nodded, as if I had said what she had expected, and stepped into the hall.

"Elvis is dead," she said.

Then she turned away and walked to her bedroom. She went inside and closed the door. I stood in the hall, not thinking, not doing anything. Ready Teddy came to me, his toenails clicking on the hardwood, and nuzzled my hand.

Eventually, I took a shower and went to bed. That night I dreamed of a bloated corpse singing "Hound Dog." Naked, it writhed on its back, its fingers coming off as they clawed at the stage. Cheryl appeared wearing nothing but cutoff jeans and went down on the corpse, her breasts bobbing with the music. I awoke in the dark, my chest thundering, my erection hard as diamond.

I was still awake when the alarm went off at 5:00 A.M. I got up, dressed in jeans and a T-shirt, fed Ready Teddy, and ate cereal and toast. I heard the newspaper hit the driveway just before 5:30, and I went out for it. Before bringing it inside, I read the front-page head-lines. One of them was HEART ATTACK CLAIMS ELVIS PRESLEY. It was not in particularly big type.

I took the paper inside and found Mother in the living room. She was wearing her terry-cloth robe and kneeling before the album rack. Her copies of *The Sun Sessions, Elvis Is Back!*, and *Elvis—TV Special* lay on the carpet beside her.

"The station got rid of a lot of records last year," she said, "so I thought I'd take some of ours, just for today. The disc jockeys will want them."

"Good idea," I said. I lay the paper on the coffee table and left for the fields.

All through the hot day, the guys and I listened to
the radio that was hung over the truck's outside mirror.
On every station we tuned in, even the country ones, we
heard Elvis; but only KKAP was playing the really good
stuff, the stuff he'd recorded in the days before the high-
collared, jeweled jumpsuits . . . back when he was Elvis
the Pelvis, every boy's sexual role model and every girl's
fantasy.

"If I hear 'Love Me Tender' one more time I'm gonna
puke," someone said.

That evening, Cheryl called. "I've been thinking
about this Saturday," she said. Her voice dripped with
promise. "I've been thinking about it so much that I can't
wait until then. I know it's late and you've been working, but . . . let's go for a drive."

I had been tired, but Cheryl's voice revitalized me.
I said that I would pick her up in ten minutes, and
then I ran to my room for my car keys and a couple of
Peacocks.

"Mother!" I yelled as I charged back through the
house. "I'm going out!" I had my hand on the knob of
the front door before I realized that there had been no
answer. Mother always answered.

I yelled again, and still there was no answer, so I
looked for her. She wasn't in the house, but her '74 Nova
was still in the garage.

I found her in the backyard. She was sitting on the
ground and gazing up at the just-emerged stars.

"You're going to get chiggers," I said.

She remained silent.

"Mother, Cheryl called. We're going for a drive."

Still she said nothing.

I glanced up at the patch of sky she seemed to be
gazing at. "What are you looking for?"

"Elvis."

"No such constellation." I was trying to joke. But of course she was serious.

"When Buddy died," she said, as if I had not spoken, "Elvis was in the Army. In Germany. He sent a tele-gram of sympathy to the Holleys, in Lubbock. He'd been on the road a lot too, and he knew that it could have been him."

I turned to go. Cheryl was waiting.

"Elvis played in Lubbock more than once in his early days," Mother said. "He met Buddy before Buddy be-came a star. Buddy was encouraged and inspired by him. They were so different, and so much alike. Elvis sent the telegram from Germany, knowing what had been lost. So I'm looking for him in the sky now, to wave good-bye. He'll appear like a shooting star in reverse. I would have seen Buddy's star too, but it was cloudy that night."

Cheryl was waiting. I turned back and sat down a few yards away from Mother.

"Elvis's star would have appeared yesterday, wouldn't it?" I asked.

"No. A man like Elvis would wait a day, to be sure he was really supposed to go."

We waited and watched. Soon, we saw a meteor.

"There," I said. "We should go in before the chiggers eat us alive."

"That wasn't him. It fell. Elvis will be going the other way."

Another meteor fell then, and another, and another. Later, I discovered that they were the stragglers of the annual Perseid shower, but Mother had another expla-nation. "Ancient Atlanteans," she said. "They're flying down to show Elvis the way."

Chiggers were chewing my ankles, mosquitoes bit-ing my arms and neck. In Topeka, a suntanned girl waited to make love to me, and I was sitting in the backyard, staying with my lunatic mother until her crisis passed. I had the bitter thought that her crisis would never pass until she herself flew up to join Elvis and Buddy, so I might as well take off. Then I hated myself for thinking that, and I knew that I wouldn't budge. Not even to telephone Cheryl and tell her that I couldn't make it.

Hours later, we saw Elvis leave the planet. He was a ball of orange light with flickers of blue that shot up from the southeastern horizon—from Memphis—and disappeared near the zenith. I had never seen anything like it.

Mother waved.

We went inside then. After Mother went to bed, I sat in the kitchen for another hour, staring at the phone. I hadn't heard it ring while I had been in the yard. Cheryl hadn't called to ask where I was, and I couldn't call her now because it was 2:00 A.M. and her parents would throw a shit fit. In three and a half hours I would have to leave for the fields, and it would still be too early to call. I wouldn't have a chance to explain until evening.

And what explanation would I give? That I had preferred sitting in chigger-infested grass to thrashing in a back seat with Cheryl? That I had turned my back on carnal nirvana to watch for the ghost of Elvis?

Thursday dragged on for months, but when it was over, the summer was over too. We cleared our last field, and at 9:45 P.M. I threw the last bale from the truck to my buddies in the hay shed. Our boss told us to come by his place Friday or Saturday, and he'd give us our final checks.

I didn't care about that. All I cared about was getting home and calling Cheryl before it was too late.

Her mother answered the phone and told me that I
shouldn't be calling after ten, and in any event Cheryl
didn't want to speak with me. Before I could protest, or
plead, the line clicked.

I tried again in the morning, and I did speak to
Cheryl this time, but it would have been better if I hadn't.
She and her parents had fought about me on Wednesday
evening, she said. They had charged that I had a crazy
mother and that I was no good either. Then, when I hadn't
shown up for our drive, Cheryl had decided that they
were right.

She told me that she wouldn't keep our rendezvous
the next day because she had another date. I called her
a bitch and slammed down the receiver.

That afternoon I picked up my check and went out
with my hay-hauling buddies. One of them was eighteen, so he took some of our money and converted it into
five cases of Coors. We drank a case, and then we bought
our way into the various topless bars that lined the
southernmost mile of Topeka Boulevard. We drank more
beer at those places (two of which we were thrown out
of because I tried to join the girls onstage) and tipped
lavishly, and when our cash was gone, we went in search
of female companions to help us with our remaining four
cases. We didn't find any. But we were men, we bellowed. We could drink them all ourselves.

I was sick twice that night that I remember, and
probably more times that I don't. My friends went home
before dawn, and I called them all pussies. Sometime
after the sun was well up, I awoke in the Dart on the
edge of a country road. My eyes had been rubbed with
handfuls of sand, my tongue was a lump of dry cotton,
and my stomach was bubbling into my throat. Sections
of my skull were pulling apart. The Dart was full of
empty and half-empty Coors cans, and beer slimed the

seats, the floor, the dash, and the steering wheel. The stench was unbelievable.

I rolled down the window and got my head outside before heaving, but I had emptied myself in the night. The strength I had gained over the summer had drained away, leaving chewed gelatin in place of muscle.

It took me awhile to figure out that I was only a few miles from home. I didn't remember getting there, but was glad that I had. A few miles was as far as I would be able to drive.

I managed to park in the driveway, and then, stooped over because of the agony in my head, I went around to the back door in hopes of avoiding Mother. But I had to go through the kitchen, and she was eating lunch.

"Would you like a sandwich?" she asked.

It made me furious. Just once, I wanted her to act like a real parent. Just once, I wanted to hear the I-sacrificed-to-raise-you-and-now-look-at-what-you've-done speech that everyone I knew had gotten on such occasions. The only speech I had ever gotten was the don't-get-anyone-pregnant one.

"What's the matter with you?" I yelled. "I got *drunk*! I'm underage, and I went to *topless bars*! I stayed out twenty-four hours! Weren't you afraid that I was *dead*?"

"No," she said. "My friends and I held a seance last night. We contacted Elvis, and he told us that you were drinking, but that you would be fine. He said that you would sleep in your car on a country road close to home and that no one would bother you. I asked to talk to Buddy, but Elvis said he didn't see him anywhere."

I went into the bathroom and locked the door behind me. The next day I left for K-State.

I didn't come back until Friday, October 21.

I went to two morning classes that day, and then I

read a newspaper during my lunch break. Afterward, I got into the Dart and headed for home. In so doing, I skipped a Calculus exam and failed to turn in a U.S. History essay.

The newspaper had told me that the night before, a plane had crashed near Gillsburg, Mississippi. Three members of Lynyrd Skynyrd, including Ronnie Van Zant, had been killed. Ronnie had sung "Free Bird" for the last time on earth. His next concert would be in the Spirit Land.

If they had died any other way, I might have stayed in Manhattan. I would have mourned, but I would have taken my exam and turned in the essay. But they had been in a small plane, flying from one gig to another. And three of them had died.

I had been home for two hours when Mother returned from work. She didn't ask why I was there. What she said was, "I'm glad you're here, Buddy." I let it pass.

We didn't sit in the backyard that night. The musicians who had just passed on had not been like Elvis, who had believed in his own immortality. They would not have waited a day before leaving.

When the weekend was over, I went back to K-State and finished the semester, although I received a C in History and a D in Calculus for an eighteenth birthday present. I even started the spring '78 semester, but Fate had decreed that I was destined for something other than a Bachelor's degree. I came home at spring break and didn't go back. By April, I had a job as a salesman at a stereo shop in Topeka.

Mother was delighted that I was home, so I warned her that it would only be until I could afford my own apartment. She said that was fine. Infrequently, but often enough to irritate me, she called me by the name of a dead man.

In June, I went to an ophthalmologist and ordered contact lenses. When they arrived, I put my glasses away in a drawer.

*

I fell asleep on Pete's couch again, so I didn't leave on Sunday night as I was supposed to. When I awoke, it was Monday morning, and I told myself that it had been better to stay at the Holdens' and blow my travel strategy than it would have been to fall asleep at sixty miles per hour. I was rationalizing, but because of the way things were about to happen, I was right. For the wrong reasons.

Mike and Laura were in the dining room arguing with Pete about going to school. "Nobody'll be there today," Mike said. "There's a world crisis in progress, Dad."

"No school closings have been announced on the radio," Pete said.

"So where's the bus?" Laura asked. "It's twenty minutes late."

"Take the Dart," Pete said.

I got up from the couch and staggered toward them. "You have a Dart?"

"Behind the garage," Pete said.

"It's junk," Mike added.

"But it runs," Laura said. She and Mike went out through the kitchen.

"Mother and I used to have a Dart," I said.

Pete looked at me quizzically. "You feel okay?"

I didn't. Not only was I groggy, but I had slept with my contacts in, and my eyes felt like balls of vacuum-cleaner dirt. I shuffled past Pete, through the kitchen, and into the bathroom to try to revive myself. While there, I found my clean laundry folded on the sink counter, so I changed out of Pete's coveralls.

When I emerged, Pete was sitting at the kitchen table drinking coffee. A radio on the table was murmuring to him.

"Guess I lost the advantage of driving at night," I said.

Pete nodded. "Yeah, but I figured that if you were that tired, you weren't in any shape to ride anyway. Daylight or not, though, you have to go now, because my friend Curt will be back." He took a piece of paper from his shirt pocket and dropped it on the table. "I've refueled Peggy Sue and drawn a map of a route to Lubbock that ought to keep you clear of cops."

"I'll pay you for the gas."

"Don't be stupid. Just grab some breakfast and get going. Cereal's in the cupboard, milk's in the fridge."

I went to get the cereal, and Pete turned up the radio.

"—can only speculate on how the grave came to be disturbed," the announcer said, "but the primary theory is that Oliver Vale came to Lubbock and exhumed the casket. No one, however, has any idea of how he could have done so, by himself, while the cemetery was being watched by police officers and several civilian volunteers. One officer was heard to say nothing of this earth could have done such a thing. . . ."

I dashed back to the table.

"Once again, this morning's top story," the announcer said. "In Lubbock, Texas, the grave of Buddy Holly has been discovered open, and the casket is gone. No explanation is apparent, although Oliver Vale is believed to be in the city and is being searched for. We'll have more details as they become available. Meanwhile, the space-based broadcast purporting to be of Holly is continuing to supersede all terrestrial video signals." The announcer paused. "God help us."

Pete turned the radio down to a murmur again.

"Didn't ride to Lubbock and back overnight, did you?"
he asked.

I sat down heavily. "I was going there to see if Buddy
had arisen, and now they tell me that he has. Besides
which, they're searching for me there. . . ." I hadn't
thought beyond my destination, and now that the reason for that destination had been obliterated, I felt pur-
poseless.

"So go home," Pete said.

"What home? It'll be picked to pieces by now."

"You don't know that. But even if it is, you still have
to go back. Now that Lubbock is out, your home is your
only link to what's happening. Buddy's been giving out
your address and telling people to contact you there,
so maybe it isn't you that's important, but the address.
The place."

Something in my brain went *whang*. "Mother's dish,"
I said.

"What's that?"

I stood and began to pace. "The SkyVue satellite dish
she bought in '83. In Volume VII of her diary, just before she died, she claimed that it helped her communicate with a weird 'other world' populated by the ghosts
of ancient Atlanteans. She had done it before with seances, she said, but the dish was better. When she bought
the thing, I thought she only wanted more channels.
Should have known."

Pete stood as well. "That's it, then."

I stared at him. "Pete, my mother was *crazy*."

"So is the idea that Buddy Holly is performing on
Ganymede. Look, I learned from your uncle that when
the universe turns out to be insane, the wise man em-
braces insanity. Your mother's claims for her satellite
dish were crazy when the world was sane, but now they
make as much sense as anything else. Maybe she really

did communicate with another world through that dish. Maybe she put the idea of Buddy Holly into alien beings' heads, or whatever they have instead of heads. Maybe that dish is a link to whoever's responsible for mucking up television—and for pointing a finger at you."

"If that's the case," I said, "then I don't want to go back."

"I'll take the Kamikaze and go with you," Pete said. "If the aliens come for you, we can outrun 'em."

That too was insane, and so it made perfect sense. I agreed to go home, as long as I could ride Peggy Sue while Pete followed in the Kamikaze. I couldn't abandon the Ariel after all we'd been through, could I?

"We'll be conspicuous in daylight, but we can't wait until dark," Pete said. "So let's get going. I'll leave Laura and Mike a note. They're old enough to take care of themselves for a day or two, especially with Ringo for protection."

"What about Gretchen?"

Pete shrugged. "I guess she's old enough to take care of herself too. And I don't think she needs any protection."

We prepared to leave. I was in the Moonsuit and waiting for Pete in the living room when Ringo burst up the basement stairs and began barking furiously.

Pete came out of his bedroom with an olive-drab backpack slung over one shoulder. "What's with the dog?" he asked, raising his voice to be heard over the barking. "Did you hit the button on your remote?"

I was sure that I hadn't. "I put it back in its pocket before supper last night, and I haven't touched it since."

"Maybe you bumped it while you were pulling on your coveralls." He headed toward the basement door. "I'll enter a message for the kids on Laura's computer.

That's the first place she'll go when she gets home." As Pete went downstairs, the Doberman, still barking, went with him. I followed.

Laura's room was dominated by a long table that held a Mac, a video monitor displaying a stretch of country road, and oscilloscopes, receivers, transmitters, and other gadgets, including Ringo's blue eye.

"Impressive, huh?" Pete said as he sat down at the Mac and began typing. "I paid for the flying lessons, but she bought all of this herself. She does systems consulting at eighty bucks an hour, when she can get it." He saw me looking at the video monitor. "The road surveillance camera was Mike's idea. They started setting it up while you and I were working on your Ariel yesterday. It took them longer than they thought it would, though. If they'd had it ready sooner, I'd've known Curt was coming. Not that it would have made much difference."

"They should've asked me for help," I said. "I'm a whiz at that sort of crap." I thought, not for the first time, that it was the only thing I *was* a whiz at.

Ringo let out a howl, put his front paws on the table, and rubbed his nose against the monitor. Pete and I looked at the picture but saw nothing. Ringo barked at us.

Then, far down the road, a black speck appeared.

I yelled and ran for the stairs, Ringo bounding ahead of me.'As we reached the living room, Gretchen emerged from the spare bedroom.

"What's all the goddamn noise?" she asked.

"The Bald Avenger's coming!"

I must have run to the utility room, pulled on my helmet and gloves, and sprinted to the garage with Pete and Gretchen close behind. The next thing I remember clearly is being on Peggy Sue, following the Oklahoma Kamikaze down the driveway at gravel-slinging speed.

Gretchen was in the Barracuda with Pete, and Ringo was running alongside me and the Ariel. The Doberman stopped at the mouth of the driveway.

As Peggy Sue bounced onto the road, I saw that the Bald Avenger's Jaguar was within a hundred yards. The Kamikaze ran right at it, and the Jaguar swerved toward the ditch. The Kamikaze blew past, and the bike and I squeezed by just as the Jaguar began to swerve back to block our path.

I didn't look behind to see whether the Jaguar was able to turn around in the narrow, muddy road. I knew, though, that Ringo wouldn't let it use the driveway. He had elected to stay behind and guard the Holden homestead.

When we reached the highway, Pete waved for me and Peggy Sue to take the lead. "We slipped him!" he yelled out his window as the Ariel and I passed, and indeed, the Jaguar was nowhere in sight. But I didn't expect that to last long. When the Bald Avenger reached the highway, he would know what direction we had taken by the trail of mud we would leave behind.

For the first time in days, the sun was breaking through the cloud cover. I would have a scenic ride until the Avenger ran me into the ground. Which would happen eventually. Pete and I had ten cylinders between us, but the Avenger had twelve.

When he caught up, he was going to set his foot down on me and never lift it.

SHARON

Notes on client Oliver Vale, continued . . .
Monday morning. After holding us in custody for

twenty-four hours (we slept on vinyl divans in our inter-rogation room), the Texas Rangers have released us.

The reason: Buddy Holly's grave is empty.

Either Oliver is already in Lubbock, or the world as we know it has come to an end. Either way, the Rangers see no purpose in holding us any longer.

Likewise, I have told Bruce that there is no point in continuing to Lubbock. If the authorities can't find Oliver there, then we have no hope of finding him either. I still want to help him, but I will have to wait until he con-tacts me or is captured.

Bruce is relieved that I have "come to my senses."

Yet I feel that I have done just the opposite. There are things going on that I cannot understand and that I can do nothing about. But I have always felt in control of myself, of my friends and clients, and of my world. Thus my sense of failure. Thus my anger at Bruce, who is connected with that failure.

I know, rationally, that I cannot be responsible for everything. The radio tells us that there is panic, even looting, in every major city of the world and many of the minor ones. I'm not responsible for that, am I?

The radio also tells us that the Buddy Holly TV broadcast does in fact originate on Ganymede. Oliver is either an innocent or an extraterrestrial.

And I *know* I don't have anything to do with that.

. . . unless the clues have been there all along in his behavior and in the things he has said in private and in the Group. In his stories about his mother's UFO studies and her belief that he is the reincarnation of Holly. . .

Perhaps we should be paying more attention to what the broadcast has said: "For assistance, contact Oli-ver Vale."

Perhaps he has been chosen as liaison between us

and Whomever. Like in that old movie with the giant
chandelier.

The radio says that the Ganymede signal has not
repeated itself since it began. Technology aside, no human being would have the patience to create three days
of that.

But whatever he is, human or alien, Oliver is my
friend. And I wish that I could help him.

RICHTER

Early Monday, his leg and mind well rested, Richter
left his Lawton hotel room and drove to the Comanche
County sheriff's office. There he presented his FCC
identification and asked to see all reports of regional
"Oliver Vale sightings." He made it clear that, for security reasons, there was to be no record of his visit.

Most of the "Vale sighting" reports were the rav-
ings of crackpots, but two caught his eye. The first stated
that an elderly couple had spotted Vale at two-thirty in
the morning, and that he had been in the company of a
muscular woman. The second stated that a housewife
had observed a certain Peter Holden hauling a motorcycle on his flatbed truck a short time later.

Richter hadn't seen the vehicle that had stopped at
the rest area while he had been hiding under the Jaguar, but its engine noise had been that of a truck. It
could have been a flatbed.

He handed the second report to the sheriff. "Directions to Holden's," he said.

The sheriff shook his head. "Don't bother. A deputy
checked this out, and it turned out to be nothing." He
chuckled. "Lucky for that Vale character that he *wasn't*

there. My deputy says Holden's got himself a big old Doberman that like to bit his arm off."

Richter's leg began throbbing.

"Directions," he said.

He would have them this time, and since he was no longer on the assignment, he would have no one to answer to for what he did.

They wouldn't even know that he was coming.

Except that, somehow, they did. He was driving slowly, looking at names on mailboxes to be sure he found the right place, when a white muscle car exploded from a stand of trees and came at him. It happened so quickly that he couldn't see who was inside, and he was barely able to swerve to the edge of the road in time to avoid a collision.

Then he saw Vale. He swerved back, hoping to block the motorcycle or hit it, but he was too late.

Ahead of him, standing beside a mailbox, was the dog who could spit bullets.

For an instant Richter was torn—but if he stopped to try to kill the Doberman, Vale would disappear yet again. Richter turned the Jaguar around and pursued. The muscle car and the motorcycle were already out of sight, but that meant nothing. This time the chase was in daylight. He would find them again soon.

And when he did, he would not aim for the tires.

SKYVUE

The two smiling, dark-suited ministers of the Corps of Little David emerged from the projection room. Khrushchev glared at them.

"Everything all right?" Eisenhower asked.

"All of our equipment is in working order, praise the Lord," the taller minister said. "Satan's hellish waves have no effect on our video projector."

"The Reverend Willard blessed it before we brought it up from Oklahoma City," the second minister said.

"Satan's hellish waves wouldn't bother it regardless of whether it was blessed," Khrushchev said. "It's closed circuit, without broadcast reception capability, right?"

The tall man nodded. "Indeed, brother—"

Khrushchev growled. Eisenhower elbowed him.

"—for the Reverend Willard wishes to be seen and heard by all in this community and the surrounding region who wish to see and hear him. Even as he stands atop this building, preaching courage during this campaign of the Antichrist, his image shall be relayed from our cameras to the projector, and thence to the screen of this theater, larger than life, a beacon of Truth—"

Khrushchev put a finger into his mouth and made gagging noises.

The minister stared. "I beg your pardon?"

"My associate is grumpy because he hasn't been able to watch reruns of *My Mother the Car* on his five-inch color set since Satan's broadcast commenced," Eisenhower said.

"And if you jerks broke that little TV while you were futzing around in there," Khrushchev added, "you can forget about getting your deposit back."

The second minister cleared his throat. "I believe we agreed on a rental fee of six thousand dollars." He handed Eisenhower a check.

"That's right," Eisenhower said. "You do understand that we can't provide security officers?"

"No matter," the tall man said. "The Corps of Little David will provide its own security. After all, the Reverend William Willard himself will be here."

"We *know,* we *know,*" Khrushchev said. "And we aren't going to collect the admission fees for you either."

"We wouldn't want you to," the second minister said. "We'll have a member of our Ladies' Auxiliary in the ticket booth."

"And I believe that concludes our business for now," the tall man said. "I trust that our equipment, tools, and accessories will remain undisturbed until our projectionist arrives."

"Of course," Eisenhower said.

"Assuming that the blessing holds up until then," Khrushchev muttered.

The two ministers left.

Eisenhower regarded Khrushchev sternly.

"What're *you* looking at?" Khrushchev snarled.

"Are you trying to ruin everything?" Eisenhower asked. "What if they'd taken offense and called the thing off?"

"I'd be delighted. As it is, this place is gonna be packed with several thousand Willyites who'll be whipped into a frenzy by their Fearless Leader's apocalyptic hysteria. It's bad enough that your Buddy Holly stunt has instigated violence in major metropolitan areas, but now it's going to happen out here in the sticks too."

Eisenhower looked thoughtful. "Could be," he said.

"Doesn't that bother you?" Khrushchev bellowed. "Don't you *care?*"

"Yes."

"Then why let Bill Willy come to our birthplace and pollute it until it's as rotten as the rest of the fleshbound world?"

Eisenhower went to the projection room's doorway and looked inside at the video projection equipment.

"Because," he said, "everybody likes a good show."

4 · raving **on**

10

OLIVER

The last entry in Volume VI of Mother's diary is dated Monday, December 8, 1980. My twenty-first birthday.

Mother wrote, *The radio has just given me the news. John has left for the other world.*

Now I understand.

It was almost midnight when I arrived home. I had worked late, and then I'd had dinner with a woman to whom I'd sold a tape deck. The fact that it was my birthday hadn't induced her to give me anything special.

When I came into the house, "Peggy Sue" was playing. That in itself wasn't unusual, but the version being played was not the original, but the cover that John Lennon had recorded. Mother was sitting on the living-room floor in the midst of scattered Beatles and Lennon albums. I had seen this sort of thing before and would have been afraid, except that she was smiling and happy.

"Oliver!" she cried over the music. "Happy birthday!"

I went to the stereo and turned down the volume. "Is everything all right?" I asked.

She beamed at me. "Haven't you heard?"

"Heard what?"

"John Lennon has been shot."

Stunned, I sat on the floor beside her. "Is he dead?"

Mother put a hand on my shoulder. "So they say. But they're wrong. Buddy, it's all right. I understand now."

I looked at her eyes and saw the glow of her insanity. "What do you understand?"

"That I've been wrong all this time," she said. "I thought there was a battle raging in the other world, and that the agents of the malevolent ones were making us destroy ourselves. But now I know that can't be true, because the Seekers who love us would *never* let John die."

"Why not?"

"Don't you see? John was one of our best, like Buddy. He was 'Strawberry Fields' and 'Give Peace a Chance.' If death were bad, he would have been protected from it. The only way that someone could kill him would be if the body's death were in fact a transition to the other world, where humans exist as energy, as ships of light."

"Ships of light."

She shook me. "The Unidentified Flying Objects! They're the visual manifestations of the other world! Remember when we saw Elvis leave? His body died, but that was all right because the ancient Atlanteans, the Seekers, showed him how to reach the other world!"

"But you mourned for Elvis," I said.

"No. I mourned for us, because we had lost him."

"And we haven't lost Lennon?"

The bright madness flickered. "We never had him," she said. "We never *deserved* him. He always was of the other world, but he loved us and wanted to help save us from ourselves, so he stayed. Until now, when he decided to leave."

"You said he was shot."

"His *body* was shot. By a man in New York."

"Then he didn't leave of his own will," I said. "He didn't 'leave' at all. He was killed. And not by an Atlantean, but by some shit of a human being."

Mother looked back to her scattered albums and stroked the cover of *Abbey Road* with her fingertips.

I went to my room. I wanted to believe that John Lennon lived on somewhere, but I knew better. There was no "other world" except in Mother's mind. She had chosen delusion over reality. Over death.

I saw that being an adult would mean that my mother would no longer take care of me. Instead, I would have to start taking care of her.

Throughout the next few months, I tried to persuade her to see a psychological counselor, but she would have none of it. She wasn't the one with the problem, she said; I was. She was able to accept the existence of the other world, and I wasn't. So which of us needed help, hmmm?

Eight years later, I still don't have the answer. How crazy, after all, is Mother's "other world" in comparison to my own "Spirit Land"?

Of course, I don't really believe in the Spirit Land. It's just something I got from a John Wayne movie. It's only a concept. A thought construct.

And I'm not afraid to die . . . just so long as I can keep my eyes

*

At each flat stretch of road, I looked back and saw that the Jaguar was within a few miles, but getting no closer. Peggy Sue's pace was eighty-five miles per hour,

which is nothing to a Jag—so I figured that the Avenger
didn't want me or the Kamikaze to crash, but preferred
to catch us standing still so that he could shoot us.

Since there was no point in sticking to the back roads
if we were dead anyway, I took Peggy Sue onto I-35 just
south of Oklahoma City. Pete was able to stay close, so
we weaved in and out of the city traffic to put more
space between us and the Avenger. I saw only one cop,
and he was busy in the southbound lanes with a jack-
knifed tractor-trailer. I congratulated myself on my
shrewdness.

Then we reached the city's northern edge and hit
the biggest tent-revival and traffic jam in the history of
the interstate highway system. We made a little headway by driving on the shoulder, but then we stopped
dead still.

Vehicles crammed the pavement, and people packed
the ditches and fields on either side. Men and women
stood on vans and preached through bullhorns; others
blew their car horns; others sang; others merely screamed.
Fences had been trampled flat, and power poles and bill-
boards had been toppled.

With Peggy Sue in neutral, I backpedaled so that I
could talk to Pete. A ruddy, overweight man who occupied the Jeep beside us gave me a dull look and spat a
stream of tobacco juice onto my left Nike.

Pete rolled down his window. "Ain't this a bitch?"
he shouted.

Gretchen turned in her seat and looked back. "At
least the Avenger's nowhere in sight. Then again, he
could be three cars away in this mess, and we'd never
know it."

I leaned down. "He's only part of our troubles. If we
don't get out of here soon, the natives are going to recognize me and Peggy Sue. And then we're skinned."

Gretchen raised an eyebrow. "What you mean 'we,' paleface?"

"She's kidding," Pete assured me.

"Bull*shit*," Gretchen said.

"Any ideas?" I asked.

Pete looked around at the mob. "Nothing on the pavement is moving, so let's go off-road until we get around the jam."

"And give those holy rollers the chance to mob our car and cannibalize us?" Gretchen asked.

"I guess it could work out that way," Pete said. "But if Oliver goes first, and fast, they'll jump out of the way. Then we can come along after, and they'll jump farther. Keep in mind that this is only a theory."

"Hey, you!" a voice bellowed.

I turned and saw that it was the ruddy man in the Jeep. His dull gaze had become a malevolent glare.

"Yeah, you!" he roared. "Ain't that bike an Ariel?"

I rapped out Peggy Sue's engine, skidded around the Kamikaze's front end, and plunged into the crowded ditch.

Pete's plan worked until I had gained about fifty feet, and then I was yanked off my motorcycle and hoisted into the air. I struggled, but could not break free.

"We have him!" someone screamed. "We have Vale the Antichrist! Find a Corps minister!"

"Let him be! He's a prophet!" someone else screamed.

"Satanist!"

"Communist tool!"

"Kill him!"

"But don't let him bleed! You'll get AIDS!"

They pounded on my helmet, ripped the Moonsuit with their fingernails, and flung me into the air over and over again. Peggy Sue disappeared under a sea of flesh.

"Leave my Ariel alone!" I cried.

The Kamikaze was mobbed. A man swung a tire iron against the passenger window, knocking a hole in the center and cracking the rest into greenish rectangles. Before he could swing again, Gretchen reached through the hole, grabbed his hair, and smacked his head against the roof. As he fell away, she snatched the tire iron from him and pushed her head and shoulders out through the rectangles, yelling, "Don't any of you people have *jobs*?"

Pete pulled her inside, and the Barracuda's 426 roared. Its rear tires spun, flinging chunks of mud, and it charged the maniacs who were tossing me like pizza dough. They dropped me, and I landed headfirst on the Kamikaze's hood as the car stopped. Dazed, I rose to my hands and knees and found myself gazing through the windshield at Gretchen, who screamed, "Duck!"

The Barracuda lurched, I fell flat, and a metal fence post swept through the space where my head had been. It hit the windshield, which became a brilliant white spiderweb, and I rolled off the fender to lie on my back in the mud.

Above me stood the ruddy man who had been in the Jeep. He spat tobacco juice onto the Moonsuit, then raised his fence post over my faceplate. At that moment Gretchen's tire iron thunked him across the bridge of his nose. He stumbled backward, and I scrambled to my feet and tried to dive into the car through the now-glassless passenger window. I made it halfway, ending up with my head in Gretchen's lap.

Pete hit the gas, and the Kamikaze slogged forward. Outside, hands grabbed my right foot, and I kicked something soft with my left. The hands let go.

"Dorkhead jerkface!" Gretchen yelled, prodding me with the tire iron. "Get off!"

I floundered into the back seat, and when I faced forward, I saw that the starred windshield was completely opaque. Pete had rolled down his side window and was driving with his head outside. A few of the maniacs were throwing things at him, but most were either diving out of our way or fighting each other. From what I could hear, it seemed that a large number of Bill Willyites were busy beating the hell out of a group of fringe cultists who thought I was God's personal representative on Earth. That battle, I was sure, was all that kept the mob from rushing the Barracuda and stomping it flat. We began to pick up speed, sliding and fishtailing on the mud and flattened grass, and I saw that other vehicles were now opting for the ditch as well, increasing the chaos and helping to distract the maniacs.

Several hundred yards farther on, we discovered that the traffic jam was the result of three overturned church buses and a number of smaller vehicles (including an Oklahoma Highway Patrol cruiser) that were crammed against them. As soon as we were past that mess, Pete took the Kamikaze up to the pavement and continued north. The car accelerated to almost eighty, but after only a few miles, the right rear tire collapsed. The Barracuda almost flipped, but Pete struggled with the wheel and was able to bring the car to a stop on the shoulder. The three of us clambered out.

Pete had a gash on his forehead, but other than wiping it with the back of his hand, he ignored it. "Break out the windshield so we can see to drive," he said. Gretchen went to work on the glass with her tire iron while Pete sprinted to open the trunk.

I followed, intending to help, but as he pulled out the spare tire and jack, I looked to the south and saw smoke rising from near the spot where I had lost my bike.

The Willyites were burning Buddy Holly's motorcycle.

Pete tackled me from behind as I ran, and I fell into the ditch. He threw me onto my back, put a knee on my chest, and held a tire cross against the sky as if about to brain me.

"Every religious movement has its martyrs," he said.

Then he dragged me back to the Kamikaze and had Gretchen hold me while he jacked up the car and began removing the flat. I looked away and stared at the smoke.

"If your mother's aliens are going to rescue their prophet," Pete said, kicking the flat away, "they might want to show up now."

I heard the whine of approaching engines, looked down from the smoke, and saw cars and pickup trucks speeding toward us. Wild-eyed men and women leaned out of the windows waving ax handles, shovels, baseball bats, Bibles, and shotguns.

The first three cars were moving so fast that they were a quarter mile past us before they came to a stop. The fourth one, though, was approaching more slowly. It was a four-wheel-drive pickup that had men in camouflage fatigues hanging all over it. They aimed rifles at us and, although they were still two hundred yards away, started firing. Gretchen yelled a garbled obscenity, released me, and ran for the Barracuda's driver's seat.

Pete was spinning the fourth of five lug nuts onto the new wheel. It was enough. I leaned down and grabbed the tire cross from him, then whirled like a discus thrower and flung it at the approaching truck. It spun toward the windshield like a giant shurakin, and the truck swerved into the grassy median, dropping paramilitary goons like dead leaves. The cross bounced off the pavement with a triumphant *clang* and buried itself in the grill of the next car, which also headed for the median, causing more problems for the goons.

I hoped that none of them were hurt, but if any were, better them than me. That wasn't an appropriate attitude for a prophet and potential martyr, I suppose, but screw that. I'm a consumer electronics salesman, and consumer electronics salesmen don't make good martyrs. We've seen too many replays of *The Terminator* on the big-screen Mitsubishis in the showroom.

As the second vehicle hit the median, Pete grasped my wrist and pulled me toward the Barracuda's passenger door, leaving the jack up and the trunk open. Gretchen was already in the driver's seat, so I dove into the back while Pete jumped in beside her. The left rear tire squealed, and we whanged off the jack, heading toward the three cars that had overshot us. They had turned around and were coming at us head-on in a V formation.

"You're going south in the northbound lane!" Gretchen yelled at them. "Peabrains!" She put the Kamikaze on the dotted line, closed her eyes, and punched it.

I closed my eyes as well and experienced a stomach-knotting sensation of déjà vu. I felt as I had when I'd passed the SkyVue Drive-In Theater and Satellite Dish Emporium in El Dorado—as if there were something important going on, something that I should know about. That struck me as weird, because what I should have been feeling was abject fear at my impending death.

Several seconds past the moment when I should have been crushed by compacting metal, I opened my eyes. The highway ahead was clear, and when I looked back past the bobbing trunk lid, I saw the three cars far behind us. They were blocking the road in front of the rest of our pursuers.

I pulled off my helmet. "How'd you do that?" I asked

Gretchen, shouting to be heard over the blast of air that was the result of no longer having a windshield.

"I don't know," she answered. "I wasn't looking."

"I was," Pete said, blotting his forehead with a handkerchief, "but I've had a nasty blow to the head, so what I saw didn't make sense."

I would have been surprised if it had. "What did you see?"

He put the bloodstained handkerchief into his jacket pocket. "A silver blob of light appeared between us and them," he said. "Sort of like a fluorescent spoon the size of a boxcar. When it disappeared, they were behind us." He grinned at me. "Guess those aliens showed up in the nick of time after all. Just like John Wayne and the cavalry."

Maybe not just like. But close enough.

Traffic reappeared as we passed the next three exits, and by the time we reached Guthrie, the streams of vehicles were as thick and single-minded as ants. Without the usual soap operas and game shows to watch, everyone who was normally at home on Monday afternoons had decided to go for a drive. No one seemed to be pursuing us, though, so instead of trying to force our way through, we accepted the traffic as natural cover. The Kamikaze was banged up and windshieldless, but it didn't look much worse than some of the cars around us. And without Peggy Sue, we weren't as conspicuous as we had been.

I didn't want to think about Peggy Sue.

"I think we're rid of the Bald Avenger," Gretchen said. "I haven't seen that Jag since before Oklahoma City."

Pete chuckled. "Those Willyites probably tore it to

bits. I doubt that they care much for machines made in England."

I bit my lip.

Pete turned on the dash radio, and the first words out of it were that the stock market was crashing. No one in the investment community was able to think about anything except what had happened to their TV sets, and Wall Street was going to hell. By the end of the day, the Dow would be down by anywhere from six hundred to seventeen hundred points.

"Whatever that means," I said.

Gretchen began to explain the Dow and the implications of such a drop, but I tuned her out. How it was happening and what it meant didn't matter; all that mattered was that it would be blamed on me. Buddy had named me as the person to contact "for assistance," and now the mass-communication-based American and world economies were in flames. The Authorities would hang me from a flagpole and play tetherball.

Well, they could go ahead and do it for all I cared. Buddy Holly, Ready Teddy, and Mother were all dead; Julie "Eat shit and die, Oliver" Calloway had left me and wasn't coming back; any chance I might have had with Sharon Sharpston had been fantasy; my home was probably splinters on the ground; and my beloved Ariel had been burned by religious zealots. I'd had enough. I didn't even want to go back to Topeka. Pete had to be wrong about my SkyVue dish being a possible key—and even if he wasn't, the odds were good that the dish didn't even exist anymore.

So I wouldn't go home. I would give myself up.

But first, I would go to El Dorado. I had to know why the SkyVue Drive-In Theater had seemed so important to me when Peggy Sue and I had passed by.

"Highway patrol," Pete said, pointing at the south-bound lanes. "He's slowing down. Must've gotten word on us from the Oklahoma City jam."

Gretchen looked at the mirror. "Shit! There go his lights!" The Kamikaze accelerated.

I scanned the blurring road signs. "Exit for State 33 East coming up," I said. "Take it."

"Who died and made you God?" Gretchen snapped.

I had an answer, but I kept it to myself.

"It's a good idea," Pete said, looking back. "The hypo's having trouble getting across, so we might be able to exit without his seeing it."

Gretchen scooted the car in front of a semi and took the exit. As we sped down the ramp, the semi blocked our view of the hypo, and thus his view of us. Three miles later, we were sure that we had lost him.

"We'll swing north again soon," Pete said, opening the glove box and digging out a map. "Maybe U.S. 177 or something near it."

"I want to go through El Dorado, Kansas," I said.

"How come?"

"That's where Mother bought our satellite dish. I have a feeling about the place." I didn't tell him that I was planning to give myself up there.

He looked at the map. "It's on the way. Want me to drive yet, Gretchen?"

She smiled at him. "I'm okay. Except for my hands, which are freezing."

I pulled off my gloves and handed them up. Now that my Ariel was gone, I wouldn't be needing them.

"Thanks," she said grudgingly, letting Pete steer as she put them on. She glanced at me in the rearview mirror. "Hey, are you crying?"

I looked out the window and murmured, "Peggy Sue." Like everything else that mattered, she was gone.

SHARON

Notes, continued . . .

We entered Oklahoma City on I-40 early Monday afternoon. Bruce was driving, and he switched to I-35 to head north despite what we had encountered there the day before. I tried to convince him to go another way, but he argued that the mass revival that had slowed traffic to a crawl on Sunday could not still be in existence on Monday. In a way, he was right. The revival had metamorphosed into an ongoing mob riot and pileup. Bruce made some headway by driving on the shoulder for a half mile, but then even the shoulder was blocked.

"Why don't the police do something?" Bruce fumed.

"They wouldn't have any more luck penetrating this than we've had," I said. "Nor would the National Guard."

Bruce steered the car off the road into the shallow ditch, honking for people to get out of the way.

"What are you trying to do?" I shouted. "You're going to hit somebody and be sued!"

"I'd like to see 'em try! I'm a fuckin' *lawyer!*"

I stared at him. His eyes were wide, his nostrils were flared, and his mouth was set in a crooked smile. This was not the same Bruce who had left Topeka with me, or even who had been held by the Texas Rangers with me. I was strangely attracted to him even as I was enraged by his recklessness.

Our Chevrolet churned along the slope at eight or nine miles per hour and was pelted with beer cans and curses from the televisionless hordes who scrambled out of its path. Up on the pavement, a number of other drivers were also steering their automobiles into the ditch.

I began to fear that instead of escaping the traffic jam, we were expanding its boundaries. In addition, the assembled Willard worshipers were furious at us. I even saw one car overturned by the mob.

Then I spotted the motorcycle. It was lying on its side, and the crowd was piling sticks, paper, cardboard, and brush on a ring of bare earth surrounding it.

It was Oliver's Ariel.

I grabbed Bruce's arm. Startled, he hit the brakes. A car that had come into the ditch behind us began honking, and there was the sound of a backfire.

"Look!" I cried, pointing at the motorcycle. We were some distance past it already, but what was happening was still obvious. "They're going to burn it!"

"So?"

"So it's Oliver's, and if it's here, so is he! *They'll burn him too!*"

I had no doubt that it was true. After all, that's what you do with witches, or with the Antichrist, or with extraterrestrials: You burn them. At least, that's what you do if you're a follower of the Reverend William Willard.

I reached for my door handle, intending to rush out and find Oliver, but stopped at the sound of another backfire—which I now realized was not a backfire at all, but a gunshot. Immediately following that sound, a bald-headed man appeared beside the motorcycle, waving a pistol at the crowd. They backed away a few steps, and he kicked some of the trash away from the cycle. Then, with surprising strength, he grasped a handlebar with his free hand and pulled the machine upright.

A burning scrap arced from the mob, hit the trash, and set it ablaze. The bald man put his gun in his jacket, then jumped onto the motorcycle, started it, and plowed into the crowd, carrying sparks and flames with him. He disappeared in the swarming mass.

"Was that Vale?" Bruce asked. "Did he shave his head?"

"How should I know? Follow him and let's find out!"

Bruce drove on. I didn't think that Oliver was the sort to shave his head or to brandish a gun . . . but I hadn't seen the bald man's face, so it *could* have been him. He might have shaved his head to disguise himself, and almost anyone would start carrying a weapon if an entire nation called him a monster. Who knew what he'd been through the past three days?

We eventually reached clear pavement, and now we are rushing northward, trying to overtake the man who must be Oliver. Soon after regaining the interstate, we passed wrecked cars and armed men wearing camouflage fatigues. I became even more sure that Oliver had come this way.

Traffic is increasing. Bruce must speed up and slow down, speed up and slow down again, and my handwriting scrawls across the page in what may be indecipherable squiggles. Despite that, I am glad for the traffic, for we are not the only ones it has slowed. I can see the bald man on the motorcycle several vehicles ahead of us. As soon as I catch his attention, everything will be all right.

Bruce remains unconvinced.

RICHTER

His pursuit of Vale was slowed when the Doberman pinscher appeared at the end of the mud road, blocking the way onto the highway. The dog would have had to run cross-country at an impossible speed to get here first, but here it was. It stood at the edge of the pavement, snarling.

The dog's right eye was missing, and Richter decided to put out the other one. He readied his pistol and touched a button to lower the window.

With the first electric whine, the Doberman was beside the door. Richter took his finger off the button. If he lowered the bulletproof glass far enough to shoot, his gun and his hand would be in the dog's stomach before he could squeeze the trigger.

But now that the Doberman was beside him—

He hit the accelerator, and the Jaguar leaped toward the highway.

The Doberman was there first.

The Jaguar struck the dog, throwing it into the opposite ditch. Richter turned the wheel and sped north, then looked in his mirror. The Doberman was standing in the highway again. It didn't follow, but Richter knew that it could do so if it chose.

He shuddered, and then was angry with himself. Fear was counterproductive. If he should encounter the beast one more time, he promised himself, he would find a way to kill it. It was only a problem to be solved, like anything else.

Despite the lost time, he soon had the white muscle car in sight again. It was easy to follow, so he would be able to wait for the kill until he could see Vale's face.

When he hit the traffic jam, he knew that he should have run Vale off the road when he had the chance. Even when he stood on the Jaguar's roof, he could see neither the motorcycle nor the white car, which meant that Vale and his friends had found a way to break through.

A few vehicles were making headway by driving in the ditch, so Richter climbed down from the roof, drew his pistol, and pointed it at the driver of the car that was occupying the shoulder beside the Jaguar.

"Move," Richter said. The car skittered into the ditch and almost ran down a cluster of men and women who were singing hymns. One singer jumped onto the hood off the car, and the others dove aside, hitting the trampled mud face-first.

Richter almost smiled.

He reentered the Jaguar, took it into the ditch, and drove north. It was slow going because of the wet ground and because of the slope of the ditch, but Richter knew that he would make it as long as the throng of idiots got out of his way. The singers were now running on the uphill side of the Jaguar, shouting curses at him. He gave them the finger and considered lowering the window to take potshots.

He considered too long. The singers rushed the Jaguar, shoving it, and it slid down the muddy slope. Richter pushed the accelerator to the floor, but that only spun the tires and made the slide worse. Richter lifted his foot, and the Jaguar stopped. He started to lower the window, but then the singers and fifty of their friends came at the car in a human wall and turned it onto its right side.

Richter wasn't wearing his shoulder harness, and he clutched the steering wheel to keep from falling. His pistol clattered onto the passenger window. Outside, the mob was cheering.

He switched off the ignition and swung his legs out from under the wheel. His wounded thigh struck the shift lever, and he collapsed onto the passenger door beside his pistol. His leg felt as if it were filled with acid, but he had no time for pain. The car had begun to rock, which meant that the mob was going to roll it onto its roof.

He picked up the pistol and holstered it, grabbed three ammunition clips from the compartment under the seat, and reached up to open the driver's side window. As the glass slid away, a blob of mud flew in and spattered his suit. He stood, pulled himself outside, and sat on the edge of the roof.

The people surrounding the Jaguar bellowed and began rocking it wildly, so Richter drew his pistol and shot the nearest one in the stomach. The people screamed and surged away, taking the wounded man with them.

Richter stood up on the door and surveyed the area. There were plenty of vehicles, so if he couldn't push the Jaguar onto its tires again, he would be able to commandeer something. He would have to hurry, though, because the mob would return as soon as their rage overwhelmed their cowardice. Even now, some of them were flinging rocks from a distance. He started to sit again so that he could slide across the roof to the ground with a minimum of trauma to his leg.

Then he saw Vale's motorcycle. It was lying on its side less than a hundred yards north of him, and some members of the crowd were piling trash around it. The white muscle car was still nowhere to be seen, so he suspected that Vale might have escaped in it; but he had to know for certain. If Vale was here, he belonged to Richter, not to these crazed subhumans.

Richter slid to the ground and headed for the motorcycle in a limping run. When he reached the cluster surrounding the Ariel, he punched and clubbed his way through. Two people turned to fight him, and he shot one of them. The other backed off, and Richter broke through to stand beside the pyre of trash.

He turned his back to the motorcycle and scanned the mob's front line, waving his pistol. He had thought that they might be forcing Vale to watch his machine being destroyed, but Vale was nowhere to be seen. Another possibility was that Vale was buried in the pyre, so Richter began kicking the trash away. He didn't find Vale, but he discovered that the trash had been splashed with either gasoline or charcoal starter. He knew then what would happen if he stayed any longer, and with a surge of adrenaline, he jerked the motorcycle upright.

A paper torch flew from the crowd and hit the trash, igniting it. Richter holstered his pistol, then leaped onto the Ariel and kicked the starter. The engine caught, so he twisted the throttle and released the clutch. The rear tire threw flaming scraps at the crowd, and the motorcycle surged northward. Most of the people in its path jumped aside, but one didn't, so Richter ran him down.

Vale had escaped in the muscle car. Richter was sure of that now, because this mob would have been burning Vale with his bike if they'd had him. Abandoning the Jaguar was hard, especially since Richter didn't like motorcycles, but he couldn't stay here any longer. The frustration of losing Vale time and again had given way to a cold determination. He would not stop. Not now, not ever.

He regained the interstate and sped toward Guthrie, his long gray coat flapping behind him like a cape. The wind chilled and then numbed him, but he didn't care. He would obtain a better vehicle if and when it became necessary. For now, though, he knew that he was close to Vale, because the mob could not have had the Ariel for long. The white car was no more than a few miles ahead of him. He hoped that it would stay on the interstate until he had it in sight again.

He was actually beginning to be glad for the hardships he was enduring. They would make the kill, when at last it came, all the more sweet.

CATHY AND JEREMY

The Datsun puttered southward on I-35 while Cathy cursed both it and Jeremy. "Junk, the both of you," she said. "Poor design. Poor craftsmanship."

"It's not my fault that my flesh-brain didn't retain everything Ringo saw," Jeremy said.

"It most certainly is. You designed it."

"Yes, but according to normal fleshbound parameters, because we're supposed to appear normal. Besides, things aren't hopeless. Ringo didn't take this highway, but I'm sure he was on roads near here. We're still getting where he was going, only faster."

"You say."

"Look, if you don't want—" Abruptly, Jeremy turned in his seat and gazed out the back window.

"What? What?" Cathy snapped. "What is it?"

"That white car that just went by. Going north."

"What about it?"

"The people inside. Ringo saw them before he lost the link. I only got a peripheral glimpse just now, but as I did, I felt a tremendous sense of loyalty. Ringo *likes* those people."

"Could they be the ones who popped the eye?"

"Maybe. They flashed by too fast for me to tell."

Cathy studied the rearview mirror. "So should we go after them, or continue toward a place that we may or may not find and where Vale may or may not still be hiding?"

Jeremy faced forward, took Ringo's eye from his pocket, and rolled it between his fingers. "Beats me." He sighed. "Do you suppose that the fleshbound feel this in-decisive very often? It's awful."

Cathy didn't answer. She was now staring at a point on the southern horizon.

"Cath?"

"I just decided," she said, pointing.

A motorcycle appeared in the far northbound lane. As it approached, Jeremy saw that the rider was bald and that he was wearing a mud-spattered gray overcoat.

"The government man," Cathy said. "On Vale's bike."

The motorcycle flashed past, and Cathy hit the Dat-sun's brakes. Jeremy's forehead bounced off the dash, and his human-eye popped out of its socket.

"Thanks one whole hell of a lot," he said, leaning down to grope the floor. "Now I can't see anything."

"You don't have to. I know where I'm going, no thanks to you." The Datsun lurched onto the clumped grass of the median.

Jeremy pressed the dog-eye into place as Cathy started to pull into the northbound lanes. "Look out!" he yelled. "There's a car coming!"

"Screw it," Cathy said.

The approaching car braked, and Jeremy saw terror and anger in the faces of the man and woman who oc-cupied it. He rolled down his window and called, "Sorry! We're fifteen thousand years old, and we don't obey traffic laws!"

"Oh, shut up," Cathy said. She accelerated after the motorcycle.

With the help of Ringo's eye, Jeremy found his own and replaced it in its socket. He looked back at the car that Cathy had almost creamed.

"You know," he said, "that woman looks familiar too."

"They all look alike, if you ask me," Cathy grumbled.

RINGO

He watched the Jaguar speed away and decided against pursuing it. He had given his friends a head start, and that was good enough. His days of chasing vehicles across hundreds of miles were over. His new job was to be the protector of the Holden estate, so he left the highway and trotted home. Once there, he curled up on the porch and dozed until Laura and Mike drove in that afternoon.

"The garage is open and the Kamikaze's gone," Mike said as he emerged from the Dart. "That means that Dad has taken Mrs. Mussolini to the bus station, but the buses won't be running, so we'll be stuck with her for another night. Assuming that Dad doesn't get caught in a couch potato riot."

"Just because we almost did doesn't mean he will," Laura said. "Dad can take care of himself. I'll bet that Ms. Laird can too." She patted the Doberman, who was dancing and jumping to demonstrate his joy that they were home. "Want to watch me take apart Ringo's rejected eye?"

"I suppose so. There's not much on TV."

Ringo followed them inside and downstairs to Laura's room. Mike sat on the worktable in front of the Mac while Laura picked up the eye and held it under a lamp. "The division between the halves is a hair-thin line," she said. "I don't see any notch to accommodate a tool."

"Just hit it with a hammer," Mike suggested.

"Oh, sure. And destroy the works."

Ringo whined. Pete had wanted the kids to look at

the Mac screen, but Mike was blocking it. He nudged the boy with his nose.

"See?" Mike said. "Ringo agrees with me. The worst that can happen is that the thing will explode and kill us."

Laura grasped the eye and twisted the halves counterclockwise. They parted. " 'Hit it with a hammer,' " she sneered.

"Unscrewing it was going to be my second choice."

Laura examined the halves. "The inner surface of the posterior half is coated with a silvery substance," she said, "but the anterior half contains what looks like a camera." She held that half before her own right eye. "Hey, it's projecting! But the images are too small for me to see what they are."

Mike jumped down from the table, went to the wall switch, and turned off the ceiling light. "Get the lamp," he said, returning to the table and tearing a sheet of paper from the computer printer.

Laura switched off the lamp, leaving the video monitor and the Mac screen as the room's only sources of light, and Mike held the paper behind the half eye. He moved the sheet back and forth until the projection resolved into an inverted image of a two-lane highway as seen from a moving automobile.

"Rad," Mike said. "Can you get it right-side-up?"

Laura turned the eye, but the image remained inverted. "Not without an additional lens. Apparently, the image projected onto the artificial retina is upside-down, and since we're looking at the projection from the wrong side, it's backward too. That road sign really says 'U.S. 177 North.' " She took the paper from her brother. "Turn off the monitor and the Mac, will you? I want to see if I can make out what's on the road ahead."

Mike blanked the video monitor and was reaching

for the Mac when Ringo put his nose on the screen. Mike
saw the note at last. "Message from Dad," he said. "He's
escorting Mr. Vale to Topeka, expects to be back tomorrow. We're supposed to take care of ourselves and stay
out of trouble. 'P.S. Don't forget to feed the dog.' "

"Oh-oh," Laura said.

" 'Oh-oh' what? We've managed by ourselves before."

"That's not it. Look at this." The projection was
clearer in the reduced light, and it showed an upside-
down motorcycle and rider. "That's Mr. Vale's Ariel."

"But Mr. Vale isn't bald," Mike said. "And he has
blue coveralls, not a coat."

Ringo squeezed between the brother and sister to
get a better look at the projection, and then he growled.
He recognized the bald man. He should have stopped him
that morning . . . except that the only way to stop him
for good would have been to kill him, and Ringo couldn't
do that.

"He doesn't like what he sees," Laura said.

"Neither do I. Why is someone else on Mr. Vale's
bike? And if Dad was going with him, where's the Kamikaze?"

Laura shifted the paper. "Maybe that white speck
down the road?"

"Could be." Mike turned the lamp back on. "Do you
remember Ms. Laird saying something about a 'Bald
Avenger' who was after Mr. Vale?"

Ringo snatched the sheet of paper from Laura's hand
and chewed it to shreds.

"He's telling us something," Laura said.

Mike nodded. "Dad's gotten himself into trouble."

"We don't know that for certain."

"Ringo does. Let's call the highway patrol." He
started for the door.

"What?" Laura was incredulous. "Mister Anti-Es-

tablishment wants to call the cops? Mike, Dad's with
Oliver Vale. Besides which, the Bald Avenger is probably a cop of some sort himself. If we're going to help,
we'll have to do it ourselves." The Doberman nuzzled
her arm. " 'We' including Ringo, of course."

Mike stopped and glared at her. "We can't very well
catch up with Dad in an old Dodge Dart, can we?"

"No." Laura smiled a thin, sure smile. "But we can
in an old Beechcraft Bonanza."

Ringo yipped and ran for the stairs.

The red-and-white V-tail Bonanza stood out like a
mutant in a row of Cessnas and Pipers. Ringo thought
it was beautiful.

"Have you ever flown in the dark before?" Mike
whispered as he and Laura unfastened the tie-downs.

"Once. I almost collided with a smokestack. Instruc-
tor Bob practically wet his pants."

They climbed inside. Ringo took the copilot's seat,
and Mike sat behind.

Laura put on a headset and flipped switches, and
the instrument dials glowed. "Fuel's almost max." She
bit her lower lip. "Listen, I know this was my idea, but
tell me again why it isn't stealing." She activated the
starter.

"Taking this aircraft for personal gain would be
'stealing,' " Mike said, shouting to be heard over the
sudden roar. "Taking it for the purpose of helping someone else is 'commandeering into the service of the people.' Besides, you have to perform a solo for your license
anyway, and we'll pay for the fuel and flight time. Eventually."

"I'm not even sure we'll be able to find Dad!" Laura
shouted as the Beechcraft taxied across the field toward
the grass runway. "I won't be able to help you interpret

the eye's projection and fly the plane too!"

Ringo barked.

"We accept your offer," Mike said. He took the eye halves from his coat, screwed them together, and pushed the sphere into Ringo's right socket.

Ringo blinked. If he concentrated, he could see and hear what Jeremy saw and heard. It was unpleasant, but he would put up with it.

"Two barks warm, one bark cold," Laura said. "Got it?"

Ringo barked twice.

"Lassie should have been a Doberman!" Mike yelled.

Laura revved the engine. "This is against the law!"

"All laws, both of nature and of man, have been suspended!" Mike cried. "Haven't you heard? Buddy Holly is alive and well on Ganymede!"

The Bonanza roared down the runway and rose into the February night.

11

OLIVER

I've never dropped acid, but I've read Volume VII of Mother's diary. In February 1981, she wrote, *The signals of the other world crackle about me like miniature ships of light. They hop along my sweater and jump to the TV screen and back again, zip zap. Soon I will discover how to decipher their meaning, and then I shall prepare the Earth for what is to come. In the meantime I glimpse cosmic jellyfish and the whale that swallowed Jonah. Buddy rides astride its back, singing "Blue Days, Black Nights."*

Other than UFOs, mystical beings, and vintage rock 'n' roll, the only things that Mother now recognized as marginally real were me (when she wasn't calling me "Buddy"), Ready Teddy, a few TV shows, and her job at KKAP. The latter wasn't to last much longer; she became critical of the station's Top 40 format, and she often entered the booth and told the midday disc jockey that if he didn't play "Rock Around with Ollie Vee," he was a traitor to the human race.

Before the station could fire her, I suggested that she quit and let me support us. I was making good money because Cowboy Carl's Component Corral had expanded to include Cowboy Carl's Computer Corral, and Apples were selling better than amplifiers. Mother agreed to early retirement, and I sold her Nova. Thus, since I drove the Dart to work every day, she was trapped safely at home.

She was only forty years old, but I treated her as if she were a doddering crone. By encouraging her to leave her job, I forced her to abandon her one concrete link with the here-and-now. Father, forgive me. The seances in the basement became more frequent, and flakehead magazines filled the coffee table.

One day in June 1982, Mother called me at work to tell me that Ready Teddy was dead. When I rushed home, however, I found him bouncing in the driveway, as energetic as ever. I asked Mother what the big idea was, and she explained that she'd had a *vision* of him lying dead. Muttering about sending her to Menninger's, I drove back to Topeka . . . and that evening Ready Teddy didn't appear for his supper.

I found his body on a gravel road a mile away. He had been run over and scraped to the side by a county grader. We buried him in the backyard.

Neither Mother nor I said another word about her premonition. What we said instead was that we would go to the shelter and adopt a puppy as soon as the hurt of our loss had subsided.

But a few weeks later, I bought my Ariel Cyclone, and the subject of getting a puppy never came up again. Mother didn't approve of the motorcycle, but beyond a few obligatory you're-going-to-get-yourself-killed comments, she let it be. Even in her "other world" dreamland (perhaps especially there), she must have known that it's easier to love a machine than to love a living thing. When machines break, they can be fixed.

The next year, Mother made an impulse purchase of her own. I came home one spring evening and found a partially assembled satellite dish next to Ready Teddy's grave. Mother stood beside it, gazing into the parabolic shell. I was not happy.

"I used my own savings account and cashed in some bonds," Mother said. "You'll still have money for new shingles."

"That isn't the point," I told her. "If you absolutely had to have one, I could've ordered a better brand through work, and we'd've gotten it at a discount."

She patted my shoulder. "This is the one I want, Oliver. It will provide a direct link to the other world, and we'll get free HBO to boot." She produced a shiny new ten-inch crescent wrench. "Here, this came with it. Be a dear and put it all together, will you?"

But the SkyVue malfunctioned from the beginning. I connected everything properly (by now I was Topeka's fastest and greatest expert on video hookups), but at random intervals, whatever channel we were watching would dissolve into snow. Adjustments made according to the manual and according to my experience were never effective for long, and my calls to the El Dorado factory were never answered. Finally, I ran out to the dish and whanged the block converter with the crescent wrench.

"That's it!" Mother cried from inside the house.

From that day on, whenever our picture went screwy, I would go out and whang the SkyVue until Mother shouted that the reception was fine again. What I didn't know until after her death was that she believed my violence against the converter put her in touch with "other world" beings.

She wrote, *I had begun to think that the SkyVue was*

*improperly aligned, but then Oliver went into a rage and
hit it with the wrench that came packed with the electronics. At that moment, the snow cleared and Buddy
Holly appeared. "Hello, Michelle," he said. "C. can't come
to the camera, but he wants you to know that he's waiting
for you. I myself want to thank you for remembering me
even when almost everyone else has forgotten. Sam and
Elvis say hello." Then he vanished, and the baseball game
reappeared. I called to Oliver and told him that he had
fixed the picture.*

*Now, whenever the TV warps into fuzz, I will know
that Buddy is calling me. I will send Oliver to hit the
SkyVue, making sure that he uses that special wrench,
and I shall commune with my gods.*

Perhaps they will let me talk to C. sometime.

And so they did.

*

At 11:30 P.M. on Monday, February 6, I found myself on the same blacktop road on which I had fled El
Dorado the preceding Friday. This time I was slouched
in the back seat of a '68 Barracuda instead of straddling
a '57 Cyclone.

Soon after turning north on U.S. 177, Gretchen had
become convinced that we were being followed, and she
had taken the Oklahoma Kamikaze onto various back
roads for the next several hours, racking up so many
miles that we had to stop at a middle-of-nowhere gas
station to refuel despite the car's extra tank. We had
crossed into Kansas well after sundown, and now, at last,
we were only some twenty miles south of the SkyVue
Drive-In Theater and Earth Station Emporium. My cir-
cular pilgrimage was almost over. It would be ending as
it had begun, in full darkness.

Pete was fiddling with the dash radio, and he

found a Wichita station that was talking about us. He
had to turn the volume up high so we could hear it over
the wind.

"—citizens report spotting the white Barracuda that
was involved in the Oklahoma chase and that is believed to be occupied by accomplices of Oliver Vale. The
vehicle was seen northeast of Winfield—"

"Rats' asses!" Gretchen said.

"—on Haverhill Road, and another report states that
Vale himself, still on an Ariel motorcycle, is trailing the
automobile by several miles."

"What are they talking about?" I yelled. "Peggy Sue's
dead! They burned her!"

"Maybe it's risen from the grave too," Gretchen said.
"Maybe it's become one of the Undead."

I thought she might be more right than she knew.
If anything could find its way back from the Spirit Land,
it would be Peggy Sue.

But who was riding her?

There was only one possibility. If Peggy Sue were
able to come back, she would bring Buddy with her. Except that he had already left the Spirit Land for Ganymede. . . .

The radio was still going on about us. "—Cowley
County Sheriff's Department states that due to disturbances at Southwestern College, they will be unable to
send a car to verify the report. Kansas Highway Patrol
officials will not comment, and we have not yet been able
to reach the Butler County Sheriff . . ."

Pete pointed ahead. "Oil pumps and a holding tank
on the right. If we hide there awhile, we can watch to
see whether this road's being searched. If it is, they'll
probably go right past us, and then we can continue."

Gretchen took the Kamikaze onto the oil pumper's
road, and we bounced across river gravel to the tank,

which sat sixty or seventy yards from the blacktop. When we were hidden behind it, Gretchen killed the engine and lights, and the radio went dead as well. The tank hulked over us like a small butte, and the silhouettes of the pumps rose and fell like rocking horses. The smell of crude oil, the stink of ancient death, was heavy. The only sounds were the *squeak-whirr-squeak-whirr* of the pumps and the *tic-tic-tic* of the Kamikaze's cooling engine.

"This is just putting off the inevitable," I told Pete. "In fact, I was going to give myself up at SkyVue anyway. Tell you what—I'll walk north, and the Authorities can pick me up while you and Gretchen cut back south."

"Sounds good to me," Gretchen said, opening her door and stepping out. She tilted the driver's seat forward so that I could get out as well.

As I did so, Pete said, "The radio claimed that your bike is following us. Don't you want her?"

I didn't answer, but left the car and walked around the oil tank to stare toward the south. The night sky was blackened by clouds, and I couldn't see anything in the distance except the weird shadows my imagination conjured up. They were shaped like spaceships, women, dogs, patrol cars, motorcycles . . .

Pete's shoes crunched on the rocks beside me.

"Do you think Peggy Sue's coming back to me?" I asked.

"I wouldn't put it that way," he said. "My guess is that Bill Willy has a bounty on your head, so somebody from the revival, maybe even a Corps of Little David minister, is using her to get to you. But he'll have to pass by here, so we might be able to get your Ariel back if he doesn't wreck her when I run the Kamikaze up his butt." He put a hand on my shoulder and steered me behind the tank. "But whether we recover Peggy Sue or not, I promise that I'll get you to SkyVue. So don't take off on your own yet."

We sat on the Barracuda's fender and watched for headlights approaching on the blacktop. Evergreens partially blocked our view to the north, but the south was clear. During the next twenty minutes, only one vehicle passed by. It was heading toward El Dorado, and although it was neither a patrol car nor a motorcycle and didn't even slow down, I worried. Its engine noise sounded familiar and unsettling. When I spoke that thought aloud, Pete replied that it sounded like any other old Datsun to him.

Soon after the Datsun passed by, Gretchen leaned close to Pete and said, "It's so peaceful out here that it's hard to believe there's anything wrong in the rest of the world."

"We can take care of that," Pete said, jumping off the fender. "The kids gave me a pocket TV for Christmas. It's in the glove box." When he brought it out, its three-inch, black-and-white screen was displaying the same view of Buddy Holly that had driven me from my home and instigated worldwide chaos. Pete spun the tuner, and the picture popped off and on as the receiver caught different stations.

Buddy was sitting in the dust, plinking the strings of his Stratocaster. He look stranded and forlorn. I turned away and stared toward the black road some more.

"What the hell's that?" Gretchen said.

I scanned the night. "I don't see anything."

"Not out there, mush-for-brains. On TV."

I looked at the picture. The camera had drawn back so that Buddy was a minuscule figure at the bottom of the screen, and he was gazing up at an object that floated several feet over his head. It was a shimmering, oblong, Cadillac-size thing that blazed as if made from the stuff of supergiant stars.

"I've never seen anything like it," I murmured.

"I have," Pete said. "That's what appeared when we were about to have that head-on crash. See, it's shaped like a spoon."

The object rotated on its long axis with ponderous slowness, its nebulous halo shrinking and swelling as if with a gargantuan heartbeat. As I watched, I became aware that its shape was not that of a spoon.

"It's a guitar," I said.

Gretchen shook her head. "No. A crescent wrench. Or maybe, it's more like . . . well, *you* know."

A spoon, a guitar, a wrench, a rocket, a phallus: It was all of these, and none.

Whatever it was, Buddy was glad to see it. He stood, leaving his Strat at his feet, and raised his arms.

"Hey, you finally showed up!" he cried. "Thank you, Oliver Vale! I'm ready to go home!"

But Oliver Vale sat on a fender in Kansas, shivering, knowing that Buddy had waited in vain. The glowing thing would not bring him home. It stayed out of his reach, rotating and pulsing in silence.

After a while, Buddy lowered his arms. He looked at the object for a few more minutes, and then, with a shrug of resignation, he picked up his guitar and began playing.

He sang "Crying, Waiting, Hoping." It's one of his best, written in New York and recorded in his apartment with a custom-made Guild acoustic just weeks before his death. It's a song of love, loss, and yearned-for redemption.

"Jeez, what's that?" Gretchen said.

"Whatever you want it to be," I said.

"Not that, pruneface. Over there."

She pointed toward a wavering red light that illuminated the clouds over the western horizon.

"It's Wichita," Pete said. "It must be on fire."

We reentered the Kamikaze with Pete behind the wheel. He turned on the radio, and it told us that angry religious groups and couch potatoes had set massive bonfires outside TV stations not only in Wichita, but in cities across the country. Stations in Denver, San Diego, and Baltimore had already burned to the ground, and others were sure to follow. Some of the fires had spread far beyond their points of origin.

And the fires were not the only civil disturbances.

In New York City, the mayor had declared martial law. The consensus of the radio commentators was that he didn't have the power to do that, but he had done it anyway. With or without the governor's consent, he had rallied two or three thousand National Guardsmen to assist the police in squelching the rioters who were tearing apart the RCA Building. At the latest report, however, the rioters had been squelching the Guardsmen, who were retreating to Wall Street to regroup. There, it was predicted, they would be attacked by berserk stockbrokers.

In Boston, the infamous downtown Combat Zone had actually become one. A horde of overweight men who normally spent their evenings at home watching television were fighting in the streets over the peep shows and prostitutes.

In St. Louis, crazed people wielding cutting torches were attempting to topple the 630-foot, stainless-steel Gateway Arch, claiming that it was the broadcast antenna for the Buddy Holly disturbance.

In Tokyo, everybody was trying to work extra shifts

so that they wouldn't have to watch television. Factories were becoming overcrowded as workers refused to return to their dormitories.

In London, Labour leaders were blaming the Tories for failing to deal with the crisis, and the Tories were blaming Labour. Skinheads had burst into Parliament and had chain-whipped M.P.s regardless of party affiliation.

Reports from Warsaw and Moscow suggested that Polish and Soviet citizens were enjoying the change of programming.

Six Flags Over Texas had been overrun by entertainment-starved Dallas Yuppies.

Movie theaters everywhere had been reduced to rubble by throngs battling for tickets.

Burbank was being sacked.

The reports were horrifying, hilarious, bizarre, and devastating. The more we listened, the more it seemed as if it all had to be a colossal joke—but the picture on the TV in Pete's hand proved otherwise. Buddy was in his Jovian heaven, and all was wrong with the world.

Besides which, the Oklahoma Kamikaze had been sitting behind a rural oil tank for over thirty minutes, and neither the cops nor Peggy Sue had passed by. I was beginning to feel SkyVue tugging at me, telling me that it had the answer I needed if I would only hurry up and take a look. . . .

"Let's go to El Dorado," I said.

Pete started the Barracuda, and we left our hiding place just as a constellation of headlight beams appeared from behind the evergreens to the north. Pete killed the Kamikaze's lights and tried to back up, but it was too late. The first of a gang of fifteen motorcycles and pickup trucks had already turned onto the pumper's road, and there was nowhere for us to go.

Gretchen grabbed her tire iron and jumped out of the car as it stopped. "If I die because of you, Vale," she yelled, "the ghost of Buddy Holly is gonna be the least of your worries!"

Pete shut down the Kamikaze and smiled in the glare of the approaching headlights. "She's a bitch," he said. "I like her." He got out, and I followed.

The gang's lead vehicle was a monster Harley. It stopped twenty feet from the Kamikaze and sat idling, pinning us with its beam. Several more bikes and three pickups crowded behind it, and their combined noise was like the growl of a tiger the size of a 747.

Gretchen swung her tire iron as if she were warming up for batting practice. "Come on!" she yelled. "None of you weenies needs a head anyway, right?"

I stepped forward, hoping to intervene before Gretchen could get us shot, or worse. "Listen," I shouted to the gang, "I know that everybody blames me for what's happened, but I'm innocent! Have you seen *The Ox Bow Incident*? Same deal!"

"Piss on that!" Gretchen yelled. "Wimp!"

A massive shadow detached itself from the Harley and strode toward us. "Where'd you find her, Vale?" a booming voice asked. "She seems fuckin' dangerous."

"Come a few steps closer, shitheap, and find out how much," Gretchen snarled. She raised the tire iron.

Pete reached inside the Kamikaze and turned on its lights, and then I saw that the man who stood before us—his red hair wild, his crescent wrench gleaming in the bib pocket of his overalls—was Boog Burdon.

"Heard a rumor on the radio that you were heading this way again," Boog said, "so I thought I'd bring fourteen of my closest friends to give you an escort, if you want one."

"Rave on!" a voice behind the cluster of headlights

cried, and a dozen others answered, *"Rave on!"*

"Throwback city," Gretchen said, lowering her weapon. "What have we got here? A bunch of middle-aged beer-guts who all think they're Fonzie?"

I moved between her and Boog. "Boog Burdon, meet Gretchen Laird and Pete Holden."

"Fuckin' pleasure." He squinted and looked from side to side. "Hey, where's the Ariel?"

My chest twinged. "The last time I saw her, the Bill Willyites had her."

Boog scowled. "Some of those snake-handling pud-knockers are having a prayer meeting at the drive-in a few miles north. That's why I wanted to find you. You either need to have some protection or avoid 'em altogether."

I considered. I didn't want to deal with another mob of folks who thought I was the Antichrist, but whatever secret was hidden at the theater was tugging hard now, as if it were the magnetic heart of the planet and I were the needle of a compass. I had to go there.

"I'll take the protection," I said. "If I can get into SkyVue, I think I may be able to help Buddy." Although I didn't know how.

Boog's eyebrows rose. "Bitchin'. Me and the boys ain't been in a good fight for three or four hours."

I turned toward Pete, who was sitting on the Kamikaze's hood. "I can ride with Boog from here. You've done too much already, and your kids are going to wonder what the hell's happened to you. And, Gretchen, well, you've got to get on to Houston. I've messed up your life enough."

"Big of you to admit it, roadapple," she said.

Pete entered the Kamikaze through the windshield gap. "Oliver," he said as he buckled himself in, "I trust

Laura and Mike to take care of themselves. I'm not turning back until I see you dead or in jail."

Gretchen rolled her eyes. "That could take hours. I'm not going to stand here and wait."

"So let's rock 'n' roll!" Boog shouted.

"Rock 'n' roll!" his gang roared back.

"Bunch of microcephalic sixties goobers," Gretchen muttered.

She and I joined Pete, and the Kamikaze followed Boog's Harley to the county road. The other vehicles fell in beside and behind us, and we accelerated toward El Dorado.

If I survived SkyVue, I told myself, I wouldn't mind going to jail . . . because if I lived that long, I was sure to have found some answers.

If, on the other hand, Boog and his brigade couldn't keep the Bill Willyites from burning me at the stake—

Then that would be the will of Fate, or of whoever was in charge. Maybe John. Maybe Elvis. Maybe Sam. Maybe Buddy. Maybe, baby. In that case, I was ready to go to the Spirit Land. Mother could fix a pot roast.

I had my army and my gods around me, and despite the loss of Peggy Sue, I was no longer afraid.

No more crying. No more waiting. No more hoping.

I had indulged in enough of that for one life. Now it was time to *do* something.

SHARON

Notes, continued . . .

Bruce drove as if possessed, but so did the man on the motorcycle. The one time that we almost caught up, a Datsun cut across the median in front of us. If we had not been wearing our safety belts, both Bruce and I would have gone through the windshield. A man leaned out of the offending car and shouted at us, but I could not hear what he said over the things that Bruce was shouting himself. I suspected that the people in the Datsun had recognized Oliver's motorcycle and had decided to pursue it, either for a reward or for the opportunity to do Oliver physical harm.

Soon thereafter, Bruce thought that he saw the motorcycle leave the interstate for a two-lane highway; in any case, the Datsun did so. Although I had not seen the Ariel, I decided not to protest Bruce's decision to take the exit. He had become a wild man. His face was peppered with black-and-blond stubble, his hair was tousled, and his eyes were wide. I hoped that I would not have to restrain him from killing Oliver when at last we encountered him.

We zigzagged up and down highways and back roads until well after dark. I could see the Datsun's taillights, but nothing from the motorcycle. Bruce insisted that it was just out of the range of my vision.

"I can count all seven Pleiades," he told me in an excited rush when we stopped for gasoline. "Trust me, baby, that bike's there. And we're gonna *get* it."

I wanted to ask whom he thought he was calling "baby," but I was busy running for the rest room. When I came out, Bruce stuffed a twenty-dollar bill into the nozzle of the gasoline hose, dropped the nozzle to the pavement, jumped back into the car, and was accelerating before I had both feet inside. The entire refueling stop, including my trip to the rest room, had taken perhaps forty-five seconds.

"Too long!" Bruce cried, pounding his fist on the steering wheel. "We'll have to go ninety to catch up!"

He proceeded to go ninety, and I wished that I had stayed in Topeka and let Oliver take care of himself.

We encountered the stopped Ariel on a desolate stretch of road in Kansas. The Datsun had apparently gone on.

As we pulled up behind the motorcycle on the dirt shoulder, the machine itself was all that could be seen. I feared that the occupants of the Datsun had captured Oliver.

Bruce left our car idling and stepped out to have a closer look at the motorcycle. "The engine's still hot," he called. "Maybe he's just taking a whiz in the field."

As Bruce spoke, the driver's door of our car opened, and a bald man got inside. He must have been hiding on the other side of the road. He was not Oliver. I shouted.

The bald man produced a pistol and pointed it at me. The greenish light from the dash instruments gleamed along its barrel. "Out," the man said.

I exited the car. Bruce had noticed that something was wrong and was starting back, but it was too late. Our Chevrolet started toward him, forcing him to jump into the ditch, and then sped off to the north.

After he climbed back to the road, the first coherent words out of Bruce's mouth were, "Was that your little piece of shit friend Vale? If it was, he's a goddamn dead man." In the dark, I couldn't see Bruce's face, but I imagined that it looked like that of an enraged anthropoid ape.

"It wasn't Oliver," I said. "But he was bald, so it was him that we saw on the motorcycle."

"Oh, gee, really?" Bruce said, bitterly sarcastic. "Tell me something I don't know, like why did the son of a bitch stop here?" He went to the Ariel and sat astride it, turning on the headlight.

"I would guess that he either had engine trouble or became too cold to ride farther," I said.

"Well, his ass is grass," Bruce said. "We're gonna *get* the cocksucker." He began kicking the Ariel's starter.

"I think you should see a colleague of mine when we return to Topeka," I said.

"I'm not going back to Topeka," he said, breathing heavily as he continued to kick the starter. "Not until I *get* that ball of putrid spit." He stopped kicking. "Hah! The damn thing's just out of gas!"

"I fail to see how that's any better."

"It's better," Bruce said, "because that dickhead didn't know jack about bikes. The reserve tank's good for twenty or thirty miles, so as soon as I find the valve—hah!" He kicked the starter three more times, and the engine sputtered to life.

"Since when did you know anything about motorcycles?" I asked.

"Since before law school, baby!" he cried. "Since before I started my life of crap! Now get on or walk!"

I was wearing a skirt, so I had to hitch it up. I climbed onto the seat behind Bruce and put my arms around his waist, hating what was about to happen.

The motorcycle accelerated hard, and I almost fell off. The wind cut through me like icicles. My only saving thought, my mantra, was that the town of El Dorado was less than twenty miles ahead. Bruce would have to stop there for gasoline, and then I would end our pursuit. Bruce's firm's Chevrolet had been stolen; Bruce himself had reverted to his white trash ancestry; civilization was crumbling; and Oliver could be anywhere from Lubbock to Topeka.

I was going to cut my losses and call it quits. Even being a good psychologist has its limits.

RICHTER

He had almost killed the man and woman in the Chevrolet, but now he was glad that he hadn't wasted the bullets on either them or on the Datsun that had whisked past earlier. Judging from the sight ahead of him, he might need all three of his extra clips.

The motorcycles and pickups were spread out over the width of the blacktop so that he couldn't pass, but when one of the pickups shifted so that he could see the white Barracuda, he was content to stay behind the cluster. He had overtaken his quarry. No matter what his superiors believed, he was still the best. The thought warmed him, driving away the chill he had caught on the motorcycle.

Richter counted three heads inside the Barracuda. One of them was Vale's. It was too bad that he couldn't get a clear shot now, but if he had been able to wait this long, he could wait a little longer. El Dorado was not far ahead. He hoped that they would stop there.

Several of the bikers were turning to give him glares of warning, so he dropped back to quell their suspicions for the time being. There would be plenty of opportunity to eliminate any of them who interfered with him later.

He counted twelve bikers and three pickup drivers. Even if he used two rounds apiece, he would have more than enough ammunition. When the time came, though, he would try to be more conservative than that.

He was, after all, a conservative man.

CATHY AND JEREMY

The government agent was dismounting the motorcycle as Cathy and Jeremy approached. He raised his arms to their Datsun as if in supplication.

"Oh, sure," Cathy said. "We stop, you shoot us. I don't think so." She drove past.

"What a break!" Jeremy exclaimed. "Lucky for Oliver Vale that he doesn't maintain his motorcycle well. If he did, Baldy would still be after him."

"Baldy's only been slowed up a little."

"Maybe, but Vale and his friends aren't even in sight." Jeremy frowned. "Of course, that's bad for us. If only we had Ringo . . ." He put a thumb and forefinger on his dog-eye and jiggled it. "I'm sure that I felt the link being replaced a while ago, but it still isn't working. It almost feels as if Ringo is willing a transmission block."

"Can he do that?"

"I dunno. He's a dog. He might as well be an alien."

"As usual, you're full of excuses," Cathy said. "But we don't need Ringo to track Vale, because I know exactly where he's going. You've been so busy fiddling with your eyeball that you haven't even been paying attention to where the chase has taken us."

Jeremy looked outside. "It's dark. The ground is flat. I see oil pumps. It could be anywhere from South Dakota to South Texas."

"Try South Kansas. We're near the ancient physical site of our city, on the same road that we took out of El Dorado on the way down. That means—"

"Oh, no!" Jeremy cried. "Vale's going to SkyVue!"

"What's wrong with that? If we know where he's going, we know where to find him. Our pro-flesh cousins won't dare interfere with us."

"It's not them I'm worried about. Don't you remember the words on SkyVue's marquee? There's a Willard rally there tonight!"

Cathy looked stunned. "How could I have forgotten that?" She glared at Jeremy. "Your stupid brain design, that's how!"

She pressed the accelerator to the floor, but the Datsun would go no faster than sixty-five.

"Oh, please, please, don't let them shred his flesh before we can help him!" Cathy pleaded.

"To whom are you speaking?" Jeremy asked.

Cathy looked puzzled. "I have no idea."

SkyVue became visible when they were still four miles away. The marquee was brilliant white with splotches of red, and the visible sliver of the screen flashed with blues and greens. Searchlight beams swayed inside the viewing area, and diamond-bright strobes played about their bases. The yellow flame of the refinery burned above them all.

"I see flashbulbs," Jeremy said. "They must be standing on their cars and taking pictures of the Reverend. Look at that! There are hundreds of them!"

"Enough to blind the bastard, I hope."

"That's an awfully fleshbound thing to say, Cath."

"I'm in flesh. I don't have a choice."

As they reached the theater entrance, a string of motorcycles and pickup trucks rumbled past, heading south. The riders and drivers were all large and hairy.

"If we missed Vale, I hope that he doesn't run into that bunch," Jeremy said. "They don't look like the sort to show him any mercy."

"And if we didn't miss him and he's here, the Wil-
lardites will show him plenty, I suppose," Cathy said,
steering the Datsun into the drive.

Two men in dark brown three-piece suits blocked
the drive beyond the ticket booth, and a woman with
blond hair as stiff as a helmet leaned out of the booth
and smiled a beauty-queen smile. Cathy stopped the car
and rolled down her window.

"Two adults to hear Reverend Willard denounce Satan's broadcast?" the blonde said brightly. "You're in luck.
The program is running just a teensy bit late, and the
Reverend himself hasn't spoken yet. Forty dollars,
please."

"Take American Express?" Cathy asked.

"Of course, sister."

Cathy handed over the card, and when the blonde
handed it back, the brown-suited men stepped aside. As
the Datsun rolled past, Jeremy shuddered. "Ringo's eye
tingles when I look at those guys," he said. "Think they
have something bad in their jackets?"

"No doubt. I've seen those suits on TV. They're ministers of the Corps of Little David."

The Datsun passed through a gap in the tall wooden
fence that hid the theater grounds from the road, and
Cathy and Jeremy became engulfed by the rally. Cars
and trucks crammed the lot, and people stood on the roofs
snapping flash photographs. Others wandered among the
vehicles, clapping and shouting. Women spoke in tongues
and men writhed on the asphalt. Children cried and dogs
fornicated. On the movie screen, a woman who might
have been the twin of the one in the ticket booth was
singing "He's Got the Whole World in His Hands." Her
voice spewed from a thousand speakers hanging from
poles and car windows.

The Datsun crawled as Cathy looked for a place to

park and tried to avoid running over several hundred
people who seemed unaware that they were standing in
a roadway. Meanwhile, Jeremy craned his neck to gaze
at the screen. "I wonder if that's real-time," he said.

Cathy pointed at the snack bar/projection building,
which sat in the center of the ten-acre lot. The woman
whose face was on the screen stood on a platform on the
building's roof, surrounded by floodlights, musicians,
video cameras, and Corps ministers. A cameraman on
the boom of a small crane hovered over her like a mech-
anized angel. A crowd thronged about the building,
singing along with the woman.

"Say, I wonder if the snack bar's open," Jeremy said.
"I could use a hot dog."

"Wonderful. We're trying to save Oliver Vale's life,
and you want food. It was your idea that we had a responsibility to help the jerk in the first place."

Jeremy looked abashed. "Sorry. The spirit is willing, but the flesh is hungry."

Cathy finally parked the Datsun at the back of the
lot, beyond the last row of speaker poles, and she and
Jeremy climbed onto the car's roof to scan the crowd.
The people atop the snack bar were silhouetted against
the movie screen that displayed their images.

"Vale isn't here yet," Cathy said.

"How do you know?"

"Because if he were, these fleshbound larvae wouldn't
be singing or listening to anyone who was. They'd have
what was left of Vale's body hanging from the crane,
and they'd be fighting over the remaining pieces."

"But he was ahead of us, and we didn't pass him,"
Jeremy said. "Perhaps he just hasn't been recognized.
The Willyites wouldn't expect him to be in a car with
two companions."

"Well, do you see the Barracuda anywhere?"

Jeremy squinted. "Can't tell. These eyes aren't working properly."

The woman on the snack-bar roof stopped singing, and the crowd cheered. Simultaneously, the crane boom sank to the ground and was encircled by brown suits.

"Thank you so much!" the woman's voice rang from the myriad speakers. "Thank you and God Bless! It's now a little after midnight, and time to hear from the leader of our cause, the defender of our freedoms—"

The crowd erupted in a roar.

The boom rose, and a gray-pinstriped figure in the basket raised his fists. Every floodlight on the snack bar swiveled toward him.

The beefy, white-toothed, tanned, movie-star-father-figure face of the Reverend William Willard appeared on the screen. His expression was one of self-satisfied determination.

When the basket touched down on the roof, the Reverend stepped out as if he were the first man to set foot on another planet. He opened his fists to quiet the roar of his congregation.

"My dear friends!" he cried, his voice exploding from the speakers with the force of a bomb. "It is clear to me now that the Lord brought me to El Dorado, Kansas, tonight for a purpose. Friends, I have just been informed that the Antichrist's representative, the man who stole our God-given American freedom of mass-media expression—"

The crowd booed.

"—has been seen coming this way! Yes, friends, Oliver Vale—how my tongue burns to speak the name!— is being delivered into our very hands!"

The crowd cheered.

"I have sent ministers of my Corps of Little David into the countryside to watch for his approach. If the

Lord wills it, they shall bring him here to us—although I have no doubt that the Lord *will* bring him here one way or another! And when that happens, friends . . ." Bill Willy's voice dropped, and the crowd hushed to hear him. "And when that happens, I ask for your Christian mercy. Vengeance belongs to the Lord, and I ask that you allow me to ensure that He gets it. Do not pummel this Vale creature into submission; do not rend his flesh; do not pull out his forked and flicking tongue."

"Amen!" someone screamed, and the crowd's voice broke free again.

Cathy and Jeremy climbed down from the roof of the Datsun and gave each other grim looks.

"Christian mercy, my fleshbound ass," Cathy said. "He might as well have told them to shred him."

Jeremy took a deep breath. "Cath, we aren't going to be able to stop it. Not by ourselves."

"So you want to give up?" Cathy sounded almost relieved.

"No. We need help, and our cousins are right here."

Cathy was ahgast. "The pro-flesh? This whole mess is their fault!"

"All the more reason why they should be able to help us find Vale. He's their boy, and I can't believe that they really want him to die."

"Why not?" Cathy snapped. "Others have already died. Maybe the pro-flesh *want* a few martyrs."

"Maybe," Jeremy said. "I'll ask them." He began walking toward the distant movie screen.

Cathy hurried after him. "We don't even know what their fleshbound shells look like! There are thousands of bodies here, and they could be in any two of them! And if they *aren't* in the flesh anymore, we won't be able to commune with them, because we *are*."

Jeremy shrugged. "They're here somewhere, Cath.

We'll just have to hope that our flesh hasn't dulled our sense of them so much that it doesn't intensify when we're close."

"We'll have to comb the entire place!"

"Vale's life, and perhaps the lives of others as well, are at stake," Jeremy said. "If you have a better idea—"

Cathy charged ahead of him. "All right, all right! Let's start at the snack bar!"

"Why?"

"Because I'm starved!"

They bought hot dogs and then searched for their fellow Seekers as the Reverend William Willard continued to exhort his flock.

Their cousins were nowhere to be found.

12

OLIVER

In the early morning hours of Friday, February 3, 1984, Mother died and left me alone in her house. In the early morning hours of Friday, February 3, 1989, I was driven from that house by Buddy Holly's video resurrection.

I cannot help believing that the second event depended upon the first. After all, Mother's death itself resulted from what had happened a quarter century before. The events of our lives affect each other not as a line of toppling dominoes, but as the links of a chain being used as a whip.

Mother would not have become pregnant if my father C. had not made love to her; my father C. would not have committed suicide if Buddy had not died; I would not have been born a bastard if my father C. had lived to marry Mother; Mother's life would not have been so hard if I had not been a bastard; Mother would not have become obsessed with her "other world" if her life had not been so hard.

She would not have died as she did.

I knew that Mother thought of the "other world" as a place where one's spirit would live on, where Buddy Holly and Sam Cooke and John Lennon all sang without tiring. I knew that she believed her mission on the corporeal plane had ended when I became an adult, and that she was only marking time until she could rejoin her lover and her gods. I knew that the twenty-fifth anniversary of my conception, and of Buddy's and C.'s deaths, would be a critical day.

I did nothing.

On Thursday, February 2, 1984, a coworker took me to lunch and introduced me to a twenty-seven-year-old bank secretary named Julie Calloway, with whom I made a date for that evening. I had ridden my motorcycle to town, so I would meet Julie at her apartment, and we would go out in her car. I called Mother to tell her that I wouldn't be home for supper. She said that was fine.

By the time Julie drove us back to her place that night, it was after twelve. We both had to go to work in the morning, so we agreed that I wouldn't come in . . . but as we kissed, we wound up in the same bucket seat. Julie murmured that she was on the pill and that she hadn't done it in a car in ages. Neither had I. It was like going back in time.

The car radio was tuned to KKAP, and as Julie and I struggled, we were bombarded with pop rock. REO. Billy Joel. Van Halen. Huey Lewis. Then, as we were about to climax, the soundtrack changed.

"It's one A.M.," the disc jockey said. "Twenty-five years ago at about this moment—"

I fell into ice water.

"What is it?" Julie asked. "What's wrong?"

"I'm sorry," I said, opening the door and grabbing

the Moonsuit from the back seat. "I'm sorry, I'm sorry."

As I ran for Peggy Sue, I heard the opening riff of "I'm Gonna Love You Too." I ached to stay so that I could listen with Julie for the chirping cricket at the end.

I found Mother in the garage, sitting in the Dart with the engine and radio on. Buddy was singing "Heartbeat." The garage was full of fumes. Mother's skin was cold.

I dragged her into the yard, where I forced my breath into her lungs and pummeled her heart. I shouted for a neighbor to call an ambulance, but the nearest houses were dark, and no one shouted back.

I ran inside, leaving Mother on the dead grass, and found Volume VII of her diary lying open on the kitchen table. Beside it was a white sticker on which she had written, "January 19, 1981 to February 3, 1984. Conclusion."

The entry on the last page was brief:

My son will do well without me. Buddy's spirit sings in his blood, and he is old enough now that he needs no other protector. I am free to do as I wish. C. is waiting.

Remember, world: Even Jesus had to die at least once, but rock and roll lives forever.

I pasted the sticker on the spine and telephoned for an ambulance.

By the time I returned from the hospital, the Dart was out of gas and its battery was dead. Eight days later, I sold it.

I sent a telegram to Grandmother, who in 1980 had written a letter saying that she was moving back to Des Moines and that she wanted nothing further to do with us. We'd had no contact with her since, and I wasn't even sure that she was still alive. In any case, she neither appeared at the memorial service nor sent flowers.

The service was held at the funeral home and had only myself, some KKAP employees, and three of Mother's seance companions in attendance. The organist refused to play any Buddy Holly songs, so the whole thing was a waste of time.

Afterward, I rode Peggy Sue to Clear Lake, where I scattered Mother's ashes in a field that a farmer told me was the one where the Bonanza had crashed. Even if it wasn't, it was close enough. I had done the best I could.

But only in that.

I could have helped her find a way to make her corporeal life worth living. Instead, I had abandoned her on the most crucial night of her adult life, and she had died.

After I came home from Clear Lake, that thought recurred with increasing frequency. Whenever it did, I got on Peggy Sue and rode far away until my only thoughts were of the road, and the trees, and the sky. Until my Ariel and I became a meteor burning through the night.

In April, Julie Calloway called. She didn't make love on the first date with just anyone, she said. Something special had passed between us, and she would not let it get away if she could help it.

Which she couldn't. We began seeing each other again, but whenever a problem or argument seemed imminent, I rode away. Sometimes I was gone for two or three days.

Julie was patient. She knew what it was like to lose a mother, she said, and would give me the time I needed to overcome my grief. My grief, however, had dissipated at the moment that I had scattered Mother's ashes in a holy place. Grief is easy. Guilt is hard.

We were together for almost five years. She even lived with me for a year in the middle. When she moved

back to her own apartment, she warned that if I ever
ran away again, we were finished. She told me this in
colorful, obscene terms that made me love her more than
I already did.

I ran away six more times. After the sixth time, I
brought her a bag of cheeseburgers, and she told me to
eat shit and die. I took the burgers home and snarfed
them while watching *Beat the Devil* via satellite from
Vancouver. When they were gone, I rode away again,
but I returned after a few hours. I felt too heavy to run
anymore. Besides, Cowboy Carl was getting pissed at his
star salesman for missing so many days. A man has to
make a living. Mother's house still wasn't paid for.

*

Boog halted our convoy a half mile south of SkyVue.
The night was dominated by searchlight beams and the
flame of the refinery tower, and the taste of burning fuel
scorched my mouth. It was almost 1:00 A.M.

Boog dismounted his Harley and walked back to the
Kamikaze. "You sure you want to go in?" he asked me.

The crowd of Willyites was hidden behind the theater's wooden fence, but an oceanic murmur of voices
gave me an idea of its size. I did *not* want to go in, but
the tugging sensation that had drawn me here had become overwhelming, as if I were a lemming unable to
stop running for a seaside cliff. I still couldn't imagine
what I was supposed to find, but I knew, just as I knew
the locations of my feet and hands, where it was.

"I have to get to the snack bar," I said.

Pete was watching the rearview mirror. "Better
hurry."

I looked back. Two of the bikers were immediately
behind us, but beyond them, a Chevrolet sedan was
coming to a stop. Even through the glare of its head-

lights, I saw that the driver was the Bald Avenger.

"Go!" I yelled, ducking. "Go go *go!*"

Boog ran for his bike, and his gang charged forward. The two that had been behind us sped past.

Our radio dial exploded, throwing plastic flak. I glanced up and saw that the Barracuda's rear window had a bullet hole. The Kamikaze leaped ahead.

The gang swerved into SkyVue's driveway, formed a ragged phalanx, and paused as Boog's Harley and the Kamikaze pulled up behind the pickup truck at the point. Ahead was a ticket booth lit by yellow tubes. Two men wearing the dark brown suits of the Corps of Little David stood beside it. One of them waved, and ten more brown-suited men emerged from behind the satellite dishes on the lawn. Out on the road, the Bald Avenger's car was approaching the entrance.

Boog brought his machine alongside the Barracuda and grinned in at me. "A good fuckin' day to die!" he said, and raced his engine. His gang did likewise. A woman ran from the ticket booth and hid behind a satellite dish. I pulled on my helmet.

"I hate this," Gretchen said, gripping her tire iron. "I really hate this."

Boog popped his clutch, and the phalanx surged. The Kamikaze screamed like a tyrannosaur, and I was slammed back in my seat. Sixteen representatives of dead technology burst from their collective grave and raced to meet the forces of SkyVue.

One of the pickups hit the ticket booth, which burst into a shower of plaster and glass, and the two Corps ministers in the drive scrambled away. The fence splintered as the lead pickup rammed it, and then we were past, and through, and swallowed by chaos.

The way to the snack bar was clogged with men, women, and children, and our phalanx disintegrated to

avoid plowing into them. Two pickups collided, and three
motorcycles went down. The Kamikaze slid sideways,
pinning Boog's Harley against a post. The third pickup and the rest of the bikes veered off among the rows
of cars.

Pete killed the Barracuda's engine, and he and
Gretchen crawled out via the windshield hole. I clambered through the glassless passenger window and
slumped across the fuel tank of Boog's motorcycle.

Boog pointed up at the movie screen. There, the forty-
foot visage of the Reverend William Willard, looking like
the offspring of Edwin Meese and a Komodo dragon,
glared in displeasure.

"WHAT IS THIS?" he demanded, his voice thunder-
ing. "YOU CAN'T DISRUPT A PEACEFUL GATHER-
ING OF GOD-FEARING AMERICANS. WE HAVE A
PERMIT."

Gretchen, standing with Pete on the hood of the Kamikaze, raised a fist and extended the middle finger. For
an instant, I was six years old again, watching my mother
defy the elemental beast that would try to kill us.

The crowd roared and began to gravitate toward us,
compressing its mass as if we were a singularity at the
heart of a black hole. Four members of Boog's gang were
caught in the crush and beaten with flashlights.

As they approached, the Willyites gathered white
rocks from the theater lot. The first one they threw shattered the Harley's headlight, and the second ricocheted
from my helmet. Then there were too many to count.
Gretchen swung her tire iron and batted away an in-
credible number, but it wasn't enough. We were going
to be killed.

Boog leaped from his bike and dove at the rock
throwers, swinging fists like sledgehammers, while I
jumped onto the Kamikaze's hood and tackled Pete and

Gretchen. A searchlight beam swung down to trap us in brilliance.

"What do you think you're doing, shithead?" Gretchen screamed beneath me.

"Protecting you from the rocks! I'm wearing a magic spacesuit!"

"But we already have something better," Pete said. " 'Let us therefore cast off the works of darkness, and let us put on the armor of light!' " He broke free of me and stood. The rocks came flying faster and thicker than ever, but Pete smiled in the electric blaze and was not touched.

I relaxed my grip on Gretchen, and she stood as well. When she swung her tire iron at a flying stone, it curved away as if repulsed by a magnetic field.

"BROTHERS AND SISTERS, STOP," the face on the movie screen commanded. "ALLOW THE MINISTERS OF THE CORPS TO BRING THE TRESPASSERS TO ME."

The stones stopped, and I stood up beside Pete and Gretchen. Shielding my eyes from the welding-torch-bright light, I watched as Boog, bloodied but still grinning, shoved his way out of the crowd and leaned on the Barracuda's fender. The other members of his gang, minus their vehicles, began struggling toward us as well.

"BRING ONLY THE FOUR ON THE AUTOMOBILE. THE OTHERS ARE PUPPETS. THROW THEM OUT WITHOUT THEIR SHOES."

Boog's friends were seized by a multitude of Willyites and dragged away. Boog started forward as if to rescue all fourteen of them, but as he did, eight men in brown suits appeared before us. Four of them held wrist-braced, rubber-surgical-tubing-powered metal slingshots loaded with ball bearings the size of marbles. The ministers were pointing them at our heads.

I jumped down and grasped Boog's arm. "If you make

a move, they'll nail us. And I'm the only one with a helmet."

Boog stopped, but his massive body remained tense. "Tell me again why you wanted to get here," he said.

"BRING THEM TO THE SNACK BAR," Bill Willy commanded.

"Oh, yeah," Boog said. " 'Why did the Antichrist cross Oklahoma?' 'To get to the snack bar.' "

They took us out of the light and marched us through the mob to the center of the lot, where the Reverend waited atop a cement-block building. A truck with a cherry picker sat nearby, but our captors lifted us by hand to fellow ministers who hauled us up and threw us onto the tar-and-gravel roof as if we were tuna.

I was the last one. The gravel bit into my bare hands, and energy thrummed into my palms as if I were touching an electric fence. I was almost where I was supposed to be.

When I raised my head, I saw the life-size version of William Willard standing on a platform and looking upon me with contempt. My contact-weary eyes hadn't recovered from the searchlight, so I saw him bathed in a greenish aura.

"SO THIS IS THE MAN WHO CLAIMED HE COULD SAVE THE WORLD," Bill Willy said.

I rose to my knees. "No. Buddy read a sign that said to contact me for assistance, but I didn't have anything to do with that. Besides, that only meant assistance for *him*."

Pete was on his knees beside me. "How do you know?"

It occurred to me that I didn't.

"Your Reverendness," Gretchen called out, "I agree that this schmuck"—she indicated me— "couldn't save

his way out of a wet paper bag. But he doesn't pretend
to be able to, either." She and Boog were both kneeling
as well, and a Corps minister stood behind each of us. I
didn't like it. In the movies, the gangsters make you kneel
like that when they're going to open up the back of your
head.

Bill Willy laughed. "HERE THEY ARE, FLAP-
PING THEIR FORKED TONGUES, SHOUTING THAT
THEIR LEADER HAD NOTHING TO DO WITH THIS
INVASION OF OUR WAY OF LIFE! OF COURSE YOU
DIDN'T, SATAN. YOU'RE AS INNOCENT AS A BA-
BY'S BEHIND. WE BELIEVE HIM, DON'T WE, GOOD
PEOPLE?"

The crowd screamed, *"No!"*

"Shit heel Mickey Mouse!" Boog bellowed. "Y'fuckin'
morons! It's only television!"

"MORE THAN THIRTY YEARS AGO," the Rever-
end continued, "I WARNED THE PEOPLE OF THIS
NATION ABOUT THE DEMON EMBODIED IN ROCK
AND ROLL. 'BUDDY HOLLY AND HIS ILK SING
MUSIC TO STEAL HUBCAPS BY,' I TOLD THEM. BUT
THEY WOULDN'T LISTEN, AND NOW THE DEMON
HAS INVADED EVERY TELEVISION SET IN THE
WORLD SO THAT NO ONE CAN ESCAPE IT! IT
CONTAMINATES OUR LIVES, SCREECHING ITS
DARK HYMNS OF DEGRADATION—"

A red mist replaced his aura, and I recognized him.
His was the face of the pastor from 1967, the one that
Mrs. Stummert had dragged me to when I had sung
"Sergeant Pepper's Lonely Hearts Club Band" in Vaca-
tion Bible School. His was the face of the pastor who had
called me a piece of dogshit and put his hands on me. . . .

I lurched up from my knees and stumbled toward
him. "You don't talk about my life like that, fat butt!"

I was within four feet of the platform when I was

knocked down from behind and kicked onto my back. A
minister stood over me with his legs spread in a macho
stance on either side of my feet. His slingshot was aimed
at my crotch.

"AND NOW HE REVEALS HIS TRUE NATURE!"
the Reverend said triumphantly. "A SNARLING, WEAK-
KNEED SERVANT OF EVIL!"

"So's your mother!" I cried, and scissored my legs.
My heels hit the macho minister in the ankles, and he
fell on his ass. The slingshot's aim was ruined, and its
ball bearing smashed one of the floodlights shining on
Bill Willy. The crowd shrieked like banshees, and the
Corps ministers on the roof were distracted.

Pete tripped his guard as the man came to assist
the one I had toppled, and Boog grasped his own minister's lapels and flung him off the building. Gretchen
grabbed her guard's slingshot tubing and whirled him
from the roof as well. Boog threw mine after Gretchen's.

Pete's minister was still down, but as I stood, he
managed to ready his slingshot and point it at me. Other
Little Davids emerged from behind the lights and equipment and stood in a semicircle, all aiming at me.

I have no innate courage, but whatever had drawn
me to that place had damped my usual cowardice, and I
saw what would happen if the Corps let fly. I spread my
arms wide. "Fine! Drill me full of steel! Meanwhile, my
friends can take bets on how many shots'll hit the Reverend!"

That gave them pause, and I took advantage of the
moment by leaping onto the platform and putting my
arm around Willard's shoulders. He tried to twist away,
but I held him tight and faced the bizarre image of my
helmeted self hugging him on the movie screen.

The crowd, enraged and screaming, began to flow
up the sides of the snack bar.

"Make them stay down," I said into the Reverend's ear, "or I'll do something perverted to make your ministers shoot, and we'll both be Swiss cheese."

The Reverend gave me a malevolent glare and spoke into his microphone. "REMAIN WHERE YOU ARE, BROTHERS AND SISTERS! THIS CREATURE CANNOT HURT ME."

The crowd melted back to ground level, and the ministers on the roof froze.

I tightened my grip. "Now tell the Corps that if they hurt my friends, I'll put my fingers through your eyes into your brain." I was pretty sure that I couldn't really do that, but it sounded John Wayneish.

"NEITHER CAN HIS MINIONS. LET THEM BE."

Boog, Gretchen, and Pete stepped past the ministers and joined me and the Reverend on the platform.

"What now, yorkface?" Gretchen asked.

"Beats me," I said. "I'm just following a cosmic impulse, and it hasn't told me what to do next. Except to ask the Reverend to order his boys off the roof and out of the building. This snack bar is mine."

Bill Willy covered his microphone. "All right. But if anything happens to me, all these people are gonna chew you up and spit you out on the fucking dirt."

"Hey, he can talk like a normal person," Boog said.

The Reverend took his hand from the mike. "BROTHERS, LEAVE THE ROOF. EVERYONE INSIDE PLEASE EXIT. I WILL DEAL WITH THESE DEMONS."

The Corps ministers were reluctant, but they and the technicians climbed down to the mob. When they were gone, I handed Willard to Boog, removed my helmet, and spoke into the microphone.

"I need to get inside," I said. My voice didn't boom the way Bill Willy's did, and on the movie screen, my

eyes looked uncertain. "At least, I think I do. So I want
that cherry picker to take us down, and I want everyone
to back away at least fifty feet. If you don't clear the
space, or if anyone attacks us, then whatever happens
to the Reverend will be on your heads. I'm serious."

"Spoken with all of the authority of Barney Fife,"
Gretchen said.

The crowd, muttering darkly, began to back away.
The air vibrated with engine noise, and the cherry picker
rose and swung toward us. The basket set down beside
the platform, and then I saw the flaw in my plan. We
couldn't all squeeze into the basket with our hostage,
but if we didn't, whoever was left behind might take a
ball bearing in the skull.

"Anybody have any suggestions?" I asked.

Pete pointed south and yelled, "Hit the deck!"

The engine noise had not come from the cherry picker
alone. Flashing wingtip and belly strobes were bearing
down on the snack bar from an altitude of less than a
hundred feet. A red-and-white fuselage flashed through
the searchlights; we flattened; and the plane cleared
the roof by three yards. It was a V-tailed Beechcraft
Bonanza.

As it flew past the theater's north fence, it went into
a climbing turn and almost clipped the oil refinery tower.
Then it swung to the east and dove to buzz us again.
This time, a window popped from the starboard side and
fluttered down to the crowd like a scrap of cellophane.
A massive, pointy-eared head poked out of the hole, and
there was no mistaking its identity: Ringo.

The Bonanza had to pull up sharply to avoid flying
through the movie screen, and the Willyites went into a
thrashing panic.

Pete shook his fist at the sky. "Those rotten kids!

Laura doesn't even have her license yet!"

I stood, holding my helmet strap in my left hand, and spoke into the microphone. "Folks, we're coming down in two groups. The first will consist of the Reverend and this guy." I nodded at Boog. "They'll enter the snack bar, and if anything untoward happens while we're waiting for the basket to return, the Reverend will be made into Bill Willy burgers. In addition, our friends"—I looked up at the circling Bonanza—"will strafe you with an Uzi." I lowered the mike to Willard. "Kill the searchlights, Reverend. I don't want your boys testing the range of their slingshots on the airplane."

He complied. "WE HAVE NO FURTHER NEED OF OUR SIGNALS OF FAITH, BROTHERS. THE LORD HAS SEEN OUR LIGHT." A few seconds later the searchlights went off.

Boog pulled Bill Willy to his feet, and they entered the basket, which rose a few inches and moved toward the edge of the roof. Pete and Gretchen stood as well, and Gretchen looked at me with something almost like respect in her eyes.

Pete was watching the Bonanza. "You two are in big trouble!" he shouted. "You're grounded for a week!"

"But they saved our tails," I said.

Gretchen groaned. "Guess again."

Twenty feet away, at the south end of the roof, stood the Bald Avenger. He took a pistol from his jacket and walked toward us, his face rigid with determination.

In the cherry-picker basket, Boog put his hands on the Reverend's throat, and Bill Willy waved his arms at the Avenger. "No, brother! If you harm them, this creature will harm *me!*"

The Avenger ignored him. As he walked, he aimed his pistol at the floodlights illuminating the roof and shot them out one by one. I began to feel the February chill.

The crowd moved toward the building again.

Boog released the Reverend and vaulted back to the roof. Willard leaped from the basket as well, knocking over the video camera in front of the platform. The movie screen went black, and Bill Willy scrambled off the roof into the arms of his followers.

With the screen dark, I, my friends, and the Avenger stood on an electric island in a sea of shadowed flesh. The Avenger shot out the last four lights on the roof, and then the only illumination was the orange flickering of the refinery flame and the yellow glow of the snack bar's interior. Flashlight beams stabbed up from the sea and dappled us with dancing spots.

The Avenger stopped walking. "I want you to die in the dark," he said. He was looking only at me. The pistol rose to point at my forehead.

Boog charged him, and the Avenger spun and fired. Boog fell, and the crowd cheered.

The Avenger turned back toward me, but shifted his pistol so that it pointed at Gretchen. "Accomplices first," he said.

The Bonanza was coming in low again, but it would not be low enough to knock the Avenger from the roof.

The Willyites were chanting: "SHOOT-SHOOT-SHOOT—"

The Avenger's expression changed, as if he wanted to kill, but didn't want the mob to *want* him to. . . .

The Bonanza roared overhead. As the Avenger looked up, I felt for the lump of my garage-door remote control in the Moonsuit, found it, and pressed hard.

The aircraft's starboard door burst open, and a black shape plummeted into the crowd. The Willyites churned and parted, and Ringo, his galvanized chain collar gleaming, leaped up to the snack-bar roof.

He started toward me, but when he saw the Bald

Avenger he changed direction and bared his teeth.

The Avenger shot at the Doberman, but the bullet sprayed gravel, and Ringo was on him. The man fell on his side, and Ringo shattered the pistol with one chomp.

Boog sat up, rubbing his chest, and I went to him. He grinned and pulled his crescent wrench from his bib pocket. "Better than a Bible," he said. The head of the wrench was bent where the slug had hit it.

Pete and Gretchen joined us and helped Boog to his feet. Meanwhile, the Bald Avenger was rolling toward the eastern edge of the roof. Ringo was going along, tearing coat fabric as he went.

"He's had enough," I called. Ringo ripped one more strip and then trotted across to me.

The Avenger, however, had not had enough, and he stood and ran toward us with his hands set in claws and his mouth in a rictus of rage. Ringo dashed at him again, but this time the man sidestepped, and the dog went off the roof.

The Avenger's hands closed on my throat. Stumbling backward, I flailed at his head with my helmet and pried at his fingers with my free hand. We began whirling in a mad waltz, and the faces of Boog, Pete, and Gretchen flashed by in an instant.

Then the Avenger and I fell from the western edge of the roof. My helmet tumbled away like a small white moon.

We landed atop three Willyites, who crumpled. They and the Moonsuit protected me, but the Avenger hit the rocks on his back. He released my throat and stared.

Someone cried, "We have them now, brothers!" and I was hoisted over the heads of the crowd. A hand knotted in my hair and pulled my head back, and I was spread-eagled. A hundred fingernails ripped into the

Moonsuit. The world turned upside-down, and I fell into the sky.

The mob swayed and spun, and the sky swayed and spun with them. In an accelerating blur, I saw my friends trying to fight off a swarm of Willyites who were ascending the snack bar. I could not see Ringo anywhere.

The sky spun faster. My tongue and fingers swelled. The glow of the snack bar became a dying sun. The Bonanza's strobes streaked like meteors. The roar of a tidal wave drowned the voice of the mob, and my vision became suffused with an ochre wash.

Then gravity slammed down like Maxwell's silver hammer, the lights went topsy-turvy, and an electric jolt spiked into my hips and shoulder. The ochre wash burned away in a white blaze brighter than a supernova.

A primal voice pierced through the roar. "All right, you pithecanthropoid freaks! Get away from him! He's my client, and you're all in deep legal shit! I'm a lawyer, and we're SUING!"

"Oliver!" another voice called. "Are you hurt?"

"Mother?" I croaked.

Someone grasped my shoulders and pulled me up and away from the blaze. When I was standing, her face came into focus: Sharon Sharpston. Beyond her, I saw the angry brown-and-blond-eyebrowed features of Bruce Werter.

The white blaze was the headlight of my Ariel.

Peggy Sue had found me. Her engine raced in recognition, then sputtered and died.

"Goddamn!" Bruce exclaimed.

The mob had retreated a few paces because of Peggy Sue's raucous arrival, but now several ministers of the Corps of Little David appeared in their midst with slingshots at the ready. The Reverend Willard had vanished, as had the Bald Avenger. Up on the snack-bar roof, five

Willyites were approaching Boog, Pete, and Gretchen.
The mob began to close in again.

"You shouldn't have stopped here," I told Sharon.

"I didn't want to," she said, pulling me toward the
snack bar's open west door. "It was Bruce's idea. Somehow, he knew you'd be here."

"Thanks for the reprieve," I called to Bruce, who was
jumping on Peggy Sue's starter.

"Reprieve, my lily-white ass!" he said. "A reprieve
is a postponement of punishment, and you haven't been
convicted of anything!" He snapped down the bike's
kickstand, stood on the footpegs, and addressed the mob.
"As a member of the Kansas State Bar Association, I
order you throwbacks to cease and desist this pissant
vigilantism! Get a writ of habeas corpus!"

The mob kept coming. Overhead, the Beechcraft
was diving again, but the Willyites had become oblivious to it.

Bruce took a deep breath and hollered, *"Church and
state are separate!"*

The mob shrieked and lunged forward, knocking
Bruce from the Ariel with enough force to throw him
against me and Sharon. The three of us fell back against
the snack bar's concrete-block wall, and Peggy Sue was
trampled. The Willyites reached for us.

Ringo sprang from the open doorway and positioned
himself between us and the mob. His black eye burned
with a brilliant blue spark, and his lips were curled back
from his teeth. An amplified snarl tore from his throat,
and the Willyites hesitated.

"Shouldn't we get inside?" Sharon asked. As she
spoke, three of the Reverend's flock came flying off the
roof and toppled several of their brethren like bowl-
ing pins.

I glanced up and saw Boog's face. He was lying prone

on the roof and looking over the edge. "Nobody left here but us heathens! Come on up and we'll hold them off!"

I looked back at the mob. The Corps ministers were fighting their way to the front, where they would have easy shots at the three of us against the wall. We could enter the empty snack bar as Sharon suggested (and as I had wanted to do anyway), but then they would shoot through the windows because I didn't have the Reverend for protection anymore. If we went to the roof, though, we could flatten and make ourselves hard to hit. We might even have a chance to survive until the Authorities showed up. If they did.

Bruce and I lifted Sharon to Boog just as a ball bearing chipped the concrete next to my head. Bruce and I both yelped, but when Sharon was on the roof, we each cupped our hands to boost the other.

"You first," I said. "If I leave you down here and you die, Sharon'll never forgive me."

"Are you kidding? A published case study of you could make her famous. If *you* die, she'll never forgive *me!*"

Gravel peppered our heads, and I looked up to see Gretchen's face next to Boog's. "Assholes," she said.

Bruce was about to reply when a ball bearing hit his shoulder. I heard a crunch. His knees bent, but he didn't fall. Grimacing, he put his right foot in my hands.

Boog and Gretchen were still pulling him up when another ball bearing hit the concrete, and then another, joined by white rocks. I imagined that I was back in Vacation Bible School playing sinners and saints, and I spread my hands to try to catch the next projectile. Then my left knee became as nothing, and I collapsed.

In the moment that I sat dazed, Ringo launched himself at a Corps minister who was reloading. The mob shrank back as he charged, but then they poured ahead

344   Bradley Denton   Buddy Holly Is

like lava, engulfing both minister and dog, and coming on toward me.

I crawled to the doorway and into the snack bar, dragging my left leg after me. Once inside, I slammed the metal door and twisted the button in the knob to lock it, but I knew that wouldn't do much good for long. For one thing, the east door was still open.

A window beside the locked door shattered, and rocks bounced off the counter onto the grill. I reached up and flipped a switch, but that only killed half the light in the place. The Willyites would still be able to see me.

Faced with imminent destruction, I did as my mother had taught me: I prayed. I didn't have much time, though, so I just sang the first few lines of "Tell Me How."

Another window broke, and a shadow filled the east doorway. I crawled for the north wall. There was an inner door there, and no matter what was behind it, that was where I wanted to be.

I opened the door, flopped through, and kicked it shut with my good leg. It was only then that I saw the bright circle of a flashlight.

"Oh, great, just look at him!" a voice said over the noise of the mob outside. "Some rescuers we are!"

The flashlight beam passed over a face that I recognized as that of my next-door neighbor Jeremy.

"Hold still!" he exclaimed. "I can't see what I'm doing!"

"You don't *know* what you're doing!" the first voice said, and I recognized it as Cathy's.

Strangely, I was unsurprised. "What are you trying to do?" I asked.

"It's a complicated story," Jeremy said. "We're fifteen thousand years old, and we no longer use bodies unless we have to, which we do now, because, well—"

"Your mother spoke with our enemies," Cathy said.

"Not enemies, Cath. Rivals, perhaps, although that isn't right either, is it?"

" 'Enemy' is the only term the fleshbound understand."

"And there's the rub, Mr. Vale. We have one opinion of how far to trust your kind, which is as far as you could throw Andre the Giant, and our rivals have another, which is that you deserve the benefits of what we've learned—"

"And in which they are utterly wrong," Cathy said. "Which isn't to say that we wish you any harm—"

"Which is why we're here—"

"Except that we can't find our cousins—"

I interrupted. "What I meant was, what are you trying to do right now?" More glass broke in the snack bar, and I heard a scream from the roof. "Tell me fast," I said, crawling toward the flashlight. My eyes were adjusting, and I saw that we were in a cubicle dominated by machines. This was the projection room, where Bill Willy's show had been piped before being flashed across the lot to the screen. Cold air rushed in through the open window in the west wall.

"You see," Jeremy said, "we thought that if we could provide a diversion, that maybe you could—"

"Except that Jeremy designed inferior brains," Cathy said, "and we can't figure out how to do any of this."

I was beside Jeremy now. He was squatting over a toolbox and was fumbling with a tangle of cables, a screwdriver, power cords, and a portable AC/DC television. The toolbox was sitting next to the biggest video projector I had ever seen. And I had seen some big ones.

For the first time in my life, I knew my duty.

I had been charged to help Buddy Holly, and had not known how. But now I saw that all I could do, all I had ever been able to do, was help myself.

And that was the same thing.

I heard shouting Willyites enter the snack bar.

"Get out of the way and hold the light," I said, taking the cables and reaching into the toolbox. I had not dropped out of college and become a salesman at Cowboy Carl's for nothing. Fate had not made a mistake. Fate never did.

I became separate from time. My universe was defined by a mammoth video projector, coaxial cables, and a five-inch color TV. I hummed the "Holly Hop."

When all was ready, I turned on the TV and projector. The TV screen flickered, but the projector remained dead.

Time started again. The door opened, and a figure with a slingshot was framed by yellow light. Cathy cried, "Darling!" and leaped on him, riding him down as a steel ball ricocheted from the ceiling. Another figure appeared, and Jeremy yelled, "Darling!" and leaped on him as well.

I found a crescent wrench in the toolbox and whanged the projector's power supply seven times.

Three dazzling beams speared through the night to the movie screen, and a blast of sound with the energy of an atomic bomb exploded from a thousand speakers. Buddy was singing the chorus of "Rave On," and singing it loud.

On the floor, Cathy and Jeremy looked up.

Beneath them, two ministers of the Corps of Little David looked up.

Beyond, at the counter and grill, a cluster of William Willard's followers stared through the west windows.

I braced my hands on the projector and stood. Then I hobbled past Cathy and Jeremy, past the ministers and Willyites, and out to the crowded theater lot.

Everyone faced the screen. In the sky to the north, even the lights of the Bonanza seemed motionless.

The song ended with a sharp staccato chord, and Buddy Holly looked down upon us while the echoes died beyond the refinery. Jupiter hung in the black expanse behind him, and the guitar-shaped silver object pulsed above his head. A low thrumming sound accompanied each pulse.

Buddy shifted his Stratocaster and spoke.

"I don't know just how to say this." His words reverberated throughout SkyVue with a calm power that made the Reverend's voice seem puny in retrospect. "I've been hearing a voice." He pointed upward.

The crowd murmured.

"It's been telling me things," Buddy said, pushing his glasses up with a forefinger. "Like how it might be decades or centuries before anyone comes to find me. Like how thirty years have already gone by as it is. Like how the world has changed, and how it wouldn't be home anymore."

The Bonanza passed over the theater, flying slowly. Buddy tilted his head to look at the silver object, and it was as if he were gazing at the airplane as well.

The object began to descend to him.

"So I'm taking this thing up on its offer," Buddy continued. "At first I couldn't decide, so I tossed a quarter. I'm going on tour." He unslung his Strat and lay it at his feet. "I'm told that I won't have a body while I'm gone and won't need one to make music, so I'll leave this here. If anybody shows up before I do, you're welcome to use it. So long as you return it when I come back."

The silver object was so close now that its glow permeated his tousled hair.

Buddy grinned and nodded to us. "See you in the big time," he said.

The silver object sank lower, and lower, and Buddy
melted into it, head to toes, until it touched the ground
beside his guitar. Then it rose, passed the image of Jupiter, and shot off the screen. A silver afterimage glowed
for a moment before fading away.

All that was left was gray rock and dust, the impassive striped planet, empty clothes, black-framed glasses,
and the woodgrain-and-white Stratocaster. SkyVue's
speakers were silent.

We stood as silent as they. The only sound was the
buzz of the Beechcraft's engine.

The picture on the movie screen became faceted, like
a mosaic, and gradually dissolved into white light. The
speakers crackled.

And the whiteness blossomed into Technicolor. John
Wayne returned Natalie Wood to the bosom of her family, and then, satisfied that he had done a man's job,
turned and strode away into the great Western desert.
The music swelled, the cabin door closed, and the credits
rolled.

The crowd, bathed in reflected warmth, stood mes-
merized.

Then the credits vanished and were replaced by an
ugly dog dancing on a bartop while pouring beer for a
softball team. On a stage in the background, three women
in gold bikinis sang, "It's the winner's brew/It's the one
for you/Buy me one too/And you won't be blue/Oop-boop-
be-do."

The crowd erupted, cheering, waving, laughing. They
leaped into the air, hugged each other, rolled on the rocks,
humped the speaker poles. Tiny TV screens flickered to
life throughout the lot, and all of the pictures were different.

Regularly scheduled programming was back. God

was in his Heaven, and all was right with the networks.

In the sky, a meteor flared and was gone.

William Willard's flock, including the Corps of Little David, forgot about their captured demons. Whether they believed that their rally had defeated the Antichrist's broadcast, or whether they didn't care what had happened so long as TV was back to normal, I don't know. In either case, they were finished with SkyVue. One minute after the conclusion of *The Searchers,* scores of vehicles were trying to leave at both the exit and entrance. Although united in spiritual matters, the Willyites became divided in their cars, and they honked and cursed at each other.

I was swaying and would have fallen if Pete hadn't shown up to steady me. Gretchen, Boog, Sharon, and Bruce joined us, and I saw that although Bruce was holding his shoulder, he was standing without help.

"Well," Sharon said, looking around at the departing Willyites, "thank God for short attention spans."

"Or whoever the fuck's in charge," Boog said.

Ringo emerged from among the crowd's stragglers, dragging the Bald Avenger across the rocks to us. The Avenger's body was limp, but as the Doberman released his coat collar at my feet, he looked up at me.

"All of you," he said hoarsely, "are under arrest."

Gretchen raised an eyebrow at his torn pants. "Cute butt," she said.

The Avenger closed his eyes and sighed. "Okay, forget it." He sounded relieved. And old, and tired.

Above us, the Bonanza's engine throttled back, and we watched as the airplane, illuminated by a diaper commercial, descended to land in the field east of the theater lot. Ringo bounded away and leaped over

SkyVue's back fence to greet Laura and Mike.

"Rotten kids," Pete said with pride.

I saw the plane come to a stop just short of the re-finery fence, and then, my eyes stinging from a breeze full of oil-rich smoke, I looked away and down.

Several speaker poles away, Peggy Sue lay tram-pled on the white rocks. A black pool had formed be-neath her. With Pete's help, I hobbled to her, and my friends followed. We left the Avenger behind.

My Ariel's chrome was bent, her headlight smashed. Her handlebars were twisted, her fuel tank crushed. Both tires were flat, and spokes jutted like exposed bones. Her drive chain had snapped and fallen from the sprockets.

All of the violence that had been aimed at me, she had taken upon herself. I heard distant, mechanical wailing.

"I'm so sorry, Oliver," Sharon said.

"Me too," Pete said. He was looking across the lot at the Oklahoma Kamikaze, which seemed intact except for its missing glass.

Boog squatted beside the bike and touched the car-buretor, then grinned his usual grin. "Don't be sorry yet. My hands have the power to heal the sick and raise the dead." Hearing him say it, I knew that it was true.

Light snow began to fall as Mike, Laura, and Ringo ran to us. While the kids collected hugs from their fa-ther, the first carload of Authorities rolled through a jumble of civilian vehicles into SkyVue.

"I hope there's an ambulance," Sharon said, shiver-ing as the snow came harder. "Bruce and Oliver need a doctor."

"Bullshit," Bruce said. "Just get me a goddamn pair of pliers to pull out the bone chips."

I laughed. Bruce had transformed since the last time I had seen him.

"You seem to be in a surprisingly good mood, Mr. Vale," Mike said, "for a man about to be taken into custody by the musclemen of bourgeois repression."

Gretchen glanced at the approaching car. "Uh, Oliver," she said, "the cops are coming."

My contacts were hurting me, so I removed them. "I know," I said, my hands before my face. "That makes it tough."

When I lowered my hands, the movie screen had gone black. The refinery flame blurred. I leaned back and opened my mouth so that I could catch the last snowflakes before the end of the world.

CATHY AND JEREMY

They sat on the bench in the dark projection room, staying quiet long after the sirens had droned away and SkyVue was silent.

"It didn't turn out the way I expected," Cathy said at last.

"What way was that, love?"

"I don't know. I had a vague notion in this defective head that we could distract the crowd long enough to hustle Vale away. But when you couldn't get the projector working, and Vale had to do it himself . . . things happened."

Jeremy patted her hand. "We couldn't have known that Holly was about to end the broadcast."

"Even if we had," Cathy said, "I wouldn't have guessed that a mob of the fleshbound would just *stop* like that."

"Me either. We didn't do a damn thing to help Vale, and we didn't have to. I can't figure it."

There was a low chuckle from the doorway. "Can't, or won't? The truth is that you did do something to help him, but you aren't willing to admit it."

A light came on, and Dwight D. Eisenhower entered the cubicle, followed by Nikita Khrushchev.

Cathy and Jeremy stood. "Where the hell have you two been?" Cathy demanded. "This mess was your fault—"

"—and when it hit the fan, you were gone," Jeremy concluded.

"We were around," Khrushchev said. "In fact, I butted in when Vale was about to die in a head-on collision, and again when he was being stoned." He glanced sidelong at Eisenhower. "Even though I wasn't supposed to."

Eisenhower smiled. "Oh, no? I swore that I wouldn't intervene, but I didn't say anything about you."

Khrushchev glowered. "You're a jerk!"

Eisenhower chuckled again. "Despite that, our job is finished, and we can return to noncorporeality."

"What do you mean, 'your job is finished'?" Cathy said. "If anything, the violence of tonight's mob, and of the mobs all over the world, has proven that the flesh-bound have no right to Seeker status. You were wrong, and we were right."

Eisenhower raised an index finger. "Except that you two are already Seekers, and yet you also committed violence. You each leaped upon a man and forced him to the floor without considering that you might harm him."

"That was necessary!" Jeremy said.

"And spur-of-the-moment!" Cathy added.

Khrushchev gave them a stern look, and they bit their lower lips.

"Gotcha," Eisenhower said.

"We tried another way first," Jeremy said. "You've got to give us that."

Eisenhower nodded. "Indeed. By projecting Holly's image—or rather, by helping Vale do so—you achieved our pro-flesh goal. In effect, you defeated yourselves."

Cathy crossed her arms and glared. "How's that?"

"First," Eisenhower said, "you proved that Seekers themselves still possess the capacity for violence. How, then, can we deny Seeker status to the fleshbound on the grounds that they too possess this capacity?

"Second, you gave a crowd of the fleshbound a chance to prove that they possess qualities beyond violence. When they saw what was happening to Holly, their anger became wonder—which is precisely what started us on the path to becoming Seekers so many centuries ago."

"They were just drugged by television!" Cathy snapped.

Khrushchev shook his head, and his jowls quivered. "Regular programming didn't resume until after Holly left Ganymede. Besides, the subversion of violence didn't only occur here, but everywhere that Holly's departure was seen."

Jeremy made a noise in his throat. "Uh, Cath, maybe they're right. Maybe we—"

"No! the fleshbound don't deserve the galaxy. I won't be a party to giving it to them."

"You don't have to be," Eisenhower said. "Our faction has compromised: If we're right, and the fleshbound are worthy, this episode will persuade them to put aside their violence and let their wonder take them to Ganymede. Only then will they find the key to our existence as Seekers."

"It's hidden in the guitar," Khrushchev added.

Cathy and Jeremy looked at each other, then at the floor.

"Nick and I must be going now," Eisenhower said. "Thank you both for your help. We'd stay longer, but we're tired of the flesh." Smiling and waving, he left.

Khrushchev scratched his head. "This might be against the rules of party politics, but you guys look beat. If you want to get out of those bodies without driving back to Topeka, you're welcome to join us. The device is in the refinery stack." He followed Eisenhower.

Jeremy scuffed a shoe. "You know, Cath, if the fleshbound can't squelch their violence, they'll waste all of their off-earth technology on orbital war machines. They'll never get to Ganymede."

"Not for a long time, anyway," Cathy said. "Maybe we won."

"Maybe nobody won," Jeremy said.

They looked at each other again.

"Let's go *home,*" they said together.

Three minutes later, four bright spheres rose from the refinery tower's flame, spiraled up to the snow clouds, and were gone.

EPILOGUE

*S*unday, *March 19, 1989*. I never did make it to Lubbock, but that's okay. Lubbock is eternal.

After the events at SkyVue, the Authorities questioned my companions and released them. I, however, was kept in "protective custody" for ten days, first in Wichita and then in Washington, during which time representatives of the KBI, FCC, FBI, SEC, BIB, NSC, CIA (probably), DIA (possibly), and various other sets of initials took turns interrogating me. I was X-rayed, CAT-scanned, HTLV-tested, probed, poked, and prodded. They no doubt would have kept me forever if not for two things: I had become famous (network news crews pounced every time I was moved), and I was the client of one of the most obnoxious attorneys in the history of the profession. Not an evening passed that Bruce's face didn't appear on the tube, yammering that I had committed no crime (other than Resisting Arrest, Interstate Flight, Attempted Kidnapping, Trespassing, and Disorderly Conduct, none of which he mentioned), that there was no evidence to suggest that I had, and that the Authorities had better brace themselves for one humongous monster daddy of a lawsuit.

Eventually, they had to kick me, but they made it clear that I had better be willing to cooperate if they should need me for anything. They didn't specify what "anything" might be, and so far, I haven't had to find out.

Bruce and Sharon brought me home on February 18, and I found my mother's house in a shambles (although in better shape than it would have been if Boog hadn't stayed there while I was in Washington). The pieces of my SkyVue dish were strewn across the backyard; shingles were missing from the roof; records and CDs were jumbled on the floors; and my black Stratocaster was smashed.

Beyond refiling the music, I did little to repair the damage. This was because Sharon told me that she detected signs of stress in my behavior, and that in order to avoid "problems" (i.e., a trip to the state hospital), I should take steps to purge myself. Such action might also help me, she said, to "integrate" my recent experiences with the rest of my life. I found it amusing that she assumed I would want to do that.

Nevertheless, I took her advice, and for the past thirty days I've been constructing what amounts to my own Volume I. Frankly, I don't feel much better; but it seems to have made Sharon happy.

All of my new friends, plus Boog's seventeen-year-old son, "Spud," arrived this past Friday to spend the weekend helping me put the house back together. Even better, Boog has completed the restoration of Peggy Sue. In fact, my knee is so much improved that I even rode the bike to Topeka yesterday to fetch some parts Laura needed for the earth station. The road felt as smooth as blue sky.

From here in my bedroom, I can hear Laura and

"Spud" working on the SkyVue . . . Gretchen and Mike
arguing about the Strategic Defense Initiative . . . Boog
and Pete hammering shingles . . . Bruce and Sharon
struggling to make lunch in the Meltdown Machine . . .
and Buddy singing "Listen to Me" on the living-room
stereo. Ringo is lying on the floor beside my chair, chewing on an old railroad spike.

I have gained a family, with all of the mingled love
and squabbling implied therein. It seems a miracle that
they all joined me at SkyVue when I needed them, and
it seems an even greater miracle that they still haven't
abandoned me. If I believed in Mother's "other world,"
I would say that somebody up there was taking care
of me.

However, despite all that I've seen and heard, I am
unwilling to follow in her footsteps that far. I have decided that my former neighbors, Cathy and Jeremy, were
crazy. The Spirit Land, where warriors go after death,
exists only in the movies.

But when a thirty-years-gone Texan appeared on TV
and his grave was found empty, "death" became a relative term. . . .

My Volume I is ending with good omens, I think:
Bruce has turned out to be likable despite his an-
noying personality and repulsive eyebrows, and he and
Sharon seem stronger in their Relationship. (Sharon, by
the way, is embarking on research into the mass psychological effects of the Holly broadcast, and she claims to
have already discovered one startling worldwide statis-
tic. Despite the angry mobs, she says, there were actually fewer deaths by violence during that four-day
period than during any comparable period throughout
the preceding year.)

Pete and Gretchen became engaged while repairing

the Kamikaze. They have yet to have a fight, although that may be because Gretchen does all of her arguing with Mike.

Mike and his New Radicals are driving their local school board berserk. By May, they hope to have extended their influence north to Oklahoma City and west to Amarillo.

Laura has gotten over her crush on me and is making googoo eyes with "Spud." It will be interesting to see what develops, because she's going to MIT in the fall, and he's going to Baja to eat peyote.

Ringo is happy with his blue eye again.

As for me, I've received a letter from Julie "Eat shit and die, Oliver" Calloway. She hadn't been able to find my new, unlisted telephone number, and she wanted to know if I was all right. I called her, and she's coming for supper tonight. It probably won't work out this time either, but it'll be nice while it lasts. I miss her.

The unlisted phone became necessary because my answering machine was about to explode with crank calls. While my fame helped me regain my freedom, it does have a down side.

Then again, as Bruce has explained, fame also means power.

So I've thought about it, and I've decided what to do.

I'm going to campaign for manned bases on the Moon and Mars. A space station. Orbital industrialization. L-5 colonies. All of that leaving-the-terrestrial-cradle stuff that the wild-eyed rocket boys claim is coded into our DNA.

Between you and me, though, I have an ulterior motive. Screw human destiny; I just want to get to Ganymede.

And it isn't as if I'm alone in that. After all, no one

can forget that *something* once usurped and replaced every TV program in the world. No one can forget, you see, because there's still one channel—one obscure, satellite-fed broadcast—that displays a tableau from another part of the solar system twenty-four hours a day.

It can't be turned off. It can't be changed. No one has to watch it, but everyone knows *it's there*.

I've already made one public announcement relative to my upcoming campaign:

I have dibs on the guitar.

Laura has just informed me that although she and "Spud" have reassembled my earth station, they can't make it work. Clearly, this is a job for me and my magic crescent wrench.

One last thing—I finally decided that I was sick of contact lenses, so I'm wearing my trusty black-framed glasses again. True, there's a slight loss of peripheral vision . . . but as my Ariel and I have discovered, you don't miss peripheral vision when you're running flat out. You can see straight and clear, forever and always, on down the line to the Spirit Land. See you there, Mom.

See you there, Buddy.